Praise for
A DAGGER OF LIGHTNING

"Meredith R. Lyons delivers a fresh, science-fiction romance with dagger-sharp writing and lightning-quick wit to prove that sometimes being the chosen one means choosing yourself."
—Matthew Hubbard, author of *The Last Boyfriends Rules for Revenge*

"In her hotly anticipated follow-up to her award-winning debut, Lyons spins a wonderful fantasy epic with an unforgettable heroine, ingenious worldbuilding, and a page-turning plot. *A Dagger of Lightning* is guaranteed to leave an indelible impression on readers of speculative fiction. Fans of Jemisin, Hobb, and Grossman take note."
—Julian R. Vaca, Daytime Emmy award-winning writer and author of *The Memory Index*

"Meredith R. Lyons's *A Dagger of Lightning* hits you like a glass of sparkling rosé: a fizzy, flirty, and fun space opera about a satisfyingly badass forty-year-old chosen one whisked off to a planet of sidhe against her will. The tale shakes up classic tropes in a delightful potion that will keep you turning the page."
—Yume Kitasei, author of *The Stardust Grail*

"Meredith R. Lyons deftly mixes space opera, fantasy adventure, and paranormal romance into an irresistible combination in *A Dagger of Lightning*. Oh, and did I mention there's an unforgettable forty-something heroine? Get this book."
—**Gwenda Bond**, *New York Times* bestselling author of *The Frame-Up*

"Wildly original and wholly unexpected, Meredith R. Lyons' sophomore effort does not disappoint. I was swept away into the story just as Imogen was and rooted for her every step of the way as she gains back her sense of self and comes into her powers. Smart, sexy, and absolutely memorable, I can't wait to see what happens next."
—**J. T. Ellison**, *New York Times* bestselling author of *A Very Bad Thing*

"*A Dagger of Lightning* begins with the mystery of a sci-fi novel, punches hard with the humor of a paranormal romance, and grows into a truly epic fantasy. If you like to have fun, this is the fantasy romance you need in your hands right now."
—**Alisha Klapheke**, *USA Today* bestselling author of the Dragons Rising series

"Lyons (*Ghost Tamer*) cleverly subverts the abduction-romance trope, celebrating a middle-aged, sensible, and spirited heroine. Narrator Freeman's technical skills make this sci-fi romantasy an unputdownable delight in audio. VERDICT Lyons's terrific new novel sparkles in audio. Share widely, especially with fans of Demi Winters's *The Road of Bones*."
—*Library Journal*, **starred review**

"Combining sf, fantasy, and romance with a soupçon of political intrigue, the latest from Lyons (after *Ghost Tamer*, 2023) will delight readers with the interesting paths the story takes. Imogen is an easy character to root for and her strong chemistry with Wells will captivate romance fans. The book ends on a cliffhanger and readers will be eager for a sequel."
—*Booklist*

"Lyons (*Ghost Tamer*) puts a fresh spin on the romantasy genre with this entertaining romp helmed by a spunky heroine in the midst of a midlife crisis. It's a pleasure to watch Imogen come into her own, learning both how to kick ass and how to make herself emotionally vulnerable. The fascinating worldbuilding, vibrant characters, and tense cliffhanger ending will have readers clamoring for more."
—*Publishers Weekly*

A Horn of Onyx

THE SIDHE CHRONICLES

A Horn of Onyx

MEREDITH R. LYONS

Violent Unicorn

Violent Unicorn Publishing
Nashville, TN 37208

This is a work of fiction. Names, characters, places, and incidents are either products of the author's imagination or are used fictitiously.

© 2026 by Meredith R. Lyons

All rights reserved. Printed in the United States of America. No part of this book may be used or reproduced in any manner whatsoever without written permission except in the case of brief quotations embodied in critical articles and reviews.

Hardcover ISBN 9798993233802
Paperback ISBN 9798993233819
eBook ISBN 9798993233826
Audiobook ISBN 9798993233833

Library of Congress Control Number: 2025927857

Book and cover design by Maryann Appel

5 3 1 2 4

For Dean

Thanks for being in the trenches with me.

PROLOGUE

EIGNEACHAN/DELANEY MATING ACCEPTANCE CEREMONY

*I would become a monster to protect my children.
Why is it so surprising that I'm also willing to become prey?*
—Queen Iphigenia Eigneachan Metellus

The room was a flurry of activity. Queen Iphigenia rolled her shoulders back and surveyed the room as if observing the servants unpacking all of Llewellyn's and Imogen's possessions with tidy haste was her only reason for being in Llewellyn's old suite.

These rooms would serve as her youngest son's gilded cage once more.

She let out a soft sigh, indistinguishable from the rustling of her gown, as she drifted from the main room into one of the bedrooms. A servant used his kroma to float the neatly pressed blue and silver army uniforms into the large closet.

Those uniforms would soon see true combat for the first time. And Llewellyn would be tested as the youngest General of the King's Armies to have ever served.

Her son's position had granted him several decades of freedom. He'd earned it, no doubt about that, but neither of them should have expected it to last forever, she supposed.

Iphigenia drifted over to the nightstand, finding the strange rectangular "phone" that Imogen had brought with her from Earth. She traced a finger over its dark surface, flinching back when it illuminated with a disturbingly lifelike image of Imogen and Llewellyn. The newly turned sidhe's short dark hair flying back from her grinning face as she leaned against Llewellyn, his long red hair shifting in the same breeze.

In spite of the fact that prince Aloysius had taken Imogen from Earth against her will—a horrible mess that Allestair had expended much energy hushing up—the former human had found love with her youngest son. The pair had even been blessed with a mating bond.

She gave the image one final glance. They both looked so happy and free.

They would learn.

She turned away from the phone. She had once leaned into Allestair and smiled like that. She had once thrown her opinion around like Imogen. Although Allestair had never defended her like his stepson did his mate. In some ways her youngest reminded her so much of his biological father—except Llewellyn was kind. And Allestair had not been able to crush that kindness from him.

She left the bedroom, pausing in the main room with her eyes on the exit. Two servants swept by carrying a large trunk and she halted to let them pass. The moment was enough; her stomach clenched, and she turned away from the door to stride onto the terrace.

She was procrastinating and would have to leave soon. Find her son and pull him away from the elaborate mating acceptance celebration Allestair had insisted on throwing them. She could wait another moment. Give both Llewellyn and herself a few more minutes of happiness before she gave him the news. She crossed the terrace, softly lit in the fading sunset, and dragged a lounge chair across the stone balcony, setting it where it might catch the light during the day. An excuse to linger a bit longer. She nudged the chair an inch to the right. Trying to picture Imogen and Llewellyn relaxing in the sun. And failing.

She hadn't argued when Allestair had tasked her with the onerous duty of letting Llewellyn know that neither he nor his new mate would be free any longer.

It would be better coming from her; at least she could deliver the news kindly and answer her son's questions, rather than simply informing him like he was a servant being reallocated.

The drive to protect her children, to make landings softer when she could, never eased, no matter how many centuries passed. And Allestair had used that against her. He was good at discovering what a person cared about. Threatening it, going so far as to destroy it if necessary. It was how he maintained control. With a sigh, the queen plopped gracelessly into one of the chairs.

It wasn't as bad when it was just Aloysuis, perhaps because he was Allestair's own son. Perhaps because he'd already made her life smaller. She used to do so much outside the palace. Now she couldn't remember the last time she'd been away from the grounds.

Iphigenia had Allestair's enthusiastic blessing when—long after giving him the prince—after centuries of childlessness, she sought to try outside their marriage. It was common for royal families. Sidhe often had difficulty conceiving and any child born to a royal was understood to belong solely to the palace, the contributing parent giving up all rights and disappearing into the unknown. Allestair had seemed just as pleased as she when she'd become pregnant again.

But Allestair treated Llewellyn much differently. And it went badly for both of them when Iphigenia tried to step in.

She'd learned—along with both of her children—that it was much easier to bend than be broken. She never once regretted either of her sons; indeed they were often her greatest sources of joy, and she learned to grab onto her small delights where she could. To struggle against King Allestair's will was to invite further pain and strife, so Iphigenia shrank herself to fit around him. She had little choice. Marrying a king was not the soul-deep permanence of a mating bond, but there was no dissolving that partnership. She had known that when she accepted.

Llewellyn had been clever; rising through the ranks of the army with Captain Marcellus's guidance. Although she'd missed him when he'd left, she was so proud of him for carving out his own life. It wasn't an easy thing to wiggle out from beneath Allestair's thumb.

A selfish part of her heart warmed at the thought of having him nearby again. To see him daily, to get to know his mate.

She'd have to speak to Imogen. The youth was too honest, to the point of being artless, and much too willful. Imogen wasn't the bending type. And if she didn't bend, Iphigenia was afraid Allestair would delight in breaking her. And what would that do to her sons?

The queen inhaled deeply as she gazed out over the landscape. The terrace was perched on the edge of the mountain, giving her a view of all Molnair City, down to the sea. Imogen and Llewellyn might have remained in his quaint townhouse a mile away had she not antagonized Aloysius, who still wasn't over the fact that she'd chosen his brother.

Iphigenia pulled in a deep breath. What Aloysius truly wasn't over was losing Imogen's grandmother, Solange, who had decided to remain on Earth a century ago rather than continue her on-again-off-again relationship with the prince.

Prince Aloysius had fed his father the perfect lines when he carefully brought up Imogen's growing abilities. Although she was certain Allestair didn't completely buy into Aloysius's theory that Imogen was the Chosen One, where he had initially only been interested in burying the story of her kidnapping, he now saw her as something he could potentially use.

Aloysius knew his father would covet that power and strive to bring it under his command, likely intending her to be taken from Llewellyn and brought to live in the palace. Imogen herself had unwittingly verified her abilities by using her lightning to rescue her friend, Cilla. Aloysuis didn't anticipate Alistair pushing the mating bond as a way to link Imogen forever to the royal family and thus have control over her.

He had pivoted quickly however, and here they were.

Humans who were turned sidhe usually honed their kroma at a predictable rate, but Imogen's grandmother had been anything but predictable before she gave up her powers for Henry Delaney.

Already Imogen was exceptional, mastering telepathy, ripping down wards, even wielding lightning, a power no one had seen in living memory. After Imogen's acceptance of the bond, Iphigenia had bitten her tongue to the point of blood while she listened to Aloysius carefully enumerate Imogen's extraordinary powers during a formal meeting. She watched her son's face when he dropped his final opinion that Imogen would listen to no one but Llewellyn. And that her mate loved her too much to take her in hand.

Her chest tightened at the memory as she gazed up at the stars from the balcony that would comprise her son's prison. Her boys hadn't had the relationship she hoped for. Aloysius was one-hundred-seventy-seven when Llewellyn was born. Yet he'd been so careful with his brother, truly happy to hold him, feed him, teach him, play with him. He loved Llewllyn—the same way one might love a favorite pet. Someone to care about, protect, and have fun with, but also below him. Belonging to him. And that was Allestair's doing.

So Aloysius brought his brother to heel, knowing there was nothing the king despised more than power existing outside of his control. Iphigenia let her eyes drop shut for an instant. As clever as Aloysius was, he hadn't considered the inevitable fallout of his machinations. Yes, he would pull Imogen closer to him, more under his control—that was his father's influence—but it wouldn't go well for the willful sidhe he claimed to love.

By presenting Imogen as both powerful and willful, Aloysius had—perhaps unintentionally—activated his father's domineering tendencies and presented Imogen as a challenge to be won. She would either submit to Allestair or he would break her.

And he would go through Iphigenia's youngest son to do it if necessary.

Aloysius wouldn't see how badly he had miscalculated until it was too late. His father was not above using Imogen to manipulate him as well.

Iphigenia shoved herself upright. She would speak to Imogen. The mating bond was strong; she'd seen the way Imogen and Llewellyn looked at each other. More importantly, she'd watched Llewellyn stand up to his family for once rather than fading into the background. And Imogen had given up any hope of returning to Earth when she accepted their mating bond. Their love for each other had pushed each of them past certain fears.

If she could get Imogen to see reason, to bend before Allestair did any real damage, it would be better for everyone. She just needed to stay quiet. Keep her eyes down. And if Allestair asked her to do something, she needed to acquiesce. Whether it was to stop taking her contraceptive tonic or using her powers as directed for Molnair. For both her own and Llewellyn's sake.

Imogen loved Llewellyn. Iphigenia just hoped she would understand what was at stake.

The queen took a breath and stood, finally striding into the palace to find her youngest.

CHAPTER ONE

FIVE LUNAR CYCLES LATER

Never underestimate the strength of a person fighting for someone they love.
—Captain Marcellus Tibercio

I realized my mistake as soon as I burst into the humidity of Sephrya's air ... one thousand feet above the ground. Aloysius's screams, "Imogen, wait!" seemed to follow me across continents. I fought to orient myself; I'd only winked across the ocean once before, accidentally, when rescuing my best friend, Cilla—another former human—from the Sephryans who had kidnapped her.

This morning, I'd fled Molnair's palace at mountain height and at mountain height I'd arrived, so intent on escaping King Allestair I hadn't taken logistics into consideration. Free falling, I clamped down on the instinctual panic that shot through me and forced my breath even as I called the wind again. It came willingly, whipping my hair back as it buffeted my body.

My stomach swooped as I stalled in midair and then descended more gently, twisting onto my belly like a flying squirrel, taking in the lay of the land. My body fizzed with adrenaline. Or perhaps it was the after-effects of the potion I downed to get through the castle wards. Pushing past it, I searched the mating bond for any flicker of Wells, while I scanned the terrain below.

My feigned interest in private dinners with Al had taught me that Sephya—a country three times the size of Molnair—was most deadly at it's center, which was continually baked by an unforgiving sun. Even now, near winter's end, the only relief came in the form of short, violent bursts of rain. Below, it was as if the maps I'd obsessively scoured had come to life; flat, muddy plains interrupted by an occasional canyon or copse of hardy trees clustered around the damp swamps.

I floated directly above a battle, which gave every indication of having raged for a while. The ground was scraped and marred by the fighting. Bodies dotted the field. My mouth dried out, but I forced myself to take in the details. I saw no sign of a campsite. It was either well-shielded or located some distance away.

Wells was here. Somewhere. Our mating bond glowed inside of me. No longer shadowy and indistinct as it had been when I was trapped behind King Allestair's blood wards. Anger bloomed anew. Allestair had lied when he reported Wells's death just moments ago. Although looking at the battle below, it was easy to see how he'd assumed it would come to pass. How had the king orchestrated this? Although he was young—for a sidhe—Wells was a fantastic general.

The bond's pull went more urgent, screaming that my mate was in mortal distress. My heart thundered against my ribs once my mind parsed what I was looking at: the steel-gray and blue of the Molnarian uniforms. Easy to pick out, surrounded as they were on all sides by the red and gold of the Sephryans. Three Sephryan units to Wells's one. That they had held out at all was astounding. Molnarian soldiers were being felled with every breath. This was a slaughter. *Why is one unit out here on its own?*

Rage at the injustice, the unnecessary peril my mate—the General of the King's Armies, for fuck's sake—had been placed in, boiled my blood.

The lightning answered my call almost before I had summoned it. As if it were tethered to the anger and terror pulsing against my breastbone. I breathed into it, fighting for control. As a human on Earth, I'd had no particular powers, but all sidhe had kroma, which took different forms. For whatever reason, mine was the only one that called lightning and wind.

And I needed to give Wells's unit help *now*.

Still gliding downward, electricity enlivening the air around me, I slid my dagger from its sheath, wishing I'd had time to grab a sword from the palace weapons' room. I'd just have to take someone else's once I landed.

My breath lodged sideways in my throat. I'd only practiced the lightning a few times on my own during thunderstorms when I'd been trapped in the palace. Aside from when Cilla and I had escaped a Sephrya compound several months ago, I'd never used lightning against anyone. I'd learned the consequences of using too much and I had better control over it, but I'd never wielded this kroma in a battle.

I'd never been in a battle.

My bond with Wells gave a sharp tug and I shoved those concerns to the back of my mind.

Clouds darkened and converged over the battlefield as I dropped nearer. Thunder rumbled across the plain. My eyes scanned the Sephryan units, picking out the strongest. The one applying the most pressure to the Molnairians. I gritted my teeth, trying not to think about the destruction I would cause. This was war, my people were dying too, this Sephryan unit needed to go first.

I chose my landing spot, flipped my feet downward, and punched my fist to the sky. Lightning wrapped my hand, crawled down my arm, zipping through me as I pulled it in . . . in . . . in . . . Hugging it to my center. Then, using my dagger to hone the charge, I flung my power outward.

Toward the unit of Sephryans I was fast approaching. Dozens of them went down instantly. The lightning arced farther than I'd anticipated, jumping from person to person and even traveling down their weapons in some instances.

I took a breath. This was new information. I'd have to be careful to avoid hitting our own soldiers.

The air around me crackled as I siphoned even more lightning. Packing it down into my core. Curling my spine around it. Pulling everything in tight. My skin prickling, my insides vibrating as I held it hard, let it cling to my nerves and wrap my bones.

I let go of the wind. Releasing it fifteen feet over the middle of the Sephryan regiment I'd chosen. Free-falling into them. A cannonball of lightning. I counted to five, then opened. My arms and legs splayed out as I launched electricity from my center in all directions. The impact of my blast rocked the battlefield and obliterated anything and anyone within fifty feet. Those nearest were vaporized, their remains mixing in with the dust now permeating the air. The ones farthest out collapsed as the lightning burned them from the inside out.

I crashed into packed earth, my spine barking as I slammed into a crater of my own creation, my own blast cushioning my fall. Still trembling, lightning aftershocks leaping from my limbs like staticky fleas, I pushed myself to my feet, coughing against the dust and impact.

The air smelled of ozone, blood, and seared flesh. I swallowed down rising bile, brushed myself off, and checked my bow and arrows. I climbed out of the crater with lightning still crackling across my body like a plasma globe from Spencer's Gifts.

Sweat already slicked my spine as I stepped over the lip of my crater and scanned the flat, barren field. The middle of this country was an odd dust bowl punctuated by random bayous. I shaded my eyes, squinting toward Wells's unit through the airborne particles across the wreck I'd just made. My stomach dropped when I saw one Sephryan unit had switched course and was now charging toward me.

"It's cool, it's cool, this was . . . kind of the plan," I muttered under my breath, coughing a little when Sephrya's dirt hit my lungs. I realized I didn't even know where to wink if I needed to get away. I had no coordinates here. And although my energy was charged from the lightning, winking back to Molnair was not an option. *Don't freak out, you can handle this.* I adjusted the grip on my dagger, baring my teeth as I marched to meet them. If they were focused on me, they weren't slaughtering Wells or his people.

I pulled more lightning from my hovering thunderclouds and used my dagger to fling a blast Zeus-like, straight into the front lines. The three directly in its path dropped like stones but not before the lightning bounced like a hungry snake to the soldiers immediately surrounding them. I yanked up a cloaking shield as deadly offshoots streaked down their weapons and right back toward me, ripping clods of earth from the pockmarked field as they struck.

It was tempting to keep my shield wrapped around me like a security blanket, but I needed them to stay engaged. Not to mention I'd be a sitting duck if I remained on the defensive while I had the element of surprise. Heart in my mouth, I dropped the shield and tossed out a few more short blasts.

I need to get my bearings. Formulate some kind of strategy...

When one of my blasts bounced off a Sephryan shield, shooting right back at me, I tucked into a shoulder roll, throwing a cloaking shield around myself as I rocked back to my feet. My own power zipped by a foot to my right, the vibration of its impact jarring my bones and dropping me into a crouch. Though the cloaking shield kept me from arcs or burns, I wondered if it would have saved me had I been hit head-on.

Panting, still hunched, I scuttled forward and grabbed an abandoned sword. Each of my blasts took out twenty to thirty fighters, but the lightning was unpredictable. And my control was spottier than I'd anticipated. I'd discovered weapons could direct my power, however, I hadn't given any thought to the fact that I wouldn't be the only one with steel on the field. Stupid. I dropped my cloak and flung one last blast down the sword, hoping the longer weapon would be more effective at directing the electricity.

It was. Slightly.

All of their units—save one, the smallest—were now focused on me. I'd bought the Molnairians—and Wells—time to regroup. I just didn't know what the hell I was doing. I was one too-slow reaction away from getting barbecued by my own lightning. I cloaked myself again and moved closer to the approaching units, this time on a diagonal, hoping they'd expect me to move away from them and I could get some wiggle room. I just needed a few seconds . . .

My blood was giving me that telltale tingle. I knew from my clandestine lightning work on the terrace that this meant it was time to take a breather from Thorkrieg or suffer serious consequences. I'd crippled the original unit I'd been facing, but the other was closing fast. I still had no real plan and I couldn't continue to use the lightning without a break. I'd do better out of the spotlight for a few seconds if I could manage it.

A vibration shook the earth beneath me, traveling up my bones before the rumble reached my ears. The very ground trembled, small rocks at my feet bounced away from each other. Something big was coming.

The fresh Sephryan unit parted to make a path for a large, pod-like vehicle hovering six inches above the ground, its surface mirrored, reflecting the land around it. Clever camouflage. It reminded me of a sculpture in Chicago that everyone called "the Bean." Although this bean had narrow viewing slits in the front for pilot visibility. They tapered as they reached the middle giving the appearance of glaring down on those it attacked. The thing sparked with kroma, gliding over the vibrating earth beneath.

A quick scan had me thanking whatever kromatic gods existed that I'd been granted the ability to view auras, allowing me to read people's emotions, detect falsehoods, even see when Wells was telepathically speaking to someone, and—most immediately relevant—many shields and spells invisible to most eyes. Their military vehicle was shielded in all but a few strategically placed areas, ostensibly to allow those within to fire kromatic attacks.

A sidhe tank?

"Oh, absolutely not." I tucked the sword into my belt and sheathed my dagger. I thumbed open a pouch at my hip. I hadn't been idle during my palatial incarceration. My nerves fizzed anew as I popped one of my golf ball-sized experiments into my palm and stripped its shield. While I'd been trapped, I'd found all the ingredients for explosives within the palace storerooms. It had been a matter of putting them together and weaving some kroma through them.

"Time to test this baby out." I dropped my cloaking shield, lit the fuse with a snap of my fingers, and 'ported it into the tank. Spearing it through one of the openings in its shield. I started counting.

Made it to three.

The left side of the tank blew out. One flank dropped to the ground, gouging a trench in the mud as it skidded in a wide arc barreling straight toward me, clumps of dirt flying in all directions. I panic-winked, aiming myself at a space behind the Sephryan lines at the last second.

I stumbled out of the wink, tripping on bodies, and forced myself to yank my cloaking shield back up while I staggered away from the dead, the smell of blood and ozone nearly choking me. When I looked up, the tank had shuddered to a stop, plowed into the mud like a beached whale.

"At least I know they work," I muttered, my heart still galloping. I pulled my attention to the Sephryan fighters. Many of them searched for what took out the tank. Several were even slinging stunning blasts toward the empty air in front of them, as if hoping to catch the person they had glimpsed.

Others were refocusing on the Molnairians, who still fought the remaining Sephryan unit about a football field's length away.

Go there or finish here? With a sinking feeling I knew I should do more here. As much as I wanted to join our own fighters, as much as I wanted to see Wells, I needed to keep these other units occupied. More of our own would stand a chance at breathing another day. I steeled myself for more killing.

Taking a leaf out of the tank's book, I kept myself wrapped in a cloaking shield, but allowed a small hole to form. An exit for my arrows. If the grenades worked, the arrows would too. They'd probably be easier to track if someone looked my way, but I wouldn't have to 'port them or aim them especially precisely. A few Sephryans were still hurling kroma indiscriminately.

Tossing up a silent thanks to Past Imogen for all those archery lessons she coaxed from Al when trapped in the palace, I strung my bow. A Sephryan blast hit too close to comfort. Clods of earth smacked against my shield. I could tell by the way it ricocheted that these weren't stunning shots. If they'd been paying close attention they would have seen how the dirt their blast threw up didn't penetrate my shielded area. Giving my position away. I didn't have much time.

I took a chance, whipping the shield off all my arrows, I nocked the first one, lit the fuse with a thought as I pulled it back, and let it fly into the center of the encroaching mass. I had the second arrow ready before the first explosion had even detonated, releasing it toward an undamaged area of the unit. As soon as it left my bow, I stumbled, the blast of the first arrow rocking the earth.

The arrows were highly effective. But unlike the lightning, these deaths were not clean.

Bodies blown asunder fell in meaty heaps. I tried not to let my gaze linger, swallowing hard against the roiling in my stomach. Tried to keep my thoughts on just the physical act of readying and shooting the arrows.

At least most of them died quickly.

How does Wells do this?

I couldn't stop my legs from trembling, although I did my best to lock up my heart. Pulled other, more useful feelings forward. Rage against King Allestair still simmered under my skin. Fear for Wells swirled in the background. *Stay alive. Just a few more minutes. I'm coming.*

Exhaling to steady my aim, I loosed six arrows into the Sephryans in rapid succession. In spite of my ineptitude, I'd managed to cripple these units. Once I stopped firing, those who remained were focused on saving the few living injured around them. They weren't hunting for me. I knew I'd pay for this later in my nightmares. But now the Molnairian unit was evenly matched.

Heart hammering against my ribcage, I completely sealed my cloaking shield, fully invisible from sight and scent, unstrung my bow, and shielded the rest of my arrows. It was time to join the Molnairians, still fighting and likely depleted. Get closer to the people who knew how to fight a damn battle. Closer to Wells.

What kind of shape would he be in?

As soon as my throat closed I ruthlessly shoved that thought into my locked box of feelings. There was no time for that now. Only surviving the present.

I stalked across the muddy field toward the center of the clash, keeping a firm grip on my cloaking shield. I didn't want to disrupt any tactical maneuvers Wells may be trying to orchestrate. I should probably observe first. And I wanted a better sword. A Molnairian sword.

As I neared the heart of the battle, I came across more and more downed Molnairians. A distant part of me felt the trickle of abject despair sliding down my soul. I selfishly hoped there were none I knew among the crumpled heaps dotting the mutilated plain.

I caught a flash of red hair in the distance. Splayed across the muddy ground. Dirt clinging to some of the flaming strands, and to the blue and gray uniform. The body still. Lifeless. My heart stopped.

It's not him, it's not him, you'd know . . . I told myself, pelting toward the soldier. I skidded to a stop by that crimson hair, draped across the filthy field like a cloak spread over a mud puddle. Choking on my own panicked breaths, I forced my fingers to grip the shoulder of the blood-splattered uniform and pull it around.

Female. Throat torn out. She must have been drained. Her body unable to heal before she bled out.

My eyes locked on her lifeless face, her vacant green eyes. A fierceness to her expression, even in death. No aura. I wasn't even sure why I checked, but it somehow made her death more palpable.

I coughed against the rising nausea, my throat tightening with unshed tears for this stranger. My cloaking shield flickered.

Enough, Imogen, you can do this part later. Get a sword and let's go.

I looked at her one last time as I carefully locked those feelings away with the others. Those green irises must have been beautiful when she was alive. She still clutched her sword. Bloodied to the hilt. She had gone down fighting. I swallowed. Then dropped my short, fat Sephryan sword to the mud with a splat and reached for the redhead.

"I'm just going to finish what you started," I told her, my eyes burning as I unbuckled her sword belt, tugging it, muddy and stained from beneath her, and slung it around my waist, securing it with trembling fingers. "I'll take a couple more down for you." I gently eased the Molnarian sword from her hand. "Rest easy." I gave her fingers—already clammy in spite of the humid air—a squeeze before I stood.

I was directly behind the Molnairian lines now. I glanced around, fighting—not entirely successfully as the bond wailed at me—the impulse to search only for Wells and focused on how best to lend aid.

It seemed a mess. I'd had enough of a breather that I could judiciously use lightning again, but there was no way I could safely wield it back here. Before I could overthink it, I dropped my cloaking shield and winked to the front lines.

Right into a blast of kroma. Instinct threw up a shield for me, but I was knocked back. Fortunately, the Sephryan I faced was drained and I recovered before he charged me with twin short swords. Two strikes, a killing blast, and he was down. I tried to make the deaths quick. Hand-to-hand, I could do.

A barely deflected graze of metal across my throat promptly reminded me that I wasn't wearing armor. Unlike everyone else on the field. *And yet to the front lines you winked*, I scolded myself. Protracted engagements were not practical.

My one advantage over everyone around me was that I was fresh and full of lightning juice. Most of these fighters were struggling to focus on the area a few feet around them. I could keep one eye on the big picture.

Another Sephryan sidhe tank rumbled toward our unit's flank.

"Just bothers me," I gritted out, disarming the golden-haired Sephryan in front of me and running him through with my redhead's sword. I wrapped a cloaking shield around myself long enough to grab another kroma grenade, light it, and 'port it into the tank. This time I considered its speed and direction.

A Molnairian soldier to my right was overwhelmed—battling two attackers—and fell to a knee. I dropped my shield and leapt upon one. *Head, neck, heart*, I chanted, reminding myself of the three certain ways to kill a sidhe. Another thing to go over with Wells later. Three seconds later, my explosion rocked the field, stunning everyone, knocking some off their feet. The tank plowed through several Sephryans in its path before it crashed. I took out three who turned to look with quick thrusts of my sword and dagger, almost dropping my weapons when his 'path hit me.

Where are you?

Wells! My heart swelled painfully. A laughing sob burst from my throat even as I blasted the Sephryan in front of me with sticking-fire kroma—my new favorite thing—and pushed him back into five others who were shortly engulfed. Wells was alive! And he was near! He tugged at me through the bond. Pulsing stronger than ever within me.

I'm here saving you! I 'pathed, a tear breaking free. Telepathy was a rare kromatic skill, and though both Wells and I possessed it, I hadn't 'pathed anyone aside from one clandestine conversation with Cilla since he'd been forced from the palace. I'd missed his voice.

I didn't want this battle to last any longer. I wanted it done. I needed to see him. My mating bond was practically writhing within me. The bond between my soul and Wells's had been shadowed behind the blood wards of the palace, but now I felt everything. I sheathed my weapons and risked absorbing more lightning. The arc forked through the clouds I had drawn earlier and plunged toward my fist. I flung a shield behind me, expanding it wide to protect the Molnairians in my immediate vicinity. Already breathless, I yanked my arm from the current, clapped my hands together, then thrust them outward. It was slightly easier to direct the arcs where I wanted them when I was close enough to push straight from my hands. A wave of electricity pulsed from my chest, down my arms, and barreled over the hundreds of sidhe directly before me. They dropped like stones.

Imogen, you don't have any armor, stand down!

The corners of my mouth lifted. The unequivocal command in his voice—the voice of a general—was new to me, but . . . his voice was in my head again. I wrapped my consciousness around it like a hug and risked a glance to the side. In the direction of that constant tug at my bond.

There he was. His face lined with exhaustion; uniform splattered with mud and blood. Fighting furiously about a hundred yards away. I winked over.

He'd just dispatched the Sephryan in front of him when I appeared. "But saving people is what I do best." I hurled two forks of lightning far back into the crowd of Sephryans pressing in. Anyone touched crumpled into heaps. I tracked the arcs with my heart in my throat, sucking in a gasp when a Molnarian was singed and had to drop his sword. I needed to figure this out if I was going to be of any use.

A short, sharp horn blasted through the air. The Sephryans immediately disengaged, stumbling back or winking out. The enemy unit had called a retreat.

A few Molnairians whooped and several gave chase until Wells ordered them to let the remaining Sephryans go. His aura split as he 'pathed the medics to get to the field. I watched in a haze as one lieutenant winked over, saying the other was drained but she would relay orders back. Wells gave clipped instructions to locate any wounded and collect the dead.

Then he turned to me. His aura swirling and twisting with a mélange of colors. I couldn't read it. My blood was hot with excess electricity. Whitecaps of emotion broke over me at the sight of him. Here. Alive. My heart cracked open. *I thought you were dead,* I 'pathed. Unshed tears from this morning staked their claim anew, choking me. My remaining lightning crackled up in defense.

"Imogen . . ." Wells's voice was hoarse. He crossed to me.

I shoved him violently away.

CHAPTER TWO

Often anger is merely love that's incredibly frightened.
—Queen Iphigenia Eignechan Metellus

"A note? You were going to die and leave me a *fucking note?*" Two tears cut trenches down my blood-splattered cheeks. Pent-up emotion, too long shoved down, burst from me in uncontrollable waves of electricity. I couldn't hold back the lightning still in my system. It skittered to the surface and wreathed my arms, crackling over my shoulders and torso.

"Imogen," Wells's voice broke. He reached for me and I backed up.

"You can't touch me right now or you'll get electrocuted," I said, my words cracking. "And that would be tragically ironic, which I really fucking hate."

His brows drew together, russet eyes shining. "They weren't supposed to give that letter to you unless I was confirmed dead," he said. As if that was going to calm me down.

"Well, I'm glad they gave it to me early!" I choked out, my breaths hitching. We were attracting a small audience but I didn't care. "Because now I can yell at you about it! And also . . . they told me you *were* . . . dead . . ." Lightning undulated over my body in spasmodic ribbons. "I thought you were dead for an entire *minute*!"

My hands clenched around the leather of my jacket at the center of my chest. The crack of my heart behind my rib cage replayed those horrible seconds when I'd believed him to be gone.

The lightning fizzled over my skin. My blood was beginning to boil. I couldn't control it. I needed to get rid of it before it arced to someone nearby and/or overwhelmed me.

I flung my arm out, tossing the lightning into a distant tree. It split down the center with a crack like a shotgun and exploded into flames. My insides cooled and a fraction of the emotion I had locked away crashed forward. I glanced up, throat tight, lips trembling.

Wells's arms were still outstretched, reaching for me, his eyes bright with worry.

My gaze locked on his.

One sob bubbled out. Tears sprang to my eyes. I pressed the heels of my hands into my sockets to stem the flow. I could no longer speak. My breath hitching.

His arms curled around me. "I'm so sorry, Demon."

I dragged my hands from my face and wrapped them around him, squeezing him back as hard as I could. Awkward, and painful in places, with all my paraphernalia and his armor. But I didn't let go. I heard him telling someone that yes, this was his mate. And yes, that was her lightning.

My eyes were still squeezed shut, face pressed into the hard plates of his armor, when his hand smoothed the back of my certainly wild hair and he pressed a kiss to my crown before murmuring, "Imogen, I'm nearly tapped, if you lend me some energy, I can wink us back to camp."

I only squeezed him tighter, the bond inside of me finally calming. *Go ahead*, I 'pathed, eyes still closed, and let all of my shields fall away, trusting him with my body and life force. I felt him pull from me. We slid into the cool black void of a wink.

As one might expect, the war camp was not glamorous. Wells's unit had found a box canyon miles from the fighting that they'd been unable to leave. They'd planned to march to a new location—closer to their rendezvous with the rest of the army—and wink fighters back to relocate the medics and wounded once they'd established a safe area, when they were attacked and surrounded. The dusty, worn tents remained within the dubious safety of the canyon. The unit unable to make progress.

As the general, Wells had a larger tent than most, but it was still canvas cloth over poles with a cot, regardless of how many shields and spells may be protecting it. He did have a desk with multiple maps and papers strewn across it, a table with some roughhewn chairs, similarly occupied with papers and scattered weapons, and a few worn rugs covering some parts of the dirt floor.

Once inside, Wells relaxed his hug and gazed down at me, pushing my hair back from my face.

"I'm sorry I shoved you," I said, sniffing. "I didn't want to accidentally barbecue you."

"You had just finished slaughtering our enemies, I suppose I should be glad you dialed it down to a shove." He half smiled.

I squeezed my eyes shut and pressed my cheek against his armor-plated chest, breathing him in, listening to his heart. "I'm sorry."

He cupped my face in my hands, tilting it up until I was gazing into his sunset eyes. "I forgive you." He gave me the softest kiss. "Thanks for coming to save us."

"Thanks for not actually being dead," I said, pushing the tip of my bow away before it stabbed him in the eye. "Can we take some of this stuff off so I can hug you properly?"

He nodded, gave me another kiss, then paused, pulling the fingers of his right hand away. They were red. "You're bleeding, Imogen."

I reached up and touched my arching ear, hissing when my fingers brushed over a divot in the shell. Wells grabbed my arm and turned my left wrist over, displaying another long cut, already healing itself. Accelerated healing was one change I hadn't complained about since being yanked from humanity and turned sidhe.

"I've never been in a battle before." I sighed and touched my ear again. It was no longer bleeding. "I was lucky to do some damage from a distance but—"

"You're lucky you weren't killed," Wells said sharply. He yanked open a drawer in his desk and dug out a small jar of salve, pushed my hair out of the way, and dabbed a bit onto my ear. "Unless you *wanted* a permanent notch there."

"Thank you," I said. "Maybe you can teach me how to . . . battle better."

His lips twitched up into that half smile I'd missed so much and some of the hardness left his eyes. "Don't touch that for five minutes." He carefully tucked my choppy, dark hair behind the injured ear, then crossed to the other side of the desk and removed his armor piece by piece, placing the components on racks evidently designed for them. I divested myself of my bow and arrows, setting them carefully near the cot, then stripped off my jacket and warm shirt, neither necessary in Sephrya's heat. My tank top was plastered to my skin.

"Did you bring that sword with you from the palace?" Wells asked. He hadn't taken his eyes off me while he removed his accoutrements.

"No," I said, my voice tightening. "I didn't have time to take anything that wasn't already in the bedroom." I cleared my throat. "She was dead. I can give it back if . . ."

He shook his head, retreating behind the mask I knew so well. "It's standard issue, it doesn't look like it was a personal family item. I just wondered . . ."

"I was forced to exit the palace rather dramatically."

"I can't wait to hear—what *are* those things on your belt?" He had finished with his armor and crossed to me, down to a T-shirt, almost transparent with perspiration, and the reinforced leather pants that were part of the uniform.

"Oh, yeah. I have shields around these, and the arrows, but I should put them someplace safe. They're explosive." I carefully unclipped the pouches from my belt and set them on the cot.

"Explosive? Like guns?" He raised his eyebrows. Guns had been banned on the entire planet. No one from Molnair would dare bring any back from an Earth expedition.

"They're not guns, they're . . . like grenades . . . or bombs." I flushed but held his gaze. "I made them here. I wasn't even sure that they'd work."

He whistled, fingers skating across my now bomb-free waist. "That's what took out the hovercrafts . . ."

"Is that what those tank things are called?" I put my hands on my hips. "I found them offensive."

He hauled me into his embrace, tucking my head beneath his chin. "You really are a demon from hell."

"But I'm *your* hell demon," I said, wrapping my arms around him, my face splitting into a wide smile against his shirt. For a few minutes we stood like that. Letting our bond dance within and between us. *It's worth it*, I thought. *Everything I had to do to get here was worth it. If I'd been too late . . .*

We were interrupted by one of Wells's lieutenants—I recognized the delicate strawberry-blonde with the pixie cut—politely clearing her throat. We broke apart, my cheeks warming just a bit, but Wells kept one hand on my waist as he brushed a hand down my sweat-soaked hair and pointed me to a flap at the back of the tent to wash up. He gave my waist a squeeze, then turned to receive her report.

Determined not to interfere with military processes I undoubtedly knew nothing about, I busied myself digging out the running shorts I'd packed, then pushed my way through the flap. I stepped into a small, sectioned-off area in the back of the tent with only a water basin on a stool.

A mirror with no frame hung from the tent pole in front of it. Wells had been roughing it.

I dunked my entire head in the basin. Scrubbing the blood from my hair, face, neck, and hands with the rag hanging nearby. The water was a muddy pink when I finished. I didn't know where to 'port fresh water in for Wells, so I rinsed the rag as best I could, rung it out, and hung it neatly, stripped off my pants—which also needed a wipe down at some point—draped them over a crossbeam, pulled on my shorts, and stepped back out into the main tent.

The lieutenant was still in the midst of her report. I'd seen her on several occasions but never been formally introduced. I slipped past them as unobtrusively as possible and took a seat on the cot.

"I don't think it's a good idea to break camp tonight and Lieutenant Kendran agrees," she was saying. "But we've only got a few with the energy to burn the dead. No one has the strength to cloak the camp or set up wards. We'd be taking a risk."

Wells let the smallest sigh escape, his face perfectly neutral. I doubted anybody but me would have noticed the tightness around his eyes. "Do we have anyone who hasn't done a double-watch the last two nights?"

"Once I've gotten a confirmed list of who survived, I should be able to tell you," she replied.

"I can cloak the camp," I volunteered, then flushed in spite of myself when they turned to look at me. "I have energy. I usually have excess after the lightning."

The left corner of Wells's mouth lifted. "Celphia, I don't know if you've ever officially met my mate, Imogen. Imogen, Celphia, my first lieutenant."

After Wells cleaned up we walked the perimeter of the camp. He borrowed some of my energy to demonstrate, then I took over, spreading the cloaking shield across the entirety of camp. It was delicate work and I hoped I'd be able to live up to my boast. Even as I directed the shield, I marveled that such an enormous thing was possible. We'd anchored it to a point above the center of the camp and connected that to a spot on the ground outside the tents. Wells said that once I'd wrapped the shield around the entire encampment, I could pull the edges together to meet and weave them into each other.

While I directed my blue-black sheet of power as if I were handling a parachute of Saran Wrap, I confessed to Wells that, although I'd worked my lightning at the palace, controlling where it went on the battlefield had been shockingly difficult. I left out the part where I'd almost been obliterated by my own offshoots.

"Although your power is unique, Imogen," he said, following me as I edged behind some tents pitched close to the lip of the canyon's entrance, "I believe—as with most energetic kromas—if you learn to control how much you give and take, the energy that disperses afterward will be more predictable as well. Think of it like the shield you're creating now. If you just flung it up as hard as you could, it would expand in all directions until the source energy, you, were drained or stopped pushing. We'll work on it, Demon. Your powers were definitely an advantage today, even as untrained as you are." He watched me carefully furl my shield around a sticky point between a jutting overhang and a sloppy cache of weapons. "I might have enough energy to ward against detection once you finish, just in case any Sephryans decide to put out a search party and come across a massive shield."

"Do you want me to 'port you a block?" I kept my eyes on the shield as I stepped carefully around the weapons. "I have the rest of the ones Captain Marc gave me in my pack." A light sweat already coated my skin. Both from the work and the weather. New Orleans had nothing on Sephrya.

"Keep them." He sighed. "We've been having a difficult time getting requests for provisions filled so we've had to hunt and scavenge. I can't guarantee there will be anything pescetarian on the menu."

I 'ported a block into my palm and offered it to him. "If I have to eat meat, I'll eat meat. I'm not an idiot, I just don't like killing animals when I have a choice." I shrugged. "If I don't have a choice, I don't have a choice."

He accepted the block, his eyebrows drawing together. "You let Allestair nearly starve you in the palace—"

"That was about more than my diet and you know it," I said, adjusting my grip on the shield as my voice took on an edge. "There was food going bad in those food stores—which he warded against me, by the way. Me specifically, no one else—and he chose to serve the one thing I prefer not to eat almost exclusively.

If he'd even served normal meals without worrying about what I ate, I probably would have been fine. But no. That was deliberate. So of course I wasn't going to break." I refocused on my shield work, stepping over a rotting log as I continued.

A soft sigh escaped Wells as he swallowed his block. "Imogen, sometimes bending is necessary so that we don't break. I know you're not used to such a restricted life, but—"

"A few things changed after you left." I kept my voice steady even as my shoulders tightened. This was as good a time to tell him as any. I trained my gaze on my hands as I pushed my blue-black kroma up around the dusty canvas tents and people milling about. "I was allowed to skip formal dinners and eat in my rooms occasionally. If I ate with Al."

I glanced sideways to check his aura. Little red shoots pushed through the calm blue-greens. His face was set in a neutral mask.

"They also stopped beating me up in training." I arced my shield around a cache of weapons being cleaned and repaired by two sidhe with blackened fingers near a fire pit. "I only trained with Al."

"And how often did you have private dinners with Aloysius?" Wells's voice was bland, but a few hotter-red shoots burned through his aura. "Did he—"

"He was still forbidden from . . . *interfering* with me while I was mated." I let him catch the subtle implication there. "The worst he did was snuggle me and kiss my head."

"And what did you do?" he asked. Anyone else would have thought his voice unchanged, level, calm. But I heard the quiet fury beneath. Not directed at me, not entirely, but fury at the situation we'd been forced into. The betrayal his family had shown him.

I had reached my start point again, once again slick with sweat. I concentrated my energy and let everything else go as I hauled the edges of the shield together, then pressed and pulled them toward each other until they were indelibly joined. The entire camp was now encased in a glittery, transparent, blue-black dome. I turned to Wells and looked him in the eye.

"I let him," I said, wiping moisture from my forehead. "Every time Al came in I made him bring me maps of Sephrya and Molnair. I asked any questions I wanted and he told me everything he knew. I needed the food. I needed the information. And I needed the king to think I was slowly folding. You told me to survive first. Everything else second. So I did what you said. And I let him." I blinked away the burning in my eyes. Took a deep breath against the constriction in my chest. "I talked about you every time though. Asked where you were. What you were supposed to be doing. It was the only news I ever received. And I never let him forget . . . ever . . . who I was in love with."

He closed the distance between us, brushed his knuckles gently across my cheekbone, then dropped his fingertips to the glittering augur stone, now visible on the delicate silver chain around my neck. My gaze fell to where he touched the necklace.

While in the palace, I'd kept it hidden under my clothes for fear it might be taken, but I hadn't removed it since he'd given it to me: the night he knew he was going to be sent away, the night he told me to survive.

"You learned to play the game," he said, his voice thick with emotion.

My eyelashes flicked upward. His aura swirled calmly again, red shoots fading away. "How's that for bending?"

CHAPTER THREE

Love does not belong near war.
To win a war, you must be willing to be cruel.
—King Allestair Metellus

"Those boots with those shorts are—" Wells glanced over his shoulder at me as he pushed back the tent flap.

"Ridiculous, I know, but I couldn't bring any other shoes." I ducked under the flap, crossing to the cot. My tall boots freed puffs of dust from the worn carpets beneath them.

"I was going to say distracting," Wells said, reaching his desk, picking up a stack of reports, and leaning a hip against the scuffed wood without taking his eyes off me.

The cot creaked as I perched on its edge facing him. I raised an eyebrow.

"Well, I was about to take them off, but maybe I shouldn't . . ." I leaned back on my elbows and stretched my legs out in front of me.

He shook his head slowly, dropped the papers back onto the desk, and prowled over to me. "Demon," he said, but his sunset eyes gleamed as he settled beside me, propping himself up on one elbow. His fingers traced my collarbone, his voice low. "Alright, I'm not sure how much time we'll have alone—there's not much privacy here—but I'm sure you have questions. I know I do."

I squeezed my thighs together. Although there were a few personal things I wanted to take care of, I did actually have several important queries and it was the middle of the day in a war camp. "Yeah, I have questions— actually I am going to take these off, it's hot here," I said, reaching for my boots. He tugged on the one nearest him, helping me free my feet as I asked, "How come you're having trouble getting supplies and aid? And how come you're in the middle of the most dangerous part of Sephrya with *one unit*? Aren't you in charge of the entire army? Because this seems like poor planning."

He threw back his head and laughed, pulling me in for a hug. "I've missed your unabashed bluntness." He released me with a kiss to my forehead. "Did you really just accuse me of poor planning?"

I kept a hold of his arms, staying close when he would have let me fall back, grinning when those russet eyes darkened and skated down my sweat-soaked shirt. I stretched, draping my arms over his shoulders. "I merely asked a question. I'm sure you have some kind of answer. I haven't been allowed in any meetings since you left."

His fingertips danced over the back of my damp shirt and visible goosebumps pebbled my skin in spite of the heat. We both pretended we didn't notice. "Yes, this would be poor planning, had it been my strategy." I noticed a strain at the corners of his eyes. "We were supposed to be meeting up with five other units. The king has apparently slightly altered several of my generals' plans from what we originally agreed upon. Nothing egregious if you look at the plans individually. But it did leave us high and dry for several days. Still, we may have been alright running into one or maybe even two Sephryan units, but three at once was terrible luck."

"But you're in charge of the armies, correct?" I dropped my arms and twisted, crossing my legs on the cot to face him. "How can he just bulldoze you without—"

"They're the king's armies. Or if you want to get very specific, they're Molnair's armies," he explained patiently, brushing sweat-dampened hair out of my eyes, although I caught a flicker of... something in his aura. "Yes, I run them, but they're Allestair's tool. He can override any decision I make. And as I'm a relatively untested general—this is my first major conflict—no one would think it unusual if the king were to... make changes."

I uncrossed my legs, letting one drop over the edge of the cot, glaring at the worn, red-patterned rug on the floor, pounding my heel into it, heat flaring low in my belly.

"What is it, Demon, what's the rug done to you?" He squeezed my shoulders, his fingers automatically finding the knots. My eyes drifted shut as my muscles begged for more.

I could easily have melted into it, but...

"Allestair was trying to kill you." I jerked my chin toward the entrance, barely holding a tirade at bay. "And he was willing to kill every other person out there to do it." I locked eyes with Wells. "I'm not letting you out of my sight again."

He pulled me closer, dropping his forehead to mine. "Well, lucky for you, there's absolutely no privacy in a war camp, so you'll have no problem keeping an eye." He grinned, smacked a kiss on my temple and sighed. "Although, I do have to leave camp for a bit tonight. I have to get a report together to send to the palace and—"

"Why?" I leaned back to look at him. How was he so chill? "Why do you have to send a report to the palace?"

"In addition to my regular correspondence with the king, I send a report after every battle, Imogen, it's procedure—"

"Um, is it still procedure when the fucking king tried to murder you?" I shoved out of his arms and stood up, jabbing my finger toward the tent flap. "All those deaths today are his fault, Wells, he *orchestrated* this!"

Wells rose and reached for me. "Alright, Imogen, calm down—"

I backed away. "I will absolutely *not* calm down. He told me you were *dead* this morning, Wells! He called Captain Marc back to the country to give me that letter you wrote! *Captain Marc* thought you were *dead*!" I paced furiously. Back and forth in the few feet of space between the cluttered table and the dilapidated cot. "He expected you to *be* dead. And if I hadn't already been planning to bust out of there this morning, you might be."

Wells moved back to lean against the desk, watching me pace, his arms crossed over his chest. "And I am sorry about the pain you went through, Imogen, bu—"

"We are so far beyond that right now," I sliced my hand through the air, cutting him off. "Everyone here is exhausted and sad from almost dying and having their friends die and we have maybe one day of semi-safety under this shield to recoup and you're going to send someone outside of it to send a report to a murderous—"

"I won't send anyone else, I'll go myself." His voice hardened subtly.

I stopped short and spun to face him. "No."

"You were right that everyone is exhausted and needs time to regroup. Not many people in camp are able to 'port a message that distance and it's best if the report comes from my energy signature anyway. If I can get a little over a mile away—"

An inarticulate noise of protest erupted from my throat.

"—any kroma I use won't be able to be traced back to our location should there be Sephryan scouts about. It won't take long and by tonight I should have enough energy to try to cloak myself."

"You're forgetting the larger issue." My skin was hot, burning with barely contained fury.

"And what is the larger issue, Demon?"

"You know, the whole 'Allestair Tried To Orchestrate Wells's Death And Caused The Deaths of Hundreds He Doesn't Deserve A Timely Report' issue."

Wells had the nerve to roll his eyes at me.

I exploded.

"Where exactly is the disconnect here? Have you been brainwashed? Your society literally *travels across galaxies* to turn humans in order to ensure the continuation of the species, risking getting blown up every time they land. This stupid war is because the Sephryans keep trying to steal said former humans for the same fucking reason and yet all of these people needlessly died today. *I* killed hundreds of people, Wells. How many babies are going to have to be created to make up for today? Stop looking at me like that, don't you dare . . ." I clenched my fists at my sides, vibrating with frustration while remorse tried to claw a foothold behind my breastbone.

"How am I looking at you?" His head was cocked to the side. One side of his mouth was even quirked up slightly.

"Like I don't understand something and I'm overreacting. It's making me *so mad*. So knock it off before I get punchy."

All humor dropped as he reached a hand out. "Imogen, come here, I'll explain."

"No!" I folded my arms and planted my feet. "I will not have you distracting me with your yummy smells and nice hugs. You can explain from there so I can remain furious because *somebody should be*."

He sighed and dropped his hand. "First, I *am* angry, but my feelings are tangential when I'm responsible for an army of people. Secondly, although I don't agree with what Allestair did in the slightest, it does not surprise me, and I suspected something like this might happen eventually—"

"Well, thanks for the *fucking heads up!*" I launched into movement again, producing tiny dust storms as I raged in the small circle of clear space. "My brain is exploding right now! Doesn't surprise you? I do *not* understand, you left me there *knowing*—"

Wells grabbed my wrist as I passed and yanked me to him, seizing my jaw in his other hand and pulling my face around. "If you will stop interrupting me, I will *explain* it to you, Imogen."

I jerked my chin from his grip and glared at him. Anger and frustration sparked through both our auras like fireworks. I tried to tug my wrist away but he wouldn't let go. I watched him take two deep breaths, never breaking eye contact. His eyes flashed like rubies. "I *hated* leaving you there. Don't think for a second that I would have ever done it voluntarily. I worried about you every minute of every day. I wrote you letters that I knew weren't being delivered—"

I sucked in a sharp breath. My anger banked by surprise.

"You never got them, did you." It wasn't a question.

"Not one." I stopped trying to yank free.

"I knew you probably wouldn't, but I sent them with my reports at regular intervals anyway." I let him pull me closer. I was now standing in front of him while he leaned back against the desk, one of his long legs on either side of mine. "I thought there was a chance that someone—maybe even Al—would see one and it would find its way to you.

"As much as I hated leaving you there, Imogen, I knew you would be safe. You wouldn't be happy, or very comfortable, but you would be safe until we could figure something out. I was certain that Al wouldn't let things get too bad for you, and my mother... well, she told me she would keep an eye out." A humorless smile. "She knows what it's like to be at a king's mercy. I also knew how much Allestair wanted to keep you."

He took both of my hands in his. "You said earlier that I was looking at you as if you didn't understand, and you were right. It's easy to forget that you haven't been sidhe very long. You have no idea how much our species desires power. Other beings on Perimov aren't like that. They would feel as you do. And you are right, Imogen, it is ridiculous, but it's as ingrained in our society as the desire for monetary wealth seems to be among Earthlings. It's why Allestair tried to encourage you to become pregnant before I left. He still may have tried to give you to Al eventually. To combine your power with mine in one child, and then your power with Al's in another, both of whom he would have use of when they grew—"

"That's... that's..."

"That's how our society thinks. And I'm not saying it's right." He pulled me closer, releasing my hands to cup my waist. "For Allestair to have the chance to bring someone with your completely unique power into his control, to potentially have that power in his own bloodline, it would be worth losing several sidhe of average or below-average kromatic blood. Any sidhe with any kind of high power or position considers the continuation of that power with every coupling that's made. I've often thought life is kinder in that way to those who have average abilities. They can choose whomever they like as a partner."

"But that's . . ." I blinked, trying to wrap my head around this. "You're saying everyone is basically breeding themselves like horses . . ."

"How do you think I came to exist?"

I stared at him. "I thought you didn't know who—"

"I have no idea who my father was," he said, pushing my hair back with a thumb as he examined the salve-covered cut. "But for my mother to have picked him, he must have been very powerful. And likely a telepath since the skill doesn't run through her line."

"And probably very tall," I murmured.

"More than likely." He smiled. "I'm very lucky to have found and mated someone that I love. Al was hoping to have that with Solange, and then later with you. The king and queen tolerated both obsessions because the match would have been good for the line. And yes, I knew it was possible that Allestair may consider finding a way to move me aside so that he could chain you to Al. I just didn't think it would be his first choice, nor did I think he would make that move so quickly.

"As far as sending out a report tonight, there are protocols in place for a reason. If I break protocol, not only will it reflect on me and my position, but it will trickle down to everyone here, who are all on the king's payroll. And those who were killed, who would want their families to receive compensation. For the sake of everyone else in this unit, it is essential that I give Allestair no additional reason to cause us hardship."

"Okay, I understand that." I slid my arms around his neck.

His eyes flicked to my ear again and he ran a careful finger over the healing wound. It no longer stung. "And on a more selfish note, being general gives me status and a position outside of Allestair's household. And it was one of the few paths open to me as the queen's son." He looked me in the eye. "Once it was clear I had talent as a fighter, Marc spoke to my mother about it, and they both subtly influenced Allestair until I'm sure he thought it was his idea to suggest I join the army. When I worked my way up the ranks, I was working my way to my own freedom. To set one toe out of line, to fail in my duties in any way . . ." He sighed and skated a hand absently up and down my back. "I can't just go into town and find work. I wouldn't be allowed. Because of how I was born, I must be in service to the royal family in some way. Being general allows me to do that while still having a status and position that I earned myself. It's why I was able to live independently and have my own home. I don't want to lose that when this is over."

I nodded. I had never considered this. Wells needed to succeed in this war or risk his freedom. Our freedom.

"Furthermore, although Allestair did make things very difficult for me, it's impossible that he knew exactly where each Sephryan unit was going to be. If he was trying to destroy this unit, he got very lucky that three of them happened along at once."

"But he said—"

"Once again, I don't doubt that he would take advantage if a situation were to arise, but destroying a unit of his army intentionally is a little more difficult to justify."

I decided to let it drop for now, although my hate for Allestair still burned just as brightly. I kissed Well's cheek. "I never want to go back to the palace again. Never. And I am going with you tonight. My cloaking shield is better than yours."

"Alright." He pulled me in for a proper kiss, when he pulled back, his gaze was thoughtful. I caught the tense swallow before he said, "We'll need to get you a uniform, otherwise you'll stand out. But although your lightning is useful, I don't know if we should put you in an actual battle."

I felt my brows drop. "Do we really have a choice right now? I know I'm untrained, but I can learn. I already learned from mistakes I made today. And you can't expect me to sit back while your depleted soldiers are—"

"You're right, you're right." He sighed deeply and I noticed the dark circles under his eyes. "We'll swear you in tomorrow."

I smiled, kissed him again, "No."

"I'm confused, Imogen."

I gazed into his sunset eyes, still smiling. Even coated in sweat he smelled fantastic. We'd been apart for too long. "If I am sworn in to the army, then I'm just another cog in the king's machine. He can move me anywhere he wants, to any unit he wants, and he has even more creative ways at his disposal to separate us. I'll stay with you. I'll fight with you. But I'm a free agent."

"Valid points," his fingers slipped beneath the hem of my tank top, skimming over the bare skin of my waist, "but have you considered, little Demon, that you are the king's subject regardless of whether you're an official part of the army or—"

I shook my head, brushing my nose against his, grinning wickedly. "Here's the thing . . . I don't think I *am*. I made some interesting observations while I was trapped in my tower." I leaned closer to him, chuckling deep in my throat.

Wells released my waist and pushed his fingers through my hair, moving it back from my face, russet irises darkening as they dropped to my lips. "You are wicked. I've missed you."

"Mmmm . . ." I let my eyes drift closed. I loved when he rubbed my head. "I missed you too."

The slight, pleasant tightening of his fingers at the roots of my hair betrayed his growing impatience. "Are you going to tell me about these observations of yours or are you too distracted by my . . . what was it . . . 'yummy smells'?"

I cracked my eyes open. "I think I can plow through," I said drily.

Challenge lit his gaze. "I guess we'll see," he murmured against my ear, pressing a kiss just beneath it.

I huffed a laugh even as goosebumps spread out over my skin. "Well, you know how if your king forbids you from doing something, you physically can't do it?"

His lips brushed against my jawline as he answered. "Yes, I've been forbidden on a few memorable occasions. Very uncomfortable." He moved down to my neck as he spoke. My toes curled against the carpet.

"The king caught me in the library during one of my many nighttime tours of the palace—"

"I'd like to hear about *that* also." Two soft kisses where my neck met my shoulder.

"Patience. All in due time," I teased, warming up to storytelling mode. Wells gave me a tiny nip. "Anyway, I told Allestair I couldn't sleep and wanted a new book. You'll deduce that this was a lie."

Wells snorted, then continued exploring my neck and shoulder. One hand drifted down to my waist, edging under my tank again, while the other remained tangled in my hair.

"He asked if the guards had seen me leave. I didn't want to get them in trouble, so I said no, I'd winked into the hall because I didn't want to bother anyone." My breath hitched when his teeth scraped down my uninjured earlobe. After restarting my brain, I went on. "Allestair accompanied me back to my room—for my own safety of course—and told me I was forbidden from leaving my rooms at night unless I was escorted. Anyway, I made sure to be extra careful after that when I was out at night—"

Wells stilled. He lifted his head and looked me in the eye. "You went out again? *After* he had forbidden you from doing so?"

"Observation number one," I said, smiling, a little dazed by the yummy smells. "Forbidding doesn't work on me."

"Are you sure you heard him right? Perhaps he didn't—" Wells was now gripping my waist, pushing me slightly back.

"I thought all those things too," I said. "Maybe he'd said something else. Maybe he didn't mean it. But I needed to go out, so I tried the very next night and it was like nothing had happened. Then he forbade me from cursing."

"What?" He laughed.

"Yeah, I know. I said 'fuck' at the dinner table and he was already cranky so he just forbid me from cursing." I rolled my eyes. "Anyway, I wasn't dumb enough to try it right there, but as soon as I was back in my room I described him with every nasty word in my arsenal. In several languages. The hardest part about that was remembering to pretend I couldn't curse in front of him."

A ghost of a smile still lingered on Wells's face, but a new tension thrummed through his aura. "Is that the second observation?"

"Getting there," I said, rubbing his belly. "So impatient."

His jaw tensed as he shook his head, smoldering russet eyes fixed on me, but didn't interrupt.

"Well, I was going through that record we have of when my grandma was turned human." I blushed and dropped my eyes, fiddling with the hem of his shirt. The Hall of Records included bound volumes of documents from every Earth Expedition, including the one my grandma had participated in. "I liked to look at it sometimes when I was lonely."

Both Wells and Captain Marc had signed, agreeing to turn my grandmother human so she could stay with my grandfather on Earth. My grandparents had also signed. It gave me warm fuzzies to think that they had known and trusted Wells, and would have approved. Wells pulled me into a hug, rubbing long strokes down my back. I turned my head and leaned into him, so that my cheek rested over his heart, feeling it beat, strong and steady.

"Anyway, one day I decided to look at who else was on that expedition. See which people came from Earth and got turned into sidhe. Just to check if I recognized any more names. I was reading over the whole document and there's a clause in there for the person consenting to be turned. By signing they agree to swear fealty to Molnair's current ruler."

Wells's hand froze on my back.

"And I never consented." I lifted my head.

Wells paled. "So you never signed."

"Observation number two," I grinned. "I have no king."

CHAPTER FOUR

No one wants to remember the Wind War; it was long, violent, and so many were taken from us. But if we obliterate that war from our memory, how are we to avoid falling into it again?
—*Captain Marcellus Tibercio*

Wells called Celphia and his other two lieutenants for a meeting. Without mentioning my rogue kingless status, he planned to inform them that I was going to fight with the army, but they weren't swearing me in. I tried to come up with reasons we could give them until Wells stopped me.

"Imogen, they're soldiers, I'm their commanding officer, I don't need to give them a reason for everything." He'd been tense since I'd told him about my monarch-free condition.

The amorous afternoon I'd thought we were heading for banked quickly with Wells asking who else knew, only slightly relieved when he realized I'd told him first. He'd begged me not to mention it again to anyone else. And not even to him outside of a 'path.

Just as Wells predicted, the lieutenants didn't question anything. The three of them held a loose line facing the desk that Wells and I stood in front of, at relaxed attention, all stripped down to their T-shirts and pants, glistening slightly, as if they'd been working in the heat before he'd called them in. The obvious respect and devotion shining through their auras had pride blooming in my chest. I'd seen the same when we walked through the camp earlier: massacre or not, this army revered Wells.

He'd told them that I would need a uniform, not just for the projection the armor would afford on the battlefield, but so that I wouldn't draw undo attention. While he explained I stood at his side, listening quietly.

"Although her lightning is of great advantage to us now, we're not certain of her permanent placement. She's not ranked, or sworn in, but she will take orders from me," Wells said.

"Most of the time," I added softly.

"Most of the—" He snapped his mouth shut and glared at me. "We'll have a talk later."

After that they gathered around the crowded tabletop, pulling the maps they needed from beneath piles of other papers and weapons, perching on mismatched chairs and trunks as they discussed strategy for the following days. Apparently the other five units that were supposed to have met up with them three days ago were now due in the next day or two. Once we were in their company, we'd be much less vulnerable to Sephryan attacks. However, within our shield it was impossible to contact them, and we wouldn't risk taking it down until we were rested and ready to move. Wells felt the shield would last a full day, but wanted a watch list drawn up.

They also gave him a confirmed list of the dead.

Pyres still burned on the battlefield. If anyone from Sephrya came to investigate, as was likely, we would be difficult to track through the mess that had been made of the plain. Wells said they were almost certain to be more interested in the two exploded hovercrafts lying in the mud than the pyres. The hope was that they'd assume we'd been picked up by an aerial unit and were no longer in the area. Regardless, Wells wanted to wait until the fires were cold before sending anyone out to scout for approaching friendlies. In the meantime, there was plenty to do: healing the wounded, collecting the personal effects of the fallen, and rearranging tent assignments. In many cases, tents that held ten soldiers had only one or two survivors remaining. Sometimes none. Consolidation and redistribution of supplies was necessary. Once assignments had been divvied up, the lieutenants left us.

Wells would personally send letters to the families of the deceased.

"That's a lot of letters," I said, perched on Wells's desk, running a finger down the list. It had nearly been a slaughter. My chest constricted when I asked, "Did you know—?"

"I knew all of them, Imogen." His aura splashed with indigo, although his face remained composed other than a slight tightening at the corners of his mouth. "Some better than others."

The corners of my eyes stung. "Do you want help?"

Wells sat facing me, an array of paperwork in front of him. I was wedged into the only clear space—of my own creation—with my legs dangling above the floor.

He exhaled through his nose, pulling the list toward him. "I might want your help 'porting things when it comes to that." He indicated stars next to many of the names. "Some of them had letters already written . . . like the one I left for you. So we'll need to check with their friends and commanders and see if we can locate those. They're likely among their effects. Or their friends' effects . . . Also any personal items that may need to be returned . . ." He ran a hand through his hair and blew out a breath. His aura was dim with exhaustion and fracturing in places. I slid off the desk into his lap and wrapped my arms around him, hooking my chin over his shoulder. He squeezed me tight and didn't let go.

"It's so good to have you here," he said.

"I'm so glad you're not on that list," I whispered.

For a few moments, we sat wrapped around each other, the sounds of the camp outside of the tent a backdrop to our own breathing, the feel of our hearts beating together.

"I don't know how long it's been since you've had an actual bath," I said. "But you still smell good." I felt the rumble of his chuckle against my rib cage.

"I actually noticed that you smell a bit different. Not bad," he said, as I straightened up to meet his gaze. "Just... different. I thought it might be all the kroma you used today..."

"Well, I did ingest a rather intense potion this morning," I said.

"Right." His tone shifted with his aura into hues of alarm. "Let's discuss your morning. I will need to send a report to the king, and I need to figure out how to... include your appearance here."

"Would you like me to write that part?" I asked brightly.

His eyes went hard. "No, Imogen, I would not." He shifted his hands to my waist and lifted me to perch on the desk facing him. "I want to hear about this potion for starters. What the hell did you take and where did you get it?"

"I made it myself," I said, summoning my pack and digging through it. "I needed to get through the wards and this was the best one I found." I pulled out my—now much abused—copy of the spell ingredients and handed it to him.

I watched his aura flow through several fascinating changes as he scanned it; surprise, pride, anger, relief... his expression didn't shift beyond a slight furrowing of his brow. *I should teach him to play poker*, I thought. Then made a mental note to see if there was a poker-esque game on Perimov. I would clean house with my aural sight.

"Imogen, this is an incredibly complex spell." Wells was still staring at the paper he held, his face tight as he ran a thumb down the list of instructions and ingredients. "There are *several* spots here where if you'd gone the slightest bit wrong, you could have died."

"It was a very unpleasant sensation," I said blandly.

His aura flashed with frustration. "Imogen, this is not—"

"I'm not an idiot, I did a small test one the night before," I told him, lifting my chin. "I didn't have time to look for a safer one. This one took weeks to put together as it was. I had to have a starlight picnic with Al to learn about the fucking moon cycles."

Wells snorted and his effort to hang on to his irritation seemed to slip. "I'll bet he loved that," he said, slight bitterness coating his words. He handed the list back to me and sighed, sliding his hands down my calves, giving my ankles a squeeze before releasing them and leaning back. "Alright, little Demon, tell me how it happened. Do not leave anything out please, whether you think it's relevant or not. Start with these nighttime wanderings."

"Wandering implies aimlessness," I said, tucking the spell away. "I always had a very specific goal in mind."

He interlaced his fingers over his stomach and glared at me. I flashed a grin, but started from the beginning, when Wells was sent away, going through every twist and turn, as best I could string them coherently together, ending with my grand entrance on the battlefield.

"You came in from the sky?" Wells raised his eyebrows.

"You didn't *see me*? It was *amazing*!" I smacked my hands down on the desk. "How could you not see me? I was *firing lightning from the heavens*!"

"I was a little preoccupied at the time, Imogen, things were pretty hot on the ground," he said, eyes going distant as he rubbed my leg.

"True." I deflated with a huff. "I bet it looked cool though. It was my *Infinity War* moment. I'll have to do it again."

"I'm sure Cilla would appreciate what an *Infinity*—"

"Oh, shit, Cilla! I need to get her a message and tell her I'm okay." I hopped down and hunted for a clean sheet of paper among Wells's complete mess of a desk.

He pulled me away from his piles—which he insisted made sense to him—and into his lap. "No messages are going out until we remove your shield, Imogen. So no need to start scribbling yet." He sighed. "And it's probably best for her if Cilla knows as little as possible. I have no doubt that she and Zoe were dragged in for interrogation as soon as you left. Al too, probably."

My heart jumped into my throat. My spine stiffened. I hadn't thought about the consequences to my friends.

Wells gave me a shake. "Allestair won't hurt them if he has no reason to. He'll likely compel them to tell the truth. Cilla will have to tell him about the 'path you had with her the night before, but from the sounds of it, you mostly asked her how she was doing." He rubbed my back soothingly. "Cilla and Zoe are already minor celebrities for being the first of the thirteen to conceive. And Cilla's due in a few weeks. It would look very odd if something happened to them. As you've discovered, Allestair is very conscious of his public image."

"What about Al?" I asked, guilt coiling in my stomach. I had been fully aware that I was using Al, and I would do it again to save Wells, but . . . as misguided as he was, Al still claimed to love me. And I'd taken full advantage. If he was being tortured because of me . . .

Wells gave my waist a squeeze. "Aloysuis won't go through anything that he hasn't already experienced in several centuries of being his father's son."

I stared at the ground. I knew how I'd feel if I were Al. Betrayed and left high and dry. He'd never considered my feelings, though, so I let my empathy drop. "What are you going to say to the king?"

All humor fell from Wells's face and that tense line between his eyebrows returned. "I'm not going to lie to you, Imogen, we're going to have to spin this carefully." He pulled a half-written report forward. "One advantage we do have is that your appearance was very public, both on our side and Sephrya's. Since I had requested aid and you did arrive in time to save us, I'm currently thanking him for sending said aid in such a timely manner."

I snorted.

"Imogen, I will need you to fall in line with this." His eyes bored into mine and I stilled. "Regardless of what you've managed to accomplish, Allestair is still my king, my step-father, my mother's husband, and my brother's father."

I clenched my jaw, fingers tightening over the tip of the desk, but kept quiet.

"The current line is that you were sent here as aid and arrived in the nick of time. If Allestair accepts that as the public narrative, we've gained level ground. If he challenges it, we have other issues."

My breath caught. "What would he—"

"I am hopeful that we'll be able to meet up with the other units before he can mobilize. The fact that Sephrya saw your lightning is another advantage. He would have to spin something very destructive to unseat this story, but he has had centuries of practice, Imogen." He put a hand on my knee. "Please understand that this is what I mean when I speak of bending versus breaking."

The tent flap rustled. "Excuse me, general . . ."

I hopped off Wells's lap and we both stood. When I turned around to face the tent's entrance my heart stopped. It was the dead redhead from the battlefield.

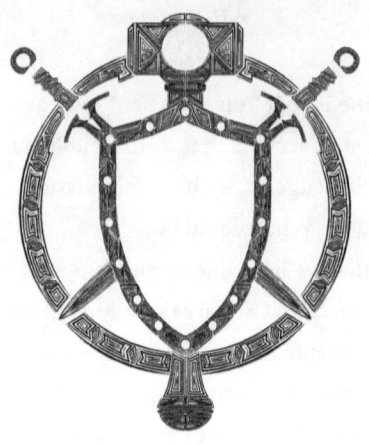

CHAPTER FIVE

I never felt like Solange was dead. Death is not usually a choice. Solange chose. She had options and she chose the one that wasn't me. I think that hurts worse.
—*Prince Aloysius Metellus*

"Kerlyn..." Wells walked around the desk toward her.

I blinked and shook my head. It wasn't the redhead I'd seen. It was a redhead who looked a lot like her. She was carrying a folded uniform and her face was swollen, perhaps from recently shed tears.

"I'm so sorry about Kaylie," he said. "Your daughter was—"

"About the size of your mate, if I'm not mistaken," Kerlyn interrupted brusquely.

I could tell she was holding back her grief by sheer force of will. Her aura was crushing indigo, with thick black fissures running through. Her throat bobbed as she looked me over. "I've got Kaylie's spare uniform here," she handed it to Wells. "They were able to get her armor back to me, and I've cleaned it, but they couldn't find her sword—"

"I think I have it," I said, hoarsely. I summoned it from where I had propped it against the cot and crossed to her on shaking legs. "I saw her after and..." I cleared my throat. Her aura was pulsing with cobalt dissolving into black, occasional pink ribbons snaking through only to shred themselves into confetti. "She had obviously taken a few down with her so I... told her I'd just finish what she started." I passed Kerlyn the sword. "You look a lot like her. Or she looks... looked like you." I swallowed. "I'm sorry."

Kerlyn examined the hilt, not taking her eyes off it when she asked, "And did you?" One tear fell when she looked back up at me, her emerald eyes shot with red. "Did you take out a few more of them for her?"

"Hundreds more I think..." I said, my own eyes beginning to burn.

"This was Kaylie's," her voice shook as she pointed to a spot just inside the loop guard where a K was scratched, an arrow making up the backbone of the letter. Her lips quivered and she smashed them together. "She chose you then." She thrust the sword back toward me.

"Kaylie was also a telepath, Imogen," Wells said, still looking at Kerlyn, his eyes soft, aura swirling with sympathetic pale blues. "Had she survived there would have been three of us in this unit."

Kerlyn snapped her gaze back to me. "You're a telepath?" When I nodded her eyes filled again. "Then I have no doubt she chose you. She was the only one of my girls to inherit the gift. From her father." A few more pink ribbons flipped through her aura, this time they didn't shatter. She squared her shoulders. "I'll be going through her trunk. Do you need anything else?"

Wells must have sensed the emotion choking me through our bond because he spared me by answering himself. "As it happens, Imogen had to leave in a rush to aid us, so she wasn't able to bring much with her." He indicated my small pack still on his desk.

"I'll just go through and see if there are any personal... things." She swallowed again. "Then I'll bring you the entire trunk. You can have what you need. Anything you don't... redistribute."

"Do you need help, Kerlyn?" Wells asked gently.

"I have help. Thank you, general." She straightened. "The three of us who survived are helping each other go through the rest before we move into our new ... anyway, I wanted to bring the uniform myself." She turned her green gaze on me again. "And I'm glad I did. Kaylie must have wanted me to know ... that she's okay." She spun on her heel and marched from the tent. I wondered how far she made it before giving in to tears.

I was trembling from head to foot when Wells crossed to me. He took the sword from my hand and looked at the spot Kerlyn had indicated, running a finger over the scratched K. "Interesting that it was Kaylie's sword you ended up with ..."

"I saw her ... h-h-hair ... first ..." I breathed, two tears cutting wet paths down my cheeks.

Realization flashed behind his eyes and his aura flowed into deep purples. He pulled me into a hug, tucking my head under his chin. "Imogen ..." I wrapped my arms around him and held hard.

The rest of the day was busy. Wells and I assisted with the dismantling and redistribution of bunks and personals. The hope was that eventually we'd meet up with the other five units and ours would be filled out from their extras. The shield would stay up until it began to fade. The estimation was about a day, but thus far I'd received a few compliments as to its opacity.

Wells had begun collecting—and writing—the dispatches to families of the dead. He'd allowed me to write to Cilla, but warned me that it wasn't wise to send it until after we'd heard back from the palace. We would be 'porting none of these communications until the shield went down. It wasn't worth the risk of sending someone outside to give away our position.

Other than the message to the king.

For that one, we would take the risk.

Wells hedged at the last minute, and tried to convince me to stay behind, resulting in a minor argument that I eventually won after pointing out that I still had more in reserves than everyone else. And since Wells didn't want his brief absence broadcast, it would also look suspicious if he left me behind on our first evening together.

After alerting Celphia, who would take charge in Wells's absence, the two of us slipped away from the box canyon camp beneath my cloaking shield. After we pushed through the barrier at the very edge of camp, I looked back. And couldn't help grinning like a jack-o'-lantern.

"I am awesome at magic," I said.

There was no box canyon from outside the shield. It merely looked like a continuation of solid rock. Even a very experienced tracker would have to know where to look or search the edge of the entire canyon to detect it.

Wells glanced over his shoulder. "Yes, excellent work, Demon, but if you could pay attention to the task at hand..."

I snapped my head forward again, testing the edges of our cloaking shield. Our plan was to walk a distance from the camp under the cloak—using no detectable kroma en route—then uncloak just long enough to port the message, recloak, wait two minutes, then uncloak for thirty seconds to receive a return if there was one. This was the agreed upon protocol in hostile territories.

Sephrya's humid air still clung to us like a wet washcloth, but beneath my shield we were undetectable. Preferable as we crossed the open plain. We aimed for the dense swamp in the distance, which wouldn't take us too long to get to. Even so, we were constantly scanning the area for telltale signs of scouts or traces of kroma. I let Wells keep a lookout and kept my concentration on our shield.

The sun was setting. Had we been here on vacation—or any non-lethal situation—it would have been beautiful. The slashes of cumulonimbus clouds cutting across the dense lavender sky reflected purples, oranges, and pinks. All colors of nervousness, excitement, and alarm, had I been reading the sky's aura. I let that thought float away.

When the sun set, my vision would be challenged. My aural sight was usually an advantage. I was able to see not only emotions, but kromatic barriers, and spells that others couldn't. However, that meant that my own shields were visible to me too. As the outside light diminished, my cloaking shield became an increasingly opaque, glittering, golden curtain dropped over us like a terrarium. And if I tried too hard to see beyond it, my own shield would make an opening in response to my need and let out a scent or a sound that I wasn't intending. This wasn't something I wanted to risk when we were exposed on a Sephryan plain.

"I know this takes a lot of concentration, Imogen," Wells said as we finally stepped into the humid wetland, leaving the vulnerability of the open grassland behind. We hoped the swampy ground would deter any scouts. "Are you up for answering some questions? I need to know a bit more about how your lightning works so I know where to direct you in battle."

My cloaking shield had improved dramatically since escaping Sephyra with Cilla. I'd honed it by sneaking around the palace anywhere and everywhere I wasn't supposed to be. Although it was draining, since we were completely undetectable this was a good time for us to discuss anything sensitive without the risk of being interrupted or overheard. I tested the edges of our cloak and my energy. I'd eaten an energy block before we left and we'd both had a large bowl of the soup being served—vegetable only tonight, happily for me, unhappily for most of the unit—but I didn't want to drain myself in the event that we did come across any enemies.

"I think if we slow down just a touch, I can answer questions and keep us covered, if you make sure I don't run into anything," I said. "I'll just pull my focus only to the shield and not worry about anything beyond it."

"I'll keep pace with you," he said. "And I'll make sure not to guide us straight into a tree." The ground was muddy, littered with puddles masquerading as terra firma. I had to keep the shield tight so that it would obliterate our footprints as it dragged behind us.

After a quick, probably unnecessary scan around the steadily darkening swamp, I dropped my focus into the area immediately surrounding us. Although there was still a bit of light left from the all-but-set sun, as soon as we'd entered the trees we were plunged into night. I could feel my sidhe body instinctively throwing all senses onto high alert in response to my nerves. I slowed us down and nodded at Wells without voicing my trepidation.

"You mentioned that you get additional energy from the lightning. I'm assuming this is only when you have access to the sky?" I dipped my chin, he went on. "What's the drawback to receiving that energy?"

I smiled. I'd found this out the hard way. Wells had warned me long ago that there would be consequences of some kind. Often the greater the power, the bigger the drawback. "If I use it for too long . . . it feels like my blood heats up. I need to stop and take a break and do other things. Or expend it, like I did when I was having too many feelings after I shoved you and threw it into the tree."

"Have you worked out a length of time? Or is it the amount of lightning pulled through you?" he asked, guiding us around one of the odd, skinny trees here. Their leaves were thick and limp, like damp feathers, and they all hung down toward the ground. Like sad, brown Christmas trees that had been forced into a wet T-shirt contest.

"I honestly don't know. I just kind of feel it," I said, intentionally resisting the urge to search my brain so that my focus wouldn't waver. "I didn't work it except during thunderstorms at the palace. I didn't want them to know what I was doing. There were three thunderstorms and I pushed it too far during the first one. By the third, I'd figured it out."

A branch cracked in the distance. We stilled. I couldn't help tightening my grip on Wells when the unmistakable sounds of something sliding through the swampy underbrush grew louder.

I clamped my other hand on Wells's arm when the feathery leaves of a low-hanging tree mere feet from us parted to reveal a long, scaly snout with three inch fangs protruding from both jaws.

"It can't see or smell us," Wells whispered, even though it shouldn't be able to hear us either.

"What the hell *is it*?" I hissed as it lumbered by on short, but powerful legs, each ending in three enormous, stained claws. Its eyes glowed an unnaturally bright green as it slid into a brackish pond, a long, thick tail propelling it away. "It's like a crocodile and a saber-toothed tiger had a baby."

Wells chuckled. "It's a surturak. Swamp imp."

"Imp? Not cool, how many of those are there?"

"I'm not worried about *them*, just keep the shield up." Before I could say anything more, he asked, "What happens if you use your lightning for too long?"

"I pass out," I said. "And . . . like . . ." I snapped my jaw shut, my cheeks warming.

"Imogen, you have to tell me in case it happens." He put his hand over mine where I clutched his sleeve and squeezed.

I took a deep breath. "I pass out, wherever I am, for an unknown amount of time." My face was in flames. I blew out another slow exhale, pushed through my shame, and focused on our shield. "Al found me afterward and . . . I don't remember most of it."

"Did Aloysius tell you what happened?" Wells's voice chilled the air around us.

"Yeah." I fought the urge to squeeze my eyes shut, embarrassment ripping through me. "We were supposed to have dinner that night. He said he found me sprawled on the terrace, soaking wet from the rain. He flipped out and carried me inside. I guess I woke up shortly after and was . . . ravenous."

I took a breath and checked the shield unnecessarily. Wells didn't speak. He pulled his arm from mine and tucked it around my waist, pulling me closer. Probably feeling my mortification through the bond.

"Al said it was like I was so hungry I was cramping when I woke up. I wouldn't speak to him, but he said it was like I was in pain and panicking."

"Al thought you were in pain?"

"That's what he said. I don't remember any of this part. Fortunately, our fish dinner was already there and I guess I ate all of it. My food, Al's food, every scrap that was there . . . I think the phrase he used was, 'like a wild dog with a fresh kill.' Then I passed out again. When I woke up—I remember this part—I was still hungry and felt a little loopy. Al had wrapped a towel around me, but otherwise I was still drenched from the rain."

Wells took several deep breaths. "And what did he believe was the cause for your... affliction? I'm assuming he knew about your lightning?"

"No," I said. "He thought Allestair's starvation techniques were finally having an effect. I never told anyone about the blocks Captain Marc gave me, so I let him believe that. I didn't want them to figure out what I was up to. I asked him not to tell anyone what happened, but I know he told his father."

I gasped as the ground dropped out from beneath me. Wells had walked us directly into an invisible puddle. My shield shuddered and a few holes opened up as I instinctively tried to see what was happening around me. I shut them quickly and let Wells reverse us back onto solid ground. He pulled me over to a tree nearby and we stilled.

My heart pounded as I watched the ripples spread out over what was now visible as a sizable, scum-covered pond. We'd just announced our presence to anything in the immediate vicinity. I wondered if the layer of algae over the stagnant water would carry our scent. Or if the hole that had opened in my shield would have let out just enough...

I wished we'd brought swords instead of just a dagger each. I'd like a little more reach if I saw one of those saber-toothed reptiles again. They looked like their skin might repel kroma.

"Maybe we should table this discussion—" I said, looking down at our legs. Wells was damp to the knees; I was soaked to the thighs. The swamp water didn't smell good either.

"I'll pay better attention." Wells was indeed, scanning the area around us intently. He pulled me in a different direction. "We'll walk a bit farther in and I'll be satisfied. What do you think that Al told his father about your... episode?"

I felt my jaw clench and forced myself to relax. "That I was starving. Some comments that Allestair made afterward made it perfectly clear that he thought I was folding. He also doubled down on meat at meals until your mother got sick of it. And it was about then that private dinners with Al became an increasingly regular thing." I risked a glance up at him. His face was set. "It all worked for my ulterior motive, so I played into it."

I could feel Wells's anger pulsing behind my own breastbone. Although it was understandable and I empathized, I worried that this wasn't the time for this kind of distraction.

"Anyway, now you know about the lightning. Where's the battlefield from here?" I asked, ready for a change of subject and for this mission to be behind us.

"A few more yards . . . that way," He pointed in a diagonal to my left. "If they did catch us here, which is unlikely unless they had someone waiting around, they would assume we'd camp somewhere nearby. Which is, of course, why we didn't."

I nodded, then dropped my eyes down to the softly glowing circle of shield immediately around our feet.

"We'll be able to wink back once we're done. If they detect that kroma, we'll be long gone and beneath the camp's shield again before they can try to track us. Now tell me about these . . . explosives you've made. How do they work, what's their range, what are their disadvantages?"

"Oh, well . . ." I cleared my throat. "The ones on my belt are pretty small. They're like a golf ball—they fit in the palm of your hand. They have a fuse. I light that. Then there's three seconds before it explodes and obliterates anything within a thirty- to fifty-foot radius."

Wells stopped walking abruptly.

"Are we there?" I looked up. I couldn't read his aura without compromising the shield, too many things to focus on, but his emotions grated against my sternum like heartburn. I tried to sort through them . . .

"Yes, Imogen, let's say we're there." He yanked me close to him. I put my arms around his waist as we'd practiced. I wanted to read his aura, but didn't risk it. Keeping my attention on our shield. He pulled the message from his pocket, held it in his hand, shifted his focus. "Now."

I let the shield drop and lent him my energy simultaneously.

"Done," he said. I pulled the shield back up. We now had two minutes to wait.

"Why are you so upset?" I asked, keeping my arms around his waist and looking up at him. "Is it—"

"Imogen, is your shield up?" He shifted his weight, glancing around, arms wrapped around my shoulders. I could feel tension running through him. His anger dissolved into something else...

"Yes," I said, testing it. "Yes, it's up and there are no holes."

For a few moments we stood there. I thought I heard a faint rustling in the trees directly behind me. I instinctively checked the shields again. *The shield's good, there are no holes.* I 'pathed, even though I knew that no one could hear us.

Don't waste energy 'pathing. Stay still and stay calm. Wells's grip on me tightened.

I hugged him back, pressing my ear to his chest. His scent was calming, but the galloping of his heart wasn't. I trained my eyes on the woods beyond us, but my aural sight got snagged on the shield. I didn't want to disrupt it again, so I buried my face against Wells and counted my breaths, concentrating only on the shield.

Near the end of the two minutes, the trees were silent again. Wells hadn't seen anything. It was nearly time for us to drop the shield and receive any reply from the palace that might be forthcoming.

"Imogen," Wells said. "The message will come to me, but if anything happens rendering me unable to collect it, I need you to get it back to the camp."

"Got it," I said. We had been over this. Protocol required a statement and an acceptance.

"I need you to take the message to camp first and then return to see if there is anything left," he said.

"I hate that phraseology but okay," I said.

"I don't have a good feeling about this, Imogen," he said.

My blood chilled.

"Back-to-back," he said. "Don't remove the shield until I say so and be ready with an offensive blast. Can you do that?"

"I can," I said, warming my hands for sticky fire. "Ready when you are."

"Drop it."

I did.

They hit us instantly.

CHAPTER SIX

Wells is not allowed to die first. I am dying first. Even if it's by two seconds. I will not have him taken away from me again.
—Imogen Delaney

I deflected the first kill shot. Right into the face of the silver-haired Sephryan who fired it. Two others materialized, dropping cloaking shields and blasting. I blocked both attacks, ricocheting them back toward my opponents. Then used both hands to fan sticky fire out in a glorious arc. I caught three of them. And several tree trunks. The limp feathers of the sad trees ignited instantly. Burning from the tips up. Leaving nothing but floating sparks and curling twigs behind. The swamp was soon as bright as day. The humid atmosphere confettied with drifting embers.

I sliced the air with my arm, throwing out blue-black blades of kroma to finish the Sephryans writhing under my flames. Splintered wood and sprays of blood joined the glowing sparks in the air. I cast out with my aural sight and detected no one else in front of me. My senses narrowed to the feel of Wells's back on mine, the muscles bunching and shifting. The thrum of kroma pulsing from both of us.

I ducked under Wells's arm to fight at his side. Arching the blade of my hand as I went, launching a cutting wave of kroma as I turned. He was fighting four. Only one of them—a tall male with golden hair—seemed to be a true threat. These were probably random scouts who had come on us by chance, perhaps detecting our scents on the water we'd fallen into. Or on the breeze if the hole in my shield had let out enough.

At this point, it didn't matter.

I let Wells handle the golden-haired threat. I focused on taking out the others. The first two went down quickly with sticky fire and a blade follow-up. Sticky fire was one of my favorite, most effective weapons. But I hated watching people burn to death. If I had time and energy, I would finish them with a cutting wave.

"Nice to see you, Llewellyn." Golden grinned, ducking a strike.

"Stian." Wells tossed an indigo immobilization blast. Stian deflected it back. We dodged. Our final, bronze-haired opponent was tricky. I let Wells handle Stian while I focused on the trickster winking around the wood.

I lit the entire area on fire trying to hit him. Nothing would be left of this swamp by morning. Not without kromatic damage control. We'd need to wink out soon or be burned. I leapt forward, determined to finish Tricky. Wells yanked me back to his side.

It was a mistake.

Stian saw it.

I lobbed a spear of killing kroma. Aiming for where I guessed Tricky would wink next, internally cheering when he appeared right in front of my blast. At the same time, Stian went defensive. Blocking several of Wells's attacks. Ducking behind flaming tree trunks which splintered. Burning feathered foliage exploded in the air, sparks flying.

Stian winked to our rear. We had only half turned before he feinted at Wells, then shot a killing curse at me. My shield bloomed on instinct. Partially deflected it.

Cold kroma sliced into my side like a blade of ice. My blood chilled instantly. But I spun with Wells to blast Stian. The two of us hit him hard. I caught him with a blade to the shoulder. Then stumbled against Wells, my legs giving out.

Wells glanced down at me. His eyes widened. His wash of dread swept through the bond before it dissolved into numbness. He threw a final shot at Stian, knocking him into one of my flaming trees. Without waiting to see if we'd finished him, Wells grabbed me and winked.

Outside the camp's shield, I collapsed against Wells with an "mmmphh." My limbs went boneless. Wells scooped me into his arms and pushed through the shield. The instant we were through he hollered for a medic. My arms and legs bounced limply as he sprinted, dodging tents and soldiers, but I felt nothing. It was as if my strings had been cut; only my mind was sluggish as well. I was barely cognizant of being laid on a cot inside a tent. The remains of my tank top were cut off and tossed aside.

Sounds went fuzzy. I was dimly aware of Wells talking rapidly over someone. His voice sharp. Panicked. I recognized the brusque female voice. Cutting him off. Giving him stern direction.

Wells came into view, kneeling beside me. He gripped the back of my hair, lifted my head and forced my jaw open. Someone else tilted a bottle over my mouth. Something warm and liquid slid down my throat, the muscles swallowing automatically. I felt as if my body were on autopilot and I was a passenger inside, passively watching. The bottle disappeared from view. Wells took my cheeks in both hands and turned me toward him. His face was bloodless, eyes wide with panic. Wells was usually so in control of his expressions, to see him obviously terrified surprised me.

I tried to reach for him, but my body wouldn't respond.

"Imogen," he said, his voice hoarse. I had to focus hard to hear him. As if my head were under water. "Stay. Stay with me. Please."

"She's not going anywhere." The brusque voice belonged to Kerlyn. Her hands glowed with rose-gold light as she fiercely pushed kroma into the gash on my side.

That doesn't look good, I thought. *I didn't know Kerlyn was a medic...*

"General, we've had a signal—" I recognized Celphia's voice through the water in my ears.

"Take care of it."

"But, sir, it's from—"

Wells didn't let go of me, but his head snapped toward his lieutenant, his eyes glinting furiously red, "Gods' bones, Celphia, I've given you command of the unit until you're informed otherwise!"

"But, sir, they don't report until you—"

Wells exploded. "Until this situation changes you are to act as if *I* am dying in this tent and you are to *take care of it!*"

I had never heard him speak to *anyone* like that. *Why is he being so mean to her?* I wondered.

Celphia hesitated. Wells *snarled* at her, looking every bit the dangerous sidhe from Earth's worst faerie tales.

"Yes, sir." She practically fled.

Kerlyn pressed on my wound with her luminous hands. Black bile flooded out. I sank farther under.

My eyelids drifted closed. Wells shook me. Begging me again to stay. *I just need a nap.* I wanted to tell him. *Sleep makes everything better.* I couldn't even 'path. I was so tired. Yet every time my eyelids blinked shut, Wells shook me. This new, stricken expression in his eyes bothered me. And he'd been so rude to Celphia. She obviously had an important message.

I stretched for him through the bond, but it was as numb as the rest of me. I fought to keep my eyes open for him. "Just . . . tired . . ." I forced out past numb lips, trying to reassure him.

To my horror, a tear dropped from his eye. He kept my head in his hands. Kept shoving my hair—ultra curly due to Sephyra's humidity—back behind my ears. *You're fighting a losing battle there,* I wanted to say. He needed to laugh. I couldn't make my voice work again.

"Just a few more minutes, Imogen, then you can rest," Kerlyn said.

Sweat gleamed on her brow. She continued to push waves of rose kroma over the wound in my side.

A few more minutes. I could do a few more minutes if it kept Wells from crying. He was much too upset. It disturbed me that I couldn't feel the bond.

Wells kept kissing me. I could feel him trembling. He kept begging me to look at him. Telling me how brave I was. How strong. How much he loved me.

Am I dying? I thought. *It doesn't feel too bad* . . .

Kerlyn's hands continued their shining dance over my wound. The black substance had all been drained. My torso warmed gradually. Starting with the gash and fanning out until my limbs were tingling. The numbness dissipated and the bond surged back to life. Wells's terror roiled within my own chest. Kerlyn touched him on the shoulder.

"Alright, general, she's out of the woods now," she said. There were dark circles under her eyes, but she was smiling. "This next part is painful, so I'm going to put her out. Otherwise you'd both feel it. Imogen, you can rest now."

Wells's shining russet eyes were the last thing I saw.

I woke in Wells's tent. Bundled up in his cot. He was at his desk working. Probably writing more death notices. For a moment, I simply watched him. Listened to his pen scratching away in the relative silence of the night. Right now we were safe. Together. I let myself bask in the peace. Breathe it in. We're alive.

I figured it was late. Noise outside the tent was minimal. No people moving about. There wasn't even a breeze to stir the air. I inhaled deep and slow, enjoying the stretch of my lungs, then exhaled a sigh. Wells's head snapped up.

"Hi," I said, the corners of my mouth lifting. I tried to sit up, but he was beside me before I could so much as push back the covers.

"Stay down, Demon, you're not supposed to try to get up yet." He pressed a hand to my shoulder and knelt by the cot, summoning a bottle of blue liquid from his desk. "I'm to give you this."

"It's impossible to drink things lying down," I complained. He pushed his hand beneath my head and tilted it upward. I grimaced, but didn't argue. Whatever I was drinking was cool and tasted of mint. *That was a nice surprise.* "I feel like I just drank Scope," I said. He laid my head back on the pillow and 'ported the bottle away. "Mouthwash on Earth," I supplied before he could ask. "Can I at least roll over?"

"Not yet," he said, one hand brushing my hair back from my forehead. "You're supposed to stay still for fifteen minutes after your potion. Then we'll see. Kerlyn is going to stop by and check you soon."

I glanced around the tent. I spotted my arrows and grenade pouches off to one side. "Did you . . ." I squinted at them. "Did you put extra shields around my . . . experiments?"

"If you mean your deadly explosives, then yes, Imogen, I did." His hand stilled and his voice went a touch sharper as he tilted my head toward him. "That's actually something I wanted to discuss with you before we got ambushed. You said these things destroy anything in a thirty-foot radius? *One* of them does that?"

"Give or take," I said. "I haven't done specific measurements. The arrows do worse."

"And you were *wearing all of them* during a *battle*?"

"I had shields on them," I said. He sank his forehead onto the cot. "I mean, I needed to get them here . . ."

"Imogen." He lifted his head. "Were you this reckless with your life when you were human?"

"I . . ." My brow furrowed. My first trip home from the police station when I was eight years old flashed through my mind. After my mother had died I'd taken up lock picking. According to the counselors, it gave me a sense of control over my environment. I'd broken into the zoo. My grandfather had come to the station to claim me. "*You can't be this reckless, Imogen.*

What if an animal had gotten out and gotten a hold of you? What would we have done if we'd lost you that way?"

I looked up at Wells. "Are shields not . . . enough?"

He sighed and dug my hand out from under the covers. For a moment he just sat on the floor, one elbow on the cot, holding my hand, playing with my fingers.

"I'm sorry," I said. "I didn't think."

"Imogen." He wouldn't look at me, gaze fixed on our hands. "As much as I love having you near me, touching you, knowing you're . . ." He cleared his throat and wrapped his hands around mine. "I wonder if it wouldn't be better for you to go back—"

"No!" I tried to sit up, but Wells's reflexes were quicker and he pressed me back to the cot. I wrapped a hand around his wrist. "Look, I know what just happened was scary. Tonight didn't go well, okay, but I can still be useful! Once I heal up, I have my lightning—"

"Demon, you were hit with a killing curse, that's not something anyone bounces back from quickly." His eyes were bleak when they found mine.

I pulled in a shaky breath, my stomach in knots. "Wells, where would I go? Think about what Allestair has already done; nearly destroyed one of his own units trying to . . . further his own agenda. That's after locking me up and starving me. What will he do if we obligingly separate? Even if I went back to stay with Cilla and Zoe he would find me and I worry about what he might do to them. Look, I know you're scared."

I wiggled my other arm from beneath the covers and cupped his face. "I was terrified when I thought you might be gone. But I think if you really sit down and think about this logically . . . I just don't think sending me back is the safest bet."

Wells was still for a long moment, his gaze internal. Then he let out a breath. "You're right, I suppose. At the very least you should stay here until we find out what Allestair's next move might be."

He leaned over, half on the cot, and wrapped his arms around my shoulders, still holding my hand, and rested his forehead against mine. The only sounds were nocturnal insects and birds and our own breathing. My stomach slowly unclenched and I decided to take that as a win for now. There was no way I was going to be separated again. No matter how altruistic his motives.

"Are you tired?" I asked. *He must be.* "I'm sure I could scoot over..." I heard him swallow.

"No," he said. "I'm not moving you until Kerlyn says it's okay." He lifted my hand to his lips and held it there for several seconds before kissing it twice and bringing it back to the covers.

"Did you get the message that Celphia was trying to tell you about?" I asked.

"No, they wouldn't respond to her energy signature. I'll have to get it when they report in person." He glanced at me. "I have spies out. They send a signal when they have a message that the watch is instructed to look out for, but they'll only report to me. I'll have to make adjustments for the future."

"You were kind of mean to her."

"I've apologized," he said softly, kissing my hand again. "I thought I'd lost you, Imogen. I thought I was watching you die."

"I'm sorry," I whispered. I knew what it felt like to lose someone. But I didn't know what it felt like to watch someone die, unable to do anything to stop it. I hoped I'd never have to find out. "I have to be honest, I figured that's why you were saying all those nice things about me."

That got a crack of a smile. "I'll have to say nice things about you more often."

"I noticed you left how funny I am off the list," I said. "For next time."

He lifted himself off the cot and shook his head at me, half smiling. "There won't be a next time," he said. "I'll just start saying more nice things about you in general. You could try it too, if you wanted."

"If we're making a to-do list, we should also have sex soon," I said. He exploded into a full laugh. "I'm one hundred percent serious," I said, his laughter warming me. "I think it's among the first things you're supposed to do after you almost die. Also, it's been awhile."

"Everyone hears everything here, Demon," he said, still grinning at me. He pulled himself off the floor to perch on the edge of the cot.

"I can be quiet," I whispered.

"You are never quiet," he whispered back, tugging one of my unruly curls.

"I've become very quiet and sneaky." I ran my hand up his leather pants. He caught my fingers before they went anywhere scandalous, narrowing his eyes at me. But he couldn't keep the smile off his face.

"Oh, good, she's awake?" Kerlyn pushed her way into the tent.

Wells squeezed my hand once before standing and moving away to give her room. "Awake and feisty," he said, eyes glinting.

"That's always a good sign." She yanked down the covers. I was still in the sports bra I'd been wearing, but my pants had been removed, and someone had put me in clean underwear. "Everything from the waist down was soaked in your blood and the bile from the death spell," she said, following my gaze. She gently probed my left side. There was a slashing, two-pronged scar, like an arrow pointing outward from my stomach. It looked years old. "Some of this may fade, but you'll always have a mark, I'm afraid."

"Scars are cool," I said.

She barked a laugh. "You gave her the potion?" At Wells's nod she asked me, "How did it taste?"

"Minty fresh," I said.

"Good! That's promising. Let's get you to stand." She helped me sit up and swing my legs over the side of the cot, then gestured Wells to my other side. "We're right here if you stumble, but I need to see you stand on your own. If you can."

I nodded. I felt a little shaky. Like I'd skipped a meal. But nothing like I expected to feel after almost dying. My legs trembled, but I stood. Wells kept a hand behind me but Kerlyn immediately began poking and tugging at me. Her hands were glowing, and left luminous, rose-gold prints on my body which faded several seconds later.

"I'm going to shove this shoulder, don't let me move you. Mmhm, now this one. Good. Now I'm going to pull here, don't let me move you ... And do you feel any pain when I press here ...? Good ... If I press here do you feel any dread? Depression? Anything like ... Good ..."

While she examined me, she glanced over her shoulder at Wells, who was leaning against his desk where he'd moved once it became obvious I wasn't going to fall over. "I hope you got the bastard?" she asked.

"You knew him," I said, my eyes finding his. "He knew you."

Wells's gaze darkened. "Stian. He's a sadist. Tortures prisoners for King Demian. Stian's responsible for killing our last two ambassadors."

"Oh," I said, then went quiet. I remembered that Al was responsible for torturing people for his father. And how haunted he'd looked afterward.

As if he could glean my train of thought, Wells 'pathed, *Al hates when his father has him torture during interrogations. Stian enjoys his job. And has a knack for knowing what his victims fear most. He's been doing it for centuries.*

Before I could let that settle and decide whether or not to ask Wells how he knew all of this about Stian, Kerlyn finished her examination. "She'll still have remnants of the killing kroma in her system for a few days, but I think she'll be alright. Extra rest and we'll dose her twice a day for a bit. She'll be able to fight."

"About that," Wells said. "Imogen, what if you didn't fight? We'll be joining up with the other units, so we're not short anymore. You could remain in camp and help with the injured or—"

"I'll stop if you stop," I said, crossing my arms.

"Imogen—"

"I know you're all freaked out right now and I sympathize." I dropped my hands to my hips. "But I thought you were dead too. So I know how much it sucks. And you forget." I narrowed my eyes. "The king sent me here as aid."

Wells glared back. *Careful, you clever thing,* he 'pathed. And although the edge in his mental tone had my chest tightening a bit, I knew I had him.

No one would understand why he refused to put me to use if the king had sent me to help the army.

"You can't ask me to hide in a bush somewhere while you go out to fight. I don't think it's fair for you to even ask me." I glanced down. "And in spite of the fact that I'm not wearing pants, I am very serious."

Kerlyn was smiling, her eyes a little misty. I wondered if I'd reminded her of her daughter in some way or if it was just the talk of death. "If you're worried about her getting fatigued," she said to Wells, "put her on a mount. I believe we've had one freed up."

"We have actually." Wells raised his eyebrows at me, the tension in his shoulders visibly easing. "Can you ride?"

"Like horses? Yeah, I learned when I was nine years old." My grandfather had decided I needed a hobby aside from lock-picking and threw me into a horse camp. "I get to ride a horse?" I loved horses.

Kerlyn's eyes were dancing. "The concept is similar, but don't compare them to horses, they get touchy. And they understand more of what we say than they let on."

"I'll take her to meet him tomorrow and see if he takes to her. Thank you, Kerlyn. For the idea and for the help." Wells accepted a few more bottles of blue liquid that Kerlyn 'ported in.

"Take me to see who? If I'm not riding a horse, what am I riding?" I was starting to want more clothes.

Wells smiled, "A battle unicorn."

CHAPTER SEVEN

Be careful of the things you desire so terribly. They already have a hold on you and frequently have hidden strings with which to tie you up.
—Queen Iphigenia Eigneachan Metellus

Wells continued as if he hadn't just exploded my brain. "We did have one lose a rider in the last—"

"I'm sorry, was the potion I drank a hallucinogen or did you just tell me that unicorns exist? And that I'm going to . . . ride one?" The last two words eked out on a whisper.

"Unicorns exist," Wells confirmed, as if this was a thing I could absorb calmly. "And you *might* get to ride one if he accepts you. They're very discriminating—"

I clamped my hands over my mouth to smother the high-pitched gasping sound that escaped from the soul of my inner child. I skipped to vent some excitement, but my knees buckled. Wells caught me by the arm, "Careful," holding tightly until I regained my balance.

"Kaylie saw her first unicorn when she joined the army. She was excited too." Kerlyn smiled softly at me, then turned to Wells and tapped the vials of potions he cradled in his other hand. "I'll let you take it from here. One of these in the morning and one in the evening. See if you can get her calmed down enough to sleep. The burst of energy is normal, but it won't last."

I managed to stammer out some thanks as Kerlyn left, then spun toward Wells, who was placing the potions carefully on his desk and thankfully didn't see me stumble again. "I know that it's inappropriate for me to be excited right now, but *unicorns exist and no one told me*," I whispered.

He turned toward me, half-smiling.

"Why haven't I seen one? Why have you kept this awesomeness from me?" My knees gave out again as I tried to rush toward him.

"Careful, Imogen." He caught me, eyes tightening with worry. "Perhaps we should get you back in bed." I threw my arms around his neck and hoisted myself up, wrapping my legs around his hips until I was hanging onto him like a koala. He looped his arms around me.

"Okay, see? No more stumbling," I said. "Please can we go see the unicorns?"

"It's the middle of the night. You want to make a good impression, so you shouldn't wake him up unnecessarily." He gave me a peck on the nose. "And you haven't seen them before because they're exceedingly bloodthirsty, so we mainly use them for battle."

"Amazing."

"Their habitat is at the center of camp, so you anchored your shield right above it. I wasn't intentionally hiding them from you." Wells's mood had lightened since Kerlyn's visit. He carried me around the tent as he explained, extinguishing lanterns and securing the tent flaps. "You must have just missed them when you winked into the sky. I had their riders signal them to wink back to camp when the last battle was becoming a massacre. They're incredibly rare and impossible to train. I didn't want to risk Sephrya slaughtering them. In general they don't like relying on intelligent animals that they can't control. Unicorns are much too unpredictable for their tastes.

They bond with their riders, but they may accept another one if theirs... becomes unavailable. In any sense. We'll just have to see if Prism accepts you."

"His name is Prism? I'm so fucking excited. Do you have a unicorn?"

Wells nodded. "Obsidian."

I stared at him. "You just became one thousand percent hotter."

Wells laughed, then patted my butt. "Alright, little Demon, you heard the medic. Time to get you settled down to sleep."

"I know one way to get me settled down." I leaned in and kissed him. Soft at first, then when he didn't pull away, I pushed deeper. His hands moved up to the bare skin of my torso. I adjusted my legs, eliminating any space between us.

He broke the kiss, grabbed my hips, and tried to shift me back, "Imogen, a lot of people are missing their partners here. It's not fair to loudly—"

"I can be quiet," I whispered into his ear, then gave it a tug with my teeth. His warm exhale brushed my shoulder.

"You better be."

Before I knew it we were down on the dusty carpet. The cot made too much noise, according to Wells. My underwear was off in seconds.

It had been too long. Our kisses turned hungry. Not bothering to come up for air while we shifted his clothes out of the way. He pulled me on top, our naked hips pressing together before he broke the kiss to move down my neck, nipping and tasting. I bit my lower lip, holding back the moans craving to escape as I moved against him, tension already pulsing through my core. He explored my breasts with hands, tongue, and teeth, as if he couldn't get enough of the taste and feel of me.

His scent and touch were intoxicating. The desire to drink him in was almost as blindingly urgent as before we had accepted the mating bond. I couldn't hold back. My hips rolled with increasing speed. His hands gripped me harder. I arched my back as that one last filament at my center ignited...

I shattered with breathtaking quickness. Sucking in a gasp. My body moving on its own now. The need to be silent increasing the intensity. "Fuck," I breathed. I collapsed on top of him. Panting.

He continued to kiss and nip my neck and shoulders. Skating his long fingers over my back and rear.

I love your ass, he 'pathed, giving it a squeeze.

My ass loves you back...

I felt him fighting back a chuckle. I lifted my head, finding his lips with mine. He moved one hand to my head, fingers mixing with my hair, holding me into the kiss while he entered me slowly. My breath quickened again. I took control. Moving us faster. He followed. His hands still roaming, gripping a little harder.

Within seconds we were both quietly losing composure. I managed to keep myself to a sprinkle of barely whispered curses as I came undone the second time. Other than a few sharp inhales, Wells was completely silent. The convulsive tightening of his hands on my hips, clutching me to him while he pushed hard into me, the only indication of his completion.

For several moments, I lay on top of him, his arms wrapped around me, both of us breathing hard, our hearts hammering against our rib cages as if they were trying to break out and join each other. Wells ran fingertips down my spine in light strokes. Both of us were slightly damp from exertion in the humid night air. Not enough kromatic energy to waste on cooling the tents.

We can't fall asleep on the floor, Demon, he 'pathed. *If someone comes in, they'll jump to the conclusion that we've been slaughtered. Not to mention that it might be a bit indecorous.*

I kissed his cheek in silent agreement as I sat up. His hand drifted over the new scar on my side, fingers tracing the jagged line. His aura dimmed. He sighed, shoved himself to a seat, and wrapped his arms around me. I leaned in and hugged him back.

I don't care how many scars I get as long as we're never separated again, I 'pathed.

I'd still like to minimize grievous wounds if at all possible, Imogen.

Once dressed—Kerlyn had brought Kaylie's trunk in, full of practical clothes—we settled on the narrow cot, sans sheets. The night was warm and so were we, snuggled together on our sides. He threw an arm across my chest, pulling me against him. My body relaxed instantly.

Told you I could be quiet, I 'pathed, sleepily. I felt him chuckle against my back.

Did you know you swear in English during sex? His amusement colored the 'path.

The sidhe spoke all languages, and so did I, now that I was one. Since I'd been turned I automatically conversed in Perimovian unless Cilla and I were together and wanted to reminisce about Earth. *I had no idea. I don't even know what I was saying really.*

He kissed my shoulder. *I liked it.*

Sleep swallowed me like quicksand.

When I finally woke, the light in the tent was noon-bright. The sheets had been tucked over me. Wells was at his desk and looked like he'd been awake for hours.

I pushed myself up with a groan, swiping my eyes.

"Good morning," I mumbled.

"Good afternoon," he replied, smiling. He plucked a bottle of blue potion from the cluster on his desk and took a seat on the edge of the cot. "You've missed breakfast, but we can get you some lunch soon."

"I never sleep until the afternoon, this is crazy." I knocked the potion back.

"You're going to be sleeping more than normal until all of that death kroma is out of your system," he said, taking the bottle from me and running a hand down the back of my head. He pressed a gentle kiss to my forehead. "I should probably get some contraceptive tonic for you today. Just in case..."

"Not necessary," I yawned, stretching my back. "The spellbook I got the potion from said I'd be infertile for four to six months afterward."

Wells stared at me. His lips pressed into a thin line as he floated the empty bottle back to the desk. "I don't like this, Imogen. You have a consistent record of risking yourself—"

"As we say on Earth, 'desperate times call for desperate measures,'" I said. "I promise I won't make a habit of concocting and ingesting dangerous potions."

Shock fizzed through me when Wells pinched my chin between his thumb and forefinger and forced me to look at him. "Listen to me very carefully, Imogen. I know how hard you fought to get here, and I appreciate your ingenuity and resourcefulness, but I cannot have you taking risks like that here."

"Okay, I won't." I tried to tug away, but he held fast. "Hey!"

"I'm not finished." His eyes flashed crimson. "That little trick you pulled in front of Kerlyn—"

This time I did yank my chin away. "It wasn't a trick. It was a reminder. And I'm pretty sure you would have cut me off at the knees if you hadn't realized I was right."

"That's not the point." He shifted closer until we were nearly nose to nose. "If you disagree with me, I'll need you to speak to me in private. I cannot have you trapping me and undermining me in front of people."

My jaw dropped. "I wasn't trying to undermine you."

"But you were fully aware that you were trapping me." He leaned back and folded his arms.

I pressed my lips together. "But I was right."

He squeezed his eyes shut and took a long breath before opening them. "I reiterate that you are missing my point. Are you doing it on purpose?"

I chewed on my lip, not quite ready to back down. Wells didn't usually mind if I pushed back on something. Finally, I shook my head.

Some of the hard lines faded, but his eyes remained locked on mine. "Imogen, you are intelligent and strong-willed, two things I love about you, but I need to impress upon you that you know nothing about war. Much less a sidhe war. I cannot have you making snap decisions especially when I have explicitly opposed an action. I don't mind a little mental sparring with you when we're home, but the stakes are too high here."

I blew out a breath. "Okay. I get it. I'm sorry."

Wells's expression remained flat. Unmollified. "I want to show that spell to Captain Marc when we speak to him next. Ask if he's ever seen anything like it."

"Fine with me." I pushed the covers back and freed my legs. He stood up to give me room. I swung out of bed and dug around in the trunk for some clothes. When I stood, he was right behind me, wrapping his arms around my waist. Some of the tension left my shoulders. "I just want to help you."

His heart thumped steadily against me. "This war has already been one challenge after another. You can help most by listening. I don't want to have to worry about you too."

My chest tightened, but I decided to let this go for now. I was ultimately here to support Wells, and I would. "Are we going to visit my unicorn soon?"

"As soon as you're dressed. It'll be time to feed them, which is fortunate. They'll be in a good mood," he said, giving me one last squeeze before releasing me. "And don't call him 'your unicorn.' For one, he hasn't accepted you as a rider yet, and secondly, they get touchy about *belonging* to anyone."

"I can get behind that," I said. These unicorns were obviously just like me. We were going to be besties. "I'll be out in a second." I headed toward the wash basin for a sponge bath.

"Imogen."

I paused at the entrance to the dubious wash area and glanced back.

He was leaning on the desk, arms folded, watching me. "What other pithy sayings do you have on Earth?"

I gave him a small smile. We hadn't fought nearly so much before and I was willing to bet he liked it about a little as I did. "We have lots. We do enjoy our pithy sayings. But another applicable one is 'all's fair in love and war.'"

CHAPTER EIGHT

Know the rules, and know them intimately. Know why they exist and what they protect. Only then can you consider bending them.
—Captain Marcellus Tibercio

I was vibrating with anticipation when we finally wound our way through camp to the unicorns' area. Wells had insisted that I get something in my stomach first. An unnecessary delay in my opinion, but I humored him, chugging soup so fast I choked. I dressed in my leather uniform pants and one of Kaylie's sturdy gray tank tops.

Although I knew it was highly unlikely, I wanted to be ready on the off-chance Prism let me ride him today. A hope that I kept hidden deep in my heart, not even admitting it to Wells.

The unicorns' habitat was beautiful. A kromatically created forest stood in the middle of our swampy camp. Trees with multicolored leaves swayed in a nonexistent breeze. There was no breeze in Sephrya. I assumed someone in camp must have earth kroma similar to Cilla's. My heart did a bittersweet wiggle thinking about her. I hoped she was okay. I also knew that she would *love* this.

"What do they eat?" I asked Wells, practically pulling him toward the swaying, vibrant trees.

He kept a firm grip on my hand. He'd already told me several times not to run at them or I'd risk getting skewered. "Pears and moonfruit are their favorites, but any fruit will do. They'll also design to eat vegetables and grain if resources are scarce, as they are now," he said with a grimace. "But I did ask one of their handlers to use a bit of extra kroma to grow this for you." He produced a small golden pear from his pocket. "You remember the steps?"

"Thanks." I took the pear. "Pear first, just hold it out and see if he takes it, let him sniff me, wait until he offers his horn to touch, then 'path him."

"They do like to be paired with telepaths so they can communicate with their riders, but as we're rare, it obviously doesn't happen often, so you have that going for you." He squeezed my hand. "Give his horn a nice, appreciative exploration before 'pathing. They can't see their own horns, so they enjoy having them touched and admired. On their terms of course."

Then we were at the edge of the enchanted oasis. The handlers had obviously waited until our arrival to unload barrel-sized, wooden buckets full of vegetables and grain from a cart. They set them around the edge of the oasis. We waited twenty feet back from the forest. Right where the enchanted grass line ceased and became muddy camp dirt.

A turquoise head with a glittering coral horn at its center appeared among the foliage. I gasped and squeezed Wells's hand, trembling with the effort of keeping still.

Please try not to explode, he 'pathed.

I ignored him. My eyes were glued to the trees.

The enormous turquoise unicorn picked her way carefully to the offered food. Her coral hooves bright against the enchanted lavender-green grass. Her muscles bunching and rippling under her glossy coat. She examined the buckets and sighed, finding them lacking. She had to be twenty... maybe even twenty-three hands high. Pushing eight feet tall for sure. She shook her long, pink mane, clearly irritated, then tossed a resigned snort over her shoulder. Shortly afterward, the trees were alive with the rustling sounds of approaching unicorns in every color of the rainbow. They were all between twenty to thirty hands high, putting any of Earth's largest draft horses to shame.

Close your mouth, Imogen, something will fly in.

I snapped my mouth shut, cutting Wells a sideways glare before turning my attention back to the small blessing crossing in front of us. I'd been informed that afternoon that a group of unicorns was called a "blessing" and to never refer to them as a herd. At least not where they could hear you.

A tall male unicorn with a coat so black it seemed to gobble up the sunlight paused en route to the buckets to look over at Wells. He gave a snort, bobbed his head, and resumed his original path.

That's Obsidian, Wells told me. *If he's in a good mood he might come say hello to me after he's eaten.*

You're so lucky.

He chuckled and shook our joined hands. *I've told him to inform Prism that he's being assigned a rider today, so he should be looking for us. And there he is. The violet one with the black mane and tail.*

I froze. Prism was the most beautiful of them all as far as I was concerned. His coat was a deep, shimmering purple. His muzzle and stockings were charcoal. His mane, tail, and gleaming horn were deepest onyx.

His head snapped toward me, his nostrils flared, and his tail lifted, floating out behind him like a banner.

Hold out your pear. Remember the steps. Wells squeezed my hand and stepped away. It was up to me now.

Heart thundering, I extended my arm and flattened my palm, displaying the golden pear.

Prism's ears pricked so far forward they almost brushed against his horn. I noticed that their edges were ringed in charcoal as well. He separated from the blessing and stepped carefully over to me. His hooves and horn were so shimmeringly onyx, they looked wet. I held my breath when he reached me. *You are absolutely the most beautiful creature I have ever seen in my life,* I thought to myself, careful not to let it slip into a 'path.

He gingerly lipped up the pear, dipping his sweeping black eyelashes once. Prism closed his dark, liquid eyes as he chewed and dipped his massive head, his long mane and forelock curtaining his jawline. His head was level with my shoulders now, muzzle near my hips and horn just over my left shoulder. He had to be twenty-five hands high.

Don't touch the horn yet, I told myself, holding still. I wanted to speak to him so badly. My stomach was twisting with excitement. I curled my fingers into fists to keep from reaching out and running my hands through his mane.

Finished with his pear, Prism raised his honeydew-sized muzzle and took his first sniff. His charcoal nostrils flared as his breath brushed my hair back. He smelled like nighttime thunderstorms. I held still as he began a careful exploration of my scent; it took longer than I expected.

You're doing fine, Wells 'pathed. *Stay patient.*

Prism reached my face again, his muzzle brushing my cheek as he worked his way down my neck. Goosebumps flashed out across my skin and I fought to keep from cringing away as his whiskers itched the spot just beneath my ear. *That tickles,* I 'pathed.

Suddenly I was thrown back. My spine cracked against the earth just as my mind rang with pain—like knives slashing across my mental body—then stopped suddenly and completely. Numb. As if a metal helmet had been clapped over my brain. Prism was tossing his head, teeth bared, eyes rolling as he backed away.

Wells dropped to his knees beside me, hauling me to a seat. "What happened? Are you hurt?"

I tried to answer him; my mouth moved but no words came out. Dread wrapped around my lungs. Something was very, very wrong. I tried again. It was as if my vocal cords were frozen. Or as if they'd never existed. I tried to 'path but I couldn't even find the muscle. I reached for Wells's thoughts but ran into a wall. Inside my mind was silent. As if I'd been locked away in a sensory-deprivation chamber. I screamed but no sound emerged. My lungs heaved faster and faster as I plummeted into hyperventilation.

Again and again I tried to scream, raking my nails down my throat as if I could claw sound free, legs thrashing against the dirt while Wells tried to physically contain me. Over his shoulder I saw Prism, nostrils flared, eyes gleaming red, looking down on me like a horror-movie devil. For a moment, I wondered if he would skewer me to the dirt where I writhed.

Wells lifted me bodily off the ground and winked us straight to the medic tent.

It took Kerlyn and Wells a few minutes to calm me down and get me seated in the curtained off portion of the tent that served as her office. I was trembling all over, my eyes burning. Wells had a hold of my wrists to keep me from scratching myself.

"All right, in order to fix it, we just have to figure out what happened, okay?" Kerlyn smoothed a hand down my frazzled hair and gave my cheek a pat. "Can't talk or 'path apparently, but let's see if she can still write."

She stepped over to a small writing desk and grabbed a clipboard-like contraption, then fixed a blank scroll of paper to the rack at the top, pulling a few inches down for me to write on. She handed this to me with a pen. Wells released me so I could take it, but hovered nearby.

My hand shook, but I managed to print legibly. "I just said, 'that tickles.'"

Wells groaned, both large hands coming up to cup my cheeks, his face was anguished. "Imogen, I told you not until *after* he offers his horn!"

I nodded miserably. I had fucked up. Wells dropped his forehead against mine, taking deep breaths, eyes squeezed shut as if he were in pain.

I moved the pen across the page again. "How long?"

Kerlyn took a deep breath. "I'm not going to lie to you, if a unicorn has trapped your voice in what he considers self-defense, the surest way to get it reversed is to try to get the unicorn to accept you again."

My stomach dropped even as Wells lifted his head and smoothed his thumbs over my cheekbones. Prism already hated me. And I never wanted to go near another fucking unicorn again.

"If he doesn't, it's possible she'll relearn to speak again in several years," Kerlyn continued. "About the 'pathing, I'm not sure."

I dropped my eyes, my vision blurring with tears. Shame and terror chased each other up and down my spine. Why couldn't I have just kept my telepathic mouth shut? Never to hear Wells in my head again? Never to *speak* again? Never to laugh? My throat closed painfully over a silent sob. My eyelids slammed shut, squeezing out two fat tears which Wells brushed away.

"We'll try again, Imogen, not today, but we'll try again." He dropped to his knees in front of my chair, pressed a kiss to my forehead, and wrapped his arms around me. I smashed my face into his shoulder, hiding my burning cheeks and watery eyes.

Kerlyn patted my back. "You may be the first in a long while, dear, but you're not the first sidhe ever to screw up their meeting with a unicorn. General, you may want to go to the habitat and speak to Koonil. He's the oldest handler and will know the apology protocol and best timing. She'll want to get it right this time."

Wells released me, but kept hold of my hands as he stood, I noticed he was shaking also. "Right. Thank you, Kerlyn." He squeezed my fingers. "Imogen, I don't think I should bring you with me at the moment."

"I can keep her busy here," Kerlyn offered. "We'll take care of the scratches on her neck and I can always use an extra hand. Better if she doesn't sit alone and sulk. And I can make sure she has her potions on time."

"Thank you, Kerlyn." He tilted my chin up until I met his gaze, shame flooding me anew, but he just gave me a gentle smile. "We can . . . process this later. Stay with Kerlyn until I come get you, or until she sends you back to our tent, all right?" He sighed. "We are going to have to try to move the camp tomorrow. To establish a base closer to the rendezvous. And since we were just ambushed by three units, I'm not holding out much hope that we'll make it without encountering at least one of them."

Kerlyn tilted her head. "Honestly, it might be better for Imogen to try again with Prism *after* she's been in active battle. Without a rider, Prism will have to sit out and he won't like that. He'll smell the fight on her and may draw the conclusion that if he doesn't choose her, he might not get to participate in the next one. They don't like missing out, especially when all of their friends are bragging about conquest."

Wells's jaw tightened and I could see him fighting the impulse to argue as he raked a hand through his hair. "I'll have to work out where to put her. We'll figure something out, Demon. Be good and I'll be back as soon as I can." With a tender kiss that I didn't feel I deserved, Wells swept from the tent.

"Now, let's see about those scratches," Kerlyn said, pulling her stool around to face me.

CHAPTER NINE

A good dose of humility rarely does any harm.
—Captain Marcellus Tibercio

Kerlyn kept me busy the rest of the day. I washed out bandages, rolled dried ones, disinfected exam tables after patients, and played gofer for Kerlyn and her medics.

Occasionally she had me sit down in her office for fifteen minutes after downing another dose of potion. The hazy outlines of auras returned after that. I hadn't seen full auras since the killing curse, but at least I was beginning to see them again.

News of my failure had spread through the camp. And as I ran errands for Kerlyn, I overheard snatches of what people were saying about me. Sometimes they seemed to think that because I was now mute, I was also deaf, and just spoke right in front of me as if I were an uncomprehending animal.

It was probably due more to the army's respect for Wells rather than any consideration for me that most of the camp tended toward pity, but nothing I heard made me feel like any less of an asshole.

"She's only been sidhe for what . . . less than a year? I'm amazed they even let her near a unicorn."

"They say she's powerful when she's at full strength, but after that killing curse, I don't see why the general doesn't just send her back to the palace."

"Why did the king even think to send the general's mate and no one else when he called for aid? She's proving more of a liability than anything."

"She's only forty-five years old. I know she was human first, but honestly, at forty-five I couldn't follow directions either."

My ego was thoroughly shredded by the time Wells came to collect me. He spoke with Kerlyn briefly, running over what Koonil had recommended. The handler agreed with Kerlyn that I should approach Prism again immediately after a battle that he hadn't been allowed to attend. And as much as I wanted to redeem myself and get my mental and physical voice back, I dreaded ever getting near a unicorn ever again. Obviously, I said nothing.

Koonil had warned that Prism's reactions to me could range from refusing to interact at all, to stabbing me with his horn. He'd advised Wells to have Obsidian on hand to restrain Prism from killing me if things went south. Although tension was obvious in every line of his face, Wells held my hand as we walked through camp back to our tent. I kept my face down, wondering how he wasn't ashamed to be seen with me.

"We're going to have a bit of dinner in the tent. Celphia is going to join us so we can discuss putting you with her battalion tomorrow. There are no unicorns in that group and she knows who you are and has seen a little of what you can do." He squeezed my hand. "You're not at full strength yet, so I don't want you in one of the front units. And I'll be keeping a 'path open to Celphia."

I nodded. I would agree to anything at this point. If Wells trusted Celphia enough to make her first lieutenant, I would have no problem following her.

Wells sighed heavily and I finally looked up at him. He tried to force a smile, but only managed to tighten his lips. "It honestly goes against every instinct I have to put you in at all at this point, but everyone from Koonil to Obsidian has insisted this is the best way for you to get your voice back."

And I desperately wanted to redeem myself.

Celphia arrived with a pitcher of soup for the three of us. She gave me a sympathetic smile which made me want to sink into the floor. Wells handed me paper and a pen in case I wanted to say anything, but mostly I mechanically spooned in my soup and listened to the two of them.

The shield on the box canyon was fading, but the unit had rested decently and scouts had reported another likely canyon nearer the rendezvous point where we would join the other units. The plan was for most of the army to march in that direction, far enough away from the wall of the canyon to divert attention from it, while the medics and those unfit to fight winked supplies to the new location and set up. Prism would be brought directly to the new location with his handlers.

There was a high probability we'd be attacked, although Wells and Celphia both thought it unlikely that we'd be on the receiving end of three Sephryan units at once. Because of the damage I had done coming in, they would be more wary, or would have assumed we were no longer in the area.

"Imogen isn't at full strength, but she does have some lightning power. She isn't adept at directing it though, so place her at the front to avoid having her accidentally hit our own." Wells said.

Celphia nodded at me. "I'll order a strike from you early on to see what it's like and we'll go from there. We may just let you use it on close-range opponents for this battle."

I pressed my lips together, but nodded. Wells told Celphia about my little grenades and explosive arrows and had me show them to her. He explained their range, glancing at me to make sure he had it correct. I felt like a bobblehead doll, just nodding along to everything. They decided on one grenade and one arrow for this battle. Since I likely wouldn't last long.

"If you see her tiring, you're to have her wink to me," Wells said. I wondered if his anxiety was as obvious to Celphia as it was to me. He didn't want me doing this. The hardness in his voice made it even more apparent. "And Imogen, I need you to do exactly what Celphia says. I don't care if you think you're fine, if she tells you you're done, you're done. Understood."

I nodded. My new favorite word. I wondered how the rest of Celphia's battalion felt about babysitting their general's liability. Once she had left, Wells dropped into a seat beside me and slid a hand beneath my hair. I pressed my cheek into his palm, letting my eyelids fall shut while his thumb softly caressed my cheekbone.

I forced myself to look at him, then mouthed, "I'm sorry," as clearly as I could before dropping my gaze again.

"Imogen," he whispered. "I can still feel you through the bond. I know how miserable you are. I know how scared and ashamed you feel. You've been self-flagellating all day. I've never seen you so sad. I know you're sorry. And I accept your apology if that makes you feel one fraction less dejected. But then you have to hear mine."

My gaze flicked up to his.

His half smile didn't reach his sunset eyes. "I encouraged this idea. I have my own unicorn, I know how temperamental they are and I know how . . . impulsive you are. I should have taken more time to explain the consequences to you before letting you attempt this. You were far too excited and, quite honestly, not scared enough. I should have seen that. And not risked you a second time." His eyes dropped to the thumb still running back and forth across my cheek.

A strand of his long red hair had come loose from its tie. I reached out and tucked it behind his ear, letting my fingers trail along his jawbone. "Not your fault," I mouthed. I wanted to say more, I wanted to tell him that he didn't deserve any part of the blame, that this was on me and my ridiculous sense of invincibility, but I had no idea how to convey that without writing it all down. And I didn't want to move away from him.

I leaned forward and kissed him, softly at first, then slowly went deeper, trying to put everything I felt into that kiss while at the same time pushing it all down the bond. My love for him, my regret, my willingness to try to make it right for his sake.

He gently broke the kiss, taking my face in both hands, eyes shining with earnestness as he said, "Please be careful tomorrow, Imogen. Listen to Celphia. Don't try to redeem yourself by being a hero or making rash sacrifices. Promise me." His grip tightened on the last words.

I nodded, then wrote "Promise" on my still blank sheet of paper. I'd contributed nothing beyond nodding during the meeting.

I was still staring at the paper when one of Wells's hands dropped to my thigh. He squeezed, throat working before he said, "Demon. Trust me when I say I know you're capable. This is just difficult for me. You know which areas to protect at all costs, corrent?"

I took a breath, then wrote, "You mean which physical wounds are fatal to sidhe?" I knew about killing curses, obviously.

He blew out a breath and leaned back, running his fingers through his hair and pulling even more strands free. "Can you name them?"

I wrote, "There are some things I assume are fatal, but I've seen people come back from wounds here that would never have survived as humans. Might not be a bad idea to make sure." My shoulders became increasingly tight as I wrote. This took so long. If I'd been able to speak I would have added more nuance. Like, of course people could be burned to death, but how much burning did that take in this world? Everyone healed so quickly.

"Agreed, let's make absolutely sure you understand." He straightened and smoothed his face into that neutral mask he donned so frequently in the palace. "Face me."

I turned in my chair, straightening my spine, and planting my feet. Soberly at attention. If this made Wells feel a tad less anxious, I'd ace it.

A half smile cracked his mask. He squeezed my knee. "I'm not used to such a serious Imogen." Wells's eyes darkened with sadness for a beat before he slid back into business mode. "Not much is fatal until you're drained of kroma. If you reach a point where you are drained; can't wink, can't shield, then you're nearly as vulnerable as a human, but a few things will kill even a full-powered sidhe immediately."

He tapped a finger to my chest. "A severed heart, unless attended to within seconds, will be fatal. Our armor protects that area heavily, so it rarely happens in battle, but it's good for you to be aware of."

For when I see Prism again and he decides to skewer me, I thought glumly, but just nodded.

He touched a finger to the side of my neck. "Beheading. There's no coming back from that."

I nodded again. I'd assumed that one, but it was good to have it confirmed.

"Partial beheading if the spinal cord is severed. Unless a healer is right beside you and manages to intervene, this is likely fatal." His hand curved around the back of my neck, fingers finding that little notch where the base of my skull met the apex of my spine. "A stab here at the right angle. Don't lose your helmet."

Now I knew why that strike was included in both offense and defense in so many drill forms. I lifted my eyebrows and touched my temple.

"Potentially fatal, but if your kroma is strong, your body will keep you alive long enough for a healer to get to you."

I pointed at my own eyeball.

"You may lose an eye, but maybe not. Again, it depends on how much kroma is in your system and how quickly you're brought to a healer. Although, avoid Sephrya's red arrows at all cost. They're rare, but tipped with poison, so nearly always fatal." His eyes searched my face, fingers massaging the back of my neck. "Any questions?" he asked softly.

I wrote, "Fire?"

"Burns can cause severe injuries, especially if the flame is inhaled. If the flame lasts for an extended amount of time, it would be fatal, but once again, not one hundred percent." He grimaced. "So unfortunately, Stian may still live." He had dropped his hand to my shoulder during that explanation, squeezing the tight muscle. "Technically, we can also bleed out. It takes a very long time and is obviously not pleasant, but it's possible. Anything else?"

I shook my head.

He lifted his other hand and brushed my unruly hair back from my eyes. "You're looking a bit pale, Demon, and it's nearly time for your potion. Why don't you go clean up?"

I dropped my eyes, nodded, but didn't move. My heart dragged, hanging inside my chest like a stone.

"Do you want me to come with you?" His voice was so gentle it cracked something inside me.

I pushed out a smile—my first since I lost my words—and shook my head. I forced my legs to straighten and lift me from the chair, putting one foot in front of the other until I was in the back room.

The silence inside my head was deafening. Even my own thoughts seemed muted. As if a blanket of snow covered the landscape of my mind. There was no echo, no reverberation. No way out. I unconsciously started to hum to fill the void, only to have my chest tighten when no sound emerged. My throat didn't even vibrate. It was truly like that stupid unicorn had removed my vocal cords.

Tears fell thick and fast as I pushed my body through the motions of sponging off. Even my shaky inhales made no sound. A bleak future stretched before me: never to laugh or joke again, other than what I scribbled out on paper. I pictured myself with a whiteboard hanging from a string on my neck like Buffy and Willow in that "Hush" episode. A choked laugh at the image made no noise, no tingle of movement in my throat and I dropped the washrag, bent into a crouch, and curled in on myself, sucking in breath, trying to pull it together.

Wells was there in moments, knees hitting the dusty rug, one sliding in front of my toes, the other bracing my tailbone as he wrapped his arms around me. "Imogen, I firmly believe that this is not forever," he whispered. He rocked me for several seconds before tugging the washrag from the sink and wiping my face. "C'mon, Demon, you have to get some rest before tomorrow." He pressed a hard kiss to my mouth, then, washrag still in hand he tilted my face up. "Worst case; if this is permanent, Imogen, we will deal with it. And I will still love you just as fiercely as I ever did. We will find a way for you to speak again, perhaps through magic, perhaps you'll relearn. And I won't give up on 'pathing, either. All right?"

I pulled in a shaky breath and dipped my chin once.

CHAPTER TEN

All it takes is one person, one yes, then you have one chance.
—Zoe Ibrahim

I did manage to sleep through the night. Mainly because my body was still shedding Stian's death magic. Wells woke me once near dawn to foist some potion upon me, then insisted I stay in bed while most of the tent was packed up around me. Normal Imogen would have felt weird and creeped out by this, but Killing Curse Survivor Imogen fell right back asleep as if people weren't dismantling camp around from her.

Sleeping also let me avoid the reality in which I was completely mute. I couldn't even claim nonverbal status as I literally couldn't make any sound.

Kerlyn roused me the second time, shoving a bright pink, fizzy potion at me and encouraging me to drink it all. Apparently, it would give me a few hours' energy boost, which would not only help me get through the march and likely battle ahead, but sustain me if I was late taking my next dose of potion. As soon as I finished it, auras bloomed all around me for the first time since being hit. I cried out in surprise and relief but the sound never materialized. Shame blanketed me, but I tried to ignore it.

Celphia came to collect me as the last of our tent was packed up. She checked my weapons, including the explosives, and briefly spoke with Wells as to whether or not a supply should be kept nearby. They decided against it for this march. It would be a short one, and hopefully we wouldn't need them.

Wells straightened my uniform and checked the position of my weapons for the umpteenth time until Celphia laid a hand on his arm, gaze locking on his, light-brown eyes clear. "She'll be fine, General. I've seen her fight, you've obviously trained her, and she has talent. She made a huge misstep yesterday, she's not likely to risk another today. I've seen how much you love each other and I know how important she is to you. Have faith."

Wells held her gaze, decades of trust and understanding passing between them. For a heartbeat, I missed Cilla so fiercely my breastbone ached. There was no one on this planet that I'd known for decades. No one aside from Wells who knew me inside and out and no one aside from Cilla who had the barest inkling of where I had come from. Al flashed through my mind but I tossed that thought out and squared my shoulders. I wasn't going to embarrass Wells or let him down again. I'd be a good soldier for Celphia and do exactly what was required. No more, no less.

Wells's mouth tightened, but he forced it into a smile as he nodded at his lieutenant. He placed both hands on my shoulders and hunched down to meet my eyes. "Imogen, listen to Celphia." The strong column of his throat worked for a moment but finally he kissed me quickly and said, "I love you and will see you afterward." He straightened, turned, and marched away. I watched him until the business of dismantling the camp swallowed him up, then turned my gaze to Celphia.

She smiled at me. "He's worried, but we'll be fine. Have you taken your potion for the morning?"

I nodded.

She dipped her chin sharply. "Good, let's go." She spun on her heel and strode in the opposite direction Wells had gone.

I kept pace with her, but stayed an inch behind just in case it was like the martial arts school where I had trained on Earth; the subordinate was never "in line" with the higher-ranking person. I didn't have the words to ask—nothing to write on—so I decided to be safe. The longer I was here the more I realized how much I didn't know.

"I'm not going to sugarcoat things, Imogen. There are a lot of people who aren't pleased to have you with our unit. I want you to ignore them if they say anything. I've given them all a talking to, but you never know what will slip out in a battle."

Ice slid down my spine, but I just nodded. I should expect this. I'd been an idiot and this was the second time I'd gotten myself hurt since arriving. Yes, I'd turned the tide in that one battle, but this was war. That battle was in the past.

"Regardless, my people are the best. They won't leave you high and dry no matter what shit they might talk. You don't have much experience working with a group, so I'll just give you a few tenants to go by. Number one: Do not injure your own. We've talked about your lightning. If it comes down to it, pull it in to give you energy, but if you cannot unleash it without risking our battalion or the ones around us, don't do it unless I specifically order you to do so. Number two: If you can help one of your own, act without hesitation. This is instinctive for you—I saw it when you came to aid us initially—so I'm not worried. Number three: When I give you an order, follow it without hesitation. General Eigneachan has told me that you question everything. You cannot question me today, you cannot try to warn me or hold back if you think I'm wrong. If there is an error, it will be mine. If I tell you to fire an arrow, for example, you do it."

Celphia stopped in the middle of the thoroughfare, forcing people to change direction and go around us. She turned to face me, tilting her head up. She was at least three inches shorter than my rather average five-foot-six.

"I'm ninety-eight years old, Imogen." She lifted her chin. "That's incredibly young for a first lieutenant. And, at two hundred and fifty-one, Llewellyn is the youngest general in centuries. He took a chance on me because he saw my work ethic. He saw my power. And he saw beyond the tiny female frame that everyone else gets stuck on. Not everyone agreed with him." She tilted her head to the side. "I know what it's like to have everyone dismiss you because you're young or small or look a certain way, but sometimes you do have to admit that you are young and you are small." Her brown eyes softened a bit. "I feel that this is a bit unfair because you can't talk back, just know that I am not trying to berate you. But my general wants me to bring you back safe and he *needs* me to fight any battle we are embroiled in effectively." She straightened. "You are an asset to this army, Imogen. I know your psyche is struggling right now, so I'm going to make it easy for you. Do exactly as I say. Let everything else go. Trust me as your mate trusts me. You may hear some snide remarks; ignore them. Can you do this?"

My gaze traveled over her face, from the warm brown eyes to the smattering of freckles across her nose. The dark blonde roots that had grown into her pink pixie cut, shaggier after months at war. I placed a hand over my heart and nodded.

The corners of her mouth curved upward. "Good, let's go."

CHAPTER ELEVEN

Respect that's been earned sticks more firmly than respect that's blindly given.
—*Captain Marcellus Tibercio*

The first several hours of the march were just dusty and hot. Celphia positioned herself at the front of her battalion, which was small, as our unit was so decimated. She didn't have me directly beside her, but on the outside corner, where she could easily see me, shout orders to me, and hopefully I would have a greater area to wield lightning if it came to that. Her soldiers tossed sidelong glances my way. I caught several whispers as we geared up to march and the one next to me, Vesen, even nudged me with an elbow while Celphia's back was turned. "Is it true the unicorn took away your entire voice? You can't even grunt? Let's see." He then slammed his elbow into my ribs, forcing the breath from my lungs.

I retaliated by driving a knee into his gut.

"Bitch!" he coughed, but Celphia turned at the word.

"Is there a problem, Vesen?" She glanced at me, and I watched her sharp eyes catch when I dropped my hand from where it had been cradling my bruised ribs. "Imogen? Is everything okay?"

"No problem," Vesen said, straightening.

I merely nodded and pretended to check the buckle on my sword belt, ignoring the new throbbing in my side.

Celphia narrowed her eyes, but turned back to monitoring the horizon.

Vesen left me alone after that. Any other mutterings or barely-under-breath joking about my idiocy faded away with the rising temperatures.

Then there was a rippling ahead. Nothing physical changed; the units continued marching without a break in pace. Instead it was as if the air grew dense with tension. I watched the auras change in a near ripple as some information or other passed through. I glanced toward Celphia just as I suspected Wells's 'path hit her. Her eyes unfocused slightly. A sharp pang of longing hit me. I missed my mate's mind. I missed my own mind being open. I felt like I was encased in ice. Stagnant. Unreachable. Alive but unable to grow.

"Sephryan army ahead," Celphia called, her voice kromatically magnified to reach her entire battalion. "The ambassadors from both armies are meeting now." Wells had told me about this, when there was a conflict, both ambassadors would meet first to see if an agreement could be reached. It was an ancient practice, but dangerous for the ambassador.

A wicked grin split Celphia's face. "The new base has been established. Our general sent scouts out with medics and a few essential personnel in the middle of the night in a last-minute decision. If you are forced to wink to the old one, stay there, someone will eventually be sent to find you. If you are grievously injured and have energy to wink, try to direct yourself to a medic. They are already settling into the new location." The sounds of swords scraping from their scabbards filled the air, amplifying the pride warming my chest. Clever of Wells, leaving nothing to chance this time.

We were one battalion from the front lines, so I couldn't see what was happening, but a tautness permeated the ranks. I heard the low, vicious whinny of a unicorn nearby and my stomach turned.

Then the first blasts of magic rippled through.

"The ambassadors have retreated with no reconciliation, we're doing this, folks!" Celphia's hands glowed white-hot with kroma.

We ran in formation, several feet behind the battalion in front of us. For an odd few moments, it felt like we were . . . just running. Nothing but the sparking kroma and breath of my neighbor to break up the thud of synchronized feet across the dry, packed dirt.

Then a Sephryan wheeled in before me, blades flying toward my middle. I blocked the strike and doused him in sticky fire before calling a bolt of lightning down to charge myself. I felt Vesen flinch away and ignored it.

I kept my focus on the area surrounding me, with one part of my mind alert to Celphia's calls. Shortly, the divisions between the battalions were less pronounced as the two opposing armies met. I fought one particularly skilled Sephryan female with short silver hair who had intertwined double hearts tattooed on her neck. A needle of regret pierced my heart when my sword sliced right through them. This was different than taking out hundreds from a distance with my lightning or charging in to lend haphazard aid at the tail end of a flagging battle. Bits of these faces were burning themselves into my memory.

"Imogen! To your right! Overwhelm. Try a strike!" Celphia yelled.

I jerked my head to the side and saw that a Sephryan platoon had worked its way back and was now chopping into the beset battalion next to ours. I shut down all the protests, maybes, and what ifs in my head and just did my best to direct a net of lightning down my sword.

It engulfed the Sephryan platoon, but offshoots hit some of our soldiers as well. I forced myself to turn away, although my stomach twisted. I'd done what she ordered.

"Imogen! Hovercraft! To your left!"

My head swiveled even as I lifted my sword to defend against the Sephryan in front of me. The hovercraft was swiftly approaching. The ground beneath my feet just starting to rumble. If I waited much longer the craft would take our own people out when it crashed. I blasted the sidhe before me with sticky fire and shoved him back, then popped the pouch, lit the fuse, and 'ported the grenade into the hovercraft, throat tightening as I awaited the aftermath.

The hovercraft blew out and crashed, carving an erratic trench in the dirt, coming straight for us. Several sidhe had to wink out of the way but I was forced to turn my attention to the fight before me, shoving down my cringe. I blocked a sloppy strike and stabbed the sidhe in front of me in the back of the neck, yanking the blade to the side and severing his spine.

But when I jerked the blade free, the person who dropped dead at my feet had brown hair. Brown. Not bronze or gold or silver.

A Molnarian. But in a Sephryan uniform.

"Imogen, heads up!" Vesen shouted.

Three Sephryans charged us. I flung my sword toward them, lightning coursing down my blade, and pushed. They were instantly engulfed, dropping before they reached us.

"Well done," Vesen said. Then we turned toward the next wave.

"Imogen!" Celphia winked over to us either hours or seconds later. "That catapult, can you hit it with an arrow?"

A catapult had been floated into the center of our unit and the Sephryans were loading something . . . dark and glowing into it.

I nodded and pulled my bow from my shoulder.

"Cover her, Vesen!" Celphia winked away and Vesen stepped in front of me as I strung my bow and pulled out my special arrow. I let my own self-defense go, put my trust in that asshole Vesen, and focused my entire being on the catapult. It was a long shot.

I strung the bow, pulled, aiming to the sky, then bent my knees to get a better angle. I inhaled, took aim, then released on the exhale, lighting the arrow with a thought as it flew.

And *just* caught the catapult on the side.

I winced as it exploded; destroying the catapult, but also injuring or killing anyone within a nearby radius. I turned back to the front just in time to see five of the rare, red Sephryan arrows arcing toward our section of the battalion. Red meant poison-tipped. Even if they didn't kill, they'd strip power from anyone they hit. These soldiers knew where some of this destruction was coming from and wanted to neutralize it.

Without thinking, I wrenched from my reserves and flung out a lightning shield. I'd been working this defense, but it wasn't perfect, nor was it practical in my current condition as it required a lot of power and control. The arrows pelted into the quivering shield, which I had expanded to cover everyone in our section, and dissolved with a hiss.

I let the shield drop, staggering a bit as I drew my sword and dagger, barely hearing Vesen call out, "Well done!"

The next few minutes stretched out like years. Vesen and I fought side by side. My breath came in hard, fast gulps. My lightning was spent and the heat in my blood warned me against calling more.

"Lieutenant!" Vesen called to Celphia. "She's done!"

I turned to him in outrage, having just dispatched another Sephryan with the entwined heart tattoo. I wondered if they'd known each other. It took commitment for sidhe to keep a tattoo permanently. Special poison had to be mixed with the ink to keep the marks from healing.

But Celphia looked me over. "Imogen, wink to the general now."

I gritted my teeth, but nodded.

Vesen grabbed my arm. "You did good."

I swallowed my surprise but winked as soon as he released me.

I stumbled out of my wink beside Wells, who was mounted on Obsidian and looked impressive as fuck. Both of them were splattered with blood. Wells was on the outskirts of the battle but had obviously been winking in and out of the action, his sword was still drawn, stained crimson.

"Imogen, you must be done then," he said, unsuccessfully trying to keep the relief from his face. "You are a bit pale. I'd like you to wink to Kerlyn, can you do that?"

I closed my eyes and found her signature. I nodded.

"Excellent, go. She'll assign you," he said just as his eyes unfocused to 'path. I couldn't help the pang of longing that tightened my chest. He refocused on me one last time. "Get to Kerlyn, do as she says. I love you." Obsidian stepped them into a wink. I realized then that I could no longer see auras. I pulled in a long breath and winked myself to Kerlyn.

The new canyon was narrower than the original and not a box. Sidhe unable to fight were already working on putting up a shield at one end, near the new unicorn habitat. Others were erecting tents along the wall.

"There you are, I was expecting you a bit sooner." Kerlyn patted my arm, glancing at the dagger still clenched in my fist, and turned back to the medic she'd been addressing. "More of them are going to be coming back, get the beds and triage stations ready and we'll worry about hauling the tent over them when we have to. Luckily it hardly rains here and the canyon is deep enough that we have shade."

She faced me. "Clean your blades, sheath them, then follow me." She strode toward a makeshift office—just her desk and cabinets in front of the partially erected medic tent.

I shoved my dagger and sword into the dry sand at my feet and cleaned my weapons as best I could, then knocked loose grains from the blades and sheathed them. I crossed to the desk.

Without glancing up from the paper she was marking—some kind of inventory—Kerlyn held a hand out behind her and a vial of blue liquid flew into her palm. "You're a bit late for this dose, but we anticipated that. Take it now."

I gulped it all down. Thinking of how I wanted to talk to Kerlyn about the battle. To ask if this was normal. If the fact that we had moved camp was already a success. If we would be waiting long to find out how it went. If I should try to help shield the entrance. I pressed my lips together, knowing the questions would remain locked inside.

My glance toward the canyon's mouth must have given me away because Kerlyn snatched the empty vial from my hand. "You don't have the energy, and even if you did, we need it open so that those who have never been here can get through. We've got people on standby. We've been managing for months before you came along, child."

The last part wasn't said unkindly and when I snapped my head toward her, those sad eyes had a tiny spark behind them. She chuckled. "I said that same thing to Kaylie when she first arrived. Trust the rest of us, Imogen. Now come on. I need this tent up. If you do have any kroma to spare, let's use it on that."

To my shock, I had no kroma to spare. Celphia—and I supposed Vesen—had timed it perfectly so that I had just enough to wink back to Wells, and fortunately again to Kerlyn. I didn't even have enough kromatic energy to soften the earth for the studs.

Which meant it all had to be done manually.

The upside was that I had done things manually for most of my life, that it didn't require much talking, and that once I was engaged in a repetitive task, I could almost forget I couldn't speak.

I wished I had my phone to listen to music, but it was packed away with the rest of our tent.

By the time I had Kerlyn's medical tent set up, both inside and out, I emerged to find countless other tents had sprung up all along the wall. I also saw several sidhe at the narrow entrance to our canyon, shoving a shield in place.

I turned to Kerlyn, pointed toward them, and raised my eyebrows.

She grinned and I noticed a dimple in her cheek for the first time. "They've been coming back in waves. The battle is done. We lost. Half of the unit retreated to our old canyon. In a moment, we'll send a few from here to go and give them reference points or help pull them in."

I couldn't stop myself from scanning the crowd. Wells was always easy to pick out with his height and red hair. My heart picked up speed as I failed to catch a glimpse of my mate in the now-crowded canyon. I ran a mental hand over the bond, relieved at the sensation of it, safe and thrumming within me, but aching for the comfort of his physical presence.

Kerlyn touched my arm. "He'll get here when he gets here. In the meantime," she thrust a pail into my hand, "I'll need water. The wounded are already coming in."

With a bucket in each hand, I walked back and forth between the water pump and the medic tent, adding water to the tub within the tent that was emptied as soon as I filled it. Fortunately, there were other things for everyone to worry about post-battle, so there were less pitying comments about my idiocy and most people just ignored me as I trudged back and forth. Eventually, Kerlyn had me stop, sit down in the supply section, and unpack the medical supplies onto their spots on her shelves. I'd removed the armored part of my uniform, but otherwise was still in my mud- and-blood stained things. It was a relief to sit in the shade.

I woke stretched out on an exam table, staring at the canvas ceiling, the noise of the camp continuing around me. I sucked in a breath and jackknifed up.

"You're safe, Demon."

My eyes darted to the side, finding a blood-splattered Wells, obviously rousing himself from a doze in the chair beside me. His face was drawn, exhausted lines of tension bracketing his mouth. "You fell asleep sorting supplies. Kerlyn had you moved in here to rest." A corner of his lips inched upward. "Celphia says you did very well."

There was so much I wanted to ask. Had my lightning killed any of our own? The arrow that took out the catapult? I wanted to ask about that Molnairian in the Sephryan uniform. My gaze flicked over to Wells, scanning him from head to toe.

"I'm not hurt," he said softly. Then he stood, reaching out a hand to help me down from the table. "We should go try with Prism. You can get cleaned off afterward."

A chill slid down my spine and my stomach turned over, but I forced myself to nod and drop my feet to the floor. Who would have thought going to see a goddamn purple unicorn would be the most dreaded part of my day?

CHAPTER TWELVE

Fear is merely a feeling. Bravery is an action.
—*King Allestair Metellus*

Wells helped me into my armor, which was also decorated with mud and blood, but he 'ported both of our helmets back to our tent. The entire medical station smelled of iron and earth. We left without saying goodbye to Kerlyn, as she and her medics had their hands full.

As we walked, Wells produced two pears from his pocket. "I stopped by to speak with Koonil before I found you. He said Prism wasn't happy about being left behind and Obsidian told me that he has asked about you, which is a good sign. Do you remember what you're supposed to do?"

I nodded, chewing on my lip. My hands were already shaking as I accepted the pears. I was to stand still, offer the pears again, and not to move until he'd taken them. Even then I was only to drop my hands to my sides.

Since I'd 'pathed him once, it was feasible that Prism would 'path me himself if he decided to lift his curse and accept my apology pears, but that did not mean he had accepted me as a rider, and I was not to 'path him. It was possible he would accept the apology, lift the curse, and leave. It was possible he'd want nothing to do with me.

I was only to 'path him if he specifically invited me to speak with him. He may or may not offer his horn. He may or may not examine me again. At this point, I didn't know that I wanted to be paired with a unicorn. Especially *that* unicorn. I just wanted this curse lifted.

Obsidian was waiting when we walked up to the edge of the habitat. I was well aware that I was visibly trembling. I watched, a hollow feeling in my chest, as Wells straightened his unicorn's dark forelock. Obsidian flicked an ear toward me, then back to Wells.

"He said it's good that you're a bit afraid. It will show Prism that you've learned your lesson."

I clenched my jaw, wrapping a fist around each pear and staring into the trees. I wanted to get this over with.

Ice trickled down my spine at the first whisper of movement beyond the trees. Wells remained beside Obsidian, but I could sense his own nerves through the bond, which didn't make me feel better. As soon as that lavender head poked into the clearing, I lifted my hands and displayed the pears, hoping they wouldn't roll off because of my shaking.

Prism picked his way toward me slowly, those onyx hooves gleaming wetly as they sank into the enchanted grass. He halted five feet away, nostrils flaring as he scented the air. I could have sworn a red gleam flashed in those depthless black eyes. He stepped closer, tossing his head, pink sparks flying from the tip of a lethally sharp horn. I kept my arms extended, though my shivering had only increased.

Prism stilled, breath loud as he stretched his melon-sized muzzle toward me and huffed. I assumed he was pulling in the scent of blood, mud, and general eau de battlefield. His ears flicked back until they were flat against his skull, a low, threatening whinny rumbling through his chest.

Through the corner of my eye, I saw Wells stiffen, but Obsidian nudged him and they stayed where they were.

Prism dipped his head and lipped up one pear, then backed up, angling sideways, one shining eye fixed on me as he pranced in place, swishing his shiny charcoal tail. He really was stunning. My arms were aching by the time he deigned to return for the second pear. I forced myself to lower them slowly to my sides although I felt like just dropping them. No one had said as such, but it felt like a bad idea to make any sudden moves.

A warm release of pressure brushed through my mind and throat as a voice like star-flecked wind swept in. *You do appear to have learned your lesson, child. I accept your apology.*

I remained where I was, my knees weak with relief. I was dying to 'path Wells, to try my voice, but I didn't dare. Although I really didn't care to be paired with Prism at this point, I resolved to wait until the unicorn was done with me before backing away.

I wouldn't have anyone watching think that Wells was mated to a coward who couldn't face up to her mistakes. I refused to do anything that could reflect poorly on him again.

You smell of battle, of conquest. Prism's 'path was rough with envy.

I didn't respond, and although my trembling had dialed down to the occasional shiver, a muscle-slackening relief at having my mind free nearly melted my bones.

You may speak. Tell me, was the battle won?

We were successful in changing camps. I nearly wept at the expression of my own 'path. *But I was told that we had to retreat and the battle was lost.*

It was lost because I was not present, Prism said, with what I thought was a bit of an inflated sense of self-worth. He stamped his hoof. *Let us speak of you. You are very young and brash, although telepathy is rare and admirable. Was it for this reason alone that it was deemed fit to offer you to me?*

I risked folding my arms. *I have other talents aside from telepathy. I can call lightning and use it in battle, I'm an above-average fighter, and when I'm at full strength, I am very powerful.*

He took another deep sniff, this time coming close enough to brush his velvety muzzle against my cheek. *You were hit with a killing curse. But you have survived?*

Obviously, I said, ready to be rejected and move on. *They have me on potions and say I'll eventually make a full recovery.*

He tossed his head, prancing to the side. *I have never heard of a sidhe calling lightning.*

That's because I'm the first one who's ever done it. I scraped up the dredges of my not-yet-replenished energy and allowed a bracelet of lightning to wrap my wrist, lifting my palm and letting it travel to my hand and play among my fingers.

Prism's ears pricked so far forward they nearly brushed his horn.

Since I haven't recovered from the battle, and I don't want to hurt anyone, I won't do more right now, but I can direct it down my blades and call it from the sky. We're still learning how to use it most effectively on the field. I shook my hand and the lightning dispersed.

I knew I did not imagine the hungry red gleam in Prism's eye when he asked, *Your name?*

Imogen.

And how do you rank in the army, young Imogen?

I shrugged. *I'm mated to Wells,* I dipped my head toward him, *who is the General of all the Armies, but I'm a free agent. I fight with Molnair, but I am not under any official command.*

That low whinny rumbled in Prism's chest again. *Mated to the general but under no command? The first of the lightning throwers, able to do battle where you will? Yes, this will do nicely. You are young and trainable. I shall achieve much conquest with you as my weapon, young Imogen.*

He arched his crest, dropping his horn to my shoulder as if he were knighting me. *You may admire my horn.*

Conflicting emotions collided in my chest as I reached up and gently ran my fingertips along the side of Prism's horn. He accepted me, which felt much better than rejection, but also meant I'd have to ride this monster into battle for the rest of the goddamn war. Glittering flecks trailed my fingers, as if Prism's horn was filled with a viscous, sparkling liquid. *It's beautiful*, I said honestly.

Prism's barrel expanded in a great sigh as he lifted his head. *Yes, I've often been told so. It's a pity I cannot see it myself. I'm certain it is stunning. Farewell for now, young Imogen. I anticipate much success on the battlefield with you in the future.* And with a swish of his tail, he turned and cantered into the forest.

Wells absently scratched the underside of Obsidian's jaw, but his eyes were locked on me. The worry, the apprehension tightening his features pulled at my heart. "He accepted me," I said, relief skating down my spine at the sound of my own voice.

My mate's face split into a grin as he hauled me into his embrace, dirty armor and all. I wrapped my arms around him, squeezing back as best I could. "It may have done something for Prism, but I do not enjoy my own smell right now," I muttered.

Wells released me only to slide his fingers through my knotted hair and pulled my mouth to his. "I missed your voice so much," he said between kisses. I heard Obsidian huff once before he turned away, trotting to the trees.

He probably thinks I'm an idiot too, I 'pathed, jerking my chin toward Obsidian.

Wells took my hand, eyes shining as he waved to the handlers and tugged me back toward the tents. I realized I had no idea where ours had been set up.

No more than the unicorns think any of us are idiots, he said. *Honestly, as traumatizing as that incident was to you and I, they see it as no more than putting a foal in time-out for stepping out of line.* When my jaw dropped open, he squeezed my hand. *I spoke to Obsidian about it at length after I dropped you with Kerlyn. He helped us remember the proper apology protocols as it's been so long since this has happened. Prism is one of the pricklier unicorns, but Obsidian was certain he wouldn't want to leave you permanently without a voice. He's* never been paired with a telepath and it's something of a status symbol among them. He won't silence you again now that you're paired.

Well, I find I am no longer as enamored with unicorns as I once was. Having my voice liberated had rinsed away an undercurrent of fear and misery I hadn't even realized I was hauling around. That, in addition to the events of the day, had me feeling every ache in my bones and longing for an actual bath to sink into. "I don't think unicorns would have enjoyed the surge of popularity they experienced in the '80s on Earth if people knew they were like that."

Wells chuckled. "They did originate on Earth. We brought them with us."

I stopped dead. "What."

His smile widened, crinkling the corners of his eyes and warming my skin. "They have kroma of their own and most wanted to come, so our ancestors decided to take them. They deduced that the humans would have a difficult time with them if we left them there. They'd end up killing each other."

I snorted. "Yeah, that's likely."

"I missed you," Wells murmured, dropping a kiss onto my mop of tangled hair and pulling me forward again. "Your voice in my head, your questions . . ."

"I have so many questions," I gushed out on an exhale.

He chuckled. "I'm delighted to hear it."

In our tent, we removed our armor but Wells suggested we wash up before sitting down to clean it. While we mopped up at the basin—I had to dunk my entire head, Wells insisted on 'porting in fresh water himself, saying I'd hauled around enough—he told me that the battle had technically been a loss, resulting in our side retreating. We'd lost still more soldiers that we couldn't afford, and those remaining were exhausted and disheartened, but at least we'd finally managed to relocate camp, which brought us closer to the other units.

My throat was tight when I said, "Celphia had me fire one of my arrows into a catapult thing." I cleared my throat. "Did it . . . ?"

Wells gently took the washrag from me and turned me around. We'd stripped down to our underwear and I was much filthier than Wells, having been on the ground and in the thick of things the entire time, then on gofer duty for Kerlyn afterward.

Wells swiped at a hard-to-reach spot on my spine as he answered. "Celphia said she could see the fear in your face when she gave you those orders, but you executed them anyway. Which is exactly what you should have done."

"Yeah, but I need to know," I breathed.

Wells kissed the damp skin between my neck and shoulder, his arms coming around me from behind. "There were injuries, but no deaths, Imogen. Not among our own."

A little sigh of relief escaped me and I forced myself to leave it there rather than ask about the extent of the injuries. This was war, after all.

As we pulled on clean clothes and straightened the bathing area, Wells grabbed a blue vial and passed it to me. "Time for your potion."

I sighed and accepted it plopping to a seat on a crate beside my hanging armor. I sipped it, turning over more questions in my mind, hoping at least the transparent swirls of auras might show up for a while after this dose. Wells sat down on a separate crate and placed a rag beside me. "I can clean your armor if you like," he said. His voice was soft but his eyes were bright with worry. "If you'd like to get some sleep. I'll wake you once food arrives."

I blew a breath through my nose as I set the empty vial on the floor beside me. Wells 'ported it away, throwing my kromatic weakness into even starker relief. "Am I a liability?"

His dark russet eyebrows nudged together. "What?"

I grabbed the rag and turned to my armor, determinedly wiping the first plate free of mud and grime. "I'm not even at a tenth of my powers. I fucked up with Prism. You're constantly having to give me special assignments and—"

"Imogen, I've heard some of the things people are saying around camp." His voice was gentle, but firm. "Do you think the same hasn't been said about me when I was coming up through the ranks? About Celphia?

Do you think you're the only fighter that wasn't at full capacity on the field today? That you were the only one ordered to retreat early?"

My shoulders tensed and I paused in my cleaning. I had not considered that. So wrapped up in my own misery.

"I can see by your face that you didn't."

I glanced at him, he offered a half smile before turning to work on his own armor. "Like it or not, you're a known and public figure, Imogen. You're going to be talked about more, judged more, and generally receive more attention and scrutiny. You'll have to learn which comments to take seriously and when to just let gossip slide. And I know you have no real basis for comparison—you *are* young and new to this world—but even as diminished as you are, your power is significant, as are your fighting talents." He took a long, quiet breath. "And we are incredibly depleted right now. We need everyone who's capable."

"I'm so self-centered," I muttered, my buddy Shame clinging to my rib cage like a monkey. I rubbed harder at my armor.

"You've had a rough entry into military life and were literally trapped, voiceless in your own mind for a while, I don't blame you for being unable to see beyond your own troubles for the past few hours." He dunked his rag in a nearby bucket and rung it out. "However, I do wonder if there was perhaps a good lesson for you in all of this."

My eyes flicked up to his.

He sighed. "Your actions have consequences. You could do with a bit more deference—"

"I defer to you!"

He snorted.

My chest tightened. "I did everything Celphia said today."

"As you should have." His eyes dropped from mine as he picked up a shin guard and took up his rag again. "But you were scared and ashamed. Once you bounce back, I'm concerned you may forget yourself again. I need you to toe the line while you're with my army, Imogen. I cannot emphasize this enough. Please try to think before you act and always follow orders."

I chewed on my lower lip as I scrubbed hard at an oily smear on my backplate. His words had me automatically going defensive. I took a slow breath. *Wells is not Allestair or Al, he's not trying to control you, he's trying to keep you safe.*

"I'll try to do better," I said finally.

He nodded. "I mean it, Imogen. I have to stay firm on this for your safety as well as everyone else's."

"Got it." I couldn't entirely keep the bite from my words. How many times did I have to agree?

We cleaned in silence for a few moments before Wells rolled his shoulders, then wrung out his rag.

I did the same, my hands shaking a bit as I squeezed the excess water free. "I have another question." If I was going to be deferring and blindly following orders, I was determined to get as full a picture as possible, not interested in clinging to my own ignorance.

"Ask away." Wells moved to stand near me, running his rag over my shoulder plates.

A glance told me that he had finished his own cleaning; his armor sat gleaming on its frame. "One of the people I . . . fought today." I swallowed the tightness down. "He . . . well he looked Molnarian, but he was definitely in a Sephryan uniform."

"It happens," Wells said. "Not often, but people from either country will defect for one reason or another."

I felt my brow crease as I asked, "What do they think is going to happen? Like what does Sephrya want if they win this war?"

Wells blew out a breath and dunked his rag again. "Without going over the entire war agreement and delving into a centuries-old history, they want access to our technology. You remember that after an early Earth expedition the Sephryans felt that turning humans sidhe was an unnatural and unnecessary magical advancement?"

"Yeah, I remember that." I dunked my own rag; the water was darkening. "That's why they just trap a bunch of humans and steal their babies."

"And you remember that they extended those beliefs, deciding that now that we were here, advancement for the sake of advancement was unnecessary, resulting in Molnair significantly surpassing them in space travel, reproductive technology, and a host of other things." At my nod he continued. "Since they're now facing reproductive issues of their own and cannot figure out what is killing their humans, they want access to all our data and more. As you know, we don't agree that letting them have unfettered access to Earth would be beneficial to the humans there." He cleared his throat. "And there are many sidhe who don't believe we should be separate countries. Perhaps separate states, but under one rule."

"I bet Allestair loves that idea." I dropped my rag into the bucket and wiped my damp hands on my pants.

Wells smirked. "I think either Allestair or Demian would be willing to entertain it if they were chosen to rule. They're similar in that way. But no, neither wants to relinquish his crown." He dropped his rag into the bucket as well. "I'll take this, please rest for a while."

He winked out with the bucket and I dragged myself over to the cot. It wasn't even that late in the afternoon, but my body was undeniably done. I owed it to everyone else to be at my best if possible. I had just plopped to a seat on the edge of the cot when Wells winked back in, holding a hunk of bread in each hand. He passed one to me and I noticed a rough wedge of cheese shoved inside.

"It's not much," he said. "But hopefully it will tide us over until something is scrounged up for dinner."

I took an enthusiastic bite. "You know, whenever I would read books about people in medieval times like, roughing it, they always talked about how they had to subsist on hunks of bread and cheese and I always thought, 'that actually sounds really yummy to me.'"

He chuckled around his own mouthful. *I've missed your voice.*

A tiny smile curved the corners of my lips as I swallowed. "Did you know Demian? Or, I guess do you know Demian?" I shoved more bread in.

Wells chewed thoughtfully for a moment; his eyes fixed on the ceiling before facing me as he swallowed. "I don't think I could claim to know him but I've met him a few times. He's only a few decades older than Al. They were princes together for a bit. From what I understand Axterius, Demian's father, had a less contentious relationship with Allestair. With both of them coming into their thrones a generation out of the Wind War, neither wanted another conflict. Recently evidenced by how reluctant Allestair was to even admit Demian was sanctioning the kidnappings this year. But Axterius died centuries ago and Demian is much less cautious. I know Allestair thinks he's an idiot."

"Is there anyone Allestair doesn't think is an idiot?" I muttered.

Wells let out a soft laugh but there was no humor in it. "Allestair does keep his own counsel much of the time and unerringly manipulates everyone into doing what he thinks is right, but I definitely don't think he views you as an idiot, Imogen. He may have underestimated you once, I doubt he'll make that mistake again."

Not exactly reassuring.

CHAPTER THIRTEEN

*The enemy will not simply relinquish his secrets;
they must be pried from him.*
—*King Allestair Metellus*

I was jolted from my nap when a sound like a hunting horn, only two octaves deeper, cut through the air. Tangled in the sheets, I thrashed, heart hammering as the horn blasted through camp again.

"It's all right, Imogen, it's all right. The scouts are rejoining us." Wells shoved aside whatever papers he'd been working on, came around the desk, and helped me free myself. "You should meet them if you're up for it, it's about time for your next dose anyway."

My aural sight had returned with the last dose, so I downed the next one eagerly as I straightened my clothes, ready to inch closer to normal.

Moments later, two scouts I had never met strolled into our tent. One had straight black hair and uplifted eyes, the other had curious metallic golden hair, like I'd seen on many Sephryans, although his skin wasn't nearly as pale. I'd always found it odd that people from such a warm, swampy place had such a pallor to their skin. I'd asked Wells about the Sephryan coloring before and apparently the Molnarians had more of a variety because of continually introducing turned human genetics into their pool. A turned human brings the DNA markers for their coloring with them when they become sidhe, adding those markers to the pool. As the Sephryans only mate with humans, their genes are dominant and obliterate the human genetics. Pure fae partnering with pure fae would always be pale with metallic colored hair and bright, jewel-toned eyes.

Although both scouts wore triumphant grins, I also saw grim mustard and brown rivers running through their auras.

Wells's aura split and I wondered who he'd 'pathed as he gestured them to the chairs around his table. Without speaking, they helped each other move the table away from the side of the tent so that we might all sit around it, as if this were something they had done many times before. Wells and the black-haired scout cleared the table of all but a few specific maps. Noticing that we were one chair short if I joined, the other silently offered me his, setting it next to Wells's. He inclined his head with a slight smile before grabbing the handle of my trunk and hauling it over to make a seat for himself.

I watched him curiously. I'd never met a half-Sephryan before.

The scout examined me just as thoroughly, a slight smile playing about his lips. I didn't take the seat he offered me. I cocked my head to the side, trying to read his aura. Excitement. Curiosity. Relief. And an interesting mixture of shame and pride.

"It's an honor to finally meet my general's mate," he said, his expression never changing, hazel eyes inquisitive. He extended his hand. "I'm Jarleth. Nice to have you with us. How did you get out, Imogen?"

So, Wells obviously trusted Jarleth enough to have told him I was trapped and not simply "kept safe" in the palace and "sent as aid" in the nick of time. I took the offered hand and shook. "Luck, talent, and some trademark recklessness," I answered.

This time his smile was genuine, if only for a second. Then it melted back to cool, collected curiosity. I sat down at the same time he did. The other scout introduced himself as Kitano. His smile was as warm as his golden complexion, although exhaustion had painted dark circles under his eyes.

The two duty soldiers Wells had 'pathed marched in with what rough food might be obtained for the scouts and even a couple bottles of wine. My mouth watered at the sight. Had I missed dinner? It was difficult to judge time of day inside the canyon, although it looked to be after sunset. I wondered how long I had slept.

Kitano announced to Wells that two other units had been spotted less than a day's march from here. The soldiers let out a couple "whoops" as they dropped the provisions, saluted Wells, then left quickly, shutting the tent flaps behind them, likely to spread the word. Jarleth nodded at Kitano and I realized that they had intentionally let that bit of good news drop before the soldiers left. Everyone served themselves without standing on ceremony. Kitano poured wine and pressed the cup into my hand before I could grab a glass for myself. When I went to fix myself a plate of hard cheese and bread, Jarleth passed me one he had just loaded.

"Thanks?" I felt my eyebrows pulling together.

"Imogen is uncomfortable being waited on." Wells smiled his thanks and ran a hand down the back of my head. "They're showing you respect, Demon."

Before anyone could react to Wells's unique pet name for me—although I thought I saw Jarleth mouth it to himself—he filled me in on Jarleth and Kitano's assignments. I learned quickly that, although they were officially known as scouts, these were definitely Wells's spies. In their dual capacity, they first reported that all five Molnarian units had been spotted and would rendezvous with us tonight and tomorrow. Wells's relief was palpable. His aura split again as he 'pathed Celphia with the news.

Then I learned about their not-so-public mission.

Jarleth and Kitano had been dispatched before the disastrous near-massacre. The king had given Wells direct orders to continue his march toward the capital as intended, although every maneuver had gone exactly opposite the original plans at that point. Their supplies dwindling, the other units days late, Wells had no choice but to do as Allestair commanded and risk a march. He did his best to mitigate damage in advance, and planned to establish a less-exposed camp closer to the larger units, wink a few soldiers back to retrieve the medics and supplies, and send word to implore those units to make haste, but he knew the dangers. In preparation for the worst, he wrote the king an official request for emergency aid, and sent his two spies to infiltrate Sephryan camps for information.

Wells hoped that if the worst were to happen, the spies might be able to assist any of his soldiers taken prisoner, or at least get word to the other generals as to who and where they were. He also hoped they could discreetly lure the Sephryans away from the camp to spare the medics, unicorns, and any survivors who made it back.

Kitano was especially skilled at glamours, making them so seamless that even other sidhe had a difficult time detecting them. He demonstrated, becoming Sephryan for me. His short black hair melding into burnished gold and his tan skin leaching of color before my eyes. He held the glamour long enough to give me a short bow, before releasing it and fading back into himself. I took quick mental notes. His seam work was brilliant. I wondered if I could replicate it now that I had seen how it was done.

As a half-Sephryan—which he told me was rare—all Jarleth had to do was pale his skin slightly with an easy glamour, making it ridiculously simple, he said, to slide into their camps. Even his scent matched, something Kitano couldn't imitate as easily, so Jarleth usually took point if they had to interact with anyone extensively.

Before delving into more official Molnarian news—Wells *had* received a response from the palace seconds after we were attacked in the swamp and had managed to snatch it from the air and 'port it into a pocket—he asked for complete reports from Jarleth and Kitano. They shared a long stare, sighing simultaneously, as though silently deciding who would break the bad tidings.

Kitano leaned forward, "General, how many fighters were unaccounted for after the last battle? Not among the dead or the living."

Wells blinked. "Nine. I had assumed—"

"You had assumed they were obliterated by kroma or sliced into pieces so small they were unidentifiable?" Jarleth finished grimly, folding his arms across his chest. "The Sephryans are taking prisoners if they can knock them unconscious without killing them or somehow overpower them. Females particularly, but they'll keep males too."

"What are they doing with them?" Wells's voice was cold with fury.

"Aside from the usual prisoner-of-war activities of torture and confinement, they're being kept for breeding," said Kitano bluntly, his face blank and hard; his aura thrashing with fury. "The Sephryans still don't know what's sterilizing and killing their humans, and they can't get their hands on our recently turned Earthlings." He nodded in my direction. "They figure ours have enough human in their blood to help them out for now."

"Any idea how many of ours they have?" Wells glared at the map of Sephrya in front of him, his aura crimping and cracking briefly before a wash of bronze determination flooded through. I laid a hand on his thigh, my own chest tight.

"Once we have all the units together and get their numbers, we'll have a better idea. But they have a sizable amount," Jarleth said. "We're not sure where they're keeping them, but they seem to have some system whereby certain Sephryans stake a claim to them, then wait for them to get worn down enough to . . . do what they want. Unless they're able to compel them."

I shuddered, my stomach turning. I'd been under Al's compulsion for days when I'd been pulled from Earth initially. Having my will taken from me had been just as traumatic as the abduction itself. And that was done by someone who claimed to love me and want me to be happy. I remembered how I'd found Cilla when I rescued her from a Sephryan keep months ago. She'd been in a stone cell, on a straw mattress with a chain around her neck. I couldn't imagine being compelled by someone who saw you as a mere vessel for their genes. I knocked back a gulp of wine.

I knew I should eat, but my stomach was roiling as if I were back on that ship, under Al's compulsion.

"Did you see where they were keeping them?" Wells asked, taking my hand under the table and squeezing.

Kitano shook his head. "We've only been able to find out what's being done. We're uncertain if they've been brought into King Demian's own compound or are being held somewhere else."

"Demian's compound would be the most secure." Wells's brow furrowed as he teased a map from beneath the topmost one. "However, he has to have guessed that our eventual plan is to lay siege and force him to surrender."

"He doesn't believe our miniscule country capable of that," Jarleth said, sipping his wine, his tiny smile still in place, although his aura was crimson with fury. "And he could use them as hostages for negotiations if we do succeed in laying siege."

"Would they be in the same place they took Cilla?" I asked, feeling as if something heavy settled in the base of my throat. I still had no idea where in Sephrya I'd been. I'd followed a sense of Cilla when I'd winked to her. There were definitely wards in place to prevent winking into the castle she'd been held in, and winking out of the entire compound. I'd assumed at the time that we were in some minor keep, but if Sephrya's king had a large complex maybe we had been in an outer area.

"No one knows where in Sephrya you and Cilla escaped from," Kitano said. "They may have had to completely rebuild the wards after you tore them down, but they did it quickly enough that neither of us have been able to notice a discernible difference in any of the locations we've infiltrated."

I swallowed, my mouth going dry. "Would you know it if you saw it?" I pulled my phone from my pocket.

Jarleth's strange little smile stretched into a more natural grin. "I was hoping we'd get to see that thing. It's possible we'd recognize the place, yes."

When an Earthling chose to come to Molnair, they had to leave all electronics behind. However, since Al had kidnapped me, my only possessions from Earth were what I'd had with me at the time. My phone was a one-of-a-kind exception to the electronics rule and most sidhe had never seen one.

"Hang on, let me charge it," I said, glancing at Wells and receiving his discreet nod before laying the phone on my palm and carefully sending it some energy. Wells hadn't been a fan of me wasting energy on charging my phone while I was recovering.

My stomach flipped uncomfortably, but I ignored it. Once the phone was charged, I pulled up the full-length video. My legs were trembling. I took a deep breath and hoped no one else noticed, but decided I didn't have to subject myself to watching the video with them. "Okay, y'all come over here for a second so I can show you how to work it and then you can take it wherever you think is best to watch." I showed them how to play, pause, and scroll frame by frame. They grasped it quickly, deciding to do a playthrough of the interior first.

Wells gently massaged the back of my neck. *Are you okay? I got some tumultuous feelings a few moments ago.*

I'm okay. I 'pathed back. *I just . . . know what it's like to be under compulsion for a long time. And that was by someone who . . . claimed to care about me.* I cleared my throat. I still hadn't learned to throw off a compulsion. Wells refused to work it with me any longer because I broke down in tears every time we practiced. It remained my Achilles heel. Wells had told me to try it with Cilla or Zoe if I was determined to keep torturing myself but he was done.

"These fuckers need a decorator . . ." my voice floated up from the phone. I'd forgotten to mute the recording. The scouts sniggered, but my stomach clenched.

"You know what, we can mute that if you just need visuals." I reached out my hand for the phone.

"No, this is fine," Jarleth said, hazel eyes twinkling. "We don't mind your commentary."

"I mind it," I said. I didn't want them to get to where I was quoting *The Princess Bride* during a sword fight. Also . . . "I don't want to hear my bullshit and I really don't want to hear Cilla screaming later." He blinked, then passed me the phone. I hit mute and gave it right back. My hand shook slightly.

Do you want to go for a walk? You don't have to stay here for this. You could go talk to Prism. You should attempt to bond with him soon.

I felt myself closing up like a fist. *No. I want to see if they find something. I'm fine.*

Yes, clearly you're fine.

I stiffened. Wells switched from massaging my neck to rubbing long strokes along my spine.

It's okay to be upset, Imogen. It's also okay not to subject yourself to this again. He had put his arm around me when he felt how hard I was shaking.

I looked at the floor, willing myself to calm down. *I had to show people this video several times at the palace, I'm not sure why I'm reacting this way, but I'll get it under control.*

You had other issues at the palace you were focusing on surviving. You're back in the country where it happened. Trauma doesn't need a reason to hit you, Imogen, and you've had a rough twenty-four hours. Please take a break. No one will think less of you. One of us will come find you if we discover something, I promise.

I finally acquiesced, if only to spare myself the embarrassment of having two people I'd just met witness my mini breakdown. I grabbed my glass of wine and another hunk of bread and cheese and went out to sit by the central cooking fire. I wasn't ready to go see Prism again just yet.

My shoulders relaxed a fraction when I saw no one else around. Wells was right that I needed to develop a thicker skin, but I was grateful for the reprieve. I peeked into the large pot of hot water hanging just to the side—ready if anyone wanted tea at any time of the day or night—then plopped down onto one of the mismatched chairs that ringed the area along with a few stumps and logs. I blew out a long breath and set down my wine. I stared into the flames and forced myself to chew and swallow the bread and cheese, bite by bite, until it was gone. I thought of the meditation techniques Cilla sometimes employed during our yoga sessions, but just thinking of Cilla had my throat tightening.

Nothing about Cilla or Zoe had been in Wells's message from the palace, although he didn't believe for a moment they weren't questioned. He promised I could 'port her letter as soon as we were on the move again, if not before.

Wells had gone through what I'd written, crossed out anything compromising, and made me rewrite it. He said it was for the best to protect Cilla and Zoe. And the baby that they'd be having any week now. A birth I was likely going to be absent for. The thought tugged at my heart like a lead weight whenever it surfaced.

I'd considered winking back to Molnair. Seeing Cilla and Zoe. I'd virtually missed Cilla's entire pregnancy trapped in the stupid palace and now in Sephrya. I wondered if she'd started her hair salon or if she was going to wait until after the baby was born. But a visit wasn't worth the risk. To me or to them.

If I were caught, I'd be dragged back to the palace. And the king would certainly do a better job keeping me contained. And probably be more thorough about killing Wells. The fact that Wells had dropped the idea so quickly after initially bringing it up validated my suspicion that returning was not in our best interest.

I was still staring into the fire, although no longer trembling, with my empty wine glass dangling between my fingers, when I heard someone approaching from behind. I knew instantly it wasn't Wells and turned in time to see Jarleth striding into the circle of firelight. I realized he'd intentionally let me hear him and my breath came easier.

He held up the tail end of one of the bottles of wine as he took the seat next to me. I dipped my chin a fraction and he split it between us, set the bottle on the ground, then leaned to the side to reach his back pocket. He pulled out my phone and handed it to me.

"Did you find anything?" I tucked the phone into my thigh pocket and took a sip of wine.

"We did." Jarleth leaned back in his chair. "The dormers of all the windows in the courtyard have a D in the uppermost decoration. Which means the building is in Demian's capital city. We had to do your frame-by-frame thing to catch it. Based on that and our own knowledge of Demian's camps, we think that's where they're being held."

I nodded. Took another drink. Noticed my knee was bobbing and forced it to still.

"The capitol is laid out in layers. An outer ring, then two inner ones. Demian's castle is the innermost ring," Jarleth said. "Your mate and Kitano are going over what new maps they'll need and how to get them."

I nodded. That meant I could probably return to the tent. I didn't move, however.

"It's okay to be upset, you know," he said, his voice so soft I barely heard it over the snap of the flames. "And it's definitely okay to be angry at the people doing this and feel empathy for the ones suffering."

My throat burned again and I clenched my jaw. I didn't *want* to be upset in front of him. Or anyone.

This was a goddamn war and bad things were going to happen. And I needed to learn how to live with that. Regardless of what had been done to me in the past.

I felt Jarleth watching me, but I refused to look away from the flames.

"My mother was an ambassador during the Wind War. Well, right before it broke out. She was there trying to negotiate an agreement."

In spite of myself, he had my attention. "An ambassador for . . . Molnair?" I glanced over at him.

He nodded, his eyes flicking to mine once before turning back to the fire. He lifted his cup to his lips.

My stomach dropped. Our ambassadors had been sent back in pieces before this war. "Did she . . . ?"

"They didn't kill her. But they did just about everything else to her and sent her back as part of a message. She had me several months later."

My hand flew to my mouth.

"In spite of it all, she was a great mother. Angry about what had been done to her, yes, but she channeled that anger into helping others who were victimized during the war. She helped a lot of people and her fury paved the way to an easier recovery for many. And our immediate friends and family were good to us while I was growing up. But not everyone we met was kind.

"I learned how to do a glamour when I was very young, to avoid standing out. My mother ended up taking me to a healer because I was draining myself doing it as soon as I left the house every day and maintaining it until I got home. Not healthy for a young sidhe. The healer was surprised I was able to do it at all. And my mother was crushed when she learned I was having such a hard time. She made me promise to stop glamouring myself everyday though. The healer said it would stunt my growth."

He paused, took another sip of wine, still staring at the fire. "Of course, things were hard for a while, but one boy still treated me the same. Still sat next to me for meals. Partnered with me for drills or projects. And eventually there was another, and another." He met my gaze. "So don't be afraid of your empathy, Imogen. And use your anger. There are people out there who need both."

Once Jarleth had left me to finish with Wells and Kitano, I decided to stop being a coward and headed to the unicorn habitat. If Prism came out, I'd try to talk to him. If not, I'd wait five minutes, then go back to the tent.

He was waiting.

His lavender body seemed lit softly from within, his ears pricked forward.

Obsidian said you might come. What do you have for me?

I sighed, I hadn't brought him any pears, but Wells didn't ply Obsidian with treats every time he saw him. They did know each other better though. I slid my phone from my pocket. *How would you like to see what your horn looks like?*

His ears pricked forward, tail lifted. *What is that thing?*

It makes a picture. Hold still. I stood next to him for a selfie, struggling to muster up a smile, but I managed. I pulled up the photo and examined it. Whatever luminescence he innately possessed seemed to bleed into me when I was near him. Both of us were clearly visible, and when I held my finger on the photo to make it live, his horn glittered.

Look here. I held the phone up to one gleaming eye. *It captures a moment in time.*

Prism went completely still. I held my finger on the screen and he flinched. A little "Huhuhu" clattering up from his chest. My lips twitched.

Do another one. I wish to see all of myself. Without your face blocking any of me.

Stand back a little farther. Over by that rut in the grass.

He did as I requested. Posing like the Calvin Klein model of unicorns. He even gave me several "looks" without any prompting. I had ten pictures within seconds and waved him back over. I held the phone before one gleaming eye and swiped through them.

Prism huffed and tossed his mane. *I look absolutely as magnificent as I have been told. This is most pleasing. Do another one. I will make light with my horn.*

I obligingly took a slow-motion video of Prism rearing and showering indigo sparks from his horn as he sliced it through the air in vicious arcs that I recognized as attack strikes. He looked like a death metal Lisa Frank drawing.

Once Prism had seen his video, he was overjoyed with how magnificent he looked in slow motion. He watched it three times. When I left, the ache in my chest had eased just slightly.

That night, after the scouts had melted away to join the rest of the camp, and Wells and I had crashed into sleep together on the narrow cot, I had my first laryngospasm since I'd left the palace. Although it had never been this way on Earth, they were now always connected to terrifying nightmares. Wells suspected that, just as my skills had been enhanced when I was turned, some of my handicaps had as well. He compelled me to breathe before I'd even struggled to a seat.

"I forgot how nice it is when you do that for me," I gasped out between coughs.

Wells paused in rubbing circles on my stomach. Then resumed when he asked, "How many of these did you have at the palace after I . . . left?"

"Almost every night," I said, nudging his arm when he stopped again.

"Imogen . . ." He wrapped his hand around my waist and pulled me closer. "And did you just . . . wait it out?"

"Yeah," I said. Ninety seconds of feeling like I was choking to death on nothing. "I couldn't exactly compel *myself* to breathe and I certainly wasn't going to 'path Al to come into my bedroom and compel me to do *anything*."

His guilt lodged in my throat as if it were my own. I rolled to face him. "I handled this on Earth every single time without anyone being able to make my body breathe until it was ready. This isn't something you've got to feel guilty about."

"Did you have them this often on Earth?" His guilt had only slightly released its hold, I could still feel it stuck there.

"I didn't," I admitted. "But it's also not your responsibility to keep me from all uncomfortable things."

He wrapped his arms around me and I let him pull me close, relaxing into his embrace, breathing in the scent that I'd missed so sorely when we'd been apart.

"I'd like to try though," he said.

"As long as you let me try back," I said, snuggling against him. I sighed, reveling in the contact. Another question I hadn't been able to voice popped into my head. "You never said what we were going to do about the king's message."

Wells had revealed the contents of the king's reply to his report once I had rejoined them after my photo op with Prism. The king wanted to be informed of my swearing-in and what rank and company I'd be joining. I knew he was looking forward to pulling me out of Wells's unit as soon as possible. The scouts had been gleefully in support of me remaining a free agent, which made me like them even more.

The army may have technically belonged to Molnair, but these people followed Wells. The two scouts were an extreme version of that. I had no doubt they would spy on the king himself if Wells asked them to.

"He didn't specifically ask for a reply. He only asked to be informed of your swearing-in." Wells kissed the top of my head, but I caught the thread of tension in his voice. "And since we don't intend on swearing you in, I don't feel the need to do anything about his message."

"Do you think that will work?"

Wells massaged the back of my neck with one hand. "Until he makes a clear move, there's not much else I can do. And you're right, swearing you in would put you under his control. Patience is part of this game."

I wiggled closer, but couldn't quite shift the heaviness settled at the base of my spine as I wondered how long the king would let us get away with avoiding him. Or if he already had some other nefarious plan in the works. As much as I yearned to be free of him, I didn't see any realistic scenario in which he let us go.

CHAPTER FOURTEEN

Betrayal is a deep, painful wound because it comes from behind, delivered by someone who turned the trust you offered into a weapon.
—Queen Iphigenia Eigneachan Metellus

Two of the other five units, led by Adgemon and Lehm, met up with us the following day. I'd heard a lot about both of them, but Wells had spoken especially highly of Adgemon and I looked forward to meeting him. Soldiers on watch reported when the units were in range and Wells sent out a small number to welcome them and guide them back to our shielded camp.

Once initial greetings were performed, they set up their camps adjacent to ours so that we could join our shields and move easily between the three units. I knew I wasn't alone in noticing how well-supplied these other units looked. The contrast was stark. I wondered if I was the only one clocking the disturbed looks on the faces of the newly arrived soldiers as they passed through our camp to set up farther down the canyon. Both generals came to Wells's tent to exchange reports. Once again pride swelled behind my breastbone when I watched their auras and saw how much respect the other generals had for my mate. They were also visibly appalled by our lack of supplies and the conditions of our camp.

"We've had no issues getting anything we've requested," Lehm said, staring around in disbelief, his short, dark-blond hair spiky with sweat. "And you said you haven't even been sent rations? After surviving out here on your own for this long?"

"The unicorns are incredibly cranky." Wells was smiling, but I felt an ache growing between my shoulder blades from tension that wasn't entirely my own. "And I think Imogen would kill for a bath."

What I actually wanted was to see what the other generals' tents looked like if ours was so horrific. What did everyone usually carry around in the middle of a war?

Adgemon scribbled something on a scrap of paper and 'ported it away. "I'm having some of our extras brought over," he said, shoving the forelock of his thick black hair out of his eyes. It looked like he normally wore it short, but hadn't had it trimmed in a few months; it fell almost to his shoulders. He was nearly as tall as Wells. "This is ridiculous. How many of your squads have been eliminated? We can fill out some holes."

Lehm 'ported out a note of his own. "We've got more pears than we know what to do with. We only have five unicorns. I'm having extra crates brought over to yours now."

Wells thanked them both graciously, but I could feel his anger at the way we'd been slighted gnawing at my own belly. Anger and . . . something else. I watched his aura carefully. He was superior in rank to everyone other than the king. If the others truly hadn't been hunting and scavenging as we had, this made it glaringly obvious that Allestair had been priming Wells's unit to fail. I was about to 'path him and see if he was all right when I was distracted by the arrival of two soldiers levitating a bathtub between them.

"Holy hell, we get a real bathtub? You're my two favorite people," I said.

They smiled at me and brought the tub all the way to the curtained-off bathing area in back of our tent.

For the next hour, Wells and the two generals talked through changing rosters to fill out our unit. I learned that Kerlyn had two other daughters in the army and one in the air force. That answered the question I'd been asking myself about why she'd stayed after Kaylie had been killed. One of her daughters was in Lehm's unit and would be transferred over immediately. The other was in one of the three units we'd be meeting up with in the morning.

Once strategy and supply talk had concluded, I ducked behind the curtain to take my first bath in days. Wells 'ported the water in for me, but I heated it with a bit of my own kroma. It was heaven. And when I finished, I came out to a completely transformed tent.

"Wow, we are totally glamping now," I said, finger-combing my damp hair. It was nearly long enough to touch my shoulders. "Cilla would call this a glow up." Our cot had been replaced with what looked like a large futon and the thin sheets swapped out for actual bed linens. The worn, dusty rugs had been exchanged for thick carpets that wouldn't have been out of place in a posh chateau. Sturdy lanterns were hung from hooks rather than the stubs of candles I'd gotten used to. And it felt like there was ... air conditioning. "Is this tent climate-controlled now?"

"The rugs repel dust as well," Wells told me, bent over his desk. "I wasn't going to have anyone waste power on these kinds of comfort charms when we barely had energy to fight, but yes, several of Lehm and Adgemon's camp caretakers are going around charming all the tents against this insidious humidity. I think everyone will sleep better tonight."

"Do we have camp caretakers?" I asked, running my hand over a deep-blue chaise before plopping onto it.

"We have a few, but they were as run down as everyone else," Wells didn't look up from sorting through his piles of paper and tucking them into drawers. He lifted an eyebrow and floated a bottle of potion to me before letting his eyes fall back to his desk. "We'll break camp in the morning after we've met with the others and then everyone will march. The hope is to eventually establish a well-shielded camp close enough to lay siege. We'll get as far as we can tomorrow without wearing everyone out. You'll ride Prism, but it's hopeful we won't see any fighting until we're closer to Sephrya's capitol. Always better to be prepared, however. And six units together will be much more difficult to ambush successfully."

I nodded, sipping my potion. All of this had been said during the meeting with the other generals. "Are you okay?" I asked him. When his mouth tightened, I added, "It's nice to see how devoted the entire army is to you. Their auras are . . ."

I trailed off when he glanced up from his papers, sighed, and gave me his signature half smile. I rose, tossed back the rest of the potion, padded across the plush carpets, and settled on his lap, wrapping my arms around his neck. He pulled me in close, the warmth of his body seeping through the stiffness of his jacket. I shut my eyes and for a moment we just breathed together.

"It's hard," he said, "to be confronted with the undeniable reality that our unit has been intentionally left inadequately supplied and vulnerable."

I combed my fingers through his long hair, resting my cheek against his head. I could feel his anger and grief ebbing and flowing under my own heart as his aura fractured and surged. His chest expanded against me in a slow sigh.

"I knew, Imogen. I knew that he wanted to break you. Allestair saw your power and wanted to command it. I also knew he hated how willful you are. I knew he would send me away and keep you from joining me, even though you're obviously an asset to any fighting force. He wanted to isolate you. I also hoped you would find a way to survive until we worked out a way to get you out."

He sighed again and squeezed me tighter. "Even after my requests for supplies and aid went unanswered, even after that disastrous battle, even after everything you told me, I couldn't believe he'd done it intentionally. But when I see what every other general received so easily and readily . . . It's undeniable, Imogen. He intentionally crippled our unit. I'm still not sure he meant for us to be destroyed—how could he have known what Sephrya's movements would be—but he took advantage of the situation as soon as he learned of it. All to give you to Al and have control over you."

"I'm sorry," I said, kissing his temple, then leaned back to look him in the eye, gathering his thick red hair into a ponytail then letting it slide through my fingers. "He failed though."

"I know." Wells took a deep breath. "And I . . . I need to get past it."

"I won't blame you for holding a grudge if you want. I mean, I certainly plan to." I dropped my forehead against his. "But please believe I would never let anyone kill you. I absolutely refuse to allow it. Hey," I leaned back and grinned sunnily, "should I assassinate him?"

He pressed a hand over my mouth. "Gods' bones, Imogen, I know you're joking, but everyone doesn't understand your type of humor. Do not jest about regicide within the General of the King's Armies' tent."

Can I 'path about it? Daydream about it? Maybe make little stick-figure cartoons depicting the event?

I'd prefer it if you didn't make . . . little cartoons.

What about just in the dirt sometimes? I am excellent at stick figure cartoons.

He took a deep breath, his gaze holding mine. "I know you're trying to lighten the mood, Imogen, but I need to impress upon you that we're walking an incredibly thin line. When it comes to the king—in any and all iterations—I need you to be very careful. Remember our talk about deference?"

My nose wrinkled. "But, Wells, he tried to—"

He touched his finger to my lips. *From here on out, we need to be very careful with what we say. And we cannot have Allestair learning about your . . . kingless status. Things would become very dangerous very quickly. You need to behave as if you are loyal to the crown.*

My jaw clenched, but the bond seemed to quiver inside of me. I felt Wells's fear. And really, why wouldn't he be afraid after what happened? I took a slow breath.

"Okay."

He brushed my cheekbone with his thumb, the bond relaxed a bit, but Wells didn't attempt to force a smile. "We'll find a way past this."

Early the next morning and we prepared to continue our march, now several units strong. Wells cupped his hands together to give me a leg up. On a horse, I would have been able to pull myself aboard, but I was forced to accept the help when mounting Prism. Not only was he obscenely tall, but unicorns refused to be tacked. No saddle, no bridle, not so much as a blanket. I was thankful that Child Imogen had enjoyed riding bareback.

"His mane is tough, no nerves, so you can feel free to hang on to it just like—" he cleared his throat. I winked at him, knowing he'd been about to compare Prism's mane to a horse's. "Just like your instincts would tell you to," he finished. He pulled a pink pear from his pocket and offered it to Prism on a flat palm, speaking aloud as he 'pathed. "Prism, you're carrying my heart. Please take good care of her."

Prism accepted the pear daintily. *Your heart can take care of herself. We shall cut swaths of destruction through hordes of our enemies. Together we shall be feared and admired. We shall create chaos and ruination. We shall achieve conquest.*

I don't know why I try, Wells 'pathed to me only, shaking his head and walking over to Obsidian, who apparently demanded two pears since Prism wasn't even carrying Wells. Thankfully, Wells had anticipated this and produced three pears. One green, one pink, and one golden.

Wells, as general, was able to 'path all the unicorns if he needed to, as long as he didn't do it too often. Other than that, unicorns preferred to only 'path with their chosen rider. I was warned to *never* attempt to path another unicorn unless they spoke to me first. That was a rule I wasn't even a little tempted to break.

Wells gave Obsidian his last pear, then ran a hand down his gleaming neck. *Do try to remind Prism that we are unlikely see combat today. We were* able to move everyone to this location effectively and secretly. That's one good thing I was able to report to Allestair. We should be able to establish a camp nearer to the capitol without incident. Your unicorn is violent. I want to manage his expectations.

Have your mate take a picture of us, Prism demanded, pawing the ground with an onyx hoof. *I want to see what you look like upon me. Especially now that you have bathed.*

"Prism wants you to take a picture of us," I said, digging my phone out of my thigh pocket.

Don't make that stupid face, Prism suggested.

"He wants one without me smiling, so let's take two if you don't mind," I extended the phone out.

Wells glared but took it. "You're not supposed to carry this during a march, Imogen, it's supposed to be packed up with the tent." But he lifted the phone anyway.

"You said we probably wouldn't battle today, so . . ." I let him take one of me smiling, making a V with my first two fingers, then I dropped my smile for a more serious pose for Prism.

Wells handed the phone back to me. "When I spoke of deference and following orders, I meant it with regards to all things big and small. Leave it with our things next time. Obsidian wants one now, of course, apparently Prism has been bragging about seeing himself. Please just take one and let's get the hell on our way." Wells vaulted onto Obsidian's back.

"Okay, I'll leave it next time, sorry. Oh damn, Cilla would be freaking out right now," I said, aiming the phone at him. "You look so hot on him with his black coat and your red hair. Yeah, just keep looking pissed like that, it makes it better." I ended up getting two pictures, one with him staring at the camera, looking sexy and pissed off, and one with him caught in surprised laughter.

"Alright, if everyone is done documenting the experience, let's get the hell on our way." Wells and Obsidian cantered forward to the head of our unit, ready to march us to our position among the other five. I glanced back behind me and saw the unicorns' handlers shrinking the enchanted forest back into the swampy soil.

Why are we marching directly adjacent to Obsidian? Prism complained. *It's not practical. There are fewer unicorns than sidhe. We should be spread out across the unit for greater efficiency and more opportunities for destruction.*

I ran a hand down his shining black mane. *Wells says that we're unlikely to see actual combat today.* I told him for the third time. *And honestly, I'm not sure he trusts us as a pair yet.*

Prism snorted with derision and shook his mane. *Ridiculous. You can understand me, unlike my previous riders. I can teach you everything you need to know. You are young and malleable. I will teach you how to shield your mind more effectively and mold you into an excellent weapon.* He tossed his head while my eyebrows climbed higher and higher. *No matter. We are free agents. When battle begins, we shall wink to the most effective point.*

Sure. I made a mental note to ask Wells how to handle this later on. Technically Prism *did* know a lot more about battles than I did, so maybe he should be in charge between the two of us? And the other unicorns were spread out among the force. It did make sense. Our unit had the most, with ten, but even so, no other pair of unicorns was even within shouting distance of each other.

We shall do shielding drills now. Your mind is too open. Prism commanded.

Okay, just remember I'm not at full strength yet . . .

If there is not to be fighting, Prism 'pathed crisply, *then you shall not need to worry about it.*

After thirty minutes of shielding drills, I could see what Prism meant. If I had known these kinds of shields when I met him he wouldn't have been able to steal my voice. Still, I was about to beg him for a break when a note fluttered down in front of Wells. He caught it and read.

"What's up?" I asked while braiding sections of Prism's shiny mane.

"Scouts have spotted something up ahead," he said, igniting the note and letting the ash blow away. "I've called them back and alerted the other generals. Could be a traveling caravan, could be an attempted ambush." He met my gaze and sighed. "Go ahead and 'port over some of your explosives."

I nodded and focused on the location of my weapons. Wells had decided I could carry one explosive arrow and two little grenades at a time. I knew where on the supply carts they were kept—well-shielded—and if I needed more, I was to 'port them from there. I caught the arrow and added it to my quiver of normal ones. Then caught the pouch with my grenades and clipped it to my belt. I checked Kaylie's sword hanging at my side, and touched my dagger on the opposite hip.

Prism lifted his nose, flared his nostrils, and whinnied menacingly deep in his throat. *I smell... enemies.* His eyes gleamed malevolently red.

"Prism says he smells them," I reported, just as I heard Wells mutter "shit" under his breath.

"Obsidian does, too. It's a full unit. Why they're out here..." He shook his head as if clearing it. "I've alerted the lieutenants and had Obsidian ready the unicorns." Wells's eyes were fixed on the horizon. I heard several vicious whinnies punctuating the even sound of marching and knew that the unicorns, at least, were thrilled. "Remember to use control with your lightning like we discussed. If you're unsure about directing it, stop using it. Imogen, pay attention to your energy level. You are improving, but I don't want to push it too far. We have enough people now so it's not necessary to wear yourself out. In fact, if you and Prism don't feel ready—"

"He's already said that we're free agents and he's going to wink us to the point of most destruction or something, so you may as well put us where you think we'd be best," I said bluntly, then 'pathed on a tight band, *Remember that the entire reason we threw me in front of him after a battle before was so he would get this chance. I really don't want to antagonize him again.*

Wells ran a hand through his hair. "I know you can take care of yourself, Imogen, it's just—yes, all right," he snapped at Obsidian, who was snorting and circling his muzzle in what I interpreted as a unicorn eye roll.

"Apparently, I'm wasting time. Imogen, I want you on the right flank, I'll take the left. Remember to be aware of Prism if you call the lightning. You don't want to electrocute him."

I nodded, my joints watery with nerves. "See you in a minute," I pushed a smile toward him. *Prism, can you win*—he winked us into position. My stomach turned over as I adjusted. *Okay, hey, can you like, either wait for me to finish or warn me that you're about to do that in the future? Thanks.*

Why did you thank me? I did not agree to either of those things. Prism pranced sideways a few steps, tossing his head attractively before settling into formation.

Because it was a reasonable request from your partner in combat and I assumed you were a reasonable unicorn, I said, clamping down on the heartburn of irritation flaring near my diaphragm.

I am a reasonable unicorn and a brilliant strategist, he said. *It does make sense that I inform you before winking so that you are aware and do not react poorly. This could thwart my plans. I shall inform you in the future.*

Well, I've already said thanks, so I won't say it again, I commented drily, then movement on the horizon caught my attention. *Prism, do you see that? Wells?*

I see it, Wells answered, his voice already in that steady, emotionless command mode. *Get ready. There are thousands of them. This is going to be a battle.*

I wondered if he could feel the nerves coursing through me. I straightened my spine, threading the fingers of my left hand through Prism's mane and holding hard. *We've got this.* I 'pathed. Wells didn't need to be worrying about me.

Keep in touch. Listen for commands and stay safe. I love you.

I love you, too. I cut off contact. The approaching army was taking shape.

I watched our ambassador, in steel gray and blue, wink to the valley in between us, thinking of my conversation with Jarleth and wondering who in their right mind would ever accept the position of ambassador. It was then that I realized that both armies were paused on the crests of adjacent hills.

I saw the red and gold of Sephrya flashing along the length of the horizon. There were thousands more of them than there were of us. *Prism, we are going to have to destroy a lot of our enemies.*

Prism flattened his ears against his skull, extended his neck toward the Sephryan army and bared his teeth. *Conquest!*

Hey, Prism, just so you know, I watched the Sephryan ambassador wink down to ours. *I have these special explosives I made that cause a lot of destruction—*

This sounds delightful. Prism arched his neck, angling his horn down toward the valley.

It—yeah, I think you'll enjoy it—just, if I use one, I need you to do what I say at that time. The Molnairian ambassador was folding her arms, shaking her head. *I understand that you're the one that's more experienced, but to avoid us getting blown up, just when I use one of those, I need to be in charge. Okay?*

I accept. This is logical. I appreciate you informing me in advance.

The Sephryan ambassador summoned two blades from nowhere and sliced at the Molnairian's neck and midsection. She barely deflected.

The battle cry went up from all around.

Prism was the first to charge.

CHAPTER FIFTEEN

Unexpected enemies are an incredible inconvenience in that they're nearly impossible to prepare for.
—Captain Marcellus Tibercio

I gripped with my legs and lifted my hands from Prism's mane, heating them for sticky fire. It was one non-lightning attack I could fling at distance that had the benefit of spreading like a virus. Unless someone was familiar with it and confident in the counter, it was unstoppable. I flung sticky fire out before we hit the Sephryans' front lines, catching at least ten. Then I drew my sword.

Winking! Prism said, less than a second before he winked us right into the center of the enemy unit. He sliced into them with his horn, skewering them and tossing their bodies aside, shielding us both from either side with kromatic barriers of his own, and trampling Sephryans with his hooves.

More warning, next time, more warning! I swiveled frantically, trying to get my bearings, then spotted the slow, menacing glide of a silver sidhe tank.

I popped a grenade into my hand, lit it with a snap, 'ported it into the tank about fifty feet from us. *Explosives, keep the shields up.* Three seconds later the tank's rear blew out. It cut a swath through the Sephryan ranks, tearing through them to crash land ten feet from us.

That was your destruction thing! Prism exclaimed, launching a gale of violet fire from his horn, catching twenty Sephryans. *Wonderful!*

I swung my sword to deflect and slice at any Sephryans that broke through Prism's shields, adrenaline zinging up my spine. We were completely surrounded. What had this blasted unicorn been thinking? Keeping my legs clenched firmly around Prism, I thought of the lightning and the clouds darkened. Electricity thrummed against my skin, tingling. I punched my fist high. The lightning connected in a bright, sky-splitting arc. Once I was charged, I took a breath—no small feat in the midst of a battle on a blood-crazed unicorn—and gathered the energy to myself. *Control.* It took more concentration because I didn't want to electrocute Prism. I used my sword to fling the energy out, focused on directing the lightning as it released. I caught an entire Sephryan battalion in my electric net.

Lightning thrower! Conquest! Prism charged forward. I was grateful for my running legs as I kept them clamped around his massive sides, one hand still receiving lightning the other tossing it out with my sword. Mentally this was easier than being on the ground, I had less personal contact with each soldier, but physically I knew I was draining faster.

Prism skewered through several Sephryans in front of us to make room for a charge. *Throw the lightning to the sides! I will drop the shields!* With no time to argue, I did as he said, pulling my arm from the sky. He raced forward, spewing flame from his horn, stabbing anyone who didn't get out of our way while I tossed short bolts of lightning to either side of us. I tried to ignore the splat of blood from Prism's kills hitting my skin. His coat was streaked with it. I had to trust the unicorn to take charge of where we were heading; my entire focus riveted to throwing my lightning and remaining mounted.

Shortly we were clear and behind enemy lines. I let the lightning go with a relieved breath and hunched forward, gripping Prism's mane.

I shall see where we can create the most destruction without causing death among our own, Prism said, spinning around to gallop behind the wall of Sephryans. I sucked in several deep breaths, taking the opportunity to let my blood cool, sheathed my sword, and grabbed my bow. I needed to rest my kroma and Prism left me no time to debate him once he made a decision. Already the auras of the crowd had faded to transparent swirls.

Once you find a good spot, Prism, let me shoot one of my explosives. I pulled out my arrow. Removed its shield.

There! Lehm's unit is overwhelmed. They are being attacked by multiple enemy units.

Got it. I pulled the arrow back, launched it into the center of the Sephryan crowd, and ignited it midair. *Shields up, move away from my arrow!*

Prism winked us fifty yards forward. We reappeared just as the arrow detonated. I spotted another sidhe tank in the Sephryan ranks.

Imogen, I don't know where you are but get back into position! Wells's voice was sharp.

Okay! I 'pathed. *Prism, I'm going to hit that hovercraft then let's head back to our unit.* I tossed the bow crossways over my shoulder and reached for the pouch at my belt.

We are doing well here! Prism argued.

I gritted my teeth, one fist wrapped around my final explosive. How to word this so that he listens? *Don't you want our unit to be the most successful? We should make sure they're coping without us. And you forget that my kroma isn't one hundred percent yet.*

I felt him grumble. *Yes, all right. Destroy the craft.*

I pulled out my last grenade. Lit the fuse with a snap and 'ported it into the tank. Prism veered away and winked us back to our unit just as the explosion reached my ears. Wells took one look at me and ordered us to the back of the unit. Obsidian had to reinforce the order with Prism.

Fortunately, the Sephryans retreated shortly afterward. The battle was a victory for our side. The explosives had surprised the Sephryans and we had suffered minimal losses. We were able to set up a well-shielded camp less than a day's march from the capital. To Prism's everlasting pride, much of the success had been as a result of his "swaths of destruction" as he put it. Wells was less than pleased. Not only was he unnerved by yet another Sephryan unit appearing where it shouldn't have been, but I was gray with exhaustion by the time he saw me. The last of my kroma sparked out while we were setting up camp, before I had cleaned off Prism or myself. Wells hauled me to Kerlyn, who had me sit in her tent and drink one of the fizzy pink concoctions. Apparently they were addictive, so I couldn't have more than one every few days.

While I waited for it to hit, Wells took the opportunity to berate me in relative privacy. "You promised me you would follow orders, Imogen."

My jaw dropped. "I absolutely followed orders!"

He leaned forward, putting one hand on either arm of my chair. "Then let me make one thing clear: when I order you back to our unit, I mean immediately."

I snapped my jaw shut. Opened it to tell him I'd been fighting with Prism, then shut it again. Maybe it wasn't a good idea to throw Prism under the bus. "Fine. I didn't realize . . . Fine."

Once I was pepped up, we went to see about our unicorns. Prism was elated as he was covered in the blood of his enemies and several people gave him pears.

Okay, that's your fifth one, can we go clean you off now? I asked, grooming bucket in hand, still drooping a bit with exhaustion. All the unicorns boasted splatters from their own kills, but Prism was by far the bloodiest. I suspected he enjoyed it.

Take a picture first. I wish to compare my clean image to my post-conquest image.

"This thing doesn't have unlimited storage, you know," I griped, pulling out my phone. "I can't take a picture of everything. Sometimes you have to just enjoy the moment."

Prism posed with one front leg lifted and his blood-coated horn angled down. I sighed and took the picture, then brought it over and showed it to him. "It's like Slayer and My Little Pony had a baby."

"Imogen, gods' bones, please put that away before the other unicorns see it," Wells came up behind me. "We're starting to convince some of them to clean off before it dries into their coats and I don't want any further delays." He glanced toward the distant battlefield, a crease forming between his eyebrows. "This close to the Briarwood Forest we need to get the dead taken care of quickly."

I did as he said, stowing the phone in my pocket while 'pathing Prism that he could look at more photos after we'd cleaned him off. "What's the deal with the Briarwood?" I followed Wells and Obsidian over to the water station. Admittedly there was something off-putting about an entire forest full of blood-red trees but I didn't see what that had to do with the collection of our dead. Although I knew several soldiers had been dispatched to check for wounded immediately.

Wells hurled a bucket of water over Obsidian's withers and promptly began scraping the blood from his coat. "It's not so much the forest as the creatures that live within. They'll undoubtedly have smelled the blood by now and it's only a matter of time before they decide to make a meal of it. We want to get the pyres lit and personal effects collected before that happens."

He was cleaning with an energetic swiftness that made me breathless. I dumped water over Prism and did my best to match him, concentrating on the actions rather than letting myself delve too far into my imagination regarding corpse-eating forest creatures.

Either Wells and Obsidian had their cleaning routine down pat or Prism was just that much bloodier, but in the end, Wells helped me finish cleaning, then to my dismay, told me to mount up. I didn't complain, but he must have read the expression on my face.

"We'll have a bath right after this, Demon, I promise." He said, hauling himself onto Obsidian after giving me a boost. "Sometimes the presence of the unicorns will deter the urzen. I didn't want to take them out without letting them come down from their bloodlust. Easier to get them to retreat if necessary."

Nerves scuttling up my spine, I clung to Prism's newly combed mane as he cantered after Obsidian, their coats gleaming damply. By the time Wells and I arrived at the battlefield, a few of the other freshly scrubbed unicorns and their exhausted riders were already there. My stomach clenched when I saw several people quickly stripping the dead of their weapons and searching their pockets for letters to loved ones, some with silent tears running down their faces.

Wells's jaw was hard, tension running through his entire body. I'd overheard him speaking to Celphia. Apparently, it was impossible to wink entire units en masse over great distances. They could be winked in increments or individually, but they'd need a reference point. Scouts had reported no units in the vicinity of camp last night.

So how did they get there?

The unicorns formed a perimeter around what appeared to be our side of the battlefield, the Sephryans were erecting their own pyres half a mile away. No one bothered anyone from either side while caring for their dead after a battle. Both kings, in agreement, had forbidden it.

I eventually let my eyes unfocus, even the magic of the pink fizzy drink ebbing away, but I kept my chin up, not wanting anyone to accuse the general's mate of snoozing on the job. It was Prism's scream of challenge and the sudden tension running through his body that snapped everything into sudden clarity.

Every unicorn on the field was screaming and rearing, swinging their horns toward the forest. Dread slid down my spine, goosebumps flashing out across my skin in spite of the heat. A punch of adrenaline had me straightening, clenching Prism's mane as an enormous pack of canines stalked across the field, half of them split off toward the Sephryan side. The Sephryans had no unicorns and didn't hesitate before winking away.

"Steady," I said, although I could have been speaking to myself just as much as Prism. They were wolves the size of grizzly bears, fangs as long as my forearm gleamed against their midnight-black coats. Their lips peeled back and they lifted their snouts, scenting blood on the wind.

My heart spun into my throat as Wells and Obsidian streaked toward these monsters. Wells was either too exhausted to focus or intentionally broadcasting his 'path as he rode. *These are our friends! Let us give them dignity in death! We mean you no harm!*

I had unconsciously grabbed onto the 'path Wells held open for the urzen as he passed, so he and I alone were rocked by the snarl in the reply as the nearest canine pounced upon two bodies, scattering those nearby into winks. *Your kind offers us no dignity in death. Why should we care for your customs? Your friends will sustain us while you torture our fields for your own petty feuds. Begone or we feast upon the living as well.*

My stomach iced over when a canine the size of a rhinoceros stalked across the blood-soaked field, giving Gmork from *A NeverEnding Story* as it scented the gruesome, ravaged ground and leveled its yellow eyes at Wells. I blinked and it was lunging toward Obsidian, who blasted out with his horn. The urzen apparently had magic of their own, however and it shielded and continued to charge.

At the same time, another urzen leapt upon a dead soldier that a sidhe with long black hair was desperately trying to haul toward a pyre. The scream that tore from her throat as the urzen tore the body from her hands ripped through my heart. For a breath, I thought she would fight the beast, but a rider on a sea-green unicorn charged by and hauled her bodily astride her own mount.

"WINK OUT!" Wells commanded, still facing down the largest urzen. And for once I didn't protest when Prism just went.

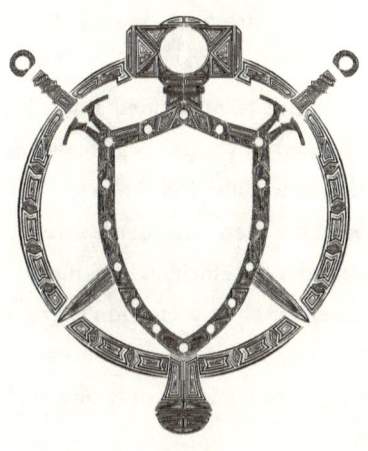

CHAPTER SIXTEEN

No one enjoys the consequences of their own actions.
—Prince Aloysius Metellus

Wells verified that no one had been left behind, gave orders that the unicorns be returned to their habitat and fed, then 'pathed the watch to keep an eye on the field. He informed the shaken soldiers that we would return once the urzen were gone if there was still light, and take care of what was left.

Wells had pulled from his own kromatic reserves to light the pyres himself before he and Obsidian winked out, ensuring he was the last on the field and that those bodies already prepared would at least receive the dignity of the fire rite.

He was nearly as exhausted as I was, his face pale and drawn, with new darkness smudged beneath his eyes, but he insisted I go clean off when we found Adgemon waiting in our tent. I knocked back my next dose of potion and obeyed. I'd originally imagined a nice long soak, maybe even falling asleep in the tub, but my mind kept replaying the image of those fangs plunging into that dead sidhe and yanking him away like a doll.

Although the heat unknotted some of the sore muscles at my neck and shoulders, my bath was brief and efficient, I was just toweling off when Wells pushed the flap aside, his steps heavy. He didn't say a word as he 'ported my bathwater away and replaced it with fresh. His eyes were dull and vacant, the mask was off, and I knew I was the only one in camp who would ever witness him like this.

Although I couldn't see his aura and there was nothing I could glean through the bond, I could tell he needed some time to himself. I was dressed by the time he sank into the water. I ran a hand down his head and pressed a kiss to his cheek. "I'm going to check the unicorns," I said. "'Path if you need anything?"

Without looking, he reached up and caught my fingers, giving them a squeeze, then let them go.

I took my time walking to the unicorns' habitat. I didn't really have much desire to take pictures of Prism, which was the likely outcome, but I wanted to give Wells some space and I couldn't image myself just sitting quietly somewhere right now.

Prism was actually happy to see me. He had tussled with another unicorn and accidentally stabbed a tree. He had a sap smudge on his horn that he needed removed. I obligingly retrieved a rag and stepped up onto a mounting block. Prism was quiet as I worked on his horn and I wondered if, in spite of his flippant personality, the carnage on the field had affected him too.

My meditative polishing was interrupted by a 'path from Wells. *The watch has just informed me of an approaching aerial unit. He believed it could be one of ours. Are you with Prism?*

Yeah, want me to check it out? I gave Prism's horn one last swipe with the cloth and tossed it in the hamper with the rest of the grooming items. *Give you time to get some clothes on?*

Please. 'Path me and let me know what you see. If it's one of ours we'll need to get them under cover before they give away the location of camp. I'll be there as quickly as I can.

After informing Prism what we were up to, I vaulted onto his back from the mounting block. We cantered to the edge of camp, as swiftly as we could go without disrupting traffic, and peered out through the shield. *Definitely one of ours . . .* I 'pathed Wells as the lead craft made a sweep of the field. *I think it might be Captain Marc!*

A beat of silence from Wells, then, *It's him! Just 'pathed him. Step outside of the shield so he knows where to land.*

Moments later, Prism and I were streaking toward the cruiser, its cargo ramp descending with Captain Marc already ambling down to meet us, the Sephryan sun glinting off his brown, clean-shaven pate. "Imogen Delaney!" He grinned, spreading his arms wide as he reached the ground and strode toward us. "On a unicorn, no less. Your grandmother would be thrilled."

"It's not all it's cracked up to be," I said, returning the captain's smile. Then, when Prism snorted his pique, I tossed a little honey into my tone. "His name is Prism. Isn't he the most gorgeous being you've ever seen?"

Prism arched his neck, lifted his tail, and pranced in place, giving Marc a side view in order to more effectively admire him. The little snot even shot some rainbow sparkles out of his horn.

"Absolutely breathtaking," Captain Marc said as he approached, giving me a wink.

He may stroke my neck if he likes, Prism informed me magnanimously.

"He says you can pet him," I told the captain.

Marc chuckled as he laid a dark hand against Prism's violet coat, his ebony eyes dancing as he lifted them to mine. "It's good to see you again, ward-breaker."

The captain joined his shield with ours so that his flying unit was cloaked as well. He'd been sent to aid in our attack on the capital. Additional units were said to be converging on the opposite side of the city. After a lengthy strategy meeting with the other generals and Captain Marc in our new glowed-up glamping tent, everyone but the captain retired to their own units to eat.

We finally got to find out what had happened at the palace after my dramatic escape. Al had indeed been questioned under compulsion and both Al and Captain Marc were forbidden from discussing the incident with anyone who didn't already know about it. Cilla and Zoe had been pulled in and questioned under compulsion also, but, as Wells had predicted, since I hadn't told them anything vital, they were safe and quickly released. They were fed the line that the king was simply concerned for my whereabouts and anxious to find me.

I'd sent my note to Cilla that morning when we broke camp. When I hadn't received a reply, they'd both assured me that she was probably waiting until I specifically told her it was okay to do so.

After Wells sent his report thanking the king for sending me as the requested aid—a part of the story that brought Marc to hysterics as he recounted it, calling Wells a brutal genius—that was accepted as the party line throughout the city: King Allestair had sent me to assist my mate, and the king would most likely reassign me as the need arose.

"Clever not to swear her in," Marc said, twirling the wine stem of his nearly empty glass between his fingers. "I don't know how long you'll be able to get away with it, but it prevents him from moving her without causing a lot of scandal. Separating mates for the sake of separating them is criminal, as we're all aware."

"Even though that's exactly what he did when he wouldn't let me come with Wells to begin with," I said darkly. Marc had put a sound shield over the tent for this conversation.

It was a tricky bit of kroma, but he was fresh and he wouldn't have been able to talk to us about the palace if it were possible that anyone else could overhear. I liked it because I could say what I wanted about the damn king.

"One thing I would like you to look at, if you wouldn't mind, Marc," Wells said, refilling everyone's glasses. "Imogen, get that spell out of your things. I want Marc to see it."

"Oh, de*light*ful!" The captain's grin was a slash of white as he accepted his full glass. He winked at me as I dug through my sack for the spell. "No one has been able to figure out what you did to get through the wards. I've been dying of curiosity."

"It was a highly dangerous spell," Wells said, brows lowered, glaring at me over a sip of his own wine. "She's lucky she didn't screw anything up and kill herself."

I passed Marc the worn paper, pulling my own glass toward me, decorating my face with a look of bland innocence.

The captain's smile faded as he read. He set his glass down and leaned forward, running a finger over the list. His aura shifted from calm blue-greens and pink-gold amusement into spritzes of sharp shock, then spun too quickly for me to make sense of. I felt the brush of his power as he reached out to test his sound shield. He stretched a hand toward the tent flaps and they fell closed.

"Imogen, where did you get this spell?" he murmured, his eyes still scanning the scrap of paper.

Butterflies danced in my chest. "At the palace. In the library."

Marc leaned over the table, eyes fixed on me. "No one saw you with it? You're absolutely certain?" His finger thumped on the table with each word.

"I'm positive. I went at night under a cloaking shield. They would never have let me near any spell books. I wasn't even supposed to know about that section. I copied it down and then researched the ingredients separately."

Wells leaned forward also, his aura shifting into the blue-blacks of concern. The three of us were bent toward each other like thieves planning a heist.

"Did you read the pages before the spell concerning the history and purpose of this particular potion?" Marc waved the paper back and forth, his dark eyes boring relentlessly into mine.

"I . . ." I glanced sideways at Wells. This wasn't going to go over well. "I read enough to know that it would get me through the wards."

"Imogen!" Wells smacked the table, eyes widening in disbelief.

"I didn't have a ton of time! I had to do a lot of things on the sly with very little sleep. I wasn't even technically supposed to be able to *see* that section."

"You told me you did a test dose," Wells growled.

"I did! I mean . . . it was a slightly different spell but with the same basic ingredients, just with smaller amounts and less prep time." My stomach swirled. I could feel Wells's fury burning my own lungs. "That spell was only for 'porting and 'pathing though, so I couldn't use it to get myself through. But since the preparation was almost exactly the same, I figured if I didn't screw that one up . . ." I trailed off. Wells's eyes flashed dangerously and I knew we were going to have it out later.

"So you didn't read—" Captain Marc started.

"There were like . . . fifteen pages of very tiny writing," I said, trying to get them to see reason. "The first time I found it, Al interrupted me and I needed to get out of the area before he saw me. When I went back to double check, I was in the *dark* crouching in the stacks with a little, tiny stub of a candle." Wells's gaze burned into me, eyes now flashing as malevolently red as Prism's. "Look, I promise I will read all of the pages the next time I do—"

"There. Will. Not. Be. A. Next. Time," Wells snarled.

I leveled a cool glare of my own right back at him. "Then don't get yourself in stupid positions where I have to come rescue your ass then."

Captain Marc swiped a hand through the air, interrupting us. "Does anyone else know about this?" He waved the paper again. "Has *anyone* else seen it? Sidhe, unicorn, any living soul?"

I cast back in my memory and I could see Wells doing the same. We both shook our heads.

Captain Marc released the paper, floating it above his hand, and flicked his fingers once. A flash of golden flame and the spell was nothing but ash. "Tell no one," he said. "No one outside the three of us can ever know about this."

Wells's eyebrows drew together. "Gods' bones, Marc, what the hell kind of spell was it?"

"A very old and rarely used spell, kept for emergencies," Marc leaned toward us, speaking barely over a whisper. "It's used when the royal line has no direct heir. Normally when a monarch is on their deathbed. So that they can pass the blood kroma on to someone of their choosing." His gaze flicked to me. "The change is permanent." He looked back at Wells. "Imogen is now in line for the throne."

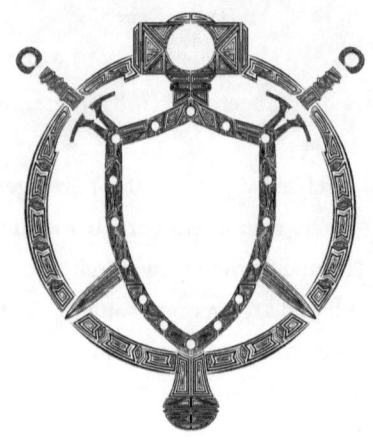

CHAPTER SEVENTEEN

*Check your blessings from every angle
and you're likely to find a curse somewhere.*
—Prince Alloysius Metellus

All the blood drained from my face. "I don't want the throne," I said, heart thudding in my ears. "I don't want anything to do with it. Ever."

"It doesn't matter, Imogen, you're of the Blood now." Marc took a long pull from his glass. "However, if the three of us keep quiet, it's possible no one has to know about it. You can go on living your . . . well, I won't say normal, but non-royal lives. If everything goes as it should, the throne will pass to Aloysius and then his children, bypassing you completely. I think . . ."

Wells squeezed his eyes shut. "You think?"

"I'm assuming you obtained Aloysius's blood for this spell and not Allestair's?" Marc's gaze fixed on me. I nodded.

"Blood?!" Wells was glaring again. "You had to get someone's *blood* for this? What were you *thinking*, Imogen?"

"I was *thinking* that it's Blood Kroma, as you continually reminded me, so that it made complete fucking sense!" Maybe I'd made a mistake but I hadn't even been on this planet a year yet and I did not regret escaping by any means necessary. "It was right there on the list. Although, it admittedly took me a while to work out what the 'iron of life which flows through the Blooded' meant, so I don't blame you if you didn't catch it."

"And how did you obtain Al's blood?" Wells gritted out, an actual vein pulsing in his forehead. I couldn't believe he was this mad.

"I told you; after you left I only trained with Al. I just pretended to get sloppy one day and cut him. It was easy." I folded my arms and glared right back at him. "Do you want a blow-by-blow?"

Captain Marc held up a hand. "Since it was Aloysius's blood in the potion you drank—"

"Ugh, you *drank* it!" Wells interrupted, his face twisting into a grimace. Enough was enough.

"Okay, Wells? First of all, it was a fucking potion, yes I drank it. There were other disgusting ingredients included that you don't seem worried about. And secondly, you've made it clear that you're upset with me about this and we can have it out later if you want, but I feel like you're getting hung up on the wrong details." I turned back to Captain Marc. "You were saying?"

Wells growled, but leaned back in his chair, arms crossed tightly across his chest, and directed his attention to Marc. I tried to ignore the steady burn of his anger behind my ribs.

"If Imogen had taken blood from Allestair, the kroma would have recognized her as his equivalent. However, as she used Aloysius's blood, she's made herself not Allestair's but rather *Aloysius's* equal. This has never been done. The kroma could pass from Allestair to either of the two of them. Normally it's the ruling monarch who gives their blood explicitly because they have no heirs." Marc gazed at me, tapping a finger on his chin.

"But Al's older than me, so it would go to him anyway, right?" I squirmed in my chair, then grabbed onto the edges and made myself stop. "I'm assuming it doesn't always pass down gender lines?"

Marc's lips twisted up in a grim smile. "It does not and age doesn't always make a difference either. Although there aren't often many legitimate children to choose between. As you know, Llewellyn is of Queen Iphigenia's line. She has very few rights not gifted to her by Allestair. She would be considered just as Blooded as you are. Were. Rather. So her offspring would not even be in contention. When there are multiple Blooded heirs, the power will often go to the one with the most offspring to ensure the continuation of the line. If there aren't offspring . . ."

"Surely it would go to Al. Surely it would recognize that his blood is legitimate and Imogen's was . . . made?" Wells's anger was melting into something like fear, tightening around my own lungs.

Captain Marc shrugged and gave me a thin smile. "This has never been done before. Once again, our Imogen is breaking new ground." He drained his glass. "If Aloysius doesn't have a family when the time comes . . . it's possible the kroma will choose Imogen because of the mating bond." My stomach dropped. He continued. "It's also possible that the kroma will be able to see that she's not originally sidhe and bypass her for that reason, but I don't think so. Turning is another permanent alteration."

"So . . . no chance of me finding a way to—" I started without much hope.

"Even if Llewellyn would allow it . . ." Marc cast a sideways look at Wells's murderous expression. "You risked your life making this change the first time. To attempt it again would be suicide. Spells that completely alter the body in this manner are one-way for a reason. I'm not even sure a counterspell exists. The fact that you survived it at all means you're an excellent candidate for the throne."

Wells groaned and buried his face in his hands. Captain Marc patted him on the shoulder. "There are most likely a few centuries to go before this becomes a true concern. The three of us will keep quiet about it. And let's concentrate on surviving this war first, shall we?"

Wells did not want to have it out once Marc left, and in fact gave me the silent treatment while we got ready for bed—the one surefire way to get under my skin during a disagreement. I did not find it an effective form of conflict resolution and it felt dismissive. Finally, I just stepped right in front of him, arms folded across my nightshift.

"You *cannot* be mad at me about this," I said quietly. The sound shield had left with Captain Marc.

"Then please explain how I'm doing it," he snapped under his breath. "Get into bed." He stepped around me.

My blood boiled. "You can't talk to me like that, I'm royalty," I snarked, which at least effectively eliminated the silent treatment.

Wells spun on his heel, eyes blazing, and latched on to my biceps pushing me backward toward the bed. "You will *not* get into the habit of joking about this, Imogen," he hissed.

My knees hit the bed frame, buckling them, giving me no choice but to sit down. He held me there.

"You seem to have no ability to control what flies out of your mouth sometimes, so we're making this taboo." He shoved me sideways onto the mattress. "Stay there." He stalked toward the back of the tent.

Rage exploded inside of me like a living thing and I shot up, storming after him. He must have felt my anger—how he could sort it from his, I wasn't sure—and spun around, meeting me halfway. He tried to grab at me again but I blocked him. "Stop it, just *talk* to me!" I whisper-yelled.

He didn't stop and we had a furiously silent grappling fight for several seconds. I was so enraged I couldn't read his aura. He knew all my tells; it ended with me pinned facedown on the bed with Wells holding both my hands behind my back. I was viciously plotting his demise when he 'pathed me.

Imogen, I will talk to you when we are in bed like everyone expects us to be at this hour. We have spies in and out of the Sephryan army, have you never considered they might have spies in ours? We've just linked up five units, in addition to Marc's aerial force, making it several times more likely that someone in camp is slithering around, looking for anything out of the ordinary. We had a sound shield over our entire tent for an hour. If anyone noticed it, they'll hang around to see if they can discover anything worthwhile. We will act like everything is normal and get into bed and then we can discuss this.*

When it was clear I was no longer fighting him, he let me go. I didn't look at him but scooted away, tunnelling under the covers with my back toward him. *You could have 'pathed to me at any time.*

You sometimes lose focus when you're upset and your 'paths could be picked up if there's another telepath around. He paused and I felt the mattress dip with his weight. *And I was angry and wanted some time in my own head for a minute.*

I curled into a tight ball. *You could have told me that too.*

I heard him sigh. A beat, then he brushed a finger down my spine. *I'm sorry.* The bed shifted when he stood up. "I'll be back in a few minutes."

I silently fumed. Trying to order my thoughts enough to make a comprehensive list of the ways Wells was a *terrible* arguer: ordering me around, grabbing me. *I did shove him pretty hard and yell at him immediately upon arriving. In front of his entire unit. I'm no angel.* I burrowed deeper into the covers. Still, he could have been clearer. He could have—*He could have compelled me.*

Any fire left in my belly died. He could have easily compelled me to stop fighting, be quiet, or get in bed and stay there. It would have been much less effort on his part.

By the time he slid between the sheets I was thawed enough to let him put his arms around me. I still hadn't turned around, so he pulled me closer until my back was flush with his front. For a few minutes neither of us said anything. We'd both cooled off and could relax simply being next to each other. Wells squeezed me, pressing a kiss between my neck and shoulder.

I'm sorry I grabbed you. A breath. *I wish you'd found a different spell.*

I dropped an arm atop his, interlacing our fingers. *I have a pithy Earth saying for that.*

Let's have it.

"If wishes were horses, beggars would ride." Usually just condensed down to, "If wishes were horses . . ." I'll adapt it for our present conditions and say, "If wishes were unicorns . . ."

He sighed.

Although, I continued. *If wishes were unicorns we'd all likely be murdered in our beds.*

His chuckle rumbled against my back. "Imogen—"

"There were no other spells," I whispered. "I looked through everything available to me. Even while I was prepping this one, I kept looking. Which is how I learned to make grenades, so not a complete waste."

"That was in a book?" He dropped a kiss to the nape of my neck.

"I mean . . . not exactly, but things in the books led me to . . . You know what, you're already mad at me about the one thing, I would rather not discuss the grenades this evening." I snuggled against him. "If I hadn't done it, you would have died. Lots more people would have died. So I don't regret it." I shrugged. "Let's just set Al up on some dates when we get back and make sure he has some kids."

He snorted. "Is there anything you *don't* joke about?"

"It's all I know," I said loftily.

"That was a serious question."

"A serious question about my joking?" I felt him exhale. "Okay, sorry. I don't know how to answer that. It's just something I do when I'm . . . trying to diffuse tension I guess." He didn't say anything. "Are you still mad at me?"

He took a deep breath as he squeezed me again. "I'm terrified for you, Imogen. I know you're smart and I know you're capable but . . . *How* could you think it was okay to perform a spell that complex without reading everything included? I just . . . please, explain your reasoning if you don't mind."

I twisted in his arms to face him. "'Kay, I'll do my best. One: I was on a time crunch and those books were warded, so I couldn't take them out of the stacks, much less out of the library, which meant I had to do all my reading sitting on the floor, hoping no one came in and caught me in that section. Cloaking shields are instantly stripped in the library. I'd been caught before. If I was caught again, Allestair would know that the forbidding thing didn't work on me and ... I don't know what can of worms that would have opened. Two: I did try to read some of it, but the language in those spells is often ..." I took a breath. "I'm not sure how to phrase this so it's not insulting?"

"Archaic and flowery?" he suggested.

"Yes, thank you, so I wasn't getting a lot out of it anyway. I interpreted enough to know that it would get me through the wards. I made sure I understood that part, then I let the rest go because I was prioritizing. I still had to figure out where to get all the ingredients, and what they were, and the fucking cycles of the moons. So, three: I had a lot going on. And four: I've never died from not reading the introduction of a book before. I haven't even lived in this hostile environment for a year yet. I'm still adjusting."

He stared at me for a second. Then his eyes dropped away from mine and his focus went inward. He pulled me closer and met my eyes again. "You've adapted so well, it makes it easy to forget how new you are. And you've been put in situations that would have tested anyone, regardless of how old they might have been." He pressed his lips to my forehead. "I apologize, Imogen, it's a mistake I've made more than once with you." His eyes traveled over my face, I couldn't read his expression. His aura danced with an interesting mixture of conflicting colors.

"What are you thinking? Your aura's all ... flippy."

He smiled. "I'm not sure how to phrase it without being insulting."

I sighed. "You wish I was more cautious by nature, but you also like how I am."

"I *love* how you are ... but ... yes. How did you know that's what I was trying to say?"

I snuggled closer until there was no space between us. He tucked my head under his chin. *It's a feeling that Keane expressed more than once,*

I 'pathed. The familiar swirling of emotions that accompanied thoughts of the fiancé I'd been pulled away from on Earth rose up to constrict my throat. *He used to say that it was like I took a leap and then waited until I was midair to check out where to land.*

I felt his silent chuckle. *And what did you say to that?* he asked.

I shrugged. *I always managed to land.*

CHAPTER EIGHTEEN

*I would throw myself into traffic for every pet I've ever had.
Even if they were the biggest asshole on the planet.*
—Cilla Ibrahim

Much to Prism's everlasting delight, we were certain to see more frequent combat as we established a base camp nearer the capital and tried to lay siege. Messages to the units on the other side of the capital's compound were 'ported at odd hours, during prearranged windows of time, when a scout would know to be outside of the shields waiting for them. The plan was to hit the Sephryans from both sides on the ground and from the sky in hopes of getting enough of a hold to drive them within their compound, then we'd cover the city with wards of our own.

Captain Marc and Wells both agreed that I should keep in contact with Marc when I initially summoned my lightning in order to prevent catching one of his aircraft in the crossfire. They suggested various 'paths I could call, but I asserted that it was my lightning, so I wanted to pick my warning phrase. They rejected "to infinity and beyond" and "by the power of Grayskull" and thus I was left with "lightning in the hole" which had been my safety.

Prism and I were sent with Celphia and a small scouting unit to check the terrain before the morning march. Our role was mainly to deter any urzen who might get curious; it was only a scouting mission. No Sephryan units had been noted in the area when scouts returned and Wells made his nightly report to Allestair detailing the successful merging of units and informing him of our plans.

I made a point of tossing a glare at these messages when Wells sealed them, hoping my animosity would somehow stick to the wax and make it to Allestair.

"I know you're not at full strength and technically not part of the army," Wells said before sending me to fetch Prism that afternoon. "But these are the types of assignments you would get as the most junior unicorn team, so this is an easy way to quiet some of those jealous mutterings about favoritism."

I nodded. "Makes sense."

"In addition, since you and Prism are so adept at winking, I thought we might keep you back with the generals and send you out when necessary." Wells's back was to me, polishing his armor, his voice falsely light.

My stomach tightened. "Why?"

He still didn't turn around, "I'm making a tactical decision."

I blinked. "Wells, wouldn't this look just as much like favoritism as—"

"Gods bones, do you have to argue about everything." He tossed his rag down, finally turning. His jaw was hard, eyes blazing, but his throat bobbed once.

I crossed to him and wrapped one hand around his wrist, his pulse fluttered wildly beneath my fingers. "I'm honestly not trying to argue." His aura was dim, but I could make out the orange flashes of panic edged with the blue black of concern. "Wells, you can't pull me back now. The army knows what I can do. It would be so obvious if Prism and I weren't out there. We'll obey you, I promise, 'path me and it's done, but you can't pull me back. For the same reason you're sending me on this mission today. You know that."

Wells dropped his gaze, expression tight.

I squeezed his wrist and slid my hand down to take his. To my relief, he wrapped his fingers around mine. I searched his face. "Did you discuss this with the other generals or . . . ?"

He shook his head, blowing out a breath. "No, it's something I've been mulling over. But you're right. I can't pull myself and Obsidian back *and* you and Prism now that the other generals are here without making it look like I've promoted you." Those russet eyes flicked up to mine. "But I'm going to keep thinking about this." Shortly after, I rushed from the tent a pear for Prism clutched in my fist. I did not want to be late to meet up with Celphia. There were still some grumblings among some of the soldiers and I didn't want to give them any more ammunition.

Fortunately, anyone who had seen me fight—so most of Celphia's unit—and the unicorn handlers who understood Prism's irascibility, weren't among those slinging barbs. Still, I'd do whatever I could to uphold Wells's image. Even my not insignificant foibles hadn't been enough to tarnish his reputation.

His soldiers mainly seemed to pity their fabulous general for being saddled with such a troublesome mate.

The day was mild for Sephrya, as their winters tended to be drier with colder evenings, and there was something beautiful about their dark winter sun gilding the blood-red forest with the violet sky as a backdrop. It was as if the colorless land lent all its pigmentation to the heavens.

I continued to sweep for any sign of urzen; the terrain made it difficult. At first glance it appeared flat, but was peppered with ridges and dips that could be hiding anything from urzen to swamp imps in their folds. But the air was dry, even though the sun was bright in its lavender home. Overall, the ride was pleasant, which I mentioned to Prism.

Pleasant? It's boring. Is that what you mean? Where is the potential for conquest?

I sighed. *We're just here to keep the scouts safe from urzen. It's a good thing if nothing happens.*

Prism snorted his disagreement, but just then, almost as if my words had poked at fate, the air stilled. The entire company went rigid. I 'pathed Celphia. *Something feels off, but I don't see any urzen.* The 'path had just left my mind when the spider-fine hairs on the back of my neck lifted.

It's not urzen, it's sidhe, she said, keeping her eyes forward as if nothing was wrong. *Can you sense how many?*

I wasn't as good at this as Wells was, but I had been learning. I cast out behind us and estimated about twenty minds, decently shielded. I swept to my right and found nothing—no big surprise as that was the direction of the forest—ten more in front of us and five to the side.

I estimate thirty-five to forty. Most of them to the rear with the right flank clear. My stomach knotted as I relayed the information. I thought it was a decent estimate. We were fifty strong, with a unicorn; this shouldn't be an issue. But what if I was wrong?

Can you relay that to the team? I'd like the enemy to think they're successfully ambushing us and then turn this around. Although I enjoyed the vindictive glee in her 'path, sending the message to the entire company would drain me. I obliged, however, and watched the auras around me drain into transparency with a sinking feeling.

I had included Prism on the 'path and he rumbled deep in his chest like a Harley revving, swishing his tail so violently its ends whipped my legs. *We shall achieve conquest.*

We shall do what Celphia tells us and then—

If we hadn't been aware of their presence they would have slaughtered us.

They did not march upright or even jump out at us, but waited until we were in a slight dip of the terrain and crawled out over the lip of a ridge, throwing blasts at our legs.

Fury burned white-hot as I realized they likely wanted to incapacitate as many of us as possible to drag back as prisoners. I wheeled Prism around just as that pressure on my back increased. He was smart enough to flame as he turned, catching half a dozen as they tried to seize us from behind. I punched my fist to the sky and was lightning charged before Prism had completed his rotation.

I jerked my sword from its scabbard and flung a net of lightning out over those at our backs.

"Imogen, to the front!" Celphia shouted.

My stomach dropped to my toes. At least twenty had been lying in wait as the others tracked us. I signaled Prism and he spun on a dime, his battle scream curdling my blood as we charged them down. I hadn't brought explosives, but this was close fighting. I had to be circumspect with the lightning.

I got one good shot in, taking down nearly ten before the rest of the unit engaged. Prism had taken his own initiative, skewering or blasting a Sephryan or two, then winking to another spot. And although he was the one doing the winking, it still took a toll on my body.

Prism, you have to warn me. I managed to throw out an arc of lightning and catch the back of the Sephryan group before our people tangled in.

If I hadn't winked at that moment, you wouldn't have had time to do that, Prism snapped. Then both of us were beset by attackers and paused our argument.

The golden-haired Sephryan coming at me from the side was practically frothing with rage, his face twisted as he flung daggers at me. "Just share your fucking technology, you controlling bitch!" His voice cracked with the force of his shout, his eyes blazed as if I had personally injured him. "You could help millions of people!"

Shock short-circuited my nerves and I froze before blocking his last dagger, which slid perfectly between my helmet and armor, carving a burning line between my neck and shoulder, right where Wells liked to kiss me, before another plunged into my side, piercing my death-magic scar.

The pain triggered my reflexes; sword jerking toward him as my lightning crawled along it like so many rabid tarantulas, leaping from the blade to his body and pulling him to the ground.

Prism winked me to the left flank with no warning.

This was taking too long. We should have taken them out quickly. Even with the twenty surprise soldiers. But Celphia hadn't given the order to retreat. Prism's erratic winking was likely helpful, but I was forced to blast lightning immediately after each wink, which he seemed to be counting on, and my blood was heating.

Prism, I can't use the lightning anymore.

We are nearly done! Conquest! We shall be the reason this battle is won!

I'm wounded and it's not a battle. My teeth clenched against the pain, I risked a quick glance at Celphia. The tension in her face told me she was close to calling this. They'd obviously been hoping to catch a scouting troop and although we were evenly matched now, the Sephryans knew the terrain and were dirty fighters.

We can finish this! Prism winked.

And came out behind the largest Sephryan group. Fear streaked down my spine when I realized he had separated us from the others just as Celphia ordered, "Wink out!"

"Prism!"

He had already launched a rainbow blast of radiation at them, but suddenly all attention swiveled to us. My heart dove into my stomach as I saw four thick spears heading toward the biggest threat: my unicorn.

I reached down inside myself and clawed up the last fistfuls of lightning I had left, then threw a lightning shield over the both of us just as my blood went white-hot, searing my brain.

I collapsed forward, my chin cracking against Prism's crest.

"Wink," I rasped, just before I tumbled from his back and the world went dark.

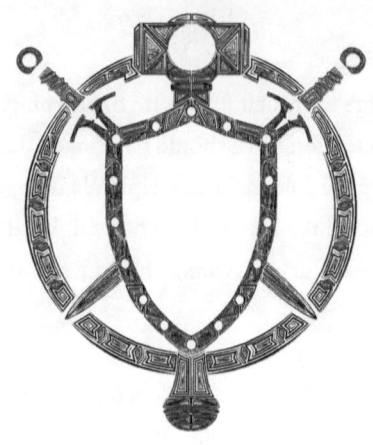

CHAPTER NINETEEN

*You never appreciate love so much as you do once you've lost it.
It makes you want to hang on to the next love harder.*
—Prince Alloysius Metellus

"Can someone get him out of here?" My body was heavy. Immobile. *Was I captured? Dead? No, I knew that irritated voice. My soul relaxed. Although my stomach cramped with hunger.*

"Get him *out*!" Wells. He was angry with someone that wasn't me. What had happened this time? Had I humiliated myself again? And how much more would I be set back?

"He won't hurt anything, General," came Kerlyn's patient voice.

"He's done enough damage already," Wells snarled, then to the intruder, "Get out before I have Obsidian *force* you out!"

An obstinate whinny answered him. Was Wells arguing with Prism?

I hauled myself back into my body, as if I were climbing up a vertical rope one hand at a time. By the time I was fully seated inside myself I was exhausted. But a different tired. As if I'd had a good workout and wanted a shower and a nap. Not as if my gas tank had a hole in it and I was constantly struggling to keep it half full.

I blinked, my eyes focusing on the canvas ceiling of our tent. Wells was seated ramrod straight on the edge of the bed, one hand gently wrapped around my forearm, glaring toward the entrance. The offshoots of several auras flashed, indicating multiple people in the room. It had been a while since I'd seen auras so clearly. I blinked at their brightness.

"You're all being very loud," I muttered, surprised when my voice came out smoothly, if a bit soft. My stomach rumbled audibly. "Also, I'm hungry."

Wells's head whipped toward mine so fast his long hair fanned out behind him. I couldn't repress the curl of a smile at the sight. His russet eyes found mine, lips slightly parted.

"You're so pretty," I sighed before he had the chance to say anything.

His entire body melted into softer lines, relief shining in eyes that remained locked on me. He lifted the wrist he had been clutching, pressing it to his heart. With his other hand he swept sweaty strands of hair from my face. "There she is. My own hell demon."

"What happened?" I tried to sit up, but Wells pushed me down. My stomach twisted as if I hadn't eaten in days. "Did everyone get back okay?"

"We did." Celphia stepped forward, still in her armor, helmet tucked under her arm. The corners of her mouth twitched upward. "No casualties. And you have . . . someone here desperate to see you." Her gaze shifted pointedly to Wells.

He sighed heavily, rolling his eyes to the ceiling. "Fine. Give me a moment to catch her up."

My brow puckered as he leaned over and pulled what looked like my backplate from the floor and set it on his lap. The metal was dented near the top. This time he didn't stop me when I shoved myself upright. I didn't remember getting hit in the back.

I reached out and ran a finger over the dents and only then realized they looked a lot like . . . bite marks?

"Prism dragged you back to my tent after you collapsed from overuse of your lightning." He gestured toward the table and my stomach plummeted.

The destroyed remains of at least three meals were strewn across it. And I was still starving.

"Oh, God . . ." I covered my face with my hands. The lightning. I'd overdone it and passed out and then . . . *Who all was in the tent?* "Who saw me like that?"

The backplate hit the floor with a thunk before Wells moved closer and ran a hand up and down my back. "Just Kerlyn and me." His hand paused. "Are you still hungry?"

"Fucking starving," I whispered.

Wells must have felt my anxiety. "Everything is fine, Demon." His face tightened. "Now that Prism has made . . . reparations."

I shook my head. "Okay." I shoved the sheets back, realized I was in a nightshift and paused, decided I didn't care and stood up anyway. "Someone needs to tell me everything right now."

"Llewellyn, just let him in," Captain Marc said, glancing toward the tent's entrance.

I felt my brows pulling together as Wells stepped up to my side and wrapped a possessive hand around my waist. "Fine."

Everyone shuffled to the side as a charcoal muzzle nudged the tent flaps apart. I stilled when Prism poked his head into the tent, swinging it back and forth as if to reassure himself he was in the correct place before stepping all the way in.

He slowly crossed to me, head bobbing side to side, ears flicking in every direction. I automatically extended my palm toward him and was surprised when he shoved his entire face against my torso.

I instinctively wrapped an arm around him, cupping his jaw. His ears brushed my shoulder while his muzzle lined up with my hips. I tentatively reached my other hand around and scratched beneath his jaw with both. "Are you okay, Prism?" I asked aloud as I 'pathed.

No.

I'm sorry. I brought my hands up to his ears, dragging my fingernails behind them in the little circles I knew he liked. *What can I do?*

He sighed heavily, his warm breath fluttering the edge of my nightshift. *There is nothing for you to do. I have already done it.* He lifted his head, closing his eyes in a long blink, those sweeping black eyelashes in beautiful contrast to his lavender hide.

I repressed a sigh. More non-answers. And I was still hungry. *You've already done what? I'm getting a little sick of no one just giving me a full answer, Prism.*

His eyes flew open, a low grumble echoing from his chest. *You told me you were at your limit. I did not listen. I endangered my rider and my soldiers. I have made it so that you will no longer need the medic's potions. You will no longer tire so quickly. It was tedious and it was inhibiting.*

Prism swished his tail violently, knocking over a lantern—which Marc quickly extinguished—then backed up awkwardly until he had the space to turn. He still managed to knock over several weapons as he swung his hind quarters around and practically charged for the exit.

Koonil, the unicorn handler, leaned in, tossed us a thumbs-up, then let the tent flap fall.

"I'm sorry, I'm still starving and I still have no idea what the hell is going on," I said. "Am I in trouble?"

Captain Marc and Celphia chuckled, which irritated and relaxed me at the same time, both of them muttered assurances while hugging me good-bye—my first hug from Celphia—and left me with Wells and Kerlyn.

"Alright, let's have a look altogether, shall we?" Kerlyn strode forward and lifted the hem of my nightshift. "There it is. Unmistakable."

I glanced down at my own body, wondering what the hell was unmistakable about it, and my breath caught. The raised white scar from the death kroma was now narrower, flatter, and a deep indigo. Like a purple bolt of lightning. I ran my fingers over it.

"Prism has marked you," Kerlyn said, dropping my hem, and grabbing my shoulders. She didn't smile, but her eyes crinkled. "You were nearly dead when he dragged you back into camp by the neck of your armor. And in fact, you might have died had he not dropped you and marked you on the spot."

"What does that mean?" I asked, my fingers traveling to where I'd felt the knife slice into my neck earlier. Nothing. And I felt no pain from my scar either. In fact, I felt better than I had since I left the palace.

"Prism poured his own kroma into you," Kerlyn continued when Wells remained silent. "It is not something unicorns do often. In doing so, he healed all injuries you sustained today and drove out the last of the death curse. He also deeply solidified the bond between you."

Her emerald eyes shifted back and forth between the two of us, then she abruptly turned toward Wells's desk. "It's true. You won't be needing these anymore." She gathered up my potions. "Still, get some rest tonight, Imogen. Being marked is a special kind of exhaustion. So I've heard. Goodnight, General." She pushed a small smile toward Wells before striding from our tent.

As soon as the tent flaps fell shut behind her, Wells flicked his fingers, extinguishing all but two candles. I barely had time to pull in a breath before he'd hauled me against the taut line of his body. My arms automatically wrapped around him; the bridge of his nose skated along the underside of my jaw before breaking away to allow his lips to brush the shell of my ear. "I should never have pushed you to meet that blasted unicorn." A warm kiss just behind my jaw had my breath hitching.

His hips flexed against mine as he held me even closer, I dipped my face into the river of his crimson hair, one hand gliding beneath it to curl around the nape of his neck, inhaling his scent. "I regret nothing," I whispered.

One broad hand slid up my spine, the fingers threading through the curly hair at the base of my skull before tightening. "You could have been killed today, Imogen. On a routine scouting mission."

He'd shed his uniform down to the tank and I relished the warm feel of his skin against mine.

"Well, I hate to break it to you." I brushed my lips across his. "But we're at war, baby."

His fingers tightened against my scalp just as his eyes went brighter. "This was supposed to be an easy mission. Out and back. I wasn't . . ." His eyes dropped from mine. His other hand trailing along my collarbone. "How are they always one step ahead of us?"

"You trust your scouts, right?" I asked, even though I knew the answer.

"With my life."

I nodded. I'd seen their auras. "Another spy in camp?"

"I've asked my lieutenants and the other generals to check, although I hate sewing distrust, especially among our own unit after everything we've been through." His gaze went flat, pained. Something huge roiled against the bond. I couldn't interpret it. I couldn't read his aura. There was too much there. And there were too many feelings grasping at me through the bond. "It's okay, I'm here," I whispered. "And back to full power, apparently."

His forehead kissed mine, eyes still downcast. "I don't know if I can do this, Imogen," he breathed. "With you on the battlefield, I don't know that I can do what I need to do."

"What do you mean?" My stomach slowly knotted but I forced my body to stay relaxed against his.

"I'm being sabotaged at every turn."

"And everyone in the army admires and respects you. You've trained them all—"

"I don't know if I can make an objective decision with you on the battlefield." The tension in his voice was nearly tangible. "At least when you were in the palace you weren't in danger of being killed."

I couldn't keep myself from tensing then. I shoved back enough to look at him. My eyes must have betrayed my shock and fear because he spoke again before I could.

"I'm not going to send you back. Not that you'd let me." A strained half smile that faded quickly. "But these are people's lives at stake, Imogen. How am I supposed to make objective judgements when you're—"

I brought my palm to the side of his face. "Let me prove myself. Let me keep trying. Prism is an asshole, but he's not likely to go rogue again and if he does, you order us back. Wells, I'm back to full power now. And I'm strong."

His eyes dropped away from mine again, his chest expanding against me.

"You're scared and you're underestimating yourself," I whispered. "We can do this. Both of us."

His gaze lifted to mine. "We'll see, I suppose."

CHAPTER TWENTY

*An argument is often just two people who care deeply
and wish they could agree.*
—Zoe Ibrahim

We did see battle the following day en route to the next camp, although by now we were starting to expect it. Although I had been called in to watch the auras of a few people questioned by Wells and his colleagues, the most egregious things we found were a few affairs and a couple of younger soldiers 'porting letters home outside of approved times. All the search managed to do was stir up suspicions among our ranks. Especially Wells's unit, which had been attacked so frequently.

On the upside, the "lightning in the hole" call to Marc worked perfectly and I didn't catch any aircraft. Prism and I also performed spectacularly now that I was no longer dragged down by the killing curse. I thrilled in his partnership for the first time.

This was how it was supposed to feel.

We winked anywhere and everywhere across the battlefield, throwing lightning and downing hovercrafts. Prism liked to go where the enemies were thickest, surprise them, wreak havoc, and it was largely because of our unpredictable performance that the Sephryan units were forced to retreat after heavy losses.

Throughout the battle, I'd been laboring under the apparent delusion that Wells would be thrilled with our performance; he very decidedly was not. Apparently, Prism and I moved around so haphazardly he had no idea where we were for most of the battle. I heard about it in bed that night.

"Are we going to have to have all our arguments like this from now on? We could be finished by now," I muttered. I was lying on my back on top of the covers with my arms folded behind my head, waiting for Wells to join me so that we could "have a discussion" about my "behavior" and my "preening asshole of a unicorn."

Even after rinsing off in our kromatically chilled tent I hadn't completely cooled down from fighting in full uniform in the oppressive humidity, and was wearing only a supportive tank top and underwear. Another heat wave pushed through. Spring was coming, which meant even the nights were warm. This weather made everyone's tempers shorter.

You have no patience, Imogen, and I daresay that's part of your problem, Wells 'pathed with an edge.

I made a face at the canvas ceiling and mouthed "daresay" while rolling my eyes, knowing I was being immature. He was right, I didn't do well with waiting to argue. I wanted to have things out as soon as they came up and damn who was listening. Waiting just caused simmering, festering, and ruminating in circles. It seemed pointless to me since we were both telepaths. Why couldn't we just 'path it out wherever we were? But Wells liked to have a time and a place for everything.

He liked to get his thoughts in order first. And he *hated* telepathically arguing with me because I couldn't stop my thoughts from bulldozing over his when I was especially riled. *Amazingly, you're better at stopping your tongue,* he'd snarked.

He finally made his way over to the bed, extinguishing all the lanterns with a snap and then rolling right on top of me so that we were nose to nose.

"Ow," I complained.

"Well, you're in the middle of the bed," he said icily, propping himself up on his elbows.

"I meant to scoot over when you got here and forgot because you took so long. What were you doing in there, anyway? Exfoliating?" I snipped quietly.

He paused, then ignored my comment and jumped into our discussion. "You and Prism need to stay with our unit unless I specifically send you elsewhere and that's final."

"You should be having this argument with him then. Want me to 'path him and ask him to crawl in bed with us?"

I could feel Wells's frustration scraping against my own sternum as he reached up and tugged my arms from behind my head by the wrists and pinned them to either side of my face. His irritated exhale cut across my cheek. "Imogen, he is *your* unicorn. He should not be the one in charge between the two of you."

"I mean, I kind of think we're a team," I said. Apparently that wasn't the correct way to deal with your unicorn if the tightening on my wrists was any indication. I took a breath and continued calmly. "I told him that I need to be in charge whenever I use an explosive and I've told him he needs to warn me before he winks us anywhere. Most of the time he listens to me when I tell him we need to get back to our unit."

My lack of concern only seemed to piss Wells off more. "One of the reasons that I agreed to try pairing you with him is because you're willful enough to handle one. I thought you had worked this out after yesterday. They are *very* aggressive creatures, Imogen, it's your responsibility to make sure he lis—"

"Wells, we took out a hovercraft that was obliterating Lehm's unit and Prism pointed out that there was another one at—"

"And what about the fact that I positioned you to work the perimeter of *our* unit? Or had you told Prism that?"

I could feel his exasperation mixing with something stronger than worry as if it were swirling around my own chest. I shuffled my legs on either side of him. He'd managed to situate us in missionary position. "Well . . . he knows I'm not sworn in and sometimes he's stubborn . . ."

"Imogen!" I definitely didn't imagine the squeeze of my wrists that time. He continued, furiously whispering at me. "I understand why you don't want to be sworn in, and I support it, but there *has* to be some form of order here. You cannot just run around doing as your unicorn pleases. You've seen how volatile they are and you are too new—"

"I know I'm new, that's why I figured Prism knew more than me so—"

"I couldn't see you!"

I snapped my jaw shut.

"I had no idea where you were because you sure as hell weren't where I'd positioned you." His nostril's flared, his aura pulsing red with anger. "My attention was already split between 'pathing Obsidian, fighting myself, and shouting orders to try to locate you with a 'path. I had to force myself to forget about you, Imogen. I had to let you go, hope you weren't knocked out and bleeding somewhere, and focus on the battle. And you promised . . ."

For a moment we stared at each other. Wells's breathing was slightly elevated. My eyes burned and I blinked. "I'm sorry. We'll do better next time. I'm sorry, I didn't think—"

"If we're going to be in this together, I need to be able to trust you. Obnoxious unicorn notwithstanding."

"I thought we were doing a good job. I'm still learning, Wells, I'm—"

He pressed into me as he hissed, "Then *listen* to me."

I tried wiggling a wrist, but he didn't let me go. "Do we have to have this discussion in this position?" I asked.

"Yes."

I squirmed slightly, testing, but he didn't ease up. "Why?" I narrowed my eyes. I realized I'd landed on the wrong end of this disagreement—I'd been concerned with Prism's bossiness myself and forgot to bring it up—but being pinned beneath Wells had me a bit distracted.

"Because I'm angry with you. I'm worried about you. And I've got you here, so I'm keeping you here until I feel like letting you up." I felt him take a breath. He shifted his hips. "And because I'm enjoying it."

My core heated. My gaze slid from his face to the colors surrounding him. The red shoots of anger were still clearly flaring. That deepest blue color floated right at the edges. I was learning to interpret that as Wells's particular aural display when he was concerned about me. I saw one or two pink ribbons, though they stayed away from the angry red flares. The deep russet of sexual arousal was also pushing through in waves. My brows contracted. I sucked in a breath. "Are you . . .?" *Are you wanting angry sex right now?* I 'pathed.

He hmmmmed deep in his throat as he dropped his face near my ear. His breath heated my skin as he grazed his lips down my neck, pausing near my shoulder. Then latched on with his teeth and didn't let go. I couldn't hold back a gasp.

I'm not sure that's a good idea, he 'pathed, still applying pressure with his teeth, not quite hard enough to bruise, but a claiming, possessive hold. *I'm still running hot I don't know that you'd be able to be quiet.*

"Well, you don't have to worry," I whispered, testing a wiggle of my wrist unsuccessfully. "I truly am sorry. I'll talk to Prism in the morning and tell him we have to listen to you."

I know you will, he 'pathed, scraping his teeth slowly over my skin as he released my shoulder. I felt him go hard against me as he moved his lips across my collarbone and up the other side of my throat, as if seeking out a new spot to bite. I tugged against his grip with both wrists and received a soft "mm mm" reprimand in response. *I've half a mind to keep you right beside me during the entire battle next time.*

Heat bloomed between my legs when he pushed hard against me. My tank had ridden up to my waist so only the thin fabric of our underwear separated us. *I'm not sure that's the most effective use of—*

I stopped 'pathing when he clamped his teeth firmly on the opposite side of my neck. *You get through one battle where you prove you and your unicorn can follow directions and then perhaps I'll listen to what you think is effective and what isn't.* He rocked his hips against me and I responded. The fabric of my shirt scraped against my nipples as they grew more sensitive. I took a deep breath, inhaling his scent. This was a form of conflict resolution I could get behind.

He released my neck and pulled both of my arms up above my head, pinning them against the pillow, and gripped both wrists with one hand. With the other he pushed hair back from my face. *Do you think you can be quiet?*

My heart hammered in my chest and I couldn't help pressing myself against him as the pressure between my legs increased. I nodded silently. He curled his fingers around my shirt where it was bunched around my waist and shoved it up, exposing my breasts. He ran his hand over my chest, taking his time, watching the quickening rise and fall of my breath, still pinning my wrists.

Good. Because I think I do want to fuck you. He released my wrists long enough to peel my tank off but shackled me again before I could touch him. He crushed my lips against his in a brutal kiss, forcing my mouth open for him. His tongue swept in and he rocked hard against me. I pushed back just as hard. The tension between my legs building. I wanted to touch him, to grab on to him, but he held me firm.

He joined my wrists again, wrapping one hand around both before rolling off me and stripping my underwear. I gasped as he slid a finger between my legs, wetting it inside me, then dragging it in slow circles around the sensitive bundle of nerves at my apex.

Quiet, he 'pathed. I could hear the vicious pleasure coating his mental voice as he tortured me with his finger. It was riding the line between just right and too much. I pulled against his hand, but he wouldn't free my arms. My body moved on its own, back arching and hips bucking as the intensity of sensation increased.

"Gods, you're beautiful," he whispered, watching me writhe while he held me down.

A press of his thumb in the right spot and I shattered completely. Biting my lip hard but unable to prevent a whimper from escaping as the tension broke, pulsing out from between my legs, down my thighs, to the tips of my toes and back up to my face. Shockwaves tore through me swiftly, crashing like whitecaps until I was gasping and limp. He released me then, but I made no move to alter my position, still breathless, aftershocks throbbing through my body in waves. I got as long as it took him to remove his underwear to catch my breath, then he was on top of me and inside of me. I reached for him again but he held me fast. *Tonight I get to touch you.*

He took his time, sometimes moving fast and hard and then slowing while he explored my breasts, nipped at my neck, or kissed me. I moved with him, riding the waves that brought me closer to the edge, then pulled me back. Meeting his energy with mine. His kisses gentled as his anger cooled. I matched my force to his, letting him lead. He had released my wrists by the time he finished. I went with him, clinging to his shoulders.

Afterward we were still for several breaths, hearts thundering in tandem, then he shifted his weight to his elbows, smoothed hair away from my face, and kissed me once, softly. "Are you alright?" he whispered.

"Yeah," I breathed. The sensation of pins and needles only just retreating from my face. "My wrists are a little sore, but I think I'll survive."

He gently lifted each wrist and kissed it. "Anything else sore?" he murmured against my cheek, dropping another kiss there.

"No," I said, hugging him back when he wrapped his arms around me. "You know I'm with you, right? All the way, I'm with you."

"I do know." He held me tighter, burying his face into the space between my neck and shoulder."

A tumult of his emotions eddied through the bond. I brushed my fingertips up and down the warm skin of his back. "Are you okay?"

He sighed then lifted up enough to look me in the eye. He was quiet for a moment, the sounds of the camp at night trickling in. "I worked so hard to build this life. To earn this spot and get exactly where I am now. And I just wish . . . for the first time I wish I had another option."

CHAPTER TWENTY-ONE

The person who cares the least holds the most power.
—*King Allestair Metellus*

Wells and I talked until we fell asleep. Which unfortunately, happened in moments. We were both still completely naked when Kerlyn roused us before dawn with an urgent message. We stammered apologies and hastily summoned clothes but she waved us off, chuckling.

"Ach, it's me." She grinned. "I'm a medic. I've seen everyone in our unit naked. And I'd be disappointed if you two weren't tumbling together on a regular basis." She handed Wells a note and glanced behind her. "However, you may want to straighten yourselves quickly. I know that the other generals and the captain are getting messages as well. I'll bring in something to eat."

We thanked her and I started to push past Wells to my trunk when I noticed his aura pulsing with concern. He stared at the message, frozen.

"What is it?" I leaned in, trying to read over his shoulder.

My hair brushed his cheek and he flinched, then his eyes met mine. He dropped the message to the mattress and curved a hand around the back of my head, pulling me into a quick kiss. Still holding me, eyes fixed on mine, he said, "The king is coming."

My entire body locked up. "Here?" A hoarse squeak.

He nodded, fingers massaging the back of my neck. "He's here because we're set to attack the capital and he wants to be close for negotiations if we successfully lay siege. Which is likely the way things have been going. He'll stay on his own airship and we'll only have to see him for meetings."

I continued to stare at him, my guts slowly contracting, the scent of my own fear pouring into the air around us even before I started trembling. The tiny part of me that wasn't traumatized and afraid was ashamed. I was taken aback by my own reaction. I'd gotten out. I'd beaten him. Why was I so terrified at the mere thought of seeing him again?

"Imogen . . ." Wells pulled me into his arms and held me against him, rocking me back and forth. I knew he could smell it too and shame flooded me. He tucked my head under his chin and rubbed slow circles between my shoulder blades. "This is our chance to discover his next move. We won't be left wondering for long, that's for certain."

"Wells, what if he asks about the potion I took?" I whispered, hating the small tremors in my voice. "What if he finds out?"

"We'll tell him about the first one you took. The practice one. Just say you used a larger dose. It will be impossible to verify without having someone repeat the process. *If* he asks. He won't want to risk people hearing about it. Remember the incident isn't public knowledge. Volunteer nothing unless he asks."

I took a deep breath and nodded. We separated and grabbed clothes before heading to the back to share the wash basin for a quick sponge bath.

"Imogen, before we go out I want you to consider something." Wells tugged on his tank and I knew we'd be sweating it out in full uniform for Allestair to look us over.

"Okay." I rung the water from my washrag and hung it neatly.

Fully dressed, Wells took my hand. "While in Allestair's presence, I need you to keep your mouth shut and your eyes down."

I stiffened.

Wells held harder. "This is exactly why I'm telling you this now. We are on very thin ice, Imogen, and although you've escaped Allestair once, you basically brute-forced your way to freedom. That won't work right now. I need you to give him absolutely nothing but polite deference until I say otherwise, do you understand?"

I took a breath. Then another. Allestair didn't deserve deference. Whether or not he'd merely taken advantage of a situation, he'd tried to murder Wells as far as I was concerned.

My mate stepped forward and pulled me into his arms. "Imogen, there are bigger things at stake here. I need you to trust me. This is a landscape you are unfamiliar with. I have overestimated your knowledge of our world too many times to the detriment of us both. I will not do it now. I know it goes against your every nature, Demon, but I need you to trust me on this. Don't think of it as doing what Allestair demands, think of it as doing what I ask."

I finally wrapped my arms around him. "I can do that." He was right; I was still so new. I wasn't used to being basically a kid, but I could at least trust Wells to guide me as I learned.

Wells coaxed me into eating what Kerlyn and one of her daughters, Kiera, brought to us and I did my best to breathe through the awkwardness that permeated our tent. At the same time, I felt myself battening internal hatches. Locking down sensitive parts. The dark creature that had been sleeping since I'd escaped the palace yawned and stretched. And waited.

At dawn, the other generals and Captain Marc joined us in our tent, which had been hastily tidied; the table divested of papers and pulled into the center, several chairs borrowed from other tents placed evenly around it. Kerlyn and Kiera set up refreshments on a side table, also hauled in from somewhere else. I thought it was ridiculous to put out wine at daybreak when we'd all just been rushed out of bed the morning after a battle, but whatever.

Everyone was in full uniform—myself included—down to our freshly polished weapons. The only thing that marked me as different was the lack of a colored band on my left shoulder indicating rank. We all stood in a loose line inside our tent while the two redheads brought in more food and drink than necessary. My gaze darted around the tent's occupants while I tried to keep from fidgeting. Kerlyn and her brood had more of an orangey red than Wells's deep crimson, I observed.

My eyes continually drifted toward the tent flaps while I forced my shoulders down from my ears. I supposed the king would come whenever he damn well pleased. I pulled in a few deep inhales and distracted myself by asking questions.

Why is Captain Marc just a captain? He's in charge of the whole aerial force isn't he? And I read that a general was the highest rank. I made sure my 'path was focused tightly to Wells.

Rieger, Marc's partner before Allatu, was the previous general of the aerial force, he told me. *She died in the Wind War, alongside several other high-ranking officers, and they tried to promote him immediately. Marc said that he would rather leave the force than attempt to take her place. The ruling king at the time—Allestair's father, Albion—simply refused to promote anyone ahead of him. "Captain" is now the highest rank in our aerial force and Marc is undoubtedly the most experienced person in the room by far. He refuses even after being mated to Allatu.*

A bittersweet warmth tugged the corners of my lips upward. Wells never asked me to get rid of my engagement ring from Earth. Never questioned why I insisted on placing it with my most precious items. He'd even pulled it out of my ruined bag after it had been torn during a march and held on to it until he could find me something else.

Keane hadn't been my mate. We were best friends for years, and although we'd promised to wed if we hadn't found anyone else by our forties, I had never felt the connection with him that I had with Wells. But I'd cared about Keane.

I understand. I 'pathed.

You understand why Marc has refused a promotion that he has deserved for centuries even after having been mated with several children? Wells remained at attention, but I saw one eyebrow lift.

It's about not forgetting a person. And the mark they left on you. A mate is eternal and the connection indescribably blessed, yes. But other relationships can be significant. And important. Marc wouldn't be who he is without Rieger. I wouldn't be who I am without Keane. The significance is different, so the honorific is different. But I understand it. I flashed a smile before falling back into my military appropriate neutrality.

Wells was silent for a moment. Then he brushed a finger lightly down my wrist. *I'd never thought about it that way before.*

"They're coming," Adgemon announced. He must have felt the pull on the wards. Milliseconds later the unmistakable sound of marching feet grew louder. The king had a retinue of at least ten, I guessed. Everyone quickly straightened into a more formal line. Kerlyn and Kiera stood at attention on either side of the refreshment table. Marc stood apart from us, in his own "line" facing them, as he would represent the aerial force. Wells stood at the far right of the army's line, the other generals arranging themselves by seniority to his left. I stood to his immediate left and slightly behind him, as instructed. As I was connected to Wells but had no official rank, we decided I wouldn't toe the same line as the others.

A moment later two palace guards lifted the tent flaps, stepped aside, and held them wide. Two more guards marched in to flank the entrance, their movements synchronized and sharp. Then the king stalked in.

Followed closely by Al.

My breath lodged in my throat and I swallowed against it so noisily I was sure everyone heard. Why hadn't I assumed that Al would be coming with his father? I wondered randomly if the queen was enjoying having the run of the palace. A brief image of Iphigenia lounging around in casual wear—that I had never seen—eating chocolate, drinking wine, and reading on a chaise with books scattered about flashed through my mind.

Al didn't look at me, but tense sienna waves colored his aura. His jaw was tight and his amber eyes burning. Although his long blond hair gleamed as he stepped in from the sunlight, I noticed dark circles beneath them that hadn't been there before.

King Allestair strode into the tent as if he'd been there a million times. His ice-blue eyes raked over the refreshments table and the two redheads standing beside it; finding nothing lacking, he marched past Marc as if he weren't there. Which I was to discover was a sign of approval—or as close as we were likely to get. He stopped at every one of Wells's generals and found something to critique. The dark thing inside of me was snarling by the time he got to us.

He was unable to find anything amiss with Wells. Other than me.

"I see why I haven't been informed of her rank," he said, his gaze scraping me from head to toe. "She doesn't appear to have been sworn in yet. I'm looking forward to this explanation."

"Why, sire, it's due to your own injunctions," Wells said, affecting an innocently surprised expression that impressed the hell out of me.

Allestair spun toward him, eyebrows raised. "My injunctions?"

"Yes, sire. When I initially petitioned that Imogen join our forces, you refused due to her lack of official training," Wells said. "Captain Marc and Admiral Kavlo also petitioned to add her and had their requests revoked for the same reason. I assumed that you sent Imogen here while we were under duress, knowing that her particular skill set would ensure our survival in spite of her lack of training. Seeing that you were correct, and knowing that we are mated, I deduced your intention for her to fight under my instruction, gaining the requisite experience."

Keeping my face neutral was an exercise in restraint. I was positive that pride oozed out of my every pore in spite of it. Wells had taken every act

Allestair had contrived in order to separate us and turned it against him publicly. I sent a wave of affection through our bond and felt a squeeze back. Wells's face didn't change. He didn't break eye contact with the king.

"I see," Allestair said, and the coldness in his eyes sent a chill down my spine despite the temperature. His gaze flicked from Wells to me, lingering a moment, a predatory gleam flashing behind his icy irises as if to say, *We're not done*. He spun on his heel then, crossing to the refreshments table and—ignoring Kiera's offer to assist him—poured himself a glass of chilled wine.

It annoyed me that he handed the bottle to Kiera, without looking at her, rather than placing it back into the ice himself. He swirled the golden liquid, sniffed, took a sip and shrugged. As if the wine we served adjacent to a goddamn battlefield was barely acceptable.

"I'd like to see how Imogen does in the next conflict before any decision is made to place her within a particular force." His voice remained even, his tone unconcerned, but I tasted venom in the air when he continued. "After we lay siege, she may want to come home regardless. She must miss her friends."

His subtle threat raised the tiny hairs all over my body. I fought to keep my face blank and my breathing even. I had to find a way to get beyond the shields as soon as possible and warn Zoe and Cilla to watch themselves. The dark creature growled behind my rib cage. *He threatens my friends...*

Calm down, Demon, remember: eyes down, mouth shut. Wells 'pathed with soothing but firm pressure through our bond. *You've already promised to speak to Prism this morning. You can take a break then. Just get through the next few minutes. Please.*

Then Allestair prowled toward us, his eyes glittering with a rather vindictive glee. My breath hitched, but all he did was pull Adgemon out of line for a personal chat, ignoring the rest of us. My forehead creased and I quickly smoothed it. I managed to stop myself from glancing at Wells. I had a nasty feeling some kind of game was starting up and I wouldn't know the rules.

Allestair had a little talk with each general; guiding them to the refreshments, one by one, instructing them to serve themselves while they talked, then concluding the discussion by pointing them to a seat at the table.

Every muscle in my body slowly tensed as each person was led away. I 'pathed Wells begging to go to Prism now, but he said there was no way to leave unless the king dismissed me. No one in the tent, not even Kerlyn and Kiera, could leave unless he excused them.

I glanced at the five guards inside who stood at the entrance, stiff and unmovable as statues. I felt for the five guarding the outside, they had on full armor and had to be baking in Sephrya's morning sun.

Eventually only Wells and I were left standing. I hadn't realized how much reassurance I had taken in hanging onto Wells's arm when we were at the palace. The physical touch had been an anchor. Now I was forced to stand one step behind him, stick straight, until told to move. I did, at least, have our bond to cling to, warm and sturdy within me.

Allestair greeted Wells like one would expect a normal stepfather to greet a stepson: clapping him on the shoulder, congratulating him on the near siege, and finally strolling with him over to the refreshment table to fill his plate and cup.

Everyone was seated except for me, Kerlyn, and Keira. All with food and drink in front of them. The auras in the room—including Al's—shifted with tension, though no one dared a glance at me.

Allestair gestured to Kerlyn and Keira to sit in the chairs provided near the refreshments, indicating they weren't going to be serving anyone anytime soon and could relax. Darting quick side-eyed looks toward me, they obeyed, but the insult was clear.

These were games I didn't know how to play. I didn't know what I could do that wouldn't reflect poorly on Wells. We were both being publicly slapped on the wrist right now, but how long was it going to continue? And what other little games was Allestair going to torture us with if we allowed this one? Wells sent me caresses down the bond, but I could see his agitated aura. I consciously deepened my breaths and tried to relax one muscle at a time.

Captain Marc rose from the table, crossed to the refreshments, poured a glass of chilled wine and selected a few fruits, which he placed in a goblet. He then walked them over to me with a smile.

"Imogen." He handed me the wine. "Being without rank, no one quite knows what to do with you, but I thought you might be thirsty. How are you holding up in Sephrya's heat?" He tilted the goblet toward me.

My lips curved upward in relief as I accepted the wine and teased a juicy-looking berry free. "Thank you. I admit to feeling a bit adrift myself when it comes to protocol." I popped it into my mouth, chewed, and swallowed. "The heat is intense, but honestly, not that much different from New Orleans, where I lived on Earth just before Perimov."

We were allowed about a minute of this before the king ordered Captain Marc back over to the table for strategy discussions. Marc offered me his arm.

I accepted.

The captain escorted me all the way to his seat and was about to place me there, when Allestair snapped, "Marcellus, don't be ridiculous, that's your place. Imogen has a seat beside her mate." He bit off the last word, his iceberg eyes narrowed.

"Oh, dear, I hadn't realized," Marc took my arm again and escorted me to the other side of the table. "I assumed if she hadn't been *inadvertently* overlooked, the lady would have been seated by now." I was certain I didn't imagine the frost in his voice. He pulled out the chair next to Wells and guided me into it, even pushing it in for me. Marc went further, placing both the wine and fruit in front of me before resuming his place.

I was really enjoying this new facet of Captain Marc. Not only had he rearranged the entire hierarchical system of the aerial forces by standing his ground around memorializing his partner, but he seemed to know exactly how far he could go with subtly undercutting the king. I wondered if he might perhaps be even older than Allestair. Regardless, Allestair didn't seem willing to tangle with him directly. At least not in public.

At least I was seated now.

Between Wells and Al.

I didn't even have to glimpse Al's aura to feel the tension radiating from him. He absolutely would not look at me. Even if he were addressing Wells, he acted as if there was an empty chair between them. On the rare occasion that I was mentioned, he feigned deafness.

Mercifully, posturing ceased and actual tactical discussion took over.

Wells's eyes flicked briefly to mine before settling back on the king. "Due to her lightning, I've been placing Imogen and Prism on—"

"Excuse me," the king interrupted, his eyes going stormy. "Who exactly is Prism?"

For the first time, I saw Wells's aura sploosh with a nervy butter-yellow. "Prism is Imogen's bonded unicorn, sire."

Sparks of surprise sprang from Al's aura as he looked directly at me for the first time. The crimson flare of anger arcing from Allestair's was impossible to miss.

"I'm sorry." Allestair slowly turned toward Wells, like a shark scenting freshly spilt blood. His eyes were nearly glowing with perverse relish. He'd found something to pounce on. "Did you say that your mate has been riding a unicorn into battle?"

"Yes, sire," Wells said. And I watched the colors of his aura gather around him, as if his psyche was rallying for battle.

It hit me like a kick to the chest. Wells had known how Allestair would react yet he let me meet Prism anyway. I prayed fervently that Allestair wouldn't find out about my initial misstep.

"That is unacceptable, unicorns are far too rare," Allestair said, as if he were saying I couldn't have a puppy for Christmas. He moved his wineglass to the edge of the table for Kerlyn to fill. "Have Prism immediately reassigned to bond with a more experienced rider."

CHAPTER TWENTY-TWO

To control the public narrative is to control the public.
—*King Allestair Metellus*

My spine locked. My throat constricted. *They cannot take Prism away from me. Not after we went through so much to get where we are.* The dark creature thrashed, begging to fight.

My breath came back only to move more quickly in and out of my lungs. I hadn't even known how attached I was until faced with the threat of him being torn from me. *Prism won't stand this,* I thought, my mind spiraling, *we'll both fight.*

"If I may, your majesty?" Kerlyn stepped forward.

The king's cold gaze shifted to her, chin lifting in assent.

"Feel free to speak to the unicorn handlers, but as a medic, I do not advise separating Imogen from Prism as the unicorn has marked her, your highness." Kerlyn smoothly refilled the king's wine. She winked at me over his shoulder. "Once a unicorn has marked a sidhe, I believe they're paired until death?"

Everyone's eyes landed on me then. Even Wells's. I turned my frantic gaze to Kerlyn, who was now toting her wine and water jugs to our side of the table. She lifted her eyebrows and gazed pointedly at my stomach.

"Is she truly marked?" Allestair demanded of Wells, who looked just as gob smacked as the rest of us. Undoubtedly as surprised by the "paired until death" piece as I was.

Still, we had to put this to bed. I stood up, unbuttoned my jacket, then pulled my shirt up to show the indigo scar that Prism had burned into my side. "Is this the mark?," I asked.

Allestair's face darkened. I could have sworn the air in the barely temperate room chilled. His voice dropped an entire octave. "When did this happen?"

Wells's gaze didn't waver as the king's cold blue eyes bored into his warm russet. Everyone at the table went stock-still, the only sound the light splashing of Kerlyn refilling glasses.

"Imogen was the freshest person in the unit when she arrived, sire." Wells's voice was the epitome of practiced calm. My blood boiled knowing that childhood abuse had honed that tone, but I clenched my jaw as he continued. "I took her with me as backup to deliver our post-battle report to you. We were ambushed. Imogen was hit with a kill shot that she didn't fully deflect and I neglected to defend her from."

The deep ocher of guilt surged through his aura. I wrapped my fingers around the base of my chair to keep from reaching out to him.

To my surprise, Al's aura thrummed with shock and concern so brightly I caught it in my periphery.

Wells gestured at Kerlyn. "Our excellent medic managed to save Imogen, even in the midst of grieving for the daughter she lost that very day on the battlefield. As you've received reports, you'll know our unit was nearly decimated." I was impressed when Wells delivered that sentence without inflection. "We knew we would need Imogen, even weakened, were we to see battle before connecting with the other units. Prism's rider was one of the many fallen that day, so we introduced her to him. After several battles together, he marked her when our scouting mission was ambushed. Imogen drained herself defending the unit and the marking saved her."

You knew about this bonded until death thing? I risked 'pathing him while the rest of them sat back against their chairs, digesting this story.

I most certainly did not, he replied. *I'm acting like I did and I'll get some particulars from Kerlyn later. She seems to know more about unicorns than I gave her credit for.*

The king's laser-blue gaze swung my way seeming to slice into my very soul. "You just grow more interesting by the day, don't you, Imogen?" His aura pulsed with an ichor-green color that I'd seen before, but only from him. It made my skin crawl. At the same time, I wondered how "interesting" he would find me if he knew about the blood spell. My mouth dried out.

I took what I hoped was a casual sip from my sweating wine glass.

My fingertips dug into the damp knees of my uniform while a brief debate about swearing me in volleyed around the table. It didn't go anywhere. Although the king initially floated the idea, he didn't push it, and I tried to unclench my hands. I couldn't help wondering if perhaps he had decided this wasn't where his biggest advantage lay.

But if not here, then where?

I ended up draining my entire glass of wine in spite of the hour.

Eventually I was dismissed and allowed to go speak to Prism. I slipped into the bathing area and smothered a sigh of relief as I stripped away most of my uniform, leaving only my sturdy leather pants and tank top.

Prism was tussling with a golden unicorn when I approached their forest habitat and waved him down. With a final rear and stab at his opponent, he drove the gold one back to the trees and ambled over to me, his head high. Shoving through a couple of grazing unicorns as he approached. *Of course I had to get the Regina George of unicorns,* I thought.

I'd brought him some pears, but as he was now getting them on a regular basis, they did little to soften him up. He was not pleased with the directive that he and I were to follow Wells's orders from here on out and not to go winking around the battlefield as he liked.

Our performance is exceptional! He stomped an ebony hoof, tearing a round clod of grass free. *There is no logical reason for this change! You have no rank. I have no rank. We are free.*

Wells is the one in charge, and rank or no, he knows more about the strategy of the army than we do, so we ought to listen to him. I tried to stroke Prism soothingly, but he wasn't having it. I sighed, dropping my hand. *We can still ask permission to do what we like. Can't you just try it for the next battle?* I considered telling Wells that we might have to get Obsidian involved.

Prism tossed his head and snorted. *That one is staring at us. Not in an admiring sort of way. I dislike it.* I glanced over my shoulder to find Al watching us. I froze. One hand on Prism's glossy neck.

Our eyes met and Al held my gaze, his smoldering amber boring into me as he walked over. His face was set, and while his aura didn't radiate hostility, it also wasn't inundated with his normal flowing, confident sea greens.

Prism huffed low in this throat and lowered his horn. Al halted, still several feet away.

Prism, he's the prince. He's next in line for the throne. I patted his neck, even as my skin prickled.

I care not. What business does he have? Prism's eyes flashed red and he didn't change his position. If anything he pressed his horn farther forward.

"Gonna sic your unicorn on me, Imogen?" Al's face was blank, hands stuffed in his pockets. His casual swagger was off somehow. Stiffer. Like he wasn't quite as sure of himself. And I couldn't help but mark the use of my full name. Al always called me "Im." Even when we argued.

"He just doesn't know why you're here and he was bothered that you were staring at us." I tugged Prism's forelock. He didn't budge.

"I'm here because I want to talk to you." Al didn't shift. His simmering glare remained fixed on me. I blew out a breath. Turned toward Prism and finger-combed his mane, hoping maybe it would chill him out. A few moments slid by and Al remained silent.

"So talk," I said, still working on Prism's charcoal tresses.

"I'd like it if we could look at each other while we talked."

I exhaled slowly through my nose and stepped back to stand next to Prism's massive head. His horn was still tilted in a manner that no one could construe as anything but threatening. I folded my arms. "Okay."

For a moment, Al just stared stonily at me. Then he dropped his gaze for a breath. His shoulders slumped. When his eyes met mine again, there was an edge of uncertainty behind the molten determination. "Was any of it real?"

My stomach twisted. "Was any of *what* real?"

"I thought we were friends, Imogen. You and I were becoming friends again, and then you—"

"Friends don't trap friends in their parents' palaces," I bit out.

"That was for your own saf—"

"Horseshit."

My spine became steel as I stared Al down, hands on my hips, chin lifted. I didn't wonder that he felt betrayed. I had used him. And even though a part of me felt guilty, I didn't regret it. He was the one who had put me in a position where it was necessary. He'd done nothing but try to control me.

The prince glared back at me, his arms folded so tightly his fine blue tunic strained across the shoulders. I tried to read his aura. To my surprise, I didn't see any anger. I did see hurt . . . concern . . . what I thought was embarrassment . . . I wasn't used to seeing such a range from Al.

A moment passed. A unicorn whickered in the forest behind me.

"Are we done?" I asked. I wasn't sure exactly what he was hoping for here.

"No, Imogen, we're not fucking done!" Al said, his voice rough. "I'm having a hard time talking to you with your unicorn threatening me the entire time." He flung a hand toward Prism's reddened eyes and gleaming horn.

"Well, stop acting like a threat then, I guess." I shrugged. "You're the one who came to us."

"This is the first time you've been alone."

"Obviously I'm not alone. I'm with Prism." Irritation clipped my words. Prism snorted his agreement. Al rolled his eyes. "Or did you mean the first time I've been away from my mate." I landed hard on the last word. He had been happy to try to take Wells's place when he'd been sent away.

"I'm not trying to get between you and Wells," he snapped.

"Only because your father has forbidden it," I said acidly. If he wanted to have it out, I was here for it.

"I guess at least I'm hearing how you really feel now."

"Isn't it funny how the only time you've actually been happy with me since you stole me from Earth—the only time you thought we were friends—was during a few weeks where I had to hide my real feelings away in order to survive your fucked-up family?" I took a few steps toward him, anger licking at my rib cage like flames chewing up kindling. "Otherwise, I've done nothing but tell you the truth, Al. And the truth is that you've only liked me when you had me trapped with no choice but to act the way you wanted or when you were able to compel me into behaving like you needed me to."

To my astonishment, Al blushed and looked down at his feet, shame staining colors surrounding him. "I'm sorry about that," he muttered.

I stilled. My anger banked as suddenly as if a bucket of ice water had been dumped over it.

Al had never apologized for that, only insisted that it was something he was doing for my own good. That it was necessary and I would thank him for it someday. I didn't know what to say. I would have accused him of lying, but I saw no indication of even a half lie in his aura.

"Can we sit down somewhere . . ." He glanced around, awkwardly.

His entire demeanor seemed . . . muted. Like he was a damp version of the Al I'd left. I jerked my chin toward a clump of mounting blocks to the side of the enchanted grassland near the grooming equipment. He nodded and we crossed toward them, walking an awkward fifteen feet apart.

I hauled one away from the others and Al did the same. Prism tailed us and stepped up to stand behind me, no longer actively threatening Al with his horn, but still eyeing him warily. Al looked out of place, all folded up to sit on the short mounting block.

"What do you want to talk about?" I asked when Al was silent again for a lengthy period of time.

"I don't really know." A brown spike punched from his aura, so I knew that was only partly true.

I waited, pressing my fingernails into the worn wood of the mounting block. Al shifted around, clasped his hands together. "I didn't know that Wells was still alive when we came into your room that day. Both Captain Marc and I thought we were telling the truth when we said he was dead. I wasn't part of any scheme to mislead you. I just wanted you to know that."

"Okay . . ." The dark thing inside of me growled and I let a little bit of it out. "Were you even sad?" I snarled.

His head snapped up, amber eyes flashing. "Of course I was. You think I actually wanted my brother *to die*?"

I shrugged, my face hard and blank.

Flames of anger exploded through his aura and he stood up, knocking the mounting block over. Prism stepped closer, placing one foreleg on either side of me and huffing deep in his throat in warning.

"I watched Wells grow up! I was there when he was *born*. How do—"

I launched to my feet. "And you were taught that you were better than him and he basically belonged to you. Which is *fucked up*, Al!" Prism angled his muzzle over my shoulder, preventing me from leaving the safety of his reach. "And you've been a dick to him since—"

"We're *brothers*, we're dicks to each other sometimes!"

"You go above and beyond! Getting us trapped in that fucking palace—" We were just yelling at each other now.

"I didn't think it would be—"

"What the fuck did you think it was going to be like? You thought we were going to just enjoy being locked up in there and all be happy friends?"

Al smashed his lips into a hard line. We'd both been leaning toward each other, flinging our arms around as we hollered, but now Al straightened, his arms falling to his sides. He dropped his eyes and kicked the mounting block upright. "Maybe eventually." He sat back down.

I stared at him. "Are you serious?"

He shrugged. "I didn't know my father was going to be . . . the way he was with you."

"Have you *met* your father? I thought you knew him your whole life too."

"He's controlling, I mean, he's controlled the entire country for centuries, he almost has to be. And he can be an asshole. He's done shit to Wells, he's done shit to our mother, he's done shit to me." He finally looked up at me. "But what he did to you was . . . a lot."

I sighed and ground the heels of my hands into my eyes as I reclaimed my seat. "Okay," I shook my head. "I have to understand what you *thought* was going to happen. Like . . . your utopian vision for . . . getting us thrown into palatial lockdown."

"I figured you'd be upset at first." He interlaced his fingers, detached them, interlaced them the opposite way. "But I honestly thought that you'd get used to it after a while and start to like it there. You'd have places to run, we could train . . . I thought Cilla would be able to visit you. Wells is a general. He's always going to have to go fight and I just thought . . ." His cheeks slowly stained pink. I'd never seen Al blush before. "I thought maybe I could look out for you whenever he was gone. Like I . . . like I did."

I stared at him. Brain frozen. I had nothing to say.

Al glanced up at me once, still blushing furiously, then looked back at his fingers. "I told you that I needed you to be in my life and be happy. And I knew that you and Wells were mated and . . . I hated it. And I was really angry. But I couldn't change it. I thought . . . this would be the next best I could do—see you whenever I wanted and . . . when you got more comfortable, I could still just . . . hold you sometimes. I don't know, Imogen, I know it's stupid now." He scrubbed his face with his hands. "But it seemed like it was working out and then . . . you left and apparently you were lying to me the entire time."

It was an effort to moderate my voice. "How could you think that I'd be that comfortable with you after what you did to me?" I crossed my arms and leaned back against one of Prism's forelegs. "With what you did to my *family*." My voice broke on the last word. "My father is going to look for me for the rest of his life and never find me, Al . . . and Keane . . ."

I stopped. I was used to the sting of this particular grief by now, but it still jumped up and bit me hard occasionally. I swallowed several times, trying to get under control. I didn't want to break down today, not in front of Al.

Al stared at the ground, chewing on his lower lip. His aura swirled like a pinwheel, the colors changing so quickly, I couldn't hold them down. "Your father knows where you are, Imogen. I told him."

Any threatening tears were chased away by the fizzing shock that swept through my entire body.

"You know I searched out all of Solange's children once I got to Earth. When I talked to your father, I knew you were going to be the one. Everything he said about you. When I saw your picture." Al flicked his eyes up to mine, then back down, as if he were afraid to hold my gaze. "I was sure. You were it. So I told him everything. Then I put a glamour on his memory so that the entire night faded out of his mind. Only to resurface if he were ever told that you were missing. If I met you, and decided not to bring you with me, the memory would have stayed hidden forever. But if I brought you with me, he'd remember the entire conversation as soon as he got the call. He knew his mother was different. He wasn't as shocked as you'd think. He agreed that you were like her. And that you'd probably do well here if anyone would.

"But he didn't want me to take you . . ." Al's voice quieted as he spoke, finishing just above a whisper.

I could hardly breathe. I didn't know if I wanted to hit Al or hug him. My fingers clenched and unclenched at my sides. Prism nuzzled my hair in concern.

"Keane?" My voice was a rasp.

"I only told your father," Al said, his aura flaring, then crumbling. "I figured he would know who else . . . could handle it. So maybe he told Keane. I don't know. I'm sorry, Imogen."

Tears burned the back of my throat but my voice steadied. "What are you sorry for exactly? Why . . . why didn't you tell me this before . . ."

"I'm sorry that you're upset. That I upset you. I'm sorry I didn't have more time before we had to leave. But I still don't regret turning you." He met my eyes briefly then. "I'm still glad you're here and that you're going to live long enough to do everything you want. And I still think you're the answer to the prophecy, even if no one else does. I'm not sorry that you're here." He swallowed. "But I'm really sorry I didn't . . . I could have done better. I didn't think about your feelings. Just what I knew was right. And I'm sorry about that."

The prophecy. I'd nearly forgotten that Al believed me to be the legendary Chosen One. A human descended of sidhe who was foretold to unite the realms and bring peace. Or something. I repressed a scoff. Unite the realms indeed. I was too busy gathering the blown bits of my mind to even comment on the prophecy.

Al cleared his throat. "I am really sorry that I compelled you. I don't think I understood what that really felt like."

"You'd never been compelled?" I could feel my brows contracting. I may have been reeling, but Al had never apologized once about anything he'd done to me. The multiple apologies were like another punch when I was down.

"I've been compelled plenty of times, but never for that long and never . . ." he cleared his throat again, his cheeks brightening. "I'd never been forced to do something I would have given anything to stop."

"So what brought this revelation on then?" I asked, willing ice into my voice. Just because he'd apologized didn't mean I was obligated to forgive him.

"After you left, my father compelled me to tell him everything about the time I spent with you. Not just what we did or what we said, but how

I felt." He swallowed. His aura burst, froze, and shattered, I'd never seen a display quite like it. "And it wasn't just the two of us when he did it. He made me tell him everything I felt about you. How I felt when you leaned against me. How I felt about the smell of your hair. Things I thought about you that I never . . . he had a scribe write it all down. Every word. Sometimes they'd read it back." He shook his head, his aura shrinking down inside him completely. "And I begged him to stop. I didn't want . . . I wasn't even going to tell you these things. I wasn't going to tell anyone. He did it for days. I was compelled to tell him everything I thought about you whenever he called me in. I would just vomit thoughts with no control. I think . . . some of it was to learn about you, but a lot of it was just . . . because he wanted to. Because he could. When he finally let me go I shut myself in my rooms and fell apart. And I thought of you. How you wouldn't eat. Or shower. Unless I threatened to make you. How you couldn't say what you wanted for days . . ."

My insides turned to ice. I stiffened, one hand finding Prism's warm hide and remaining there. I didn't want to think about that time, whether Al was apologizing for it or not. I still had a mental block around compulsion. I still couldn't throw it off. I was beginning to think it was a permanent handicap.

He glanced up at me. "Anyway, it made me think about things differently. And I'm sorry. I'm sorry it took it happening to me to be able to empathize with it. And I'm sorry I didn't tell you earlier about your father I just . . . I was used to keeping all of that a secret when I first brought you on board and I just . . . I'm sorry again, Im. And I didn't know that my father's plan was to leave Wells's unit unaided so that . . . I still can't really believe that was his plan."

"Yeah, Wells had a hard time believing it too, even after his entire unit was just about massacred," I said, bile coating every word. "Allestair must really have done a number on the two of you in the gaslighting department."

"Al."

He looked up at me. I locked eyes with him. Something hard and aching settling at the base of my throat.

"Do you remember when you found out Solange wasn't coming back?" I watched the devastation flood his aura, I watched his face break, I held his gaze. "Don't you wish you could have said goodbye?" I watched his aura dance. I watched his throat bob.

His hands tightened around each other. He nodded.

"Well that's how I feel about every single member of my family."

"I'm sorry, Imogen," Al whispered, his aura shattering again with true remorse. "I know I didn't do it well."

I wasn't ready to let up just yet. "Do you know everything I'm wearing belongs to a dead person? You met her mother and sister this morning. Your father did that. He was willing to let that entire unit die. As preoccupied with creating life as y'all are, I'd think you'd be just as interested in preventing needless death."

Al opened his mouth to respond but was interrupted by Wells stalking into the unicorn habitat, his aura snapping crimson. "What's going on? Obsidian says you're both disturbing the unicorns."

Al and I spun toward him, I stood clumsily and stumbled right into Wells's arms. The talk with Al had brought me back to those awful first days on the ship and those horrid times in the palace when I was without him. My worst days. I collided against his chest, melting when he wrapped his arms around me, breathing in his scent.

"Al wanted to talk," I said shakily. "We got shouty, I'm sorry."

Wells pressed me closer to him, glaring at Al over my head. "And what was Aloysius saying that made you feel the need to get . . . shouty?"

"Just yelling back at her," Al snapped. "Honestly, Wells, you can't believe that I . . . wanted you dead. You don't believe that, do you?"

I gently pushed out of Wells's arms. "This is a conversation the two of you can have without me," I said. Wells's embrace had calmed me enough to remember my initial errand. "Prism and I are going to take a walk."

I left them glaring at each other, jogged over to a mounting block and leapt to Prism's back. We trotted into the enchanted forest. I wrapped my fingers in Prism's charcoal mane, breathing deeply. Although I would never tell him, Prism had a horsey scent that brought me back to a pleasant time in my childhood. It focused and grounded me.

I needed to contact Cilla. The rest I had to let go for now. Prism remained uncharacteristically silent, and I gazed upward, watching the harsh Sephryan sun gentle as it moved through the enchanted leaves. My tumultuous feelings slipped away the farther we rode, as if eased by the distance.

How far do you want to go? Prism asked, pulling me into the present. I'd allowed myself to get distracted with the antics of the other unicorns flitting around the forest. Watching their flashing hides darting around the multicolored trees as they played was an additional balm to my Al-frayed emotions.

Just the very middle. Wherever that is.

Once we had reached what Prism told me was the center of their forest habitat, I stood on his back and hauled myself into the nearest tree. Prism was annoyed that he wouldn't *see* me calling the wind, but I promised him that one of these days I'd show him what it looked like, and that he'd probably be unimpressed.

Al had offered the perfect distraction for my slightly illicit errand.

I had to talk to Cilla.

I enjoyed the slight burn in my arms as I pulled myself higher, it was nice to go a full day without needing a potion to prop me up. Careful to keep my eyes on the trunk and my hands, I moved more cautiously as I approached the top. Even with all of my wind-calling, heights still tore the wits from me occasionally.

The branches narrowed and the tree swayed more noticeably under my weight. My stomach dipped, but I pressed on. Soon there were more gaps in the foliage where Sephrya's pale-pink sky cut through. I took a breath, closed my eyes and felt the slight breeze caress my sticky face. I sighed. I hadn't called the wind in so long. Right after I discovered the power, I practiced it nightly until my escape from the palace. I hadn't realized how much I missed it.

I was floating before I knew it. Lifted out of the trees. My stomach calmed as the wind cradled me. As soon as I cleared the branches, I stretched out on my back like a sunbather, allowing myself to revel in the complete peace and solitude of being away from everyone and everything. Just me and the sun and the wind. I felt myself pressing up against the shields, then I was through.

I'd written a brief letter to Cilla. I had no idea if she was angry with me, or what had happened to her. For all I knew she might be in labor right now. I wasn't just going to bust into her head with a 'path. It would be difficult at this distance, and I wanted to be sure she wanted to hear from me.

I teased the slip of paper from where I'd tucked it beneath the band of my bra just under my left arm and cast my focus toward her. Even after all these months apart, all this distance away, her energy was easy for me to lock on to. Making sure my hold was strong, I 'ported the letter to her and then counted down as I hovered. I'd written that I would stay for three minutes to wait for her reply. I could risk a short 'path with her in the early morning this far above the ground.

Sephrya wasn't known for air patrols. They saved their ships for battles. We decimated a good chunk of their aerial fleet on our return from Earth when Captain Marc obliterated them upon reentry.

I chewed my lower lip, tingling with nerves. Would she write back? Casting around for something to focus on, I twisted in midair, my eyes catching on the Briarwood Forest in the distance. We'd been marching with it on our flank for days now.

One part of my mind still tracking the time, I scanned the trees for any movement, perversely wanting to glimpse another horrifying dire wolf creature. All was quiet today, however. The forest was still and innocent looking. As innocent as a blood-red forest could be. I wondered if the trees were carnivorous. The berries and wine from this morning danced in my stomach as the seconds ticked by. Maybe Cilla didn't want to write back. Maybe she blamed me for not telling her what I was up to when I left. Maybe she was upset about being interrogated by the king. What if he had compelled her for hours like he did with Al? Made her confess her most secret thoughts? She might hate me. Perhaps that's why she hadn't written back the first time. I realized I was fidgeting in the air and had to force myself to relax or lose the wind.

There were maybe seconds left. I gazed up at the smooth, pink, cloudless sky, trying to tell myself that there were a million reasons she couldn't write back right away. And if she was angry, I could find a way to fix it when I returned. Then a scrap of paper fluttered into existence just above my nose. I snatched it.

Kristin Imogen Ibrahim. 5 lbs. 7 oz. Janus 20
We'll call her Kris. Zoe says that's a beautiful type of sword.
She's going to be strong. Labor was <u>rough</u> and early, but I'm okay.
You'll be her godmother, right?

I sobbed out loud. Happy tears streaming from the corners of my eyes. I rallied my energy, and speared my thoughts toward her. Found her after several seconds and screamed *Yes!* across the world. I felt her mental smile, then latched on.

Cilla, you're a mother! Congratulations! How are you? Are you okay? Did Allestair do anything to you? He said something today about my friends and it sounded like a veiled threat. I'm so sorry I didn't tell you I was breaking out, but I figured it would be better that way—

Her glittery, mental laugh interrupted me. God, I had missed her. *Immy calm down. Zoe said it was a blessing that you didn't tell me anything. And smart of you. We were compelled for a while, which I never want to experience again.* Her shudder rippled across my mind. *If it makes you feel better, I'll tell Zoe he said something today and we'll keep an eye out. But we're with her family now out of the city. We're fine. And little Kris is fine too.*

Are you holding her? I wanted a complete mental picture.

No, she's with Zoe right now actually. My labor was rough which is one reason we're still in Zens with the Ibrahims. There aren't as many healer facilities out here, so I can't get seen for a while and Zoe doesn't want to risk winking until I'm . . . more stable. I was sleeping when your letter hit me in the nose.

Jesus Christ, I'm sorry.

That glittery laugh tickled my mind again. *Don't be, it was the best way to wake up ever. I have missed you so much, Immy. How are you? War must be awful but you're with Wells again! What is it?*

My unease must have trickled through our telepathic link. Or maybe she just knew me well enough to take the temperature of my silences. *Cilla,* I swallowed. *Do you think kroma ever chooses a mating bond incorrectly?*

Why would you say that? You and Wells are perfect. What's going on?

I just . . . I keep screwing up. We're arguing. A lot. And the king got here today and Wells basically told me to be subservient and obey. It's like who I am just messes up his entire job. I don't mean to do it, but . . . He even admitted that as hard as he's worked to get where he is, he was wishing for other options for the first time in his life. I'm the reason for that, Cilla. I'm making him doubt things. I'm causing problems. I'm—

Stop. Her mental voice was so strong an image of her—long blond hair in one of those flowy sundresses with a palm thrust toward my face—flew down our link. *Immy, you and Wells are in a super high-stress situation. And your relationship is really new. It's completely understandable that you would have disagreements. You have no idea the fights that Zoe and I've had recently.*

I took a breath and gazed down through the branches, Prism's violet hide just visible where he paced beneath me. I really shouldn't 'path for too long. *I think I'm having a hard time wrapping my mind around "forever." Like, this isn't a marriage contract that we can dissolve if it's wrong. Our literal souls were torn apart and stitched together. And we have thousands of years. Unless we die in this war.*

Stop, you better not die or I will actually kill you. I felt her reach toward me, as if to take my hand, and my heart ached. I missed her so much. *Immy, I've made a permanent link, too. I'm not mated, but Zoe and I created another immortal being together. And yes, it's scary. But it's also amazing. And I think questioning things is okay. Good even. It's okay for you to check yourself and it's okay for Wells to want a better life for both of you. We're both still learning about this place we've been brought to. And you had even less to go on than I did. It's natural to worry, but if you want my honest opinion, you and Wells were perfectly mated. You're going to get through this and you'll be stronger.*

Something in my heart eased. *Cilla, I miss you so much.* Wells's mind brushed mine. He was looking for me. I pushed him to the side quickly. *Cill, I gotta go. I love you. I'll write again soon.* Shoving a mental hug down the line, which I felt her latch on to, I cut off contact and let the wind drop me into the trees.

I clambered down quickly and fell from the lower branches onto Prism's back, hugging his massive neck. Joy zipped through every nerve as I grinned into his mane, my eyes still moist. I let Wells feel the rest of my mind, concentrating on the elation I'd felt from Cilla's initial announcement.

What is the meaning of this? Prism pawed the forest floor twice before setting off.

I'm a godmother! My best friend had a baby! I laughed, still draped over his neck, even as he grumbled that he had no idea what a godmother was. I wasn't a god and I wasn't a mother. So it made no sense to him.

I touched my bond with Wells. He was brimming with a mixture of feelings, likely from his talk with Al. I wondered if he'd felt my burst of joy and everything that followed or if he'd been too embroiled. I was still grinning, my cheeks aching with it, when we emerged from the forest, although no longer collapsed across Prism's mane.

Prism at least understood that my best friend had a new baby. Unicorns did not procreate often, so he appreciated that joy. He pranced in ecstatic empathy, circled by several other unicorns we had passed en route, Prism having spread the news. We burst into the clearing, a riot of romping color. A few of the unicorns showered us with harmless, warm sparks from their horns. Our display effectively ended Al and Wells's conversation.

Wells waded through the massive cavorting bodies until he reached me and pulled me from Prism.

"Imogen, what is going on?" His dark red brows crinkled the skin between them, russet eyes dilating in concern when he saw the tear tracks on my face. The unicorns continued to frisk about the clearing.

I wrapped myself around him like a koala and handed him the scrap of paper that would join my ring, necklace, and phone as one of the most precious things I possessed in this world.

I watched Wells's face crack into a full grin as he read. He slapped his arms around my rib cage, spinning me around while I buried my smile against his neck. I released my legs, letting my boots float feet from the ground as the unicorns capered around us.

"Wait, Imogen." Wells set me down, pushing me back and peering at the scrap of paper again. "How did you get this?"

My stomach tightened. "I just 'pathed her for a minute..."

Any scrap of joy or humor remaining on Wells's face vanished.

CHAPTER TWENTY-THREE

My fight coach used to say that you learn more from your losses than your wins. And while I agree, it doesn't make losing suck less.
  —Imogen Delaney

Wells hauled me from the unicorn habitat, face set and jaw clenched. *I cannot believe you would be so selfish as to put this entire company at risk.* The steady pulse of fury in his aura tightened my chest even more than the arrow sharp smack of his 'path.

I rode the wind above the trees in the center of the habitat, I was careful, Wells, but you heard what Allestair said. I had to check on them. Warn them—

I stopped speaking as we approached the tents, shocked by the flurry of activity.

Wells still had my hand in a vise grip and pulled me inside. Our belongings had already been magically stowed away. He tossed me my sword. "Suit up. Allestair has ordered an immediate relocation nearer to the capital. He wants to be able to strike within hours if necessary." A muscle in Wells's jaw ticked, his eyes flared like rubies when they landed hard on me. "You're either incredibly lucky that we were already planning to relocate or you've just doomed us to an attack en route."

Remorse curdled my insides as shame heated my skin.

We were lucky. For once, the relocation was quick and uneventful. Although Wells and the other generals had to spend time drawing up additional watch rosters while we marched since we were so deep within enemy territory. Wells was still furious with me, though he kept my transgression between us. Once the new camp was established and shielded, we trudged back to our tent in silence, covered with dust from the march, our bodies limp with exhaustion Wells's face was drawn, his eyes flat with fatigue. Contrition curled low in my lungs like heavy smoke.

He pushed the tent flap open for me. "Start a bath. I'll be there in a moment." He crossed to his desk and immediately began pulling his papers out from the drawers while I did as he said.

Now that we had the full-sized tub, Wells and I occasionally shared bathtime as another quiet space to talk. I usually found it relaxing, but today my muscles remained tensed as I slid into the warm water. I didn't turn when I heard Wells enter and shuck off his own clothes. I silently scooted back to make room. He eased into the water facing away from me.

It's how we usually started; I washed his hair then he washed mine. But today his back felt like a wall between us. Sadness pulling at my heart, I wrapped my arms around him, dropping my head onto his shoulder. "Wells . . ."

I felt his sigh against my cheek as he cupped his hands over mine. "If you had just waited, just talked to me, I would have let you 'path her discreetly while we marched."

Guilt coiled through my belly like a fat eel. I squeezed my eyes shut.

"I feel your guilt, Imogen," Wells said softly. "I still love you. But we really must get on the same page about this."

"Okay," I whispered and sat back. Wells bent his knees and lowered himself into the water. Eyes meeting mine once before he shut them and dropped his head into my waiting palms.

I sudsed up his obnoxiously long auburn hair, focusing on the task to keep my mental voice as focused as possible. *I hadn't heard from Cilla. After what Allestair said, I was worried he had done something to them. I guess I panicked a little.*

I gently scratched at his scalp before drawing the soap to the ends, folding them in on themselves and working the suds through. The colors of the individual hairs were so varied in shade that it was easy to get lost in the gradations. The Sephryan sun had lightened some strands while others remained stubbornly dark. I couldn't help taking extra time running my fingers through it.

I understand, Demon, but we just had a conversation about obeying orders. That includes standing orders given to the entire company. You are intelligent enough to understand the risk you took in using kroma outside of the shield. If we'd been keeping that camp, I would have had no choice but to alert the watch that you had potentially leaked our location.

I bit my lower lip. That would have been great ammunition for all the Imogen-haters. Even Allestair. And I had to admit to myself that Wells was right. One reason I hadn't said anything to anyone was because I knew I wasn't supposed to be 'pathing home. *Do you want to send me back to Molnair? Cilla's with Zoe's family, maybe I could go there. If Allestair is here—*

I can't send you back now. Allestair is very keen to see you fight.

My guts twisted for an entirely different reason then. *What does that mean? Are we concerned about that?*

A soft moan escaped him as I massaged his neck. *We're not unconcerned.* He reached a hand back to curl around my knee with a sigh. "Imogen, I need you to stop and think before you act. Every action from here on out. We *cannot* have another misstep. You got lucky today. Please. I'm imploring you."

"I promise I will stop and think. And ask you." I let a soft sigh go myself. Something like fear curling around my chest. "Dunk." Wells obediently tilted his head back until it was below the waterline. I scrubbed his hair free of soap, keeping a firm leash on my thoughts.

I kept my eyes on my fingertips, working through the crimson and copper, planting a kiss on his forehead when I was done. He hadn't been nearly as hard on me as he should have been. Yes, being told to be quiet and meek was annoying, but I should have talked to Wells before putting the camp at risk. Especially with how abysmal our luck had been lately.

"Your turn." Wells twisted around in the tub and we repositioned ourselves the opposite way.

I let myself float back, eyes closed, my hands resting on his knees, my crown bumping into his chest. My ears slid beneath the water, muffling the sound as my eyes dropped shut. I reveled in that little bit of sensory deprivation searching for a granule of peace. I heard him soaping up his hands even with my ears submerged. He tapped my head and I lifted it so he could rub the soap in.

Something else is bothering you. Is it just concern regarding the king's machinations? Or about what Al told you? His 'path was gentle. *About your father?*

The reminder stung sharply as if a needle had pierced my breastbone. I pulled my mind within its mental shields for a moment. Sorting through my thoughts where he couldn't hear me. He patiently scrubbed soap into my hair, waiting silently.

My throat tightened. I forced a swallow. Fought the tears down and took a breath. For a beat I focused only on the feel of his fingers massaging my scalp.

I'm glad my dad knows. One tear squeezed out of the corner of my eye, but I kept my face relaxed. It could probably be taken for bath water. *I wish Al had told me sooner. My nightmares could have been ... different.*

Wells brushed the tear away from my face. So that had fooled no one. He gently lowered my head into the water and rinsed me out.

But my current feelings are related to something ... more immediate, I said finally. Heart in my throat, I asked, *Wells, do you ever worry that kroma was wrong? That maybe I'm not the right mate for you?*

A flash of shock burst through the bond. "No," he said firmly. "I believe that kroma chooses pairings that will enhance each other. And growth can be difficult." Wells continued rubbing out my hair. When he finished, he dropped a rough kiss on my lips and pushed me upright, then he hauled me against his chest and leaned against the tub so that we both reclined. He pressed another kiss to my shoulder.

We are still getting to know each other, Imogen. And you are still very, very new to this world, not to mention military life. We're both going to make mistakes. This hasn't been easy for you, and I think that's a good thing. The harder lessons stick more solidly. I still firmly believe you are the perfect mate for me. A little curl of hurt brushed against the bond as he asked, *Do you regret accepting?*

My fingers dug into his arms as if I feared he would be yanked from me. *Not at all, I just . . . I feel like I've been trying so hard and I'm barely keeping my head above water. I keep screwing up and I don't want to drag you down with me.* I closed my eyes and let my head fall back, my tense muscles slackening. I was exhausted and hoped I'd be able to sleep later. His fingers drifted across my collarbones and absently fingered my necklace. We'd asked Obsidian to put an unbreakable spell put on it at the earliest opportunity. I didn't want to lose it in battle. Unicorn charms were more difficult for sidhe to break.

How about we hold each other up instead? His arms tightened around me. *You'll get your footing, Demon, and I need you with me. If we're aligned, I can handle . . . everything else.*

The mysterious spy. And Allestair. Was Wells worried about what he might do? *The king could separate us again, right?* I pushed when Wells was quiet for too long, his worry bleeding into the bond.

He didn't answer for a long time. Just sat, with his arms wrapped around me, soaking in the warm water, idly trailing his fingers up and down my arm. *I don't think he'll try that tactic again, Demon,* he said finally. *Not with how close we are to laying siege. He does have a war to focus on. I'm still holding out hope that we'll get through this and eventually be able to go home.*

Will we be allowed to go home? I asked, my heart pounding as I finally voiced the thoughts that had been racing around my head since Allestair's arrival. *If we make it through this war, do you really think he'll let us go back to the house on the hill? That we'll be able to live our lives as we please? He may never let us leave the palace.*

If we're both together, we'll be home. He pressed his lips to my temple. *Everything ebbs and flows, Imogen, right now you're new—we're new—and he's trying to figure out where we fit—*

I knocked the soap into the water with a plunk. Like an annoyed cat. *He's trying to figure out how to control us completely.*

Wells fished the bar out and set it to the side. *I know it doesn't feel like it right now, but his focus will eventually drift from the two of us.*

I didn't answer. Wells could be right and the king would move on in a few years—or decades—but I was anxious about his immediate plans. I'd seen his aura this morning. He was not done with me. Not by a long shot.

We received word that several other units had successfully made camp on the other side of the capitol compound. Wells's spies had come in the middle of the night while we were sleeping—almost getting skewered by my dagger—and brought him detailed maps of the entire city. They wouldn't answer me when I asked how they'd obtained them.

They also had no evidence of a Sephryan spy in our midst reporting our movements.

Sephrya's capital city was walled and warded, with the king's palace at the very center. Jarleth pointed out the area where he thought Cilla and I had been. It was indeed a keep on the outer ring of the compound. They believed that the other Molnairian prisoners might be held there as well though they hadn't been able to find out definitively. Nor had they found any trace of a human. Rumor was that they had all perished, but Kitano didn't believe it.

I shoved back against the warring anger and nausea that rolled through me upon hearing that news. I shivered in my tank top and shorts, even though the night was as warm and humid as usual. Wells ran a hand down my back, still bent over the maps.

Jarleth turned his unnervingly steady gaze on me. "Does it upset you because you used to be human, or because you don't like the way they were treated?"

I stared back at him. "Why can't it be both?"

He gave me that small smile. "Is it both?"

"It's both and more," I furrowed my brow. His aura didn't show anything other than calming oceanic colors, and a few spritzes of curiosity.

Kitano and Jarleth rolled out another large map, containing some details of the palace and grabbed items at random to weigh down the corners.

I moved over to the side table to get some water while they arranged a smaller map on top of the newer large one. This one was a detail map of some battlements along the southern end of the third ring. "These battlements are connected," I heard Wells say. "Were the ones on the northern end the same?" They shuffled it aside to view the large map.

"Only the battlements in the middle ring were connected on the northern end," I said, pouring my water. "Eastern battlements on the outer ring, western battlements in the innermost ring."

Everyone went silent and I experienced the familiar tingling sensation of disbelieving eyes upon my back. I turned around to find Kitano and Jarleth staring at me. Wells was smiling.

"Imogen memorizes instantaneously," he told them. His aura was glowing softly red-gold with pride.

"You'd make a good spy," Jarleth said, his strange smile dancing on his lips.

"Except that everyone knows who I am," I retorted, leaning against the table and drinking my water.

"A good glamour takes care of that," Kitano reminded me.

I blinked. He was right. I bet I'd be even better at glamouring myself now that I'd seen him do it.

"Please don't give her any ideas," Wells said, turning back to the maps. He pointed at me. "And you, stop considering it."

I smirked, finished my water, and joined them examining the maps again. I knew they would sneak out of camp well before dawn. I wanted to learn as much as possible.

The following day Wells received word that all units were in place. We would attack Demian's stronghold from both sides in the morning. I was storing my freshly cleaned armor, aiming for an early night to rest up when Al came barging in. I ignored him, hoping Wells could take care of whatever he needed quickly and ducked into the back to wash my face.

Al's raised voice carried easily to my ears just as I was patting my skin dry. I shut my eyes and indulged in a heavy sigh before draping the towel over the basin and stepping out to deal with this my goddamn self.

"You've got the full army now, you don't need her—" Al was pacing around the tent while Wells leaned against his desk. Neither of them glanced my way as I approached.

"Al—"

"Don't give me that horseshit about her being marked by a unicorn. One less unicorn in the battle isn't going to make a difference."

"*Al*, just after you left the tent your father insisted on placing Imogen himself."

"Well, I disagree with his placement. She could try doing her lightning shit from up on the hill where we watch. It might not catch as many but—"

"And how do you plan to deal with the king?"

There was a beat of silence. I came to a stop near Wells, planted my feet, and folded my arms. Al's eyes flicked from Wells to me, then back again.

"We fake some kind of wound."

I outright laughed, earning a glare from Al.

He refocused on Wells as if I weren't there.

"You and the generals will be strategizing from the battleside camp now that your unit is at full strength. Just have Imogen wink back to you after the battle has started."

Wells had fought alongside his unit when they'd been severely depleted and outnumbered, and he wouldn't hesitate to do so again, but now that he had several units to command, he and Obsidian would remain mostly observers. Obsidian could relay commands to the unicorns from afar just as Wells could 'path any general or lieutenant on the field. And the pair of them could be anywhere in an instant if necessary.

"Let her start the battle." Al was still pushing this. "Then call her back, make some excuse to keep her on the hill and—"

"Listen," I broke in. "Not only does Allestair want to see me in action, but Prism and I want to fight. We want to help—"

Al thrust a finger in my face. "You don't get an opinion."

My blood boiled. I clenched my jaw, waiting for Wells to tell him off so I could wrangle my temper down before opening my mouth.

Wells had his arms crossed, his gaze downward, eyes unfocused. "I'll have to let her start where she is, but there is no reason I can't gradually pull her back."

"Uh, how about the fact that she's standing right here and—"

"And you said you would follow my orders from here on out." Wells's gaze slammed into me, eyes hard.

Frustration added fuel to the anger Al had stoked. I hauled desperately on the slim tether keeping my temper from exploding. "And I will follow your orders, but what you're talking about now . . ." I took a breath to modulate my increasing volume. "You're treating me different than you would another soldier."

"You *are* different, Im." Fury simmered behind Al's amber eyes. "Like it or not, you belong to the palace now. You're valuable and cannot be replaced."

I sucked in another deep breath and spun to Wells. "You said you were going to try to be objective." My voice was shaking with barely suppressed rage. "Then use me and Prism where we will benefit the army most. There's no reason to pull us back early, we've been doing fine—"

Wells shoved a hand through his hair. "I know you don't like it, Imogen, but Al isn't wrong. At some point you will have to learn how to take a backseat, no matter how you feel, and do as you're told."

I exploded. "I refuse to become your mother!"

Everything went silent and still. The temperature in the tent seemed to plunge. My anger fizzled out and my chest tightened. Al and Wells had never looked more like siblings as when they turned cold eyes on me.

"What exactly is wrong with my mother?" Wells asked softly.

My mouth went dry, but it was out now and I wasn't going to sugar coat it. "She had a talk with me one day. And basically told me to sand down my personality or be broken." When I saw Wells's jaw clench I hurried on. "I honestly think she had good intentions. But," frustration burned against my breastbone, "the amount of times I've been told to sit down and shut up, lately—"

"That's a hyperbole, Imogen," Wells snapped.

"Is it? I know I've got a lot to learn, but right now I feel like I'm doing my best to use my talents to be of service to some crown that I never," I cut a glare at Al, "said I was the least bit interested in—"

"Imogen." Wells cut me off sharply.

I snapped my mouth shut and took a breath, striding away from both of them. I had come dangerously close to claiming no fealty to Al's father. And potentially hinting at my kingless status. Behind me I heard Wells ask Al to give us a minute alone.

I'd made my way to the other side of the desk and plopped down in his chair, dropping my forehead against the heels of my hands. I heard the tent flaps fall shut then Wells's slow steps toward me. The sounds of shifting paper were accompanied by the warmth of his nearness as he perched on the desk beside me. "You have to be more careful."

"I know." I took another two deep breaths then dropped my hands from my face, though I continued to gaze at them, dangling between my knees. My elbows remained braced on my thighs. The fight had gone out of me. I didn't look at Wells. "Did you know that your mother started the Wind War Carthanacht?"

A pause. "The Wind War Carthanacht is centuries old, Imogen. I know mother was involved at one time but—"

"She was more than involved." I glanced up at him. "She started it. Allestair and Iphigenia started ruling near the end of the War. Since she was married to the prince she couldn't be drafted, but wanted to help with the war effort at home. Once Allestair came into power, he asked her to appoint some people to help her. Once the war was over, the WWC shifted their focus a bit but, as you know, they were still very busy and still very much in demand. But the Wind War was done, and Allestair slowly pulled your mother out of every external organization she had influence in. He used Al, and later you, as leverage"

I paused for breath. The crease between Wells's eyes had deepened and his aura was an ever-sifting array of colors. "She never told me any of this."

"Allestair doesn't like her to speak of it," I said, suddenly exhausted. "She told me it would be best if I left the 'loudest' parts of myself behind and created a new, softer persona for my life on Perimov. She said it would be easier for us both if I faded into the background a bit."

Wells crossed his arms, every line of him tight. "I know what she meant, but this doesn't mean you have to erase yourself, Imogen."

"Doesn't it? Al just told me I don't get an opinion. You were both standing there discussing me and telling me to butt out of it." My throat tightened, but I swallowed it down, dropping my gaze to my hands again.

"We're worried about you, Imogen." Wells's tone had lost some of its sharpness.

"Your concern is starting to look a lot like control," I said, my voice barely above a whisper. "I cannot lose myself like your mother lost herself, Wells. I—"

"I am not Allestair," Wells's voice went cold and hard. His fingers wrapped my chin and lifted it until my eyes locked with his. Tension bracketed his mouth and his eyes flamed, but there was fear running through his aura. "I don't want to crush or change any part of you, but I do want to bring you through this unscathed if I can. Can't you please trust me?"

"Like you're trusting me?"

For a moment, his lips tightened, then his fingers relaxed on my jaw, releasing it to slide his palm against my cheek. A sigh escaped him. "Alright." And I could feel a tightness, a clenching, lung-squeezing worry that wasn't my own as he said, "Let's put our trust in each other tomorrow."

I covered his hand with mine and noticed both were cold. "Done."

CHAPTER TWENTY-FOUR

*Knowing what motivates your enemy is essential.
I know exactly what Sephrya wants. And I shall never give it to them.*
—King Allestair Metellus

P rism pawed the wilted grass, excitement radiating from his violet coat even though we were not on the front lines, much to his chagrin. *We could have been the first to breach the enemy compound,* he 'pathed. *We have been unfairly deprived of the opportunity.*

After serious consideration, and a murmured conversation with Adgemon that Wells thought I slept through, he conceded that his responsibility was to the army as a whole and that he was better utilized observing the entire battle and directing us from there. Adgemon agreed that pulling me from the fight unnecessarily would raise some eyebrows. Especially those who already muttered about favoritism.

As a telepath, Wells was incredibly effective from a distance. Obsidian was definitely alpha unicorn of the blessing and would have no issue enforcing orders from afar. Obsidian was older than Prism and had worked with Wells for long enough that he trusted him, which made it easier to pull his unicorn out of the thick of the bloodshed.

Al still pushed for an early exit, but Prism and I disagreed. We both desperately wanted to bring Molnair a victory and were reveling in our new bond.

Although Prism merely craved conquest and I wanted to prove to Wells that I could be the partner he needed without being sidelined. Allestair put an end to the debate by reiterating that he wished to evaluate my performance and usefulness himself.

So no pressure.

I 'pathed Prism. *I don't think the plan is to breach the compound today. I think we're just laying siege. Let's concentrate on our orders.*

Prism neighed low in his chest. It sounded like an engine revving. That he was unhappy with these new orders was no secret. Wells even had Obsidian step in to reinforce them. We were both quickly learning that Prism was very willful, even for a unicorn, but in spite of his insistence that we had no rank, he *did* listen to Obsidian.

I patted his glossy neck. *We'll still get to do some amazing shit, my friend.*

His ribs expanded against my inner leg line as he sighed deeply. *I suppose we can't help but be amazing. Even when restricted.*

We were on the outside middle of the unit. Wells wanted us to be outside so that he could send us to other units easily. He didn't want us in the front where Prism might get blood lust and disobey me if there was too much carnage. I insisted that Prism had never *completely* disobeyed me—argued, yes—but it wasn't good enough for Wells. I didn't really blame him. Prism was a spitfire.

This was the first battle that felt like an old-school war movie. The Sephryan compound was in sight. We were arranged on the crest of a hill before it. Our royalty and generals were stationed on a hill above the valley before the impressive city walls, and the enemy army was filing out across the opposite hill, ready to defend their borders.

There were more Sephryans than I had envisioned. We outnumbered them, but they were defending a walled and warded compound. Trying to seize it might prove the more difficult job. Eels tumbled through my belly and I told myself I was excited, just like Prism.

As the ambassadors winked down to meet each other, I thought of the lightning and the clouds above us darkened. I noticed several of the Sephryan fighters glancing skyward then scanning our ranks.

They fear your lightning. Prism arched his crest, preening. *Already they quake at its herald.*

Something about the way those Sephryan units scanned our soldiers—sparing no attention for the ambassadors down below—bothered me. I couldn't read their auras from this far away, but collectively they flowed with a similar color; shifting together into a calculated bronze. Determination. But without any of the usual battlefield variances of fear or anger. The hairs on my arms rose. This wasn't right.

In the valley below, the ambassadors slowed as they neared each other.

Be prepared for everything. I will tell you what to throw. Prism tossed his ebony mane.

I'm actually supposed to listen to Wells this time, remember?

Prism snorted and circled his muzzle in a unicorn eye roll. *Charge your weapons at the very least. There is challenge in the air.*

During previous battles, I discovered that my swords would hold a bit of lightning without me continually pulling from the sky. I had to pull it with intent, like when I charged my phone, so it wasn't something I could do in the heat of battle. At least not yet. I risked a quick 'path to Wells. *Prism is really raring to go. I've told him we have to wait for you, but he wants me to at least charge my weapons. Is that okay?*

How much attention will that draw?

Depends. Sometimes I can do it just with the clouds, sometimes a bolt comes down.

Do it now, while the ambassadors are talking. You're not attacking anyone so it's not breaching protocol and no one will be paying attention to you.

Will do. I let Prism know what I was going to do and pulled out my sword and dagger. I shut my eyes and focused on drawing the energy into my blades.

One crack split the clouds. My palms warmed and I opened my eyes.

The Sephryans' collective auras shifted. Golden bursts of excitement. Even some shining triumph.

Prism, I don't feel good about this. I felt like an entire Sephryan unit was staring straight at us. *Too many people are looking at us.* I shifted my focus. *Wells...*

A roar erupted from the Molnarian army as our ambassador was felled by an arrow from the Sephryan heights.

The Molnarian army charged. Prism let out a vicious whinny as we surged with them.

Wells directed me to a hovercraft approaching our off side. Much closer and I wouldn't be able to take it out without compromising one of our units.

I warned Prism, readied a grenade, and 'ported it through as soon as the opening was visible.

Three...two...it exploded and skidded to the side mere feet from our soldiers, but they were able to divert around it.

Catapult on the near side! Prism wanted to wink directly to it, but I held him back, pulled an arrow and let it fly.

Wood burns nicely, I told him as my arrow made contact. The catapult exploded in a satisfying burst of timber. *See, we don't have to be front and center all the time.*

Prism grunted in grudging approval.

Things got messy. In spite of our position on the outside, Prism and I were suddenly crowded. Our battalion was hit harder than the others. Two Sephryan units pressed on our flank.

Launch your lightning over them. Prism ordered, his mental voice ice-cold.

I sliced my sword through the air, slinging lightning out over the crushing hordes of Sephryans. I caught dozens without hitting our fighters.

Everything immediately got worse.

Every Sephryan soldier switched their focus to our unit.

Prism blasted with his horn, slicing, using cutting kroma, he was obliterating dozens of soldiers with every strike.

And we were being overwhelmed.

I shot out with my lightning-charged weapons, but I was hampered by the presence of our own soldiers. Still I brought down Sephryans with every strike.

They kept coming. Almost as if they knew. My stomach twisted as the beach of Normandy came to mind.

Prism surged forward, shooting a rainbow beam of radiation in front of us, frying everyone in its path, trying to get space. I knew this was a draining move. We were in trouble. We had to wink. I reached out to Wells just as his 'path hit me, *Tell Prism to wink!* At the same instant Prism's radiation fizzled. A mass of Sephryans surged forward, dozens sacrificing themselves so that those behind them could surround Prism and grab on to us. It was all I could do to stay astride.

Prism couldn't wink now without either towing along everyone who touched him or ditching all including me.

They're hanging on to him! I 'pathed Wells. What did they want with my unicorn? Terror for Prism froze my mind.

With difficulty, I sheathed my dagger. Clinging to Prism's mane, I kicked and struck with my sword.

Wink out! Imogen, Prism can handle himself, Walls 'pathed. But not only was I loath to leave Prism, I was barely keeping their hands off me. I wrenched my ankle from another Sephryan, ramming my heel into his face, but for every soldier Prism and I took down, another was ready. We'd been separated from our unit entirely. Surrounded by a mass of Sephryans.

His eyes gleaming red with rage, Prism bucked and thrashed until his aura began to dim from the exertion. Soon he wouldn't even have the energy to wink.

I knelt on his withers, using my blade to defend us. I had no time to reach for my arrows and hadn't 'ported any more explosive replacements. *Prism, let's wink to a different location!* I 'pathed. Even if we brought a few with us, we could separate them from their reinforcements. *We're going to wink to you! Be ready!* I 'pathed Wells, opening up the band to Prism.

Someone grabbed onto my quiver, hauling me backward. Prism's mane was ripped from my hands. As soon as I lost contact with my unicorn, they winked me away.

My opponent ripped my bow and quiver from me as we came out of the wink and threw me on my back. We were inside a Sephryan compound. I couldn't access the sky. He went for my sword, but I slashed across his shins. He called for reinforcements. I tried to wink to Wells.

Warded. Blocked.

The thuds of multiple boots thundered down a hallway toward us. The Sephryan who had winked me lunged forward. I sprang to my feet, slashing out with my sword to hold him off. A quick glance told me I was in a prison. A large group cell. With multiple ragged Molnairians chained to the walls.

Fuck. I was dead if I didn't get out. *Leave them though?*

My hesitation was enough for the bronze-haired asshole who'd winked me to recover and pull his own sword. I yanked my dagger free, blasting him with lightning. Turned and threw the remaining energy of both blades into a prisoner-free section of wall. Four gray stones shattered. My heart leapt when daylight poured in. An outer wall.

Reinforcements arrived. I spun. Blocked a blow with my sword. Sliced my dagger down the blade hand of another. I was surrounded. Tried to call the lightning. One blast answered through my hole. Widening it by two stones. I bared my teeth, focusing my entire energy on taking these Sephryans out.

My blades were electric. I couldn't toss indiscriminate bolts without hitting the prisoners. But I could electrocute anyone who touched me.

Where are you? Wells.

Not now! I sent lightning down four of their blades and got enough space to aim a blast at the crowd of Sephryans by the door.

Where!

Prison. Fighting.

We'll follow your lightning.

I risked sheathing my dagger to punch a fist toward the sky. Pulling charge straight to me and shooting a continuous blast straight at the door. A signal to Wells just as much as fuel for me. Bodies piled up, turning my stomach. My blood was heating. Continuous flow was the most enervating.

Fuck. Imogen, you've been taken directly into the compound. No one can wink in.

I stopped pulling lightning. It crackled over my body. My lungs sucked air like bellows.

I'll have to get out then. I glanced at the prisoners. *Wells—*

A red arrow thunked into my right shoulder. Oddly, it didn't hurt. Something cool and numbing swept into my veins. Fear wrapped my spine.

I hurled lightning at the door. My sword arm dropped. Sword clattering to the ground. I grasped the arrow shaft. Prepared to pull. Another arrow hit my left forearm. My right thigh. I belatedly hauled my shield up. It felt like lead.

My knees buckled and hit the ground. *Why didn't I shield as soon as I had a charge? Stupid, stupid . . .* I fumbled for my sword with my left hand. Fired lightning indiscriminately at the door with my right. The entire room tilted and I swayed as if I'd been roofied. The famous Sephryan poisoned arrows. I couldn't lift the sword. Even keeping my fingers wrapped around it was an effort.

Goddammit, Imogen, you cannot die here, I told myself, just as the blade slipped from unresponsive fingers and clattered to the stone. *Wells will never forgive you.*

Abandoning my sword, I forced my arms level with my shoulders, one toward the door, one toward the wall. My breath sawed in and out with the effort. I dropped my shield and blasted lightning with all my might.

CHAPTER TWENTY-FIVE

Everyone is afraid of something.
It's how you react to that fear that defines you.
—Captain Marcellus Tibercio

Pain tugged first, shoving aside the shadow dreams winding through my mind, the throbbing in my shoulder hauled me into consciousness. My entire body ached. A heavy silence thickened the atmosphere. Not the quiet of solitude.

I was caught. My stomach iced over.

I lay still, kept my muscles relaxed in spite of the sharp ache in my shoulder begging me to shift. I forced myself to assess the situation before opening my eyes. Before giving away anything.

Cold metal encircled my neck and wrists. I was laying on straw. The pungent scent of other living bodies in the room was unmistakable once I caught it. Most likely the other prisoners.

If you get out, at least you can let everyone know where they are.

My shoulder was the worst, but my forearm and thigh throbbed insistently as well. I wasn't healing then.

I tried to 'path. Nothing. Tried to pull up a shield. Nothing. This was different than when Prism had stolen my voice. Then it was just gone. Now it was as if I were attempting to move an arm that had fallen asleep. It was there, I could sense it, but I had no control over it.

My heart rate increased and I forced my breaths to lengthen and slow back to that deep sleepy rhythm. No panicking. Not yet. Afraid of what I might find, I made myself search for the bond. Relief poured into me when I touched it. Shadowy and faint but undeniably whole. Almost as faint as it had been when I was trapped in the palace. I tried again to summon kroma of any kind. Nothing. I searched for wards . . . spells . . . finally concluded something in the actual chains binding me was inhibiting my powers.

I cracked open my eyes.

I was in the same large, depressing stone room. I could tell by the lack of sunlight that my "window" had been repaired. Scorch marks still adorned several stones and the door. The doorframe was almost black. The other Molnairian sidhe chained to the walls around me each had a bed of straw. It was obvious which ones had been here the longest. They were in scraps of their uniforms. I shut my eyes as nausea rolled through me.

You can't help them if you can't get free yourself.

Wells was going to be beside himself. My insides nearly cramped under the pressure of guilt, dread, and paralyzing fear that crashed through me. I forced it back and continued assessing my condition. I was still fully clothed. Only my weapons and armor had been taken. And my boots. My feet were completely bare and slightly chilled.

So the fun has yet to begin.

I did a scan for anything I could use as a weapon. Nothing. My throat tightened when I realized the dagger Wells had given me after my first lunar cycle on Perimov had been taken. *Priorities.* I told myself. Things could be replaced.

Finding no further sanctuary in feigning unconsciousness, I pushed myself upright. In addition to my dagger, my pocketknife was gone. The small knife in my bra was gone. My stomach roiled again when I realized that an in-depth search of my body had been conducted while I was unconscious.

The necklace Wells had given me was still there, although there were cuts and abrasions encircling my throat that led me to believe removal had been attempted. The unbreakable spell had held.

I still wore my button-down uniform shirt. Hope flared.

My chains clinked softly as I brought my fingers to the hem, pinching around the edge. Right at the seam. There it was. I tore at the stitching. Teased out a tiny metal rod.

I positioned the rod between my teeth and went to work on the cuffs. They slid around. I clamped my wrists together and pushed them up against the corner where the wall met the floor to get more stability. Then it was easy.

I closed my eyes and narrowed my focus to the feel of the tumblers. Grinned bitterly as that satisfying click reverberated up the rod into my gums. My hands were free. I pushed the shackles away and pulled the rod from my teeth.

My scalp stung as my hair was fisted, my neck yanked against its metal collar. A bronze-haired Sephryan materialized above me. If I'd had my aural sight, I might have sensed his cloaking spell.

"Clever." He snatched the rod and banished it with a flick of his fingers. I smacked my hands over his, holding it hard in place against my head. Twisted, torquing his wrist the wrong way. Kicked out with my legs and knocked him down. He cursed as his wrist was sprained. He lost his grip on my hair.

Bronze's shout brought in a golden-haired friend.

I pulled desperately at my dormant kroma, urging it to unlock the chain at my neck but nothing came. I still fought when they came at me. It was satisfying to get a few licks in, but the end result was the same: me back in chains. Only now I was battered and bloody. And not healing.

Once they'd wrangled me to the ground, Bronze continued to hold my arms behind my back while Golden tugged on the chain at my throat, hauling me into a semi-upright position against the wall. I recognized him: Stian. My insides felt like they'd been dipped in Novocain. So he'd survived after giving me that killing curse.

"Little lightning sidhe," Stian crooned, yellow eyes glinting with sadistic delight. "They'll be lining up to breed with you." He ran a hand down my cheek, leaning closer. "Maybe we can take first crack."

The bond shrieked inside me. "I am *mated*!" I snarled, thrashing against them, though all it did was irritate my wounds.

Stian yanked on the chain, dragging my head to the ground, and kneeled painfully on my punctured thigh. I bit my lower lip to keep from crying out. He trailed his gaze over my body before finally lifting his eyes to his companion, whose fingers were clamped onto my biceps. "I'm not sure if you heard the happy tidings, but apparently Molnair's general was mated very recently."

"How wonderful for him." Bronze dug his fingers into my arm. "And how fortuitous for us to be allowed the opportunity of hosting the general's mate."

My insides froze. *Shit*. "There's more than one mated pair in the army," I spat with as much confidence as I could muster. They were not going to use me against Wells if I could help it.

They hauled me into a sitting position and slammed my back against the wall. "Let's just confirm it, shall we? What's your name, little lightning?" Bronze purred, his face inches from mine. I clenched my jaw shut and turned away from his humid breath, my mind spinning. *Make up a name, any name . . .*

Stian wrapped his hand around the metal collar, taking up any extra space. Swallowing was now uncomfortable. "Who's your mate, darling?" His yellow eyes flicked toward his companion, one corner of his mouth sliding upward. "It might be fun to try to beat it out of her, but I don't know if it would get the job done."

Nerves fraying, I battened down my mental hatches. Prepared for more pain. At the same time, I cast about for any name to use, my mind frustratingly blank. But perhaps it would be better if it took a moment to give up my fake partner's name. How much time could I buy? *Plan, I need a plan...*

Stian pulled on the collar. When I refused to look his way, he grabbed the back of my hair with his other hand and jerked my face around. *"Tell us who your mate is."*

Compulsion. My guts swirled in horror. In vain I tried to lock my jaw shut, my entire body squirming ineffectually. The muscles relaxed, my mouth opened, and my voice emerged, flat and expressionless. "Llewellyn Eigneachan, General of the King's Armies, Son of the Queen." One tear escaped as my heart contracted in terror.

They threw back their heads and laughed. And continued laughing as they unhooked my chain from the wall and dragged me roughly from the large cell, without allowing me to get to my feet. My gaze collided with one dead-eyed Molnairian prisoner as I was dragged down the hall and into the room next door.

A torture chamber.

Blades, hooks, whips, and all manner of horrifically uncomfortable-looking clamps hung from the walls and the ceiling. It reeked of blood, sweat, and terror. They threw me onto a stained wooden table in the middle of the room.

I didn't make it easy for them.

I flung all my shame and fear into my kicks and elbows, but I was soon tied down and immobilized, face up, limbs splayed, panting with wasted effort. The collar remained locked around my throat. I grabbed my exploding emotions one at a time—terror, grief, rage, humiliation—and shoved them into a box. *You will not stink of fear. You will not scream,* I told myself. I wrangled my breathing under control.

"Wink up to the king, Elric," said Stian. "See what kind of message he wants to send."

With Elric gone, Stian strolled nearer and looked me over. He thumbed a trickle of blood from my upper lip and sniffed it before rubbing it between his thumb and forefinger, those yellow eyes never leaving mine. "Up close, you're smaller than I expected," he mused, as though I were an online friend he'd just met in person.

I stared at one spot on the ceiling that didn't have a torture device hanging from it and willed my muscles to relax. I would not start shaking. I wondered if the mountain palace's torture room was similar. I couldn't imagine Al relishing the job as much as this asshole did.

Stian gripped my chin and pulled my face around. "You know, we've never been properly introduced, have we, lightning?"

"You know my name," I gritted out.

His grin was all teeth. "Oh, but wouldn't it be polite? Since we're going to be spending some intimate time together." He smirked and sketched a little bow. "Stian. Feel free to scream it the next time you're in agony." He released my face and stepped back.

"I'm Imogen. Feel free to beg for mercy when the tables turn."

He laughed, long and hard, then patted my stomach. "I like you, Imogen." He slid his cold hand under my shirt, rubbing back and forth across my bare skin. Raising an eyebrow, he glanced down. "Nice scar. Perhaps I'll add to it." A glint of metal at his hip caught my eye.

My dagger. Something hot burst just below my breastbone.

"That's mine," I hissed.

Stian chuckled. "Don't you realize, darling?" He slid his hand between my breasts and leaned in close. "Nothing belongs to you anymore."

Elric winked back in. Stian lazily slid his hand from my chest and tugged my shirt down, closing one eye in a slow wink before crossing to Elric. They conferred in murmurs. I strained to catch what they were saying while keeping my face blank, eyes focused on the ceiling.

Stian sighed. "Well, it won't be as fun, but it does make sense."

They sauntered back to my torture table. Elric pulled a rusted knife from the array hanging from the ceiling. The adjacent ones clanked dully against each other. But Stian held a hand out, a cruel gleam in his eye that sent a chill down my spine.

"I don't think that will be necessary, Elric." An icy grin curved his lips. "*Don't move.*"

My insides curdled as the compulsion took hold. I remained where I was as they released my bonds. Once they were finished, Stian stepped up near my head and brushed his fingers across my cheek. "So nice and biddable."

A growl rumbled through my throat, but I couldn't even open my mouth. I tried to calm myself, to keep my breaths long, but I was triggered. And Stian knew it. His grin broadened and he stepped back from the table.

"*Imogen, stand up and don't struggle.*"

My body trembled as it obeyed, my injured shoulder and thigh protesting. I threw as much hate and loathing into my glare as possible since a poker face was a lost cause. Elric tucked the knife in his belt and chuckled. "I don't know how you always know, Stian," he murmured.

Stian smirked and tucked a strand of hair behind my ear. "She's already wounded; we'll need her alive. This is easier on her body," he stepped in front of me, gazing right into my eyes. "And apparently incredibly difficult for her mind."

"Fuck you," I spat.

Stian's smirk only deepened. "*Follow me and don't struggle.*"

He spun on his heel and I followed like a dog. My hands curled into fists at my sides but apparently punching him in the back of the head would have constituted a struggle. He made an unnecessary loop around the room, turning around to walk backwards, hands in his pockets, eyes glittering with sadistic amusement. Elric sniggered by the doorway.

"You're going to get your own special room, darling." With that he finally led me from the chamber. Stian even put his arm around my shoulders, probably so he could enjoy my shaking. Elric laughed and stepped to my other side, sliding a hand underneath my hair and massaging my neck like a lover.

"Get your fucking hands off me," I snarled with as much ferocity as I could muster.

"Such a mouth," Elric said, without removing his hand.

Stian pulled me closer, pressing his face to my head and taking a loud sniff. "But you smell so good, darling, even wounded with battlefield filth all over you."

"Well, I guess anything would smell good when you—"

Elric's grip on my neck tightened. "Careful, child, don't press your luck."

Stian stopped in front of a solid wooden door, lifting his hand to the keyhole. The tumblers rasped and the lock clicked. Stian dropped his arm from my shoulders and led us inside. Elric maintained his unnecessary grip on the back of my throat.

We stepped into a room the size of a closet. There were no windows, just endless gray stones, a bucket, and one heavy wooden chair at one end. Bye-bye, straw bed, I guess.

"*Sit and stay, Imogen.*" Stian gestured to the chair and my traitorous body limped over—the ache in my thigh deepening—turned around and sat.

Stian leaned over, placing his hands on the armrests. I could have shrank back a few inches until I hit the backrest—but I refused. I'd take any expression of control I could cling to. He stopped with his nose nearly touching mine, his grin sharpening.

"The bond will let your mate know you're still alive, but the muting collar," he tapped the metal encircling my neck, "will keep him from being able to 'path you. It will also stunt your healing. How long do you think you'll be able to go before you're begging us to bring you to your mate?"

Elric chuckled in the background as my stomach iced over. Separating a mated pair was considered criminal for a reason. I'd been told if kept apart long enough, a mate would do anything for a glimpse at their partner. Harm themselves and apparently even kill others.

Stian's eyes dropped to my throat as I swallowed. "A day? A week?"

I clenched my jaw. No matter what, it was better that Wells wasn't here. And I would sacrifice anything to keep him safe. Even if I never saw him again. The bond shuddered at that, but I felt the truth ringing through me. With my wounds not healing, I might not last longer than a week or two anyway. "I will do whatever it takes to keep Wells away from you," I ground out. "If I can do that, my bond is content."

Stian pushed away, his smirk disappearing. "We'll see how long he'll be able to stay away then." He yanked my dagger from its sheath. My mouth dried out as Elric 'ported in a sack and shook it open.

"Imogen, take this dagger, cut off a lock of hair, put it into the sack. Now return the dagger to me, hilt first."

I shuddered as my body obeyed his compulsions one after the other, even as I mentally struggled to hang on to my dagger. Elric produced a scroll and pen. "Time to write a little letter to your mate begging him to save you."

"No!" I shot up from the chair, that compulsion having been obliterated by the others, putting as much distance between us as possible.

Elric chuckled as Stian compelled me to take the pen and scroll carefully. I mentally thrashed and clawed, trapped within my body as it returned to take the scroll. No matter where in the room I tried to go, I had no choice but to copy what Stian dictated word by word. I was drenched in sweat by the time I returned the paper to him and attempted to stab him with the pen.

They both continued to smirk and chuckle as Stian compelled me to sit and stay in the chair. They tucked my letter into the sack with my hair.

Trembling and sore, I pulled my feet up onto the seat and curled around myself, dropping my forehead to my knees, my breaths shuddering through me. Wells would know I'd been forced to write that letter; they'd had me address it to Llewellyn. But my injuries had been accurately described—if he bought that part—and knowing I was alive and being compelled against my will might be even worse for him. My chest caved and I wished we hadn't fought last night. I wished I'd swallowed my pride and let him pull me out of the battle. I hoped Prism was okay. I hoped Wells refused to negotiate.

CHAPTER TWENTY-SIX

*The heart is more resilient than one can ever imagine.
Unfortunately, extreme suffering is necessary to witness it.
—Queen Iphigenia Eigneachan Metellus*

I was left alone for hours, maybe even a day. I had no concept of the passing of time. Although the stone room was chilly, I sacrificed my button-down shirt, tearing it up to bind my wounds as best I could. That left me in my thin tank.

I did try to break the compulsion several times, but what was already difficult for me with full access to my kroma became impossible without it. And I was fraying my own nerves and burning energy. Eventually I curled up in the chair and dozed, focusing on the bond, brushing against it, and trying to send Wells reassuring caresses through it. Occasionally I thought I felt something back, but I could just as easily have been dreaming.

Eventually Stian ambled back in, the sound of the lock jerking me from sleep. "Ah, stayed put like a good girl."

I imbued my stare with hate and death wishes.

"We heard from your mate, darling." He stepped close enough to put a hand on the back of my chair.

My heartbeat quickened, although I managed to keep my glare in place.

"We've started negotiating." He leaned in with a grin. "I don't think he's doing well with the separation."

I twisted in my seat and punched him in the face as hard as I could, a feral grin stretching my lips when I felt his septum crack.

Stian staggered back with a shout, but recovered quickly and shot forward, trapping me by the neck and pressing me down against the arm of the chair, twisting my arm behind my back with his other hand. A yelp punched from my throat as my bad shoulder was torqued.

I braced myself for a compulsion, but now that he had his weight on me, Stian seemed to be enjoying physically holding me down. Blood from his nose dripped onto my cheek as he hissed into my ear. "I hope you enjoyed that. You won't get a chance again." His fingers tightened at my throat. "You're lucky the negotiations included an agreement not to do any further physical damage to you."

He pushed off me and stepped back, taking a few deep breaths before wrenching his nose back into place with a sickening crack and a groan. I took the time to gingerly unfold my aching limbs. It was worth it to have wiped that smirk from Stian's face, even if just for a while.

"*Follow me and don't struggle.*" Stian spun on his heel and marched from the room.

My body lurched forward, but my leg crumpled beneath me, my kneecaps cracking painfully against the stone. The compulsion still yanked at my limbs and I crawled forward a few inches until my shoulder collapsed. Stian returned to see my cheek smack into the ground. He sighed as if I were the greatest inconvenience. "*Stop, Imogen.*"

My limbs relaxed and I let myself lay there, panting slightly.

"*Don't struggle.*" He reached down and hauled me up, his face hard. I guess he was still pissed I got that one hit in. "King Demian wants to see you, so I'm taking you to get cleaned up. You'll help as much as possible or I'll find some new creative compulsions to torture you with. Understand?"

He waited, staring at me until I dipped my chin in a nod.

Stian looped my left arm over his shoulder. I bit back a yell when he wrapped a hand around my injured forearm to keep me in place. With a muttered curse he moved his hand to my wrist, wrapping his other arm around my waist and getting a grip on my belt. We awkwardly traveled down the hall to one of the most depressing bathrooms I'd ever seen. Stian stayed in the room with me, although he did turn his head.

He forced me to stay at the sink longer than I would have. Compelling me to wash as much of the gore off as possible. He didn't offer me any actual bandages, but compelled me to wash out the makeshift ones and clean my own wounds. By the time he had me retying my now-soaked bandages, I was barely able to stand, my entire body vibrating with exhaustion and the trauma of being repeatedly compelled. Although, as I stopped resisting the compulsion, I learned that as long as I followed the spoken instructions, I sometimes had wiggle-room with my interpretation. I tucked that knowledge away.

In the end, Stian was forced to rebandage my injuries in the interest of time. He practically had to carry me back to my cell, where he once again compelled me to sit and stay. I curled up in my chair the instant he was gone, reaching for the shadowy bond deep within me, and passing out.

In spite of Stian's claim, the king must not have been in a hurry to look in on me. Elric and Stian returned with a flask of water, which Stian unnecessarily compelled me to drink in its entirety. My stomach cramped painfully around it, having been empty for so long.

They then forced me to eat two blocks before questioning me under compulsion about the army's movements, Wells's plans, and Molnair's state secrets.

Fortunately, nothing that I knew about the army's movements or Wells's plans were currently a surprise. I knew they planned to lay siege but beyond that, I had no details. And as long as I answered their questions, the compulsion was fulfilled. Rather than attempting to hold information back, I focused all my energy on answering without giving away more than I had to. I was able to avoid mentioning Wells's personal spies by saying I didn't know the identities of any spies in the Sephryan camps. Which was true, as the last time I saw Jarleth and Kitano they were in the Molnairian camp. Wells might have sent them to infiltrate Sephrya once I was taken, but I wasn't privy to that information.

As far as state secrets, we were safe there. As if Allestair would ever tell me anything important.

Stian and Elric were visibly frustrated with my lack of knowledge, so I was surprised when they produced another flask of water and had me drink it. Once I handed it back, Stian said, *"Don't move."* Then handed Elric my dagger.

I froze in place while Elric approached with the blade and a vial. I was unable to do anything while he pricked my neck and held the vial up to collect my blood.

"Heal that once you're done," Stian said. "We've said we won't inflict further damage and we can't have her bleeding out."

Elric did as he was told and moved away once he had a full vial. He nodded to Stian and left the room.

Stian didn't immediately lift the compulsion but pulled his chair closer until he was directly in front of me. He lifted a hand, tousled my curls, then let his fingers drift down my cheek, stopping when he had a firm grip on my chin. "I'd love to break your nose right now," he whispered. "But rules are rules." The corners of his mouth twitched. He gave my chin a little shake. "And I think Demian has plans for you." He released me and stood up. *"Go to sleep."*

As if my strings had been cut, my body went limp as it plummeted from one compulsion to another.

Hours or days later, I heard Stian releasing me from the compulsion as if from a distance. Then, as I woke from my enforced slumber, a new, cold voice asked. "Why is she on the floor?"

"It's where she landed when I compelled her to sleep, your majesty," Stian said, his entire voice an audible shrug. "*Get up, Imogen.*"

Sleep hadn't done much to restore my body and my face twisted into a grimace as my injured shoulder and forearm screamed.

"Have you been compelling her to do every small thing?" The cold voice snapped. The compulsion vanished as if it had been yanked from my bones. I collapsed back to the ground, lifting my head to see a tall sidhe with long silver hair dressed in full black glaring at Stian. King Demian.

"She *did* punch me in the face yesterday," Stian protested. So that had been a day ago? How long had I been here?

"And what had you done prior to that?" Demian's sapphire gaze was brutal as he knelt and offered me a hand.

My spine locked, wondering what kind of trick this was, but he continued reaching out, so I slowly placed mine in his, bracing for him to break my wrist or drag me along the floor. Maybe fling me into the wall.

Instead, he attempted to help me to my feet. When he saw me struggling, his other hand slid beneath my opposite shoulder. He kept hold of me once I was up, his eyes scanning my wounds. "She's hot to the touch. And these are the wounds she sustained during her capture?"

"We weren't told to heal her," Stian said. "Only to avoid causing new injuries."

Demian helped me into the chair and I froze, waiting for the compulsion to lock me there. The king watched me the entire time, his pale face expressionless. He didn't take his eyes from me when he said, "You've been doing *something* to her."

Stian's jaw worked. Still tense, my eyes darted from one to the other. Was this some sort of bad cop/good cop routine? If so, to what end? My mind was swimming and my body a ball of aches and pain. I found I didn't care, I was tired of bad cop, so I'd take whatever break they gave me.

"What have you been doing, Stian? I know how you like to . . . play." Demian's voice was deeper than I expected. And his entire persona was ice, at odds with the hot, humid country he ruled over.

"I only kept her under compulsion so I wouldn't get punched in the face again," Stian lied.

I snorted. I'd seen that glint in his eye, he knew what being compelled did to me and pounced on it.

Demian still hadn't looked away from me. He raised an eyebrow at my snort, his only shift in expression thus far. "She has been continually under compulsion since she arrived?"

I snorted again at the same time Stian said, "It's not like it hurt her."

Demian cocked his head. "What was amusing that time, Imogen?" He glanced over his shoulder at Elric. "Chair." Elric darted out of the room and returned with one in record time.

"I just like how you said 'arrived' like I came here on a visit or something." Realizing I was not about to be compelled, I pulled my aching, trembling limbs onto the seat and curled up against the backrest.

"Put your feet down and have some respect, you're talking to a king. Or do I make you?" Stian growled.

Before I could react—and I was so feverish as to have considered flipping him off—Demian's voice deepened. "Sit however you like, Imogen. Stian, wait outside. You too, Elric."

They both hesitated, their eyes bouncing between their king and me. "But sire—" Stian started.

"Do you think," Demian raised his voice slightly, flinging the words at them like blades, "that I could not handle myself against a shivering, desperately wounded female sidhe that hasn't eaten in days and is wearing a muting collar?"

They both muttered a few "No, sires," dipped at the waist in fumbling bows that Demian didn't turn around to see, and stepped into the hall.

He lifted that cerulean gaze to me. "Now, Imogen. Let's talk."

CHAPTER TWENTY-SEVEN

There's nothing fair about war. And there's nothing fair about love.
—Imogen Delaney

The Sephryan king leaned forward, dropping his elbows to his knees. I fought the urge to flinch.

"Llewellyn has been negotiating admirably to get you back, or even just to see you."

"I'm guessing you sent him nice little presents like my hair and blood in response," I said, too exhausted to filter myself. "I've been wondering if we'll be moving on to fingers and toes next."

The corners of his mouth twitched. "As Stian mentioned, he did successfully clinch an agreement not to do you any further harm. So your fingers and toes are safe for the time being. I thought we would be closer to a compromise," he let out a soft sigh, "but Allestair is such a stubborn, controlling asshole."

I blinked. Couldn't disagree with him there.

Demian leaned back in his chair. "You've had an interesting year, Imogen. New planet, new body, new mate, and now throwing around never-before-seen powers in a war you cannot possibly fully understand."

I blinked again but said nothing. Days ago, I might have felt the stirrings of anger, or indignation, maybe come back with a smart-ass remark, but all I felt now were intense body aches and a headache blooming behind my eyes. If he wanted to hear himself talk, fine.

He tilted his head. "Did you really punch Stian in the face?" Apparently the royal tactic of unexplained subject shifts was a thriving practice in Sephrya also.

"Yeah," I croaked. My throat was dry. My entire body was parched.

"I'm sure that didn't go over well."

"Worth it."

An actual smile curved Demian's lips upward. He 'ported a flask in and offered it to me. I gingerly pushed myself upright, my eyes on what he held.

"It's broth," he said. "I doubt you could handle much more right now, but I don't want you keeling over before I have a chance to speak with you."

I took the flask, my face heating when I struggled with the lid, my arms still trembling. I took a cautious sip at first. The broth was warm, but not hot. My stomach clenched at the first taste, desperate for nourishment. I tilted the flask back with both hands, my throat working as I gulped.

Demian reached out and easily pulled it down. "You'll get sick. It would be a shame if you vomited it all up, wouldn't it?" His gaze lingered on my hands still clutching the flask, the right one shaking even harder due to my shoulder wound. He glanced over his shoulder. "Stian!"

Stian darted in instantly. I guessed this place must be warded against winking if you weren't the king, otherwise I suspected Stian would have arrived that way. More stupid blood kroma.

Still holding the flask with one hand, Demian stretched the other toward Stian. "Your jacket."

Stian kept his face blank as he shrugged out of it and passed it to his king. Demian held it out to me.

"No, thank you." I'd freeze to death before I wore anything that stank of Stian.

Demian's eyes glittered, the nearly immobile corners of his mouth twitching as he passed the jacket back to Stian, his eyes still on me. "I suppose your answer would be the same if I offered you Elric's jacket?"

I nodded. He released the flask. "Slowly."

While I returned to the broth, I heard Demian order Stian to bring a blanket. "I can't talk to her while she's trembling like this."

You could just heal my goddamn wounds and we wouldn't have this problem, I thought, but didn't bother saying. They needed me weak and incapacitated.

And I was convinced this nice-guy act of Demian's was a means to some kind of end. Getting me to drop my guard.

By the time I finished my broth, Stian was back with a blanket. Demian handed it to me and 'ported the flask away while I clumsily wrapped it around myself. I wondered if they'd let me hang on to it once he was gone.

I kept my knees bent and feet on the seat, sitting diagonally, so that I could lean into the corner formed by the arm and backrest and stay mostly upright, wrapping the blanket around my shoulders and covering my legs with the ends. I still ached all over, but my shivering banked slightly. I stared at Demian and waited.

Once we were alone again, he leaned back in his chair, letting his arms relax to the armrests as if he were sitting on his throne. "Why are you fighting this war, Imogen? Are you truly so loyal to Allestair that you'll lay down your own life?"

"I'm loyal to my mate." I pushed as much bite into my words as I could. "And as to why I'm personally pissed at you, if that's what you're really asking, you tried to kidnap me and you *did* kidnap my friend—"

"You're so positive I was behind that?"

"Uh, yeah, since I had to break in here and . . ." I swallowed. "Kill the two guards that were physically assaulting her while she was chained to a wall by her neck before they brought her to *you*."

That small smile again. "So that was you. I wondered."

I didn't respond, forcing my feverish brain to turn over what I had just said. Had I given away anything? Perhaps I confirmed that there was only one lightning wielder in Molnair. Perhaps confirmed that I was the one who brought back the evidence that gave Allestair the justification he needed for war. I let the thought go. None of that was too important surely.

"So you are here for your mate?" Demian asked. "Rather than your king?"

"I go where Wells goes." I truly had absolutely no loyalty toward Allestair. Especially after how he'd treated my mate.

This time the tiny smile seemed to reach Demian's frosty dark blue eyes. "'Wells.' Your pet name for Llewllyn?"

I didn't answer. It was a dumb question and I didn't have the energy. Although I had already reached for the bond, mentally wrapping myself around it, my heart aching when I thought of how distraught Wells must be. If our places were reversed, I would have been burning the world down.

"I met him a couple of times, you know, when we were younger." His eyes bored into mine, nearly as piercing as Allestair's.

I let my head drop against the backrest. "I know. I asked him if he knew you."

Silver eyebrows lifted just slightly. "And what did he say?"

"That he'd met you a couple times," I answered flatly.

Demian's eyes flashed, any hint of amusement dropping from his stony features. "Now, Imogen." His voice dropped lower. "I know you've been questioned extensively under compulsion, and I'm just learning that you've spent the last several days under Stian's compulsion which can't have been comfortable. I am attempting to have a civilized conversation with you but for it to continue, you will need to cooperate."

I didn't lift my head, didn't move beyond a slow blink. A trickle of warning skated down my spine, cutting through the dull aches wracking my body. "You want to know everything Wells said about you when I asked if he knew you?"

He stared unblinkingly.

I closed my eyes as I went back to find the conversation in my mental Rolodex. "Al knew you better. You were princes together. You're less cautious than your father. Oh, his name was Axterius. And he and Allestair were a generation out of the Wind War and didn't want to rock the boat. And . . . Allestair thinks you're an idiot." I blinked open my eyes to find him chuckling through a smile that was all teeth.

"If Allestair wants to find an idiot he needs to look no further than his own son," Demian purred.

"Al's not an idiot about everything." Even as the words came out, I couldn't believe I was defending Al. "Just about interacting with normal people. And anything involving empathy."

Demian's eyes sparkled, a genuine close-mouthed smile lingering on his lips. I berated myself for saying more than I needed to. I inwardly put a tick mark in Demian's not-an-idiot column; he'd waited however many days until I was mentally worn down and physically weakened before coming into question me himself.

"And what does Llewellyn think?"

I felt my eyebrows pulling together. "He didn't actually say what he thought of you."

"And what made you ask him about me in the first place?"

A shudder ripped through me as my stomach roiled with nausea. I clenched my teeth and took a few deep breaths, trying to keep the broth down. I felt like I had the flu. I wondered idly if they would let this infection kill me. And if sidhe died from infections at the same rate as humans if their magic was suppressed. Demian waited in silence until the episode passed. I went completely limp in the chair, still curled upright, but no longer making any attempt to hold myself up.

"I wanted to know what Sephrya wanted the outcome to be if you won this war." I swallowed and anticipated his follow-up question. "Wells said he didn't have time to go over the nuances of the war agreement, but basically you want our technology."

"And what's wrong with that?" Demian's eyes flashed. "Your advancement could help my people. We're in need."

The last thing I wanted was an ethics debate in my current condition. Still, I forced the words out. "I thought your people didn't believe in—"

"My father and his predecessors may have been against certain advancements." Demian sat forward again, leaning toward me. "But I will do what needs to be done for my people. Must this generation suffer because of the backward beliefs of dead kings?"

I blinked. On the surface, I felt that Demian was right. If he wanted to bring his country forward, that shouldn't be a crime. And yet . . . "So are you saying you would be willing to give your humans the option of being turned? Let them live where they pleased?"

His expression iced over again.

I pressed further. "And you wouldn't go to Earth and just yank a bunch of people from their homes to put into your little containment space like cattle?" My voice was low with exhaustion, but the words were clear.

"And would it be so terrible if we did bring some humans from Earth? You came yourself; you must have seen certain advantages."

I pushed my feet against the chair arm to force myself up straighter. "I didn't choose to come here, Aloysius took me. And it sucked ass, if you must know. I wouldn't wish that experience on anyone. I got lucky with Wells."

Demian blinked. Something flickered behind his eyes before they shuttered again. So Demian's spies hadn't managed to obtain *that* bit of information. Allestair would be pleased.

"Doesn't Molnair stand on its moral superiority by claiming that it only turns humans who willingly leave Earth with them?" He lifted a silver eyebrow.

"Why do you think Allestair covered this up?" I snapped. Demian was probably thrilled with this bit of intelligence. I didn't care. I'd never been okay with how Al's actions had been swept under the rug, no matter how sorry he claimed to be now. "Wells was the only one who stuck his neck out for me during the whole ordeal. He and Captain Marc."

Demian's ocean eyes glittered. I could practically hear the wheels turning in his head.

I let my burning eyelids drop. My face was hot, but I felt so cold. A very large part of me wanted Demian to go away and let me sleep with this fabulous new blanket. Another part wondered if I would wake up again.

"Marcellus was always one for picking up interesting strays," Demian muttered.

I cracked my eyes open. Before I could ask him what that meant, he leaned forward and pinched the muting collar between his thumb and forefinger. "You've been very cooperative, Imogen. I'm going to grant you a reward and give your mate a moment to reach you." The muting collar released and I gasped as my power plunged forward.

I was unable to control my body as my spine arched, the joints popping loudly, a cry punching from my throat. The surge of kroma back into my system after days of suppression felt like blood rushing back into a limb that had been deeply asleep: painful and unyielding.

My hands released the blanket to clutch at the arm of the chair as spasms rocked me. I could feel my power rushing to fight the fever, to work on my wounds. But my focus narrowed on the bond roaring back from the shadows. A deep, cutting worry that wasn't my own swirled in my stomach. I felt it the moment his mind found mine. In spite of everything, I sighed in relief.

Imogen?

My mind curled around his. *Wells...*

Gods' bones I can feel your pain. They promised they wouldn't hurt you anymore, we agreed to a cease fire on that condition! Anger flooded through along with the worry.

These are just the wounds I got when they caught me. I've been wearing this muting collar thing so they haven't healed.

Wells's emotions went dark and turbulent. I could no longer sort out individual feelings. *I can feel your fever. They let your wounds fester.*

I'll be okay. Better me than you. My body was still twitching with the sudden return of so much kroma, but I only clung to the sense of his voice in my head again.

They've taken the collar off? Or did you find a way to remove it?

Demian said he was giving me a minute to let you reach me. I don't think he knows I'm a telepath on my own.

Wells's mental voice hardened. *He wanted me to feel this. Imogen, listen—*

But Demian snapped the collar back on and my body slumped into the chair as if my strings had been cut. I felt marginally better due to the burst of kroma flooding my wounds, but it hadn't been enough to heal me completely or even dispel the fever.

"I assume from that vacant expression in your eyes and the smile on your face that he was able to say hello?" Demian leaned back in his chair, crossing one ankle over his knee.

I scanned him, not bothering to attempt to straighten, panting slightly from the dual shock of kroma being returned and yanked away again. I dipped my chin once, nerves wrapping my stomach. Were we finally getting to the point of this meeting?

One corner of his mouth lifted, just slightly. "Allestair doesn't treat Llewellyn the same way he treats Aloysius, does he?"

I swallowed, my mouth dry again in spite of the broth and water. The hair on my neck slowly rose. Where was he going with this?

He waved a hand through the air as if he didn't need my answer. "I've seen it. I didn't meet Llewellyn often, but that in and of itself was a bit of a tell. And the few times I did meet the three of them, it was obvious." A smirk curled his lips. "Probably why you bonded with Llewellyn in the first place. He's a decent person."

I slowly pushed myself upright. Still cocooned in my scratchy blanket, eyes fixed on Demian as if he were a coiled snake. He hadn't asked me a question, so I didn't speak.

"I take it there's no love lost between you and Allestair?" Both eyebrows floated upward.

"I'm not his favorite person," I muttered. No secret there.

"I'd be more than happy to reunite you with your mate, Imogen. We don't need to deal with Allestair." He dropped that bomb and waited, interlacing his fingers in his lap.

The shadowy remains of the bond surged at his words and I found myself sitting up even straighter, my knees dropping to the seat as my chilled bare feet curled against my rear. I swallowed several times, that desperation clawing at me. Wells was right; he'd let us both have a taste, knowing we'd be even more frantic afterward. "At what cost?" I asked finally.

The corners of the king's mouth lifted. "No real cost. If you agree, I'll have your wounds healed, have a house readied for you in one of my coastal cities—perhaps Phrelia, far from the fighting—then once Llewellyn has severed his commitment to Allestair's army, I'll bring him to join you. The two of you will be provided for comfortably."

"So basically imprisoned in a nice house."

Demian shook his head, dropping his foot to the ground and leaning forward again. "You misunderstand me. Once you have sworn allegiance to Sephrya, you won't be restricted in the least. You can go where you please and I would never require you to fight against your former countrymen."

I chewed my lower lip, the bond screaming an enthusiastic "Yes!" that made it difficult to pull apart my still-fevered thoughts.

As if sensing he had gained a foothold, Demian went on. "I have nothing against Llewellyn, other than the fact that he stands in the way of what my people need by fighting this war. Allestair doesn't appreciate your mate. You don't like him yourself. You haven't even been in Molnair a year, how do you know that life in Sephrya wouldn't be better for you?"

He was right. And to be able to leave all this pain and killing . . . the bond, as shadowy as it was, continued to yank on my heart. *Whatever it takes to get back to Wells, whatever it takes . . .*

"If you both wished to participate in court, I could facilitate that lifestyle, without wasting your mate's obvious potential as Allestair has done. If you'd rather live privately, that is an option also. I would swear not to pull you into service if you don't wish it. We could write up the terms so that they're clear. And if you change your minds later, we can add a clause for that."

I couldn't think over the bond buzzing through my body, crashing against me like breaking waves. It wanted this. The quickest path to Wells. The safest. Never to fight again. No more court bullshit if we didn't want. This could be that other option Wells wished for.

But there was something trying to push through the urgency of my bond and the fog of my fever. "I have friends in Molnair," I said finally, Cilla and Zoe flashing across my mind's eye. "Wells has friends. We have unicorns."

"Give me a list and your friends are granted safe passage to see you whenever they like. And although we don't usually encourage them in Sephrya, we'll even make accommodations for your unicorns." Demian agreed easily. "What else? We can address all your concerns now, Imogen, and get you back to your mate."

My eyes flicked up to his. Did he know? Could he somehow tell how this clawing inside of me was preventing me from concentrating? *Tell him yes and get back to Wells. Tell him yes and it can all be over.*

"You . . . kidnapped Cilla." My brow furrowed as I stared at him. "Like she was just an object for you to breed with. You have dozens of our soldiers in there, I saw them."

"War creates ugly circumstances, Imogen. As far as your friend . . ." He shrugged. "Perhaps if you help us facilitate a negotiation for the technology we need then such measures wouldn't be necessary to get Allestair's attention. We could usher in an era of peace between our two countries."

Al's ridiculous "Chosen One" theory flashed across my mind, but I let it go. I clenched my jaw, trying hard to focus while the bond writhed within me, screaming, *Yes, yes, yes! Tell us where to sign!* This sounded too good to be true. I struggled to think through every pitfall. "You mean you'd consider giving any humans living in Sephrya the option of being turned and keeping their children? Let them go where they please?"

"I'm open to discussing changes," Demian said, face impassive. "As your mate pointed out, I'm not my father. We could even write that meeting into your terms. Whatever you want."

Could this be a good thing? *Yes!* The bond beat against me. *Do what he asks! Get back to our mate!* If it hadn't been muted, I probably would have agreed immediately, its desperation to get back to Wells was blindingly intense.

Wells.

What would Wells want?

I couldn't know. Wells had been working toward his position as general most of his life. Perhaps out of necessity, but it was something he had built for himself. And the army was his. If Wells defected, there was no way morale would be the same. The army would be at a severe disadvantage. I forced myself to think through this logically.

If I agreed here and now, Demian would have me sign something, pack me off to the Phrelian coast—the coast on the opposite side of Sephrya from Molnair—and tell Wells that in order to get to me, he had to defect. In order to ever see me again, he would have to give up his entire life.

I couldn't do to him what had been done to me.

"I can't make that decision on my own," I said finally, the bond wailing in agony. "Like you said, I haven't been here very long. I'm sure there's a lot I don't know. But I can't take your deal without knowing what Wells would want."

I thought I caught a flash of disappointment or anger behind Demian's eyes before he shuttered them again. "I suppose I'll have to speak to your mate, then." The king stood, waving a hand at his chair and 'porting it away. "I tried. If you change your mind, drag yourself to the door and knock. The guard on duty can summon me."

With that, he vanished. Leaving me alone with my fever and my anguished mating bond.

CHAPTER TWENTY-EIGHT

To truly love is to be willing to sacrifice everything else.
—*Captain Marcellus Tibercio*

In spite of that one surge of magic and the addition of a blanket, I got worse. Stian stopped compelling me. Either to avoid his king's disapproval or because there was no need as I wasn't a threat to anyone. I moved from the chair to the floor depending on whether I was hot or chilled. My sense of time became even more nebulous.

Stian set a flask of water and a cup of broth on the floor beside me and left. I simply stared at it. I'd stopped feeling hunger. Didn't have the energy to move back to the chair, much less drink anything. I let my eyes fall shut again, not even opening them when I heard Stian return, utter a low curse, and step out again.

He returned with a healer, claiming that he didn't want to be the one to report my death, but she pronounced me still alive.

"She's in trouble though. If these wounds aren't seen to shortly—"

"Get her to eat and drink," Stian said gruffly. "I'll see what the king wants us to do with her."

I didn't open my eyes as the healer gently propped me against the wall of the cell. She muttered something and placed a hand to my forehead. My shivering stopped and for once, I wasn't too hot or too cold. I blinked open my eyes.

She had on a gray cloak, the hood of which covered her bronze hair but her eyes were kind. "I brought your fever down temporarily. It will come back if we don't get these seen to. Can you try to drink some water?"

While I struggled through the flask of water and bowl of now-cold broth, she surreptitiously checked my wounds as much as she could without removing my makeshift bandages. She made little tsking sounds, then helped me to wrap back up in my blanket.

I closed my eyes again, but I strongly suspected she had done a little something to my wounds. I no longer felt like I was lying on Death's doorway.

Though I still didn't feel great.

As soon as the healer stopped supporting me, I used the wall to assist a slow slide to the ground. She had helped just enough that I thought perhaps I might be able to fall into a deeper sleep, one where my pain didn't follow me into fever dreams. The little shadow of the bond tugged at me and I curled around it.

The door creaked open and the warmth from the healer's body was suddenly absent. I burrowed into the blanket as she ostensibly met with Stian. I didn't open my eyes to check. I let myself drift, not even trying to parse their murmured conversation, though the healer's tone was sharp with disbelief until Stian cut her off coldly.

I jerked awake when he yanked my hands from beneath the blanket and bound them together with cord. My stomach lurched wondering if they were finally going to torture me, but he was finished before I even thought to resist.

"Doesn't matter at this point anyway," he said to the healer, who was standing near the door with her arms folded across her chest. Her shoulders a tight line beneath her hood.

Then Stian took the muting collar off.

Once again, the overwhelming surge of kroma inundating my body had me writhing involuntarily. I couldn't control my movements and some corner of my mind held embarrassment when they both just watched me spasm on the floor. Once I was reduced to merely panting and twitching, Stian shoved a plain metal collar around my neck, attaching the chain to a hook in the wall. Laughable. As if I were going anywhere. "She won't die in the next few hours at any rate." He led the healer out.

My eyes fell shut and I tried to pull the edge of the blanket over me. My limbs were still twitching and Stian had bound my wrists so tightly it was difficult to get a firm hold. Then the bond flooded me with feeling and my heart swelled. I'd get to talk to Wells one last time.

My mate slid into my mind as if I'd called him. *Imogen?*

Hi.

Are you alright?

Tired. Sore. Missing you. But I'm alive.

It won't be long now, Demon. I'm getting you out.

The 'pathing was already draining me. All my kroma was focused on pulling me back from death. I felt myself drifting away again. *Don't . . . worry . . . about me . . . I can take it . . .*

I can't take you taking it, he 'pathed, the soft agony beneath his words tugging at my heart. *I'm going to get you out and I want you to get well, understand?*

His emotions were hauling at my lungs and throat. The strength of his worry tugged at my conscience. His bond hadn't been suppressed. It must have been torture to have it screaming at him this entire time.

How long have I been here?

He pushed a caress down the bond and I leaned into it. *A week, Demon. You've been incredibly strong.*

The corners of my eyes stung, but I was too dehydrated for tears.

I didn't write that letter, they compelled me.

I know, Demon, it's all right.

Did Demian tell you what he told me? I hadn't seen Sephrya's king again. And I hadn't tried to summon him.

Yes. Wells's mental voice hardened. *Again, you have been very strong, Imogen. I love you so much.*

I love you so much. My heart ached as if my fever had cuddled into that one organ. *Is Prism okay?*

He winked to us right after you were pulled from him. He's distraught. Blamed me for not letting him wink around like a dervish, but he's fine.

Tell him to calm down. My mental voice was slurry. *I don't want you to worry about me, Wells. I just want you to . . .* My train of thought fled. I had no reserves.

Just hang on, Imogen. I'll get you out, Demon.

I love . . . you . . .

I couldn't stay awake.

Stian woke me by dragging me upright, using the metal collar around my neck as a handle. The blanket fell away and I immediately missed its scratchy warmth.

"Good morning, darling," he cooed into my face as I struggled to wake up, coughed against the strangling metal cutting into my throat, and tried to find the floor with my feet. "I've got good news for you."

He didn't tell me what the good news was. He shoved on a muting collar and removed the metal one, tossing it to the ground. My limited energy plummeted further. Stian hauled me from the cell. My feet were free, but my hands were still bound in front of me. He insisted on using the collar to steer me. I stumbled after him as best I could, not wanting to give him an excuse to compel me again, but I tripped frequently. When we came to a set of stairs he was forced to support me by my arm to help me climb them. It zapped me so much that he had to continue holding much of my weight as we trudged through endless gray corridors.

After an eternity, he pushed aside a tapestry and dragged me through what looked like the castle's great hall. There were long wooden tables, high vaulted ceilings, and one rough, wooden, throne-like chair against the back wall. Behind and above it was an enormous black pelt surrounded by several others of varying sizes. Even as depleted as I was, I couldn't help wondering what kind of animal those gigantic pelts must have come from. Then I remembered the enormous urzen roaming the forest and shuddered.

I was hustled through the room toward a large set of wooden doors. Another Sephryan guard joined Stian on my other side, grabbing my free arm. They were practically carrying me now. Spots danced in front of my eyes and I sagged against their ungentle grip. This was the most I'd moved in a week.

I blinked against the weak morning sun as we traveled through a muddy courtyard, a distant part of my brain matched the area up with the maps that I had seen. We were in an inner circle. Three in, if I were correct. My captors stopped abruptly, my bare feet smacked against the mud as I fought to remain upright. I couldn't control the shivering that overtook my body. In spite of the heat and humidity, I was freezing.

"We'll wait here until we get the signal, then wink straight out," Stian told the guard.

I glanced around the courtyard. This wasn't the courtyard Cilla and I had escaped from. So they had moved the prisoners farther inside. Perhaps with the threat of siege looming, they'd taken precautions.

A soldier on the heights unfurled a red flag.

"There it is," Stian said. "Hang on, I'll wink us. Be ready in case they try something."

The blackness of the wink lasted less than a blink. We appeared just inside a stone archway. *This* was the courtyard Cilla and I had escaped from. My knees buckled and the Sephryans hauled me back upright. Then I saw him.

Wells, with Jarleth and Kitano flanking him. Standing just feet away within the arch. A line of ten Molnarian soldiers behind them, bows drawn, aiming above and behind us at the Sephryans in the heights of the compound. I noticed Jarleth had glamoured his hair into a dirty blond to avoid being recognized.

Without conscious thought, I leaned toward Wells, my heart pounding, the suppressed bond flailing within me. Stian jerked my arm. "Patience. he's got to come to us."

Wells, Jarleth, and Kitano marched toward us, their faces like stone.

"Do you have it?" Stian asked as they approached.

Wells pulled a hand from his pocket, holding a roll of paper. He snapped it open with a flick of his wrist so that Stian could read it. "Good enough?" His voice was ice.

Stian nodded just as my knees gave way again. They hauled me back to my feet. Wells's eyes found my homemade bandages and fury lit his gaze for an instant before he removed his own cloak and threw it around my shoulders, fastening it under the muting collar. I sighed, once again surrounded by his scent. He cupped my cheek with one hand and the bond purred. Reunited. I closed my eyes and leaned in. "Wells . . ." I breathed. "I'm sorry." I had no idea what he had given up, but I was positive it was momentous. Were we defecting?

He ran his thumb along my cheekbone. "You have nothing to be sorry for, Demon." His voice softened. So drastically different than when he'd spoken to Stian. "I need you to read this. Out loud. Then we'll get you out of here."

I pried open my eyes. He was holding the paper in front of my face. I blinked a few times to focus, still leaning into his palm, then read; "I, Allestair, King of Molnair, hereby forbid Imogen Delaney from using her powers against Sephrya for the duration of the current conflict." I recognized Allestair's angular handwriting.

The Sephryan guard took the paper from Wells, whose expression changed when he placed his hand on my other cheek. Fierce love, anger, and a cutting sort of sadness filtered through the shadowy bond. He lifted my face to his and pressed an achingly gentle kiss to my lips. "I love you, Imogen. I want you to know that it was all worth it to me. Every second that I got to spend with you was worth whatever happens next." He looked Stian in the eye, his face hardening. "I want to see her winked out."

Dread sluiced through my veins. "Wells, what's happening?" I croaked. Stian unlocked the muting collar just as Jarleth and Kitano stepped forward, their eyes tight with pain.

The return of my kroma was barely a cramp this time as I hadn't been under suppression as long. But the bond rushed back to life, the stronger feelings of love swirling together with a resigned determination, and a deep sadness drenched in an aching sense of loss.

Wells gave me one more quick kiss. "Survive, Demon. I want you to live." His hands slid from my face and he stepped away from me.

Fear spiked between my ribs like knives. "Wells..."

Jarleth grabbed my arm as Stian let go. Wells pushed one last brush of affection down the bond, but didn't resist when Stian locked the muting collar around his throat. The guard released my other arm to Kitano as the bond swept into shadow again.

No.

I thrashed against them. My legs gave out as I fought to run back to him. Jarleth and Kitano kept me from falling on my face as they hauled me back toward the Molnarian soldiers. Wells watched them pull me away, slowly shutting his emotions behind that unbreakable neutral mask while the guard shackled his wrists.

"Wells! No! *No!*" My throat tore with the force of my screams. Gray blurred the edges of my vision as I struggled. Panic a living thing clawing at my rib cage. My eyes burned with tears my body couldn't produce. My hands were still bound. The two scouts were now holding me off the ground. No way to get purchase with my feet. I kicked with everything I had. "No! I won't let you! *Wells!*"

They winked me out.

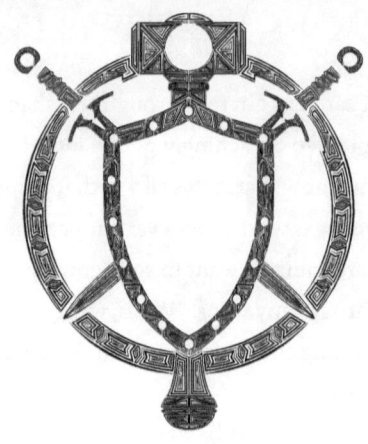

CHAPTER TWENTY-NINE

*I don't think you ever stop loving someone. I'm still in love with Solange.
I'll always love Imogen.
But maybe the way I show that love can change.*
—Prince Aloysius Metellus

I broke from the wink still screaming. Barely registering when we appeared before the camp's shield with the ten Molnarian guards behind us. And no Wells.

They left him. They left *him there.*

And I knew it wouldn't go the way it had with me. They'd interrogate him under compulsion and when that didn't work . . .

Grief and rage ripped through me, leaving no room for anything else. My vision went completely black and still I struggled as they pulled me through the shield. My legs gave out entirely but I continued to screech Wells's name. Demanded to be taken back. Cursed them for leaving him . . .

"I'll take her." Al's voice. I had no physical strength remaining when he hoisted me—still weakly shouting abuse—into his arms. I couldn't see.

My body was limp. My throat raw. I gasped between shrieks as he carried me. "I'm sorry, Im. It's what he wanted. You have to stop screaming or my father is going to make you stop."

He laid me down on the bed that Wells and I had shared only a week ago. He hadn't changed the sheets. Our combined scents hit my nose calling forth a wave of excruciating love and grief. My rage was smothered. My eyes burned with tears. Only none came out. My body sobbed, but my face remained dry.

"All the water in her system is going to her blood vessels." Kerlyn's voice, brisk and competent, but with an undercurrent of strained emotion. "We've got to get her hydrated and those wounds checked. It appears they let her start healing recently, but I'll bet they've been festering the entire time if she'd been under suppression."

Al's hand gently wrapped my forearm, steadying it long enough to cut the bindings on my wrists, then releasing me. My arms simply flopped apart. "What can I do?" he asked.

"I'm going to put her out first," she answered. "I'm surprised she's still conscious."

I felt a wave of cool mint as her kroma washed over me.

When I came to, my belly didn't ache, as if someone had dropped food into my stomach while I was out. I was clean; my hair still slightly damp, in fresh clothes, lying on our bed, with Wells's cloak stretched out beside me. Panic punched me in the chest and I fumbled for the bond. Still there. Shadowy and veiled, but he was alive. Wearing the muting collar most likely.

They could be doing anything to him. Terror shot up my spine. He was the bigger prize. Why kill me when I was a means to kill him? I should have taken Demian's fucking deal.

I pushed myself upright. Everything ached, but differently. I was healing again.

"She's awake."

I turned my head toward the desk as Kerlyn marched toward me, carrying a vial of pink liquid. Al and the king remained on either side of the desk, watching. The king sat in Wells's chair as if he belonged there. Anger smoldered beneath my skin.

Kerlyn tapped my chin. "Open." She held up the vial.

I obediently opened my mouth and let her tip its contents inside. I couldn't see her aura. I couldn't see any of their auras. Still drained.

Kerlyn placed a hand on my forehead and then ran her fingers under my jaw. "Lucky," she said. "An hour or so later and you might not have made it. Those assholes pushed the limit, letting your blood get infected."

"Wells..." I croaked, my voice hoarse from screaming. I swung my legs over the side of the bed.

"Is as good as dead." Allestair stared me down coldly. "When the Sephryans sent their proposal with your blood, he agreed to trade himself for you. I forbade him from revealing several essential pieces of information. Once they realize this, they'll try to break that injunctive with torture. When they don't succeed, they'll kill him."

Allestair stood up from the desk and pulled his coat from behind the chair, as if we were discussing the weather. "As you've been forbidden from fighting them as part of the agreement, you have no more use here. Aloysius and I will be swearing Adgemon in as General of the Armies momentarily. While we do so, you are to pack up your things. You'll be moving onto the ship with Aloysius, to be taken back to the palace."

The fire burned white hot. Rage shot up my spine so paralyzingly quick I couldn't speak.

Allestair looked down at the desk and scraped a few papers together, collecting them into a pile. "Aloysius, get whatever potions you need for the trip from Kerlyn and tell Imogen whatever you think she needs to know." He stalked toward the tent entrance. "Imogen, you're forbidden from leaving this tent unless you are in the company of Aloysius and myself." He smacked the tent flap aside and had a murmured conversation with the guards standing just outside.

I will find a way to hurt you one day, I thought viciously. Wells hadn't told him then, that forbidding didn't affect me. Good. My mating bond began clawing at the walls of my mind and my heart rate picked up.

Kerlyn packed up several vials for Al and tucked written instructions in between them. After making sure he understood them, she crossed briskly to me, gave me a swift hug, then clamped her hands on my shoulders, and looked me in the eye. "I'm a 'path away if you ever need to talk. Anytime. I know what it's like—" Her mouth tightened and her eyes shone. She straightened and strode swiftly from the tent.

Some of my internal fire shuddered, grief twisting within it, coating my stomach in a painful ache.

Al crossed over and sat down carefully next to me. As if the bed might break beneath us if he moved too fast. He stared at his hands. "Just so you know, I'm not going to make you do anything you don't want to do. Ever."

I grabbed his arm. "Al, I can't leave him there." My voice broke.

"What do you think you can do, Im?" His amber eyes were shadowed and bleak when they found mine. "You've been forbidden to fight them. And even if you weren't, you couldn't break into that compound on your own and get him out. They'd just have both of you then and make you each watch while they killed the other one." His face tightened. "Or force you into some unholy Sephryan slave contract."

Make him help, make him help! We die if our mate dies! the bond screamed. It was so much worse now that it wasn't suppressed. How Wells had withstood a week I didn't know. I swallowed, felt myself trembling. "Al, I don't want to live if he dies. I can't—"

He spun around and grabbed my wrists, his eyes shining. "Yes you can. I'm here to tell you that you can." His throat bobbed. "Wells knew what was going to happen to him, Im, and he walked into it so that you would have a life. You don't toss that kind of gift away." He dropped one wrist and tugged the silver chain around my neck, popping the Augur stone out from beneath my shirt. "He told me about this, too. You've got to try to survive, Im. Think of Prism. Your unicorn has been frantic, Im."

Allestair stepped back into the tent. "Aloysius, if you have everything you need, go prepare Adgemon. I'll speak to Imogen before she packs up her things."

Al brushed a hand down my arm as he stood. "It'll be okay, Im. I'm here for you."

As soon as Al was gone, Allestair fixed his icy stare on me. "Imogen, you will not speak, I forbid it. Just as I forbid you from leaving that seat until I say otherwise."

He snagged Wells's chair, dragging it from behind his desk and slamming it down in front of me. My fingers dug into the edge of the mattress as I trembled with barely contained rage.

Allestair settled into the chair, fixing his piercing gaze on me. "I forbid you from uttering one word of what I am about to say to anyone else. You and I are about to come to an understanding."

I pulled deep breaths in through my nose, keeping my jaw clenched shut.

"You have delayed the end of this war and flaunted your will for the last time, Imogen." He folded his arms and leaned into the backrest. Eyes never leaving mine. "You are now learning the hard way that I am not to be defied, and I want to ensure that this lesson sticks."

My brows furrowed. I had delayed the end of the war?

"Demian and I came to an agreement weeks ago. He would eliminate your mate and I would gift him one of our ships to examine at his leisure."

I sucked in a gasp and one corner of Allestair's mouth lifted in a cold smile.

"I never promised him a new ship. He can take one of our oldest. It's fit for nothing but the museum as it is. I'll allow Aloysius to take credit for negotiating the peace treaty. He's already beloved by our people. Once he's seen as Molnair's savior, working through his own grief at the loss of his brother, the people will rejoice when, after an appropriate amount of time has passed, he weds Llewellyn's mate. After nurturing her through her own heart-wrenching grief."

It took every ounce of willpower I possessed to remain seated, to keep from screaming at him. Demian was going to kill Wells for a ship. Had the deal he'd been offering me even been legit? Or just a way to get his hands on my mate with less effort?

"Had you not thwarted my initial plans, the war would have ended weeks ago. How do you think the Sephryans were continually finding Llewellyn's unit? I've been informing Demian of his movements for months." He flicked a speck of dirt from his knee. "He is a talented general to have survived, and nearly laid siege in spite of it. And he certainly is popular. It's a shame to lose him, but I felt that you needed a more intense lesson to fall in line, Imogen."

He would kill Wells to break me. My stomach wrenched at the ruthlessness even as my blood boiled. I had never hated anyone so fiercely in my life.

"Once Llewellyn dies, your bond will be severed and we'll all know it. The pain will make it obvious. I'll have Aloysius go to Demian then." He stood, shoving the chair back toward the desk. "Until then, we wait." He strolled toward the entrance. "You may leave your seat in order to pack your things, but I think I'd rather like you to remain silent for a bit longer." He left.

I shot up from the bed, grabbed Wells's light cloak and fastened it around my shoulders with shaking fingers. *Yes, yes, go, save him*, the bond urged. Heart beating quickly I searched the tent until I'd found where they'd stashed our weapons. All the time wracking my brain for an idea. Al was right, I couldn't hope to take the entire compound on my own. This was not the time for Impulsive Imogen.

I forced myself to stand still for a moment and consider my options. One: Do what I was told and stay here. Negative. I could not let Wells die in my place. Two: Find people to help me. Even when I made a mental list of who I might convince to fight with me, the number was unimpressive. Even counting Prism among them. He was always up for a fight but even his bloodthirst couldn't blast through walls. Three: Negotiate directly with Demian. See if that offer was still on the table.

I paused, thinking that through. I didn't know how to contact Demian, so it would mean me basically walking back to the compound and giving myself up. And what could I even offer him at this point? They had Wells out of the way and—as far as they knew—I couldn't attack them either. No reason to put us up in a seaside chateau. And I doubted that offer had been anything other than a ruse. I had no ships to give Demian.

I started moving again. I couldn't wait around here.

The bond quieted now that I was taking action, even though I didn't know what exactly that action would be, but my hands shook as I assembled weapons for both of us. Losing Wells would demoralize the entire army. They'd bring pieces of him out onto the battlefield. *Stop it*, I told myself firmly and shoved those images away as I stomped into a spare set of boots.

I plunked the potions and instructions into my little pack, along with my most precious things and a few scraps of clothing. I didn't know where I was going. I didn't know when or if I'd be back. I nearly 'pathed Prism, but stopped. I needed a plan before I endangered anyone else and I probably wouldn't be able to stop him from winking to me if he knew I was conscious. Not to mention hauling around a purple unicorn was anything but discreet.

I shimmied beneath the back wall of the tent where I knew it butted up against another; the front entrance was likely guarded, forbidden or not. Then I strapped on both Wells's swords, with daggers in my boots for each of us. I'd brought my remaining two grenades in a pouch on my belt and four exploding arrows.

I still hadn't a clue what I was going to do when I laboriously hauled a cloaking shield up and slipped between the tents to the warded edge. *Desperate times call for desperate measures . . . These are desperate times . . . I can't be stupid though. Al is right. I can't throw Wells's sacrifice in his face by getting caught again. What good would it do? C'mon, Imogen, think, there has to be a secret fourth option . . .*

As soon as I reached the wards, I sensed that Allestair had changed them. Only someone of the Blood could get through without permission. A grim smirk pulled one corner of my mouth upward as I pushed through.

On the other side, I took a breath and gazed at the horizon. An idea sparked instantly. A desperate one.

I could absolutely *die*, I thought. Before I could think too hard, before I could talk myself out of it, I let my cloaking shield drop and winked.

I appeared in front of the Briarwood Forest, its blood-red trees swaying ominously in the wind. I drew one sword and marched between the rusty trunks.

CHAPTER THIRTY

*Here's the thing about looking before you leap:
if you look too long it just makes the ledge seem higher.*
—Imogen Delaney

T he silence of the woods engulfed me.

I barely breathed, creeping soundlessly between the trees. Every fiber of my being on high alert. The foliage grew dense immediately, blocking out the sun within a few paces. I scanned the space between the trunks, seeing nothing. My stomach fizzed with ever-increasing nerves. Then the spider-fine hairs on the back of my neck lifted.

Get off the ground.

I obeyed my gut and leapt for the nearest tree just as a massive shadow tore into the space of earth I had occupied. A spike of raw adrenaline had me scrambling several branches higher before my brain caught up. Hearing nothing behind me, I dared to pause, my free hand locked around the next branch just in case. Balancing in a half-crouch, fingernails biting into my sword hilt, I peered between the leafy boughs to the forest floor. My gaze locked onto two yellow, slitted eyes floating just above a row of sharp, gleaming teeth. A snarl, rumbling like the engine of a vintage Corvette, thrummed from the dark shadow. I felt the vibration in my chest.

My shoulders tensed. Here goes.

I've been looking for you. My name is Imogen, I 'pathed the shadow.

Looking for me . . . A voice darker than the blackest cave scraped across my mind. *Interesting. Why do you seek your death in my forest, child?*

I don't seek death just yet. I wanted to see if you were interested in . . . an opportunity. Wells would be so angry at me if I died. I really hadn't thought this through at all. "Classic Imogen" Keane would have called it. All leaping, no looking.

No, this was different. I *had* tried to think this through. The reality of it was I was out of options and out of time. If Wells lived to be angry with me, I would bask in the glow of his fury.

I waited for an answer, every muscle tense. The branch I balanced on quivered beneath my trembling legs. My hand sweated around the hilt of my sword.

The shadow circled the trunk of my tree. Powerful shoulders shifting beneath her midnight coat. *It has steel but does not strike. It has sticks but does not shoot. It walks willingly into my home and speaks not of death, but opportunity. Curious.*

I told you my name. Can I not learn yours? I willed my shoulders to relax. Nervous was okay. Nervous was expected. Probably even respectful. But I didn't want fear coating my scent.

Im o ginnnn . . . the shadow strung out my name as if she were tasting each syllable. *My name is Varger. I am leader of the urzen. I will hear your . . . opportunity. Then I shall decide whether to cut you down and make a meal of you. Your ilk have not been friends.*

I cautiously sank into a crouch on the branch to give my legs a change of position. *Do you know of the walled city not far from here?* I was still far from full strength. My arm ached but I didn't dare sheath my blade just yet.

A growl like rolling thunder vibrated the tree beneath me. *Of course I know of this cursed city.* Varger snapped at the air beneath me, long white fangs flashing. *It has done nothing but take. Every pup I have whelped knows to stay far away.* She coiled her haunches beneath her, crouching low below my branch as if preparing to spring up and pluck me from the tree like low-hanging fruit. *Why do you speak to me of this ... city?*

I swallowed. While her hatred of the capital worked for me, her dislike of my entire species—plus her ready-to-leap position—had apprehension knotting the space between my shoulder blades. Still, there was nothing to do but go for it now.

Would you like to get inside? To ... destroy? You and your friends. Do you have a large ... pack? I hoped she had a lot of family. I didn't know what kind of powers the urzen had, but I didn't think even Varger and I together could take the entire compound.

There are hundreds of us, child. Varger rumbled deep in her chest. I supposed it could be a chuckle. A terrifying one. I swore I felt it rattle up the tree to the soles of my feet.

My brain spun, concocting and rejecting ideas to get even one of the urzen inside. Much less hundreds ... *The more the merrier,* I 'pathed, as the bones of a plan solidified. *I can get you all inside.*

Her enormous, surprisingly fluffy tail, thrashed back and forth. Her lantern-like eyes narrowed. *Why would you do this?*

They have my mate. My lungs shuddered. The bond had been gouging holes in my proverbial insides as if to urge me on. Even I heard the anguish in my 'path. *They will kill him.*

Varger straightened out of her crouch. She dropped her head, her luminous golden eyes staring off into the distance, as if watching a horrific scene play out before her. Her lips peeled back in a snarl. Talons crept from the sheaths of her paws, ever lengthening until they cut gouges in the earth beneath her. *They took my mate as well ... dumped his carcass without his skin ... we could not finish the death ceremony. He now wanders the afterlife with no coat.* Her head snapped back, nose pointed skyward, she released an anguished howl. My entire body erupted in goosebumps as a resounding chorus of howls answered her from every shadowy corner of the forest. I was surrounded by urzen.

Your people beg us to respect your dead when you desecrate ours! she snarled. *Every urzen that has had the misfortune of being killed by your kind has been stripped of skin. Their final rites forever denied.*

I remembered that day on the battlefield. Wells begging them to respect our dead. My heart thundered in my ears as I wrenched my focus back to Varger. *I believe I have seen urzen pelts. In the innermost building. Decorating the palace walls. You could get them all back...* My entire body was vibrating. There was no disguising it. The crimson leaves surrounding me trembled.

The howling ceased. Varger's predatory gaze locked on me. *Do you lie to me, Imogen?*

No. There are giant black pelts strung up like trophies. I swallowed against my sandpaper dry mouth, then risked sheathing my sword. *I was held prisoner in the capital. When I was near-death. my mate traded his life for mine. As the Sephryans dragged me out, I saw them. Hanging on a wall above the throne. One very big one at the center and others arranged around it. Unless there's another being with similar—*

Urzen fur is unique. You would not mistake it, and Skoll's was very large. My mate was the strongest of us. Varger's mental voice grated with an unmistakable growl. She sat back on her haunches and angled her massive head upward, training her lamp-like eyes on me once more. *When shall we go, Imogen?*

As soon as possible, I said, my pulse quickening with something other than fear. *I don't know how long they will keep my mate alive.*

Come down, Imogen, and let me smell you. Once I have your scent, I can convey it to all of the urzen and they will know not to kill you.

It was, perhaps, the most frightening thing I've ever done. But all I had to do was touch the shadowy bond howling within me and remind myself that every second I hesitated brought me closer to its extinction. I took a breath, then forced myself to step off the branch. I dropped down in front of Varger.

She was taller than me by twelve inches. She could have crushed my skull with a swipe of her tire-sized paw. I stood, straight-backed, arms at my sides, my fingers unintentionally curling into fists when she extended her snout toward me, the tips of her fangs gleaming wetly on either side of her lower jaw. Her juniper-and-pine scented breath pushed my hair back as she sniffed.

Very well. Let us go, Imogen. You may tell me of your plan as we walk.

My knees went watery as she stepped back. I forced a smile. *Sure. One more thing . . . do you think the urzen could work with a unicorn?*

I 'pathed Prism at the edge of the forest. The extensive berating he gave me pulled the first genuine smile onto my face since I'd been taken. The little fucker actually cared. I told him I was going to rescue Wells and asked if he could wink to me. To my surprise, Obsidian came along.

He wishes to retrieve his rider, Prism told me with a toss of his charcoal mane.

My chest ached a bit and I pushed a smile toward Obsidian as I extended my 'path to include him after receiving permission via Prism. *Good, great. Absolutely, we can use all the help we can get. So . . . this next part will be a little weird, but I want you to keep an open mind regarding the urzen.*

Both unicorns flattened their ears to their heads, rolled their eyes, and lifted their snouts.

Listen, they're going to help us. Okay? Don't freak out. They have issues with the Sephryans also.

Varger stalked to the tree line, yellow eyes glowing, pupils narrowing to naught but slits as she entered the light. *I must scent them.*

She needs to get your scent so that her pack knows not to . . . attack you. Okay?

After a lot of unicorn histrionics, Prism and Obsidian allowed Varger close enough to glean their scent. I shoved one of the remaining blocks from my original stash down my throat—mentally blessing Captain Marc's heart in the most genuine sense of the phrase—and tossed back another of Kerlyn's potions after checking the instructions.

I needed to be as hale as possible, but I had to wait before summoning lightning. The darkening sky was a clear blue. I couldn't risk the crack of a thunderstorm alerting an attentive watch. They all believed me forbidden to attack them, but my hasty plan hinged on keeping it that way for as long as possible.

May I leave a few things in your forest until we return? I asked Varger. My pack with potions and spare clothes would only be extra weight. As would Wells's cloak.

You may, she answered. *If you are true to your word, you need never fear my home again, Imogen.*

I thanked her and hung my items on a branch several paces back from the tree line. I didn't think any sidhe would dare venture that far in. The blocks I kept with me, tucked into a deep jacket pocket. I vaulted onto Prism's back using a low hanging limb as a swing.

"Alright." Jangling with nerves, I patted Prism's neck. "I've been mostly dead all week, time to storm the castle."

CHAPTER THIRTY-ONE

Never underestimate the fierce, undying love of a mated pair.
Even death cannot kill that devotion.
   —Captain Marcellus Tibercio

W*hy do you not charge your weapons?* Prism questioned every aspect of my plan. At the very least it gave me some insight into why Wells expected blind obedience from his soldiers and his exasperation with my need to understand every detail.

It's a clear, sunny afternoon. Evening. Whatever. I replied, my hands knotted into his mane, a physical manifestation of clinging to my patience. *If a lightning bolt splits the sky, the Sephryans will know it's from me and we lose the element of surprise. No lightning until we've breached the compound.*

I assumed that Prism explained anything necessary to Obsidian. I'd directed my 'paths to both of them at first, but when Obsidian never responded I stopped, wary of overstepping my bounds. The last thing I needed was another breech of unicorn etiquette. The stone archway where I had last seen Wells loomed larger in the distance. It was currently closed with an enormous, crank-operated, drawbridge-type door that appeared to have been crafted from the macabre-colored Briarwood Forest trees. Very medieval. The only thing missing was a moat. Although this was disappointing to my fantasy aesthetic, it made logistics slightly easier.

I checked in with Varger. *I'll need to put up the glamour and shield soon. Does everyone understand what's happening?*

We understand, she replied, her flinty mental voice sparking with anticipation. *I have explained our role and the limitations of your powers.*

"Limitations." I kept my internal eye rolling to myself. Cloaking an entire pack of urzen—and Obsidian— as well as glamouring Prism and myself was not "small" kroma. But the urzen had to be still until my signal. I wouldn't be able to cloak them all while they charged. I just hoped I had the energy to do what was necessary to get us inside that first ring. Then I could summon some lightning. As it was, I'd had to borrow from my unicorn.

Ready, Prism?

Oh, very well. Prism snorted and tossed his head.

It's not for long. I don't much like my disguise either. And hey, if this works, you'll get your wish and be the first to breach the compound. I turned my kroma onto Prism first, glamouring him down to a bay horse. From a distance, it should even look like he was wearing a saddle. Then I worked on myself, glamouring generic Sephryan features so that I could pass as a messenger from another part of their lands. My disguise wouldn't need to bear close scrutiny, I only needed them to lower that first drawbridge.

Disguises in place, I threw up a wide cloaking shield and stretched it out behind me. Perspiration instantly beaded my hairline. Prism pushed more energy my way so that we could haul the shield forward. The urzen trotted behind it, sporting ghastly anticipatory grins. I felt the drag as if it were physically pulling at my body, and sucked in long deep breaths. It wouldn't matter if it looked as though I were breathing hard.

I knew enough from listening to Jarleth and Kitano to have glamoured myself in the colors of a nearby Sephryan township. Far enough away to not be in constant communication, but near enough so that a solitary messenger wouldn't be questioned. I raised a scrap of cloth on a stick, glamoured to look like the orange banner that would indicate an urgent message.

The pack stopped moving at my signal. I didn't want to risk the glimmer of the shield giving me away. We were close enough now. Prism and I galloped up to the drawbridge. He kept his pace to an easy canter and I hoped to hell I'd done enough to blur his size.

I waved my flag with what I hoped was a convincing sense of urgency. Sweat now ran down my spine in rivulets. The strain on my already limited energy was palpable. I prayed there wasn't a lengthy debate among the guards. I was going to need to summon lightning soon to get us any farther. Prism rolled to a halt to the right of the obvious divot in the dirt caused by repeated droppings of the heavy wooden bridge.

Perfect, I told him, still breathing heavily. *If they open for us, this angle should be just right.*

Take more energy if you need it. Prism's coat twitched when a drop of perspiration landed on his withers.

I'll be able to recharge once we're in, I told him, my arms aching from swinging the flag. *Fucking look, asswipes.*

I continued to slice the glamoured strip of cloth through the air, my hair now damp and curling at the neck. If they didn't let us in, what was I going to tell the urzen? I'd have hundreds of angry, rhino-sized wolves to deal with. Classic Imogen. My limbs trembled with effort and anxiety.

The heavy groaning of wood shifting away from stone had my heart lifting and relief drenching my stomach. *Get ready,* I 'pathed Varger. The rumble of her growl rolled across our mental link. The bridge inched toward the ground at an agonizingly slow crawl. Arms and shoulders burning, I dropped the flag, holding it loosely across my lap. I kept it glamoured and forced myself to wait. That bridge had to come all the way down. I watched as the wooden planks dropped closer and closer. When they were inches from the ground, Prism got fidgety.

Wait for it... I told him, rallying the dregs of my energy for what was to come. I needed to focus carefully. With four inches to go, I dropped the flag and unslung my bow. By the time the bridge hit the dirt and the chains slackened, I had nocked one of my arrows. I let it fly. Igniting it just before it found its mark. The winch exploded.

I ripped off the cloaking shield and dropped the glamour.

The urzen, the unicorns, and I charged in.

I let Prism blast away with his horn as I called the lightning to me. I kept a 'path open to him and Varger. Orders to her pack bled through.

Don't feed! Kill only! You may feed later! The urzen obeyed her, tossing Sephryans about like ragdolls. I ignored the turning of my stomach, thrusting my arm into the air. A bolt of lightning tunneled to my fist as I urged Prism to the next heavy wooden drawbridge. We had two more levels to breach. Wells was in the innermost, I was certain.

Lightning swept through me. My energy soared, my very bones sighing in relief. I gripped Prism tighter with my knees, jerked my fist from the sky, drew Wells's sword and used it to cannon my lightning toward the heavy door. It hit with a reverberating crack that I felt in my bones. A jagged fissure in the wood split it down the center, but didn't fall. The urzen leapt for it, tearing with teeth and claws. I sheathed the sword and drew an arrow.

Tell them to fall back from the door! I 'pathed Varger. The canines immediately retreated. I nocked the arrow, catching the rhythm of Prism's stride for two breaths, then let it fly. It landed right in the split, exploding one second later. With a thunderous boom that even had Prism flinching, the two halves of the door dropped farther apart. The urzen fell upon them with cutting talons and glossy dark fur over rippling muscles. They took them the rest of the way down.

First two circles breached in a matter of seconds.

Prism plunged forward and I barely grabbed his mane in time. The urzen created beautiful chaos. Obsidian wreaked his own personal havoc.

If I'd had the luxury, I would have spent more time watching him. It was obvious he took Wells's capture personally. Riderless, he impaled dozens of Sephryans with his nearly five-foot horn and blasted several more with dark, glittering flames. It was cathartic as hell.

But we had to be quick.

It wasn't just Wells I had to rescue, I had to get the urzen their friends' pelts. Slinging my bow across my shoulder, I leaned over Prism's rocking crest, keeping him focused on our goal. He accomplished plenty of conquest along the way.

I'd never raced Prism, but when I told him we needed speed, he stretched out. Wind screamed in my ears as I crouched over his withers, my head to one side of his neck, my hair mixing with his mane. Tears streamed directly from my eyes into the air as we tore into the next courtyard, Varger charging at our side.

Word of our breach had obviously spread. Defenses were tighter here. I was forced to pull my own weapons rather than letting urzen and the unicorns clear a path. I could no longer keep an eye on Obsidian and hoped he stayed with us.

Dear God, I've stolen two unicorns from the king. He's going to kill me. I couldn't bring myself to worry too much. Allestair's disregard for Wells's life boiled my blood. I'd get Wells out and we'd run the fuck away as far as I was concerned. Go be hermits somewhere Allestair couldn't find us. And fuck Demian also.

Prism spewed a short blast of rainbow radiation to our front. The urzen had already learned to stay to the flank or rear of both unicorns. I could tell the unicorns were being careful not to hit the urzen and I had a sneaking suspicion they were even communicating.

The urzen were everywhere, so I couldn't use my explosives. I drew Wells's other sword and shot my remaining lightning down both blades until I had exhausted my stored electricity. I had to risk summoning another bolt from the sky. My blood heated, my fingers and scalp tingling dangerously, but I ignored them. I wouldn't be able to pull lightning once we were inside. My body would have a nice break while I found and rescued Wells and the other Molnarian prisoners.

Prism leapt over a hastily constructed barricade with a disdainful snort. The final drawbridge was in sight. This one *did* have a moat. I took a breath and leaned back to ease Prism out of his run. I'd have to take it down a little differently.

Prism, Varger, I'm going to call the wind. Cover me as best you can. I sent Prism a quick visual of my plan; something we'd only started doing recently as our bond solidified. My heart hammered in my ears.

I don't like it, Prism said, swinging his massive head from right to left, blasting a swath of Sephryans into varying degrees of injury and death with sparkling flames. *But I will shield.*

Varger didn't bother to answer. She just did as asked. Her urzen surged nearer, taking out any Sephryans that focused on me.

I had never called the wind in the middle of a battle before. My stomach sparked with prickly doubt. A fresh wave of sweat sprang from my pores.

You called it when you escaped that cursed palace, I told myself. *Wells needs you. Get your shit together.*

I gritted my teeth and pulled my knees up on Prism's wide back. I stood slowly, putting one foot on his withers and the other just before his haunches, balanced as best I could, both swords drawn. Turmoil roiled around me. Sephrya had figured out who I was by now and they were desperate to get to me. My guts tightened as I watched them slice at the urzen.

Focus, Prism cut in. *Obsidian fights for his rider.*

Obsidian hadn't left the drawbridge. He fought like a dervish. Spinning, blasting, kicking, even biting. And he was being overwhelmed. Wells would lose his unicorn. *Get it together, Imogen.*

I shut my eyes, trusting Prism and the urzen to defend me. And called the wind.

There was nothing.

The humid air was stagnant and still.

My heart stutter-stepped.

Then ... a puff of air. My hair lifted from my face. I breathed, shoulders dropping, found that small thread and coaxed it forward. The wind cradled me, my feet lifted away from Prism. Once I was stable enough, I opened my eyes, used some precious energy to shield, and climbed higher. In spite of my defenders, a few shots of kroma and well-aimed projectiles bounced off my weak barriers.

I dropped the wind just above the battlements and landed, stumbling, but forced myself upright.

Sephryans charged me from both directions.

I yanked an arrow from my quiver, spun, and dropped to one knee as I released it, high, arching toward most of the guard. I hardened my heart as I ignited it, obliterating their walkway—and probably most of them—before I twisted and threw a short blast of lightning in the opposite direction.

Panting, I pushed to my feet again. I'd saved most of my dwindling energy for the crank. I had to lower this drawbridge.

Unfortunately, they'd learned quickly. The assholes down below were shielding it.

My first blast wasn't a direct hit. For a moment I considered just charging in on my own, grabbing Wells, and getting the hell out of there.

I ducked down behind the battlements and thrust my hand into my pocket, teasing out another block. I couldn't take much more lightning without a break and if I kept this up I was going to burn out fast.

I popped the block.

Then took a chance and summoned one short blast of lightning. My blood boiled, even my skin heating as if I'd been sunburned. This was it. I called the wind once again, forced my feet onto the wall—ignoring the tingling up my legs at the proximity to the sheer edge—then leapt off the battlements into the courtyard below. The wind caught me as I swung both swords around and tossed out an arc of lightning.

The Sephryans charging me writhed in the throes of electrocution. I yanked my eyes away from them, swallowed against a rush of nausea, and turned to the cranks supporting the drawbridge. I flung my arms wide, extending one sword toward each of them, hauled up everything I had in reserve, and blasted.

I shoved the energy from me in a rush, a roar rolling up from my chest. I lost the wind a few feet from the ground. My knees cracked into the muddy earth but I managed to keep my lightning going. My shoulders tensing, arms shaking, breath peeling in and out of my lungs.

The chains released all at once. *Wait until I stop*, I 'pathed.

The drawbridge swung down with a rumble and a crack. But I had to keep it open. We'd need a way out.

I kept pushing. My entire body vibrating. My clothes plastered to my skin. I forced my lungs to suck down longer breaths.

The chain on one winch cracked.

Then the entire hub collapsed and melted. Good enough. I sliced off my last bolt, yanking the remaining lightning back. I'd need to save it, I couldn't risk calling more without a substantial break. If I passed out here, Wells and I were both done for.

The urzen charged the bridge, Prism and Obsidian at the lead. I warned them to bank to their left, then used my remaining arrow to take out the final crank.

I unstrung my bow as I ran, shoving it into my empty quiver as I pushed my legs to keep Prism in sight. Thankfully, Varger shoved her tombstone-sized snout beneath me and tossed me onto my unicorn's back.

I belly flopped onto his withers, a grunt punching from my throat, hooked my fingers into his mane and yanked myself upright, urging him faster. Varger and her four eldest sons followed me and the two unicorns as we tore into the keep. The urzen went first, tearing out throats and causing general mayhem. I simply told Varger when to change direction.

My mating bond was still muted—they had that collar on Wells, then—but I could sense we were getting nearer. Eventually flashes of recognition flared. I knew these horrid corridors. We had to be close.

The urzen spared no one. It was an effort to close my heart to each messy death. They were all quick, but they were not quiet or neat. And Varger and her sons tossed the bodies aside as if they were so many sacks of grain. I riveted my focus to the bond, to driving us in the right direction.

I recognized the hallway I'd been dragged down. We were heading toward the larger group prison where I had been held.

And the torture chamber next door.

My throat closed even as I warned Prism, Obsidian, and Varger. I was certain Wells was being tortured.

But that made it easier. All the killing we did on the way. Remembering what they had done to me, those captured Molnairians, and what Wells was going through now.

The metallic scent of his blood hit the back of my tongue before we reached the door.

Obsidian must have smelled it as well. He surged ahead. Reached the door before us. Backed up to it and with one rippling crash of his hind legs, rammed it off its hinges. One strike. Prism and I flew into the room.

My entire body went numb. My empathy fled. I was stone. The black creature within me took over completely.

Wells was strapped down to the table, paler than I'd ever seen him. Muting collar still pressing into his white throat. His eyes glassy and vacant. His fingers swollen and bent at all angles. Stian and Elric stood above him holding bloody implements.

Stian's eyes found mine.

"Tables have turned." My voice was a rusty growl. The urzen stalked through the door, lantern eyes glowing malevolently. I spoke aloud as I 'pathed. "Varger, I want the dagger off the gold one, but these two are yours."

The words had barely left my mouth when Varger's sons sprang on Stian and Elric. I barely heard their shrieks as I slid off Prism in a haze. My entire world slowed down.

Frame by frame I crossed the small room.

The gory weapons in the Sephryans' hands were nothing to the urzen. Their fangs pierced Stian and Elric's flesh, blood flying in my periphery, their screams a distant echo in ears filled with a growing roar as I rushed toward Wells.

My eyes skipped around; his pale face, broken hands, his bloodied feet . . . The urzen hauled the Sephryans away, revealing what was left of Wells.

They had eviscerated him.

CHAPTER THIRTY-TWO

As a mother, I hate being left behind while my children hurtle toward danger. But sometimes I think it might be a blessing to be ignorant of the worst of it until after it's finished.
—Queen Iphigenia Eigneachan Metellus

I threw myself forward as if the next few seconds could reverse what had been done. My palms smacked against the stone table at his side. His intestines dangled over the lip like bloody ropes. I choked back vomit, my fingers gripping the edge, and forced myself to his head.

"Wells." My voice cracked.

His eyes shifted.

He was still alive.

"Wells! No . . ." I took his face in my hands. His eyes focused on me, but there was no change of expression. Nothing to indicate mental awareness. Panic bled through my numbness. The dark creature vanished in a puff of smoke. "Prism!" I all but shrieked. "Get this off him." I yanked at the muting collar. "Prism, get this off him!"

Moisture stung my eyes as Prism's solid presence warmed my side. I blinked it back as he touched his horn to the collar. It glowed briefly, then unlatched. I ripped it off and flung it away.

No change.

Other than the bond roaring back to life and with it, echoes of Wells's pain twisting through me. I nearly dropped to my knees. My stomach clenched and I bit my tongue to keep from retching as his agony swirled through me. I dropped my forehead to his shoulder and took deep breaths. *This is just pain that's not even yours, you need to move through it.* I lifted my head and tried to glance at the damage.

My throat closed. *Why didn't I learn healing? Why didn't I spend any time trying to learn how to heal someone? What the fuck is wrong with me?* I grabbed his hand then gasped and switched my grip when his bones moved all wrong. "Wells, you have to stay. Tell me what to do. I can help just tell me how..."

His eyes rolled back.

I gently released his mangled hand. Heart pounding hard enough to bruise my ribs, I fumbled at his neck, my bloodied fingers pressing against his clammy skin. There. A pulse. But so slow and weak. Helplessness swept through me. I couldn't move him like this. I'd arrived just in time to watch him die.

One sob broke from my throat.

A voice like a midnight wind swept into my mind. *Put his guts back in. Do it now.*

Obsidian.

I turned toward Wells's wreck of an abdomen. I felt the blood leach from my face and fought the wave of faintness crashing over me. "My... my hands are dirty..." My trembling voice came out in a whisper. I tried to wipe my palms on the inside of my shirt.

DO IT NOW.

Saliva drenched my mouth as my stomach turned over. I clamped my teeth onto my tongue and held my breath as I picked up my mate's innards and carefully lifted them back into his body. *I'm sorry, I'm sorry, I'm sorryI'msorryimsorryimsorry...*

Obsidian shoved me aside with his head. *Look away.*

I jerked my gaze to Wells's face, fighting the rolling nausea. I pressed my forehead against his. So clammy. My eyes burned. "Wells... stay... please, please stay..." A light behind me glowed brighter and brighter. My eyes slammed shut just before it went blinding. Throughout it all, I held two fingers to Wells's pulse point. So slow. So faint.

"Stay with me." Eyes closed, I pressed my lips to his.

It was like kissing someone in a coma. Or someone dead. "You can't give up, Wells." My eyelids burned. The light behind me intensified. "Wells, please, *please* stay."

Prism broke into my thoughts.

Varger says there are many Sephryan soldiers blocking off our exits. She says we must hurry. They are throwing kroma which she and her sons cannot block.

My teeth clenched so hard my jaw ached. I wanted to tell them all to go to hell. That I didn't care if any of us got out of here if Wells died. But I kept those thoughts locked in the back of my mind and sectioned off a part of my heart. I'd made promises. Keeping hold of Wells, I 'pathed Prism.

Put up whatever shields you can. Go next door. Let Varger sniff all the Molnairians before you free them so they don't freak out and run away before she gets a chance. Take these blocks. Keeping one hand on Wells, I pulled one block from my remaining store, tucked it into my pocket, then handed the rest to Prism. He took the wrapping delicately between his teeth. *Have everyone in there take one. If there are any left, bring them back.*

I felt more than heard Prism and Varger sweep from the room. Two of her sons, Drauf and Ganger, remained with us. Wells's pulse beat stronger. The light behind me dimmed. I risked a glance back.

Obsidian had marked Wells.

A jagged, shimmering, black scar crossed Wells's now intact torso from the bottom of his left rib cage to his right hip. But he was alive. While I ran careful fingers over Wells's belly, Obsidian healed his feet, then instructed me to lift his mangled hands and hold them just so. My joints went watery, but I forced myself to keep breathing while Obsidian repaired the damage. I wondered how much this drained him.

When he finished, I put a hand on the unicorn's forehead, just below his horn. "Thank you." My heart ached with relief and gratitude. I tried to push everything I felt into those two words.

Go help Prism. Obsidian's dark voice swirled around my mind. *I'll fix his legs and try to revive him enough to move.*

I didn't want to leave my mate, but I knew we had to go. I held up the block I had saved. *Get him to eat this if you can.*

He can't eat anything solid this soon, Obsidian responded.

Fuck, of course. I shoved the block in my pocket. I'd figure something out later.

I couldn't resist brushing Wells's damp crimson hair back from his forehead. I pressed a soft kiss to his unresponsive lips. His eyes tracked me now, even if they still lacked the light of recognition behind them. "I'll be right back." I tucked his hair behind his ears. Kissed him again, hating to tear myself away, even for a moment. "Obsidian will take care of you." I wasn't sure if I were reassuring Wells or myself.

I forced myself to turn from him and sprint into the hallway with Varger's two sons flanking me. We were immediately blasted with a rainbow array of kromatic attacks.

I threw up a shield just in time and we rolled into the next room. Fortunately, the captured Molnairians seemed to trust the unicorn even as they appeared terrified of the urzen. Prism had freed almost everyone and they were all chewing on blocks.

"Alright, listen up, everyone," I said, trying to calm my breathing and project some semblance of authority. "We're surrounded right now and I'm going to need anyone who can to shield themselves. If you can't shield yourself, move near someone who can. Let's protect each other. Move away from the near wall."

Obsidian, can you shield yourself and Wells? I'm going to do an explosive thing.

Done.

"This is Varger, leader of the urzen. Once we're done here, her sons," I gestured to Drauf and Ganger, "will lead you to a place where you can wink back to camp. You're going to see a lot of dead Sephryans, but as long as Varger has your scent, none of the urzen will harm you. They're our friends."

I stepped to the door. *Prism, Obsidian, shields up!* "Everyone, shields up!"

I pulled my remaining grenades from their pouch, lit one with a snap and 'ported it as far to the right as I could see, lit the other and 'ported it left. Shut the door and shielded just as both blasts rocked the hallway, one second apart.

Absently swiping bits of mortar and dust from my arms, I pelted into the next room, dodging a few dislodged stones, Prism on my heels. Obsidian knelt on his forelegs before Wells, who had collapsed in a sitting position on the floor, leaning against the torture table.

He can't ride on his own, Prism told me. *You'll need to get him onto Obsidian. Find a way to keep him there.*

We must hurry, Varger said, dropping my sheathed, bloody dagger at my feet. *We do not do our best fighting inside of these insidious walls.*

"Okay, okay..." I looked wildly around the room. My gaze landed on a coil of cord, the same kind that had been used to restrain me. "Let's tie him to me. We'll both have to ride one of you. Who will it be?"

You may ride Obsidian today, Prism said. *His rider needs him more. I will clear the way ahead of you and you may speak to me.*

"All right." I hauled the cord to Wells, dropping to my knees in front of him. He was shirtless, in bloodstained pants. No shoes. Still barely conscious. "Wells," I pulled his face around to mine. "I'm going to lend you some energy. We have to get you onto Obsidian."

He fixed his gaze on me, but didn't respond. I grabbed his hands and forced a bit of my dwindling power his way.

"Imogen..." he mumbled.

Tears pricked the corners of my eyes. "Yeah, it's me. Let's get out of here." I pulled him up.

Obsidian remained kneeling as I pushed Wells astride him. I wrapped Wells's hands around chunks of Obsidian's mane, then quickly secured him to the unicorn before scrambling on behind him and tying myself to Wells. I sliced off the excess cord with my dagger as Obsidian stood up. I reached my arms around Wells's waist, balancing him as I buried my fingers into the unicorn's midnight mane.

Alright, Prism, to the left and then up the first set of stairs to the right. Varger, follow us. We've got my mate. Time to get yours.

CHAPTER THIRTY-THREE

Success is merely stamina and unflagging effort in the face of continual adversity.
—Zoe Ibrahim

My grenades had left the corridors in rubble. Thankfully the passage we needed was still intact. Prism cantered ahead with one of Varger's remaining sons, Vlad, flanking him. Varger and her last son, Ovich, brought up the rear. The others had gone with the Molnairians to guide them out.

My aching arms bracketed Wells, preventing him from slumping too far to either side. I kept my burning fingers entwined in Obsidian's silken mane. The soreness thrumming through my entire body reminded me that I wasn't recovered myself. Wells was tall, I could barely see over his shoulder, even as hunched forward as he was, but I managed to guide Prism and keep Wells from toppling. Prism and Vlad only had to fight through the last corridor before we made it to the Great Hall. They worked together seamlessly, as if unicorns and urzen were natural partners. I shuddered to think of the conquest Prism could achieve with an urzen permanently at his side. Shortly our way was clear.

The Great Hall was empty save a huddled mass of sidhe who were obviously the partners and children of those fighting. My stomach flipped, but I let the urzen decide. They allowed them to flee, but did not mark their scent.

The great pelt was stretched out above the two wooden thrones, long silken fur gleaming in the dim light from the one chandelier. The others surrounded it like gruesome flags.

Varger sprang upon the dais, knocking the throne out of her way. It crashed to its side, the echo reverberating around the enormous space. She placed her forepaws on the stone wall and stretched, her snout working to catch the scent of the pelt above her.

Then she stilled. All but her nose, nostrils still flaring, her unblinking yellow eyes darkening.

She threw her head back and howled.

My blood chilled at the sound. Her grief and rage sang against my ears, traveling down my spine and flashing out as gooseflesh across my skin. I felt Wells shudder and hugged him closer. Her family took up the howl from wherever they were. The entire Sephryan compound was filled with the bone-shredding sound of mourning urzen.

Prism, we need to get that pelt down for her, I told him. He must have communicated as much to Obsidian—who hadn't spoken to me directly once Wells was out of mortal peril—for both of them aimed their horns at Skoll's hanging fur. Their long, ebony horns glittered to life, as if filled with a turbulent, darkly sparkling liquid.

More urzen flowed into the Great Hall, sporting bloody maws and dripping fangs. They all stared fixedly as Obsidian and Prism's kroma lifted Skoll's pelt from its hooks. It drifted horizontally away from the stone, then the unicorns respectfully folded the pelt's legs toward each other, curled the fur into a roll, and floated it toward Varger. She bowed her head and they laid it across her shoulders. Vlad and Ovich flanked her.

Prism and Obsidian worked together to pull the other pelts down and deliver them to whichever urzen stepped forward. It took less than five minutes, but I felt my energy flagging, my muscles spasming from holding Wells up.

I 'pathed Varger, letting Prism listen as well. *Once we get out, I can summon lightning again, It would be best for me to wink my mate out as soon as possible. The unicorns can probably wink you as well, but not everyone.*

Varger conferred with her sons as we marched from the Great Hall. Chaos still reigned outside. The Sephryans were now aware of the urzen and were bringing all of their weapons to play.

My other children can take care of finishing our business here, she told me finally. *I have waited too long to bring peace to my mate. I will accompany you now.*

Let's go then.

I directed Prism out of the hall and to the right once we reached the courtyard. Vlad and Ovich took care of any Sephryans that avoided Prism's rainbow-death fire. My lightning was spent and my energy continued to plummet. I'd been giving Wells as much as I could spare just to keep him upright. He was still barely conscious, barely clinging to Obsidian.

Hoping that my time inside had been enough of a break, I summoned the lightning as Prism led us up the steps to battlements I'd only seen on contraband maps.

The lightning came willingly but I kept my dose short, careful to shield Wells and Obsidian from electricity. I pulled just enough to allow me to keep us both upright, and hopefully to fight if I needed to.

That eastern guard tower, Prism, Varger. Keeping one arm wrapped around Wells, I pointed. *There's a platform outside that is kept beyond the wards so that they can wink messengers to other spots in the compound. We need to take that tower.*

Most of the work was already done. The urzen had taken Varger's "kill now, feed later" order to heart and were doing their best to slaughter as many Sephryans as they could. There were a few urzen down, but many,

many more sidhe. When we reached the tower, the four guards inside it fled instantly. Vlad and Ovich gave light chase before coming back for orders.

I risked a question. *The Molnairians that we freed?*

Varger answered. *Drauf and Ganger brought them to the western tower, destroyed those who held it and occupied the tower until the last of yours had winked out. My sons now kill and feed where they choose. They will lead our people here back to our home once we are gone.*

Thank you. I swallowed. Wells slipped and I hauled him back upright, fed him some energy. I needed to find a place for us to rest. *We will wink directly to your woods. Do you mind if we stay awhile? With the unicorns?*

Imogen Lightning Bearer, you and yours are welcome in my home. My family will never forget you.

Thank you again. I peered out at the long dock-like platform. Took a steadying breath upon viewing the terrifying edge. Fortunately, I didn't have to make myself walk onto it. *Prism, tell Obsidian we all need to get out on that platform beyond the wards. Prism, you can wink Vlad and Ovich. Obsidian will wink me, Wells, and Varger. We're going to the clearing in the woods where we left our things.*

Obsidian walked to the end of the unsettlingly narrow platform. Varger followed.

I heard Obsidian's midnight voice one last time. *Tell her to take hold of my tail. Gently.*

Varger did. We were all swept up by the black void for three blinks. Then scents of blood, ozone, and sweat were replaced by aromas of leaf and wood. Wells collapsed completely.

We pulled our things farther into the trees until we were certain no random Sephryan scout would glimpse us. It had to be obvious to anyone who witnessed the lightning cracking from the skies that I had attacked the Sephryan capitol. I wondered what conclusions the kings would draw.

I'd left the tent after being forbidden and also waged my very own battle against Sephrya. A grim spark of satisfaction rooted in my chest at the thought of having pissed both of them off at once.

Once we'd picked a location, Obsidian gently lowered himself all the way to the ground. I cut myself and Wells free and guided his tumble from Obsidian, eventually propping him up to lean against his unicorn's shoulder.

"Wells." I cupped his face between my hands. "Wells, talk to me, please."

His eyes fluttered open. Locked on mine for an instant. "Imogen . . ." he sighed. His eyelids dropped shut again. I laid him back against Obsidian, brushing his tangled hair back from his face. He was so pale.

You will be safe here, Imogen, Varger told me. *I go to complete the rite and bring my mate peace. One urzen will remain nearby until you and your unicorns decide to leave. Stay as long as you need. Goodbye for now. And thank you.*

I pushed out a half smile *Thank you. I am glad we could help bring some peace to Skoll and the rest of your people.* I draped Wells's cloak around him as I 'pathed. *I'm sorry he was taken from you.*

If there were more sidhe like you, Imogen Lightning Bearer, more creatures in this world might live together in peace. She paused. Shifted the pelt on her shoulders. Checked that her sons were beside her. *Take care of your mate. Should you need anything, reach out to the urzen nearby.*

I watched as the urzen melted into the shadows, then dug into my pocket and checked my pack. There were only three blocks left after giving one to every Molnarian prisoner. I teased out the instructions for the bubbly pink liquid Kerlyn had left. As I'd feared the potion was specific to my particular affliction; nothing indicated it would help Wells. I sighed and took a dose. One of us needed to stay upright.

I dropped the empty vial back into my pack, then placed two fingers to Wells's clammy throat, feeling for that reassuring pulse. Was it getting slower, or was I imagining it?

Obsidian says we need to get him back to camp to see a medic, Prism told me.

And please tell Obsidian that I would love to do that if the king hadn't orchestrated this entire disaster. Obsidian was right though, we needed help. Wells wasn't looking good.

Obsidian neighed low in his throat, eyes glowing read as I quickly filled them in.

I plucked out a block and shoved it into my mouth. *I have to do this.* Fishing out one of the two remaining, I broke it in half, crumbling one half into the empty potion vial, added water from my canteen, corked it, and shook it vigorously until the block had mostly dissolved.

"Wells, hey, open up. You've gotta drink this." I tucked his head into the crook of my arm and tilted it upright, dropping a kiss to his temple. "Wake up just for a minute."

His eyes fluttered but didn't open.

"Here, have a sip." I gently pulled his jaws apart, then tipped my concoction in a bit at a time, watching the muscles of his throat work as he swallowed automatically. I repeated the process with the other half, my stomach fizzing with nerves. I hoped this was the right thing to do. He needed energy to heal, surely.

He swallowed the final bit and I lowered the vial. His head dropped against my shoulder, as if drinking had sapped his energy. I wrapped my arms around him and pressed my lips to his clammy forehead. I hated to let go of him, but I gently leaned him back against Obsidian, tucking his cloak up around his shoulders. Prism had already laid down as well, the two unicorns bracketing Wells and me.

"Okay, I need you two to watch out for him," I said. "I'm going to try to get some help."

After fidgeting with Wells's cloak again, I stood on shaky legs, giving him a once over to ensure he was covered and resting comfortably against Obsidian's shoulder.

Where will you go? They'll simply capture you, Prism said helpfully.

I'll glamour myself, obviously, I retorted, reining in my irritation. I unbuckled Wells's sword and left it beside him. I had no illusion that he would be able to use it anytime soon, but carrying two swords might give me away.

Who are you going to be that the king won't know? It takes great skill to make up a new being. You are new at glamours. And you have very little energy left. Prism came by his skepticism honestly, but it still rankled. Especially since he was right.

However, it didn't take me long to think of something. *I'll be someone who's face I will never forget, who the king will not recognize.*

Kaylie walked once more.

I wore her face, her clothes, her long red hair. The Molnairian camp's wards had been keyed so only those of the blood, or those the king had given exception to, could pass through.

I stepped through easily and returned to the camp I'd so recently escaped.

It was in turmoil.

I kept my head down as I dodged between soldiers crisscrossing through the camp, some singular and some in small units. The energy was high, but tense. From the bursts of conversations I overheard as I wound between the tents, they'd gotten wind of the urzen attack, and had seen my lightning, but no one had any concrete idea of what had happened.

I strode down the main thoroughfare as if I were on an errand. I held my head so that my hair slid around my face, looking up through the tops of my eyes. Kaylie had three redheaded sisters and a mother somewhere in the joined camps. As long as no one looked too closely, I'd be fine. It helped that we were the same size. I only had to alter the surface look. Basic size and bone structure could stay the same.

I walked right up to our old tent. I could tell before reaching it that it was occupied and cut to the side, stepping around the back. I tested to see what shields or wards might be in place. Smirking on discovering that only those of the blood could enter or exit uninvited, I shimmied under the back end, crawling into the unoccupied bathing room.

My own energy was flagging. I knew that my activities today hadn't been what Kerlyn had in mind when she'd prescribed those potions, so I tucked myself into a corner without cloaking, banking on no one needing to come in while I was here. I pressed my ear to the thin canvas separating me from the rest of them.

"... terms of the agreement, Imogen has been expressly forbidden, by written word, from attacking the Sephryans." I heard the king speaking to a gathered bunch. I guessed about twenty people were crammed into the tent. "Now, if she's found a loophole, or perhaps located another of her kind, of course we'll rejoice in the fact that she is safe and sound. It's also possible that she's been tortured. Traumatized. Maybe even doesn't know where she is.

"It's our responsibility to protect her if something has happened to Llewellyn." Allestair affected a tragic sigh, his voice so full of sadness that—had I not known him—I might have been fooled into believing he cared. "If anyone finds either of them, no need to startle them by trying to approach. Just wink to me immediately with their location and you will be handsomely rewarded. This applies to persons of every rank..."

I rolled my eyes. I didn't need to hear any more. There was no way I could bring Wells here right now. He wasn't himself. I wasn't one hundred percent. It would be nothing for Allestair to throw us back into that palace prison or worse. I was never going back there.

I scooted out from beneath the tent's edge, formulating vague plans to either go to the medics' tent and ask some hypothetical questions about recovering from evisceration or head over to the unicorns and ask them if they knew what to do if one of their bonded riders happened to have recently been pulled back from the brink of death.

I'd just pushed up from the ground and dusted myself off when I turned around and found myself face to face with Kerlyn.

CHAPTER THIRTY-FOUR

I've had some terrible luck for sure, but I've been incredibly fortunate in my friendships. And that makes up for a lot.
—Imogen Delaney

My stomach dropped. *Shit.* Before I could react, I felt her kroma reaching out to mine.

Every sidhe's kroma has a feel to it—and a color, which is only visible to those with aural sight, like me—the closer you get to someone, the more familiar their kroma is. Kerlyn had brought me back from the brink of death more than once. She was intimately acquainted with the flavor of my kroma. Not to mention I hadn't glamoured my scent. She knew exactly who I was.

I strode briskly toward her. "I'm sorry," I said, my voice just above a whisper, hoping she wasn't incensed enough to out me immediately. I grasped her arm and pulled her with me, away from the tent. When she didn't resist, I looped my elbow through hers and guided us back into the main thoroughfare.

"I wasn't expecting you to have to see this," I said, the words tumbling out in an awkward rush. "I just . . . I need to save Wells and I needed a face and hers was the only one I've memorized."

Kerlyn shushed me sharply, then hauled me in a different direction. I went with her, stomach in knots, praying that she wasn't turning me in. She shoved me into the medic's tent, straight into their changing area. No one else was there.

When she spun me around, moisture lined her eyes.

"You memorized her face?" Her voice broke. She reached a trembling hand up to touch my cheek. My throat burned.

"How could I not?" I said, voice cracking.

She let one sob break free, then ran her hand across my jaw, nose. Smoothed my eyebrows with both thumbs. Her fingertips brushed the dusting of freckles over my cheekbones. Her eyes moist, as if she had longed to do just that, if only one more time.

"You did a wonderful job," she said. Her voice quavered. She pushed back my long hair. "I know you didn't have as much hair as she did. Someone taught you a good glamour."

She'd mastered herself again. I recognized a kindred spirit. She wouldn't fall apart here. She'd fall apart later. In her dreams. Or in private. Curling around the wound when she felt safer.

"You did save him?" She asked me finally.

I couldn't stop my voice from breaking again. "I got him out, but . . . it's not good. And I can't bring him here." I hoped I could trust her not to bring me straight to the king.

"What do you need?" she asked, her green eyes clear, if still a bit bright with emotion.

"I honestly don't know." My limbs trembled as exhaustion tried to stake a claim. "They gutted him, broke his bones . . ." I forced back the bile trying to climb up my throat. "His unicorn put him back together, but . . ." I stopped, squeezed my eyes shut, and pulled in a long breath. Wells needed a medic, yes, but we couldn't just stay in the woods. *Think, Imogen, who would*

Wells go to? I exhaled slowly, my eyes flicking toward the tent entrance and then back to hers. "Do you know if we can get to Captain Marc?"

It took some doing.

Marc's aerial units had been dispatched to monitor the situation in Sephrya by order of the king. Allestair wanted to know what exactly was happening and know it yesterday.

To get an audience with the captain, Kerlyn had been forced to lie and say that she needed to consult him on an injury sustained by one of his aerial soldiers who would only listen to him.

I waited in a curtained-off area within the medic tent, perched on the edge of a cot, still wearing Kaylie's face. I didn't know if I'd have the energy to pull the glamour back on once I removed it, so I hoped Captain Marc wouldn't need too much convincing. My heart thundered in my chest even as my arms trembled. How long had it been since I'd eaten a real meal? The waiting was nearly as draining as the continual flow of kroma. I kept compulsively touching the bond slumbering within me. Obsessively checking that it was still there.

Sparks of excitement skittered over my skin when I heard them enter. Kerlyn held open the curtain for the captain and stepped in behind him, pulling it closed.

Captain Marc, it's me, Imogen, I 'pathed, pairing my words with a little wave. My mental voice even sounded faint. Surely he could at least tell my scent was the same? I hadn't the faintest idea how to glamour scents.

Marc started. *Imogen?*

I don't think I'll have the energy to put the glamour back on if I take it off. I opened the 'path up to include Kerlyn as well. *I need to get Wells somewhere safe. He was nearly killed. I left him with our unicorns.*

He nodded, and a wash of relief flooded me. He stepped closer. "If we walk to the edge of camp, beyond the shields, can you wink me to him?"

"Yes, if you can lend me a bit of energy."

He offered me his arm.

I let the glamour drop—nearly sighing in relief—as soon as we appeared in front of the forest. The urzen on duty stepped out from the trees, growling. Captain Marc stiffened, but I squeezed his arm and 'pathed them both.

He's a friend. Come to help my mate. Thank you for keeping watch.

The urzen bobbed his head once, then melted back into the crimson foliage. I marched to Wells as fast as my shaking legs would carry me, pulling Marc beside me.

"You befriended the creatures in the Briarwood Forest?" Marc's eyes were wide, the hint of a disbelieving laugh bouncing beneath his voice.

"I was desperate and got lucky. Turns out they had their own grudge against Sephrya." It was difficult not to launch into a sprint once I caught sight of Prism's violet hide between the trees. Once in the clearing, I released Marc's arm and dropped down next to Wells, brushing my hand over his forehead. He didn't stir.

There's been no change, Prism informed me as Captain Marc knelt at Wells's other side. *But you need to drink one of your pink things. Your energy is low.*

"They're not specifically for energy, I have to follow the directions," I said aloud as I 'pathed, digging around in the pack and double-checking the instructions nestled betwixt the vials. "It's not time yet."

"Both of you need to rest," Marc said, the edge of Wells's cloak in his hand, his eyes on the long scar bisecting his torso. He sighed. "I don't know what Allestair would do if he found you, but I don't think it's a good idea to risk discovery. At least until you're both healthy." He gently laid the cloak back over Wells. "There's an empty berth on my ship next door to mine. I keep it ready for hosting dignitaries. You'd have to be completely silent, but I could get Kerlyn to check him without raising much suspicion."

"What about Prism and Obsidian?"

"I think they'll both be fine back in the unicorn habitat. You and Llewellyn were the only two who were able to communicate with them directly. It's doubtful anyone noticed them leaving if they winked straight to you."

I nodded. He was right. Keeping Wells in the woods wasn't a viable long-term solution. And I knew that the surge of adrenaline fueling me was nearly tapped.

"I can wink you both into the berth," Marc said, carefully lifting Wells away from Obsidian so the unicorn could stand. "No need to risk encountering anyone else."

I said goodbye to both unicorns, promising them I'd keep them updated. Prism pressed me to be sure we could trust Marc. Once he was satisfied, we watched them wink out, and let the urzen know we were taking our leave.

Captain Marc winked us directly into the spare berth. The room reminded me of the small cabin I'd shared with Wells on the ship from Earth. The bed attached to the wall, with just enough space on either side for two nightstands, also attached. There was one chair, a closet sunk in the wall opposite the tiny washroom, and a small dresser.

Marc left me to settle Wells. The only spare clothes I'd had space to pack for him were underwear, which I did change out, stripping him of his blood-soaked things and sponging him off as thoroughly as I could while he lay unresponsive on the bed. My chest was tight with dread. He was so, so still. My palm continually drifted toward his face, hovering until I felt the featherlight brush of his exhale. I finally turned the covers down and tucked them around him. His skin was cold to the touch.

Marc returned minutes later with Kerlyn, who'd toted along an entire pharmacopeia in a valise. I didn't want to leave Wells's side while she examined him—as if I could keep him alive by sheer force of will and proximity—but both Kerlyn and Captain Marc insisted that I clean myself up.

I took the briefest of showers and changed into the spare shorts and tank top I'd brought.

When I emerged, Wells was still unconscious, though his color was better. Kerlyn lined up several bottles of dark-blue potion on the nightstand next to him and scribbled out instructions. She locked eyes with me.

"Get in there with him. I'm putting you out too," she said, quietly. Captain Marc had thrown a sound shield on the door for Kerlyn's visit, but insisted we not make a habit of having loud conversations in this room.

"But shouldn't I stay awake to look after—"

She shook her head, eyes narrowing. "Did you forget that you were tortured recently also? Both of you need rest; you're safe here." She twitched the covers back.

I obediently climbed in and snuggled up next to Wells. Relief unknotted my stomach when I felt his chest rise and fall evenly, his skin smooth and warm beneath my palm, no longer slick with blood or clammy with sweat. Muscles I hadn't realized were clenched relaxed as I laid my head on his shoulder.

Kerlyn handed me a vial of silvery potion and I tossed it back in one swallow.

Captain Marc said something about getting some spare clothes but I was out before he finished his sentence.

I later learned that I slept three days away. Wells didn't wake with me, remaining stubbornly unconscious despite my—occasionally lengthy—whispered monologues and questions.

When I was able to pull a bit of energy, I charged my phone and earbuds and played music for Wells while he slept. One earbud for him and one for me. I had no idea if he heard anything, but it made me feel like I was doing something. An awful feeling of helplessness clung to my skin like Sephrya's persistent humidity.

"This is that instrumental one that you like," I whispered from where I lay beside him, our heads sharing the same pillow. "The one with the violins."

Captain Marc winked into the room.

I pushed myself upright, stopped the music, and pulled the earbuds out of our ears. Marc threw a sound shield up over the door, then turned to me, holding out a flask.

"Soup."

"Thanks." I wrapped my fingers around the warm metal and unscrewed the cap, my leg pressed against Wells's side beneath the covers. As if he would vanish the moment my skin left his.

Marc pulled the chair over to my side of the bed. He indicated Wells with a nod. "Is it time for his potion?"

"I just gave it to him," I said, between greedy gulps of soup. I had over a week of meals to make up for. "I took mine too." My eyes never left Marc's. The carefully blank expression he wore had my shoulders tensing.

He nodded. "Are you up for hearing some news?"

"I think so," I said, my knuckles whitening around the flask. I pressed closer to Wells.

The captain interlaced his fingers and leaned forward in the chair, resting his elbows on his knees. "Because of your storming of the capitol with the urzen, we've been able to lay siege. The remaining Sephryans have been forced to retreat to the innermost circle of their city. We occupy the two outer rings."

"I shall await my commendations for being essential to a successful siege with bated breath," I said, my voice bone dry.

"About that." Marc's eyes dropped to his hands and my stomach tensed as if readying for a blow. He cleared his throat. "This is not something you could have known, Imogen, as Allestair kept certain things very close to the chest, but apparently the way in which you stormed the castle has violated a carefully crafted treaty between Allestair and King Demian."

I set the empty flask on the nightstand, my fingers trembling.

"I'm not privy to the details but apparently they were near ending—"

"I know the details," I whispered. "He told me before I left the camp." Trembling all over, I quickly told Marc of Allestair's plans. The captain went ashen and looked as though he might be ill. "Does this mean that particular deal is off the table?"

Marc's throat worked for a moment as he digested the king's betrayal. "Yes. And the direction everything is taking makes . . . a horrific kind of sense now. Demian told him that the destruction you caused has rendered that agreement null and void."

"Good." I glanced down at Wells. One less person actively trying to kill him.

Marc smiled grimly. "There's more." With a deep breath, he leaned back in the chair, massaging his temples for a moment before he spoke. "Reports gained from questioning captured Sephryans have left little doubt that you managed to rescue your mate and escape. Allestair has publicly offered significant rewards for the return of either of you."

"Dead or alive?" I asked bitterly, flopping back against the headboard. I pulled Wells's limp hand from beneath the covers and cradled it in my lap, interlacing my fingers with his.

"Alive, Imogen," Marc said, exhaustion behind his eyes. "I don't believe Allestair is interested in killing you. Merely controlling you."

"What about Wells?" I asked, my voice hard. Allestair had tried to get my mate out of the way too frequently for my taste. I'd had plenty of time to make and discard a multitude of plans for fleeing the country once we were better. I knew that I could wink the two of us all the way to Molnair if I got some lightning juice, but where would we go from there? What would we do? Was there anywhere on this planet Allestair couldn't find us? My lack of knowledge ate at me. To have the one person I trusted right beside me, but so out of reach, scraped at my nerves with every breath.

"I believe that Allestair is coming to learn that controlling you would be much easier for him if he did so via Llewellyn rather than by eliminating him." Marc's deep voice was heavy with resignation. I thought I detected a touch of bitterness beneath his carefully even tone. I still couldn't read his aura. I was able to discern swirls, but they were transparent and colorless. I hadn't realized exactly how drained I was when I went to rescue Wells. Kerlyn said that I had doubled my recovery time forcing complex kroma through my depleted body.

I didn't regret it.

"Imogen, I have to ask you a question and I need you to be honest with me," Marc said. His dark eyes locked, unwavering, on mine. Although his arms lay relaxed on the armrests of the chair, the tension strung between us was nearly visible. I longed to read his aura.

"Alright." I dropped my eyes first. Gazing down at Wells's hand in my lap. Played with his long fingers. My nerves jangled, but I had no reason to hide anything from Marc.

"Allestair called a few of us into his private berth today and informed us that, not only had you been forbidden to use your power against the Sephryans, but that he had forbidden you from leaving your tent unless both he and Aloysius accompanied you. He also informed us that you should not have been able to get past the wards without his permission. As Aloysius was with him nearly the entire time you were left alone, he escaped any kind of severe scrutiny."

I lifted my eyes to Marc's. He still gazed steadily at me. Unblinking. My throat closed.

"I know how you got through the wards, Imogen, but how did you manage to leave the tent when you'd been forbidden by your king? For that matter, how were you able to attack Sephrya?"

"I was also forbidden from telling anyone everything I just told you," I murmured, earning a raised eyebrow.

I blew out a breath and dropped my gaze once more to Wells's hand, wrapping both of mine around it. Wishing he were awake to tell me what to do. I squeezed, silently apologizing if I were making the wrong choice yet again, then forced my gaze back to Marc's.

"I technically have no king."

CHAPTER THIRTY-FIVE

*Secrets are heavy, but if they belong to someone else,
a good person will hold them regardless.*
—Captain Marcellus Tibercio

The tension in the room thickened to near suffocating, but I pushed the words out, explaining to Marc what I had learned about my monarchless status. He didn't move or change expression, but his growing alarm was so obvious, even without my aural sight, that I shrank deeper into the covers as I spoke, eeling around Wells's arm. Hugging it to my chest like a plush toy. The captain was silent for several seconds when I finished.

"If Allestair knew . . ." He shut his eyes for a breath. "Do you have any idea how dangerous you've become, Imogen?"

My stomach twisted. I shook my head.

Marc ticked off points on his fingers. "Never-before-seen powers, unparalleled talent and intelligence, mated to a high-ranking and high-powered sidhe, royal blood, potentially in line for the throne, no kromatically bound fealty to any monarch. If Allestair knew about those last two . . ."

"He'd kill me?" I was trembling. The icy warning in Marc's voice chilled the room.

"That's certainly one possibility," Marc said. "Allestair is already near-fanatical with his drive to bring you under his control. Honestly, I'm not sure what he would do, but it wouldn't be pleasant. For either of you." He nodded toward Wells, then sighed, scrubbing his fingers across his eyes. "I've sworn Kerlyn to secrecy and told her I'm not bringing her back here unless it's an emergency. If someone were to smell either of you on her . . ." His gaze collided with mine. "You realize that by not informing Allestair of your whereabouts, she and I are both committing treason?"

My blood went cold. My gaze snapped to Wells, eyes closed, long dark red hair drifting over one pale cheek. That desperate feeling of helplessness wrapped my lungs. Guilt curled around my stomach. Mating me had brought him nothing but pain and upheaval. *I want you to know that it was all worth it to me . . .*

I wanted to shake him awake. I longed to reach inside of him and drag his soul out from whatever deep well it slumbered in and make it talk to me. I didn't know where to leap. I had nothing solid to push off from. My fingers tightened around Wells's arm, my eyes locked on the dark, russet fringes of his eyelashes, desperate for them to flutter open. I craved his careful, logical plans, even his exasperated sighs. My heart pounded in my ears. I was so lost without him.

And I couldn't let Marc commit treason for us. Or Kerlyn. She'd lost too much already. I forced my gaze back to his. "We'll leave as soon as we can. We can't put that on you," I breathed. "Just . . . as soon as Wells wakes up . . ." I trailed off when Marc emphatically shook his head. Would he not let us leave? Was this his way of telling me that he was turning us in? My stomach plummeted. No, Marc wouldn't do that to us. "Or . . . we could go now . . . I can move him. We don't want to endanger either of you. I know Wells wouldn't want that."

Marc let out a long, loud exhale, his head and shoulders sagging. Then he sucked in a deep breath, rose from the chair, and sat on the edge of the bed facing me. "Imogen, why do you think I had so many people attend that meeting on the return trip from Earth, where we discussed what Aloysius had done to you?"

I blinked. Marc wasn't the evasive type, but I couldn't fathom what this had to do with anything. "Because... everyone was upset with Al and wanted to make sure he was being held accountable?"

"That is part of the reason, and the reason I gave Allestair, but no. I did it so that everyone on that ship would know what had happened to you and understand that you did not want to be with Aloysius, making it impossible for him to trap you in that palace against your will. As you've undoubtedly learned, the king is very conscious of his public image."

My eyes flicked to Wells, then back to Marc. "Did you know Wells would offer to take me?"

He nodded, dark eyes dropping to our clasped hands. "I suspected that he might. I also suspected Allestair may try to give you to Aloysius regardless of your wishes, which, as you know, was confirmed once I read his response. My contingency plan hinged upon my further suspicion that you would beg to live anywhere else, in the hearing of everyone present. If Llewellyn hadn't offered himself up then, I planned to bring you home to Allatu until we found you a place. She's from Earth, as you know, and would have been a sympathetic guide."

Although we had veered wildly off topic, I couldn't help but follow him down the rabbit hole. "What made you think that Wells would volunteer?"

Captain Marc's gaze rested on Wells's still form. "Llewellyn rarely went against Aloysius as a rule. Stayed out of his way, supported him, tried to keep him from making too much of an ass of himself in normal society if possible. You've seen what it's like in that palace. But Llewellyn had shown not once, but twice, prior to that meeting, that he was willing to put your safety and well-being ahead of what his brother wanted."

His eyes found mine again. "First, when he discovered that you were taken against your will and called me in to help, second when he saw how terrified you were by the mere thought of spending unsupervised time with Aloysius and 'pathed me to change the roster, giving his brother his shift so he could continue to look out for you. It wasn't a huge gamble to guess that he might volunteer to take you in. Especially after smelling your terror during that meeting when you heard you were being given to Aloysius. Oh, yes, it permeated the room."

My gaze dropped, throat tight, spine tingling with the unpleasant memories of that horrible meeting.

Marc reached over, warm brown fingers gently finding one of my pale hands and tugging it from where I clung to Wells. He wrapped it in both of his, warming my cold palm, and held it against his heart. "All this to say, Imogen, that I have been on your side since you were pulled onto our ship. I've been on Llewellyn's for two-hundred-and-fifty-one years. I'm not about to abandon either of you now."

The corners of my lips tipped upward. Some of the tightness eased from my chest, but as I gazed at his hands, gently holding mine, my brain snagged on his words. "Wells is only two-hundred-and-fifty-one years old."

I lifted my eyes and saw the moment Captain Marc realized he'd made a mistake. Watched him putting that mask back into place. He slowly lowered my hand.

My mind shuffled through my memories of Marc. He *had* always been there for Wells. Unconditionally. "How did you know you'd be on his side before he was even born?"

He could have said anything. That he'd found Wells an engaging baby, that Iphigenia had named him godfather, anything. Instead he patted my hand and released it, muttering something about a hyperbole.

This went deeper than that, I knew. Marc was loyal to Molnair, he'd fought for his country and its kings for centuries, but he chose Wells over Allestair every single time. And now he was even risking treason. "You know who Wells's father is, don't you?"

He stiffened. His eyes locked onto mine. I didn't have to read his aura to see that I'd struck.

I sucked in a breath. Marc and Iphigenia? "Are *you* Wells's father?"

He burst into laughter, snatched a pillow off the bed and buried his face in it to muffle the sound. My eyebrows dropped. I pressed my lips together. Marc continued to howl into the pillow.

"I don't see anything remotely funny about any of this."

He managed to wrangle his outburst down to a chuckle, tears streaming down his face. "Do I look like I've ever had red hair?"

My face heated. It was true, and although Marc's skin wasn't quite as dark as Zoe's, he also looked nothing like Wells. "The queen is pretty pale," I grumbled. "And I don't really understand how these outside royal pairings work. Give me a break, I'm tired. At least I'm sure you know who his father is."

His laughter died instantly. His eyes dropped to the pillow he still clutched. He passed it back to me, his eyes lifting to mine. "Alright, Imogen, you've proven to be very perceptive so I won't insult you by trying to deny it. I will, however, ask that you keep this between us for the time being. Llewellyn has no idea and there's a good reason for it."

I bit my bottom lip, but nodded. How could I refuse him anything? He'd saved me at least twice. "Does anyone else know? I mean ... well, aside from the queen, obviously."

He smiled, his face softening. "Allatu knows. No one else."

I looked over at Wells. Pushed a lock of dark auburn hair off his forehead. "Does he look like his father at all?" I dragged my gaze back to Marc.

His eyes rested on Wells's face. Something like longing softening his features. "Yes. He does."

I was wrapped up in a pleasant doze. Soft meaningless images curled through my brain while my limbs wound around Wells's. My head rested on his chest, so that I could hear the steady beat of his heart even in sleep.

I'd lost all track of time in the windowless room. Relying on Marc to let me know if days had passed. Setting timers on my phone reminding me to take my potions and give Wells his. I struggled to keep my mind from spiraling and found that sleep was best. My body was still fighting to recover after all.

"Imogen..." Wells sighed.

My heart stumbled. Barely daring to hope, I lifted my head to find him blinking at me. My chest tightened when I saw recognition behind his gaze. He was really awake. "Hi," I breathed.

"It's really you," he whispered.

My face split into a cheek-cracking grin. Tears stung my eyes. "I'm so happy to see you."

He brushed his fingertips across my cheekbone. "Are we alive?" His voice was deep, rusty with disuse.

"Yeah." My voice cracked on the word. I wondered if the bond could even transmit a portion of the bittersweet crush of joy crashing through me. A tear broke free, sliding down my cheek to drop onto his skin. "Yeah, we're alive."

"Come here." He pulled me into a hug. My heart swelled, filling my chest, my ribs nearly fracturing with the force of my elation. Tears of relief poured silently down my face, wetting his shoulder as I clung to him. His arms tightened around me, pushing out a cough when he squeezed the breath from me.

He disengaged, holding me slightly away, eyes scanning my face in the dim light from the single lamp on my nightstand. He swiped my cheeks free of tears then pulled me close again, pressing his lips to my forehead, nose, and finally covering my mouth with his.

Effervescent delight swirled through my chest as I kissed him back, parting my lips, wrapping my legs around his, as if I could find some way to bring him even closer.

I was breathless when we eventually broke apart

"What do you taste like?" he asked.

"So romantic," I murmured, grinning. "Keep your voice down, we have to be quiet. And I probably taste like potion. That's what you taste like."

Wells pushed himself into a sitting position against the wall, scanning the room. I sat up with him, flicking on the other lamp with a snap. He looked like he was about to ask where we were, then his eyes dropped to his own stomach. He froze. I realized he'd never had a permanent scar before. He traced the dark, jagged line of the mark with his fingers.

"Obsidian marked you when he saved you," I whispered. Although I couldn't see his aura, I felt the swell of Wells's emotion through the bond. I swallowed it down, but my lips curved up just a bit. "I'll need to 'path him and let him know you're awake. I'll tell him you said thanks. He's been asking about you."

"How did Obsidian get to me?" he asked, his bright eyes finding mine.

Although I was certain he could feel the joy searing through me, I fought the smile trying to burst out simply because he was awake, talking, and looking at me. I cleared my throat. "I may have stormed the castle and brought him along. Prism came too."

He raised his eyebrows. "You, Prism, and Obsidian stormed the Sephryan capitol on your own . . . and survived?"

I snuggled up to his side and wrapped my arms around him. Heart swelling when he reciprocated. I lifted my eyelashes and forced a deep breath. "Well, not exactly . . ."

Wells narrowed his eyes.

"So . . ." I sighed. "Okay, you know the ginormous canines that eat our dead sometimes?"

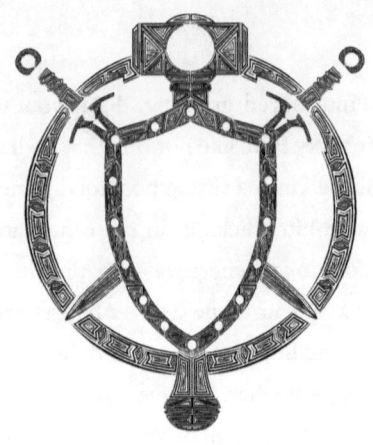

CHAPTER THIRTY-SIX

The annoying thing about true healing is it takes so long.
—Prince Aloysuis Metellus

I 'pathed Captain Marc to let him know Wells was awake.

Wells remembered nothing about escaping the capital and nothing about our brief time in the woods. Which was probably a blessing. He went even more pale when I told him about the deal Allestair had struck with Demian, and how Marc believed it was now moot, but to my surprise said nothing—aside from squeezing his eyes shut and pinching the bridge of his nose for a moment.

Captain Marc arrived an hour later with soup for both of us and threw a sound shield up. He couldn't stay long but wanted to see Wells himself and give him an opportunity to ask questions.

"Any chance of getting anything more substantial?" Wells finished his soup in record time.

"Do you not remember being eviscerated?" I asked, some heat creeping into my voice. "This is the first time your insides are processing anything aside from potion, be nice to them."

"I remember some of it." Wells's eyes dropped to the scar again. "I definitely didn't expect to survive."

"I had to put your intestines back in you." I stared into my empty soup flask, trying not to go too far into the memory. I swallowed convulsively when my stomach rolled. More than one nightmare had been inspired by those horrible minutes. My voice dropped to a whisper. "I let the urzen tear apart those two Sephryans. At least Stian will never torture another soul."

My mate's palm landed softly between my shoulder blades, sliding up to massage the sides of my neck. "Alright, Demon, I promise to take it slowly."

I leaned into him, deep breaths pulling his scent in as I tried to force those images out of my mind.

"How's the mood in camp?" Wells asked, keeping his voice low.

"Tense," the captain replied, settling into what I now considered Marc's Chair. "Although we now occupy the inner two rings, since Allestair and Demian are still flinging accusations back and forth, there has been no further movement. And Demian's responses are taking longer than usual. It's possible he evacuated elsewhere but we can't work out how. We've put our own wards over theirs, so they can't escape unless they have some method of leaving that we're unaware of, but the entire capital is surrounded on all sides. My units are doing constant flyovers of the immediate and surrounding areas."

"And what is the mood regarding Imogen and me?" Wells eased back against the wall, pulling me with him. Neither of us seemed willing to move apart from the other, keeping in constant physical contact.

Marc sighed, crossing an ankle over a knee, leaning back in his chair. "The general populace is worried. The most accepted theory is that you've escaped, taken shelter, and you're both too injured to make it back to camp. As your unicorns refuse to be paired with anyone else, very few people believe either of you to be dead. To that end, scouts are scanning the woods for you from the air; some are being dispatched to check your unit's previous camps, Aloysius has even been sent back to Molnair with instructions to head a search for you there."

I grimaced. There went my half-formed idea of finding a place in Molnair for us to hide out.

Wells let out a breath and dragged a hand through his hair. "Marc, I can't help but be concerned with how dangerous this is for you. The king has to realize by now that you're sympathetic to us."

"He's also acting as though *he* is sympathetic to you," Marc said. I noticed him subtly testing his sound shield. My aural senses were slowly returning. "He's spreading around that he'd like to give the two of you several months of rest together once you're found. Such a talented pair, so newly mated, so tragically abused by our enemies, no time to think of expanding their family..."

I made a gagging noise. "Sounds like code for 'lock us up and force us to make more lightning babies.'"

"Precisely," Marc inclined his head, lips curved in a grim smile. "Hierarchies being as they are, any children the two of you produce would belong to the palace as much as you do. Not my personal opinion," he added, in reaction to my growl. "As far as the two of you being found here, I'm aware of the risks," he said, looking directly at Wells. "And I honestly can't think of a safer place for you while you recover. We'll eventually have to come up with a long-term plan. You can't live on the ship forever, obviously, and you're both too high-profile to go into hiding easily in Molnair. You'd have to learn to shapeshift or spend your lives constantly glamoured. Anyone you hid with would also be in danger."

He cleared his throat and angled forward in his seat, elbows on knees, then lifted his eyes to meet Wells's. "You should know that Allestair has told a select few of his leaders about Imogen leaving the tent when she shouldn't have been able to and getting past wards that should have been beyond her abilities. So far no one has been able to offer him any satisfying explanation, although I suggested to him privately that perhaps you had brought more of the potion you used to escape the palace and had it hidden somewhere, implying that it allows a one-time pass. A few people have suggested that perhaps you didn't hear him forbid you to leave the tent or that he misspoke in some way. I'm not sure how much he's buying into any of these theories."

Wells closed his eyes and let his head fall back. It hit the wall with a soft thump.

I leaned against him. "At least he seems to have moved on from the killing-you plan."

My mate sighed, lifted his head, and opened his eyes. His expression bleak. "If that's the case, perhaps Imogen can stay in hiding and I can go back alone and—"

Both Captain Marc and I shook our heads emphatically. "Imogen barely survived her own capture," Marc said. "Yet, before recovering, she single-handedly found a way to completely demoralize Demian's compound and pull you out, alive, risking herself several times along the way. Allestair is not stupid. He's realized that perhaps the only sure way to control Imogen is through you. You walk in there without a plan and you may as well hand him both your leashes."

Wells deflated. I threaded my fingers through his.

"Heal first," Marc said to him, rising. "Imogen set her own recovery back with her heroics. Fortunately, the king does have a siege to concentrate on, and he's always enjoyed an excuse to hurl insults at Demian, which occasionally distracts him from hunting for you. You're safe for now. Take care of each other and *rest*. I'll try to bring in something more substantial tonight. Kerlyn has been working on gradually gathering some of your clothes. I'll bring back what we have."

"Thank you, Marc," Wells said, his face pinched, eyes shadowed. "I don't know how we'll ever be able to repay you."

"Staying alive would be a wonderful start," he said with a wink, and vanished, the sound shield dissipating with him.

Wells buried his face in his hands. I wrapped my arms around him. I wasn't used to seeing him this disheartened. "Maybe you should take a shower," I whispered. We'd 'pathed a bit, but it drained Wells so quickly that we decided to give it another day. "I always feel better when I'm clean."

"Won't that make noise?" He dropped his hands away from his face and sighed.

"Captain Marc says that as long as we don't sing it should be fine." I kissed his shoulder. "I'd offer to help, but that gets noisy too."

He gave me one huff of a laugh, then threw back the covers and trudged into the bathroom.

I did end up having to help. But only because Wells's energy tapped out while he rinsed off. I peeked in to find him sitting on the floor of the shower, pale as a ghost. By the time I got him dried off and back into bed it was time for both of our potions. I was almost done with mine.

Wells's soul-deep misery worried me.

"Talk to me," I murmured, combing the tangles out of his dark red hair. I had tucked myself behind him on the bed, turning my shins into his backrest while I leaned against the headboard.

He reached back and ran a hand down my calf, sighing. "How are you not completely overwhelmed right now? You've got to be exhausted yourself and just as stuck as I am."

I considered his question while I teased out a stubborn knot. "Well, you woke up today and talked to me and that makes me so incredibly happy you have no idea. And... my step-father didn't just try to use my life like a pawn on a chessboard." I conquered the tangle and gave his damp hair one more pass with the comb before setting it aside and wrapping my arms and legs around him, pulling him flush to my front.

"Do you want to talk about it?"

He folded his arms over mine, lifted one of my hands to his lips and kissed it, tucked it back against him, and let his head drop back to my shoulder. I laid my cheek against his temple, shut my eyes, and enjoyed the feel of him breathing with me, warm and alive.

Wells was quiet for several minutes, and when he spoke again, his voice was so low I nearly held my breath to make sure I didn't miss a word.

"On one hand, I feel as though I should be used to this. My entire life I've been told my one purpose is to be of service to the crown. Honestly, only Marc—and to a lesser degree, my mother—ever encouraged me to find something I enjoyed and felt fulfilled in while supporting Molnair's monarchy. Even that took careful planning. But outside of that small step, I've done nothing but support Allestair and Aloysuis my entire life."

"Until me," I whispered, guilt tightening my lungs.

He squeezed my arm.

"Other than stepping in to stop Al from trapping you on the ship, my relationship with you does not defy the throne. Mating bonds cannot be argued with and Allestair himself even supported acceptance. And if what he told you is correct, he was planning my death well before you escaped. Likely because you refused to have children. Which should have always been your choice. Allestair has a long history of using the people one cares about against them."

I thought of Iphigenia, encouraging me to fall in line for Wells's sake. I hadn't ever considered that she feared something like this. An uncomfortable feeling of dread settled at the base of my throat. How could we possibly get out of this?

"Kindness was never a trait Allestair cultivated. Perhaps he was kind at some time, but never in the decades since I was born. Cruelty wasn't foreign to him, but it wasn't usually his first impulse. He never treated me like a son, not really, but I never . . ." Wells swallowed, his voice dropping even lower. "I never thought he considered me quite so expendable. Honestly, the greater surprise is how much it hurts."

I hugged him hard, my heart cracking for him. "I'm sorry," I breathed.

For several long minutes, we sat in silence, listening to the sounds of the ship, occasional footfalls in the corridors, our own breathing. "Wells," I whispered, a part of me afraid to even voice the question. "Where can we go that he won't find us? Is there another country?"

Wells sighed. "Most of the beings in other parts of Perimov barely tolerate sidhe. And there are some places that are outright dangerous."

"I just . . . I just want to be able to live a normal life with you." I pressed my cheek against his, my heart sinking. "I don't want to be anyone's tool or weapon. Or breeding machine." I dropped my forehead onto his shoulder. "Even if Marc thinks he won't kill you, he's definitely going to lock us up."

He pushed out of my embrace, grabbed the covers and threw them over us. Then pulled me into his arms and pressed a kiss between my brows. "Sorry, Demon. I'm sure we'll think of something. And at the very least, if he does lock us up, we'll be together."

"I hope so," I said, but I couldn't think of anything we could do to escape Allestair's reach. And we couldn't hide forever.

CHAPTER THIRTY-SEVEN

Sometimes there are only bad plans.
And you just have to pick one and do your best.
—Cilla Ibrahim

I knew something was up when I tried to 'path the unicorns and ran up against a new shield—with a nice painful trap embedded. Fortunately, I now habitually checked before 'pathing any place hidden behind a blood kroma ward.

I let my head fall against the headboard, shut the heavy military textbook with a hollow thump, and plopped it atop the pile Captain Marc had lent me to occupy myself. "That headache spell is up around the camp."

Wells glanced up at me, mid-push-up, pausing at the top.

I glared at him but didn't say anything. I thought he should rest a bit more before adding in calisthenics. "They've changed the wards. I don't think anyone is allowed to 'path anymore. Blood or no." I checked-in with the unicorns for both of us since he wasn't of the Blood.

"I don't like the sound of that." Wells finished his set before burpeeing to stand in the small area of floor space in the cramped cabin. Weak or no, we were both a little stir-crazy now that we were recovering. And I was personally very tired of whispering.

Captain Marc winked in and tossed a sound shield against the wall almost carelessly. "I don't have much time. I've been summoned, but you should know that Aloysius returned to camp today, by order of his father, and has Cilla, Zoe, and their child with him."

"What *here*?" I jumped up to stand next to Wells, spots flashing across my vision for an instant. He shushed me. Thank goodness for the sound shield. Even so, I barely managed to modulate my voice. "Why the fuck would he bring them to a war zone?"

"Ostensibly to help search for you," Marc said, crossing his arms.

I clamped my teeth together until they ached, shoving my hands into my hair, curling my fists around the strands and biting back a scream. Terror for Cilla and her family tore through me while guilt settled low in my stomach.

Marc took a breath, then murmured, "The public line is that Cilla couldn't stand that you hadn't been found and insisted on coming. In reality, it's to draw you out."

I sucked in a long inhale, released my hair, and forced my arms to my sides. Still, I couldn't keep my fingers from curling into fists, nails biting into my palms as I squeezed my eyes shut. Wells put an arm around my waist and pulled me close. "What should we—"

"I'm going now, I'll let you know as soon as possible what's being said. I'll do what I can for them." Marc swiped a hand across his clean-shaven skull and blew out a breath.

"They changed the wards," I told him quickly. "I can't 'path you while you're there."

His arm dropped and his shoulders sagged. Obviously he hadn't expected that. "I'll be back as soon as I can." His eyes shuttered, face smoothing to neutral, then he winked out.

He didn't return.

After eight hours, Wells risked winking into Marc's private berth. He was back in less than a minute.

"His room has been tossed," he said, face tight. "I'm not sure what he's done to this cabin to keep everyone uninterested, but they suspect he knows something. We need to get out and do our best to make it look like we were never here."

We shoved clothes into our only bag with Wells's remaining potions. I used a little kroma to make the bed look as fresh and unused as possible. Wells winked into Marc's rooms to dump my final empty potion bottle down the trash chute. Our scent would linger, no matter what we did, but perhaps we could at least give the impression that we were long gone, or that no one else had known we were here.

We strapped on swords and tucked our daggers into boots. My eyes found Wells's. "If you can wink us somewhere outside the camp, I can cloak us and get us through the wards. If that's where we're going." I didn't feel the slightest bit nervous, nor did I see any signs of nerves in Wells's aura. Although neither of us were fully recovered, we weren't people who sat still well. It felt good to finally be doing something. Even if we weren't sure what it was.

"I think that's best," he said, slinging our duffel crossways on his back. "We know we're acting as Allestair expects, but—not only do I not see another option—we can't continue to operate blind. Let's try to get information without giving ourselves away before we have to. I suppose we could try to wink near the medic tent, if we're discovered there—"

"Wait." I put a hand on his arm. "How high up are we right now?"

His eyebrows pulled together. "I suppose about forty or fifty feet, why?"

I grinned up at him. "Do you wanna do something dumb?"

CHAPTER THIRTY-EIGHT

I will not throw someone I love into a fire meant for me.
—Imogen Delaney

We burst into the air above the unicorn habitat. Wells—bless him—clung to me like a backpack with all the trust in the world as I called the wind to slow our descent. Maneuvering was challenging with Wells's added weight, but I managed to safely guide us toward a space between the trees.

In spite of the seriousness of our errand, the warmth of the sun on my skin seemed to expunge a stagnant darkness from within my chest, leaving a light, fluttery feeling behind. Ages without fresh air had me taking deep lungfuls as the wind whipped around us. I didn't even mind the smack of Sephrya's humidity against my skin. Wells's heart thundered against my back, but to his credit, he didn't make a sound as we coasted closer to the treetops.

When we passed through the wards, I knew something was wrong.

I kept quiet until I'd floated us to some sturdy branches. We'd agreed it would be best not to take any chances. We would store our clothes and personal items in the trees, 'path Prism and Obsidian, get the lay of the land as best we could before even setting foot on the ground.

There was something different with the wards, I 'pathed Wells once we had clambered onto separate branches and dropped within sight of the forest floor. *Did you feel it?*

I thought so, but since passing through a blooded ward feels wrong to me anyway I was hoping that was it. His eyelashes flicked up, gaze meeting mine as he tied our duffel to a branch. *What did you feel?*

I think they let me in, but I don't think they will let me out. I secured my pack of precious things to my tree, then stepped carefully, limb to limb, to join Wells on his branch. *I don't think they will let anyone other than the king out.*

He took my hand and nodded. His aura was calm, no sparks of surprise or swirls of discomfort. "I knew that was a possibility," he said. "I can't discern anyone in the habitat that's not a unicorn. But I also can't feel Marc, Zoe, or Cilla within the camp."

With one hand pressed into the tree trunk for balance, I pushed my focus out across the camp, searching for those familiar signatures. "I don't feel them either. But not like ... not like they're not here ... more like they're blocked or something. I feel Kerlyn, so she's safe." I exhaled through my nose. "I feel Al." I didn't even reach for Allestair's essence. For all I knew he had some way of reaching back.

Wells squeezed my hand. "They've shielded them in some way. Or muted them. We'll likely have to follow Al's signature to find out where to go. But let's talk to the unicorns first."

"Do you feel your spy guys?" Maybe Jarleth and Kitano could help us out.

"As I'm no longer general, it's not really my place to call on them." He dropped his gaze and knocked his heel against our branch. "Although I know they would answer."

I squeezed his hand and raised an eyebrow when he met my eyes. The corners of his mouth tilted upward and his gaze went distant for a beat. "They've both been assigned watch and can't get away without alerting someone."

"Can't you ask what's what?" I leaned against the tree trunk, working out a knot between my shoulder blades.

"I have and they don't know." Wells placed his palms on the bark to either side of me. My face tilted upward as he leaned closer, his voice low. "Apparently since Cilla and Zoe arrived the king has stopped returning to the ship as often. He's left the running of the siege entirely to Adgemon. Kavlo was called in this morning also. Since he and Marc arrived, they, along with Adgemon and Al, have been in constant company with the king. He's not letting them out of his sight."

All lightness fled, yet we remained gazing at each other, our lips inches apart. If only I'd been of average power . . . if only we'd hidden my lightning better . . . or for longer . . . if only . . . Flashes of the life we might have lived swept through my mind but I didn't let those thoughts go any further. Now was all we had to work with. I bent away from the trunk and pressed my lips to his.

Wells responded with an ardor that surprised me. Pressing me against the bark, his tongue slid along the seam of my lips, parting them, then diving in. There was a bittersweet intensity to the kiss that cracked my heart, a kind of farewell. I gripped his shoulders, thankful that Wells was sure-footed—as if he made out in trees on the regular—and let my fingers glide into his hair. He cupped one hand behind my head, cushioning it, the other sliding beneath my shirt, over my bra. I gasped into his mouth and he hummed back.

We barely heard the soft rustle of grass beneath us. All that announced the arrival of Prism and Obsidian.

Come down. What are you doing? Prism stomped a shiny hoof.

Wells slowly broke the kiss, gaze lingering on mine. A deep ache bloomed in my chest as I realized this might be our last taste of freedom. I pulled him back in for one more soft peck before answering Prism. *We wanted to make sure no enemies were around,* I told him, as I released Wells, letting my fingers pull through his long hair as I dropped my hands away from his face.

He brushed his fingertips along my collarbone, pausing on the auger stone before he turned from me and swung down to meet the unicorns. I followed more carefully, climbing from branch to branch, giving my feelings a chance to ebb away.

Wells wrapped his arms around Obsidian's neck as soon as he was on the ground. Both their auras coalesced; flowing with colors mixing too quickly for me to grasp. Obsidian had his head bowed, angled toward Wells.

He's been very worried, said Prism. *It's not common to mark your rider and then be so quickly separated. And to be unable to 'path through the barrier. He wanted to wink to you, but I informed him that this would just put us all in danger.*

That's right, I 'pathed, the bones of an escape plan sliding into my brain. *You two can wink through the blood kroma wards. Could you wink through the ones up now if you wanted?*

Prism's horn glowed slightly, swirling with glitter. *I believe we could. Is there to be conquest? I have been bored.*

Maybe, I 'pathed. *We've got to go see what's going on with our friends, but we wanted to see the two of you first.*

The unicorns weren't thrilled once we gave them a brief rundown, but we told them we'd keep a 'path open to them when we weren't behind a cloaking shield or some other ward. We still have no idea why we couldn't get a hold on Cilla and Zoe. Prism and Obsidian walked us to the tree line. I took Wells's arm and cloaked us long before we might be visible.

The energy of the camp did feel strange. It was nothing I could specifically quantify. People were active, out and about, performing normal tasks, but something felt off. I thought perhaps it was my own nerves, but Wells agreed.

"Something's put everyone on edge," he murmured. "It's as if the entire camp is holding its breath."

"I can't read auras well through the shield," I said, stepping closer to him to avoid running into six soldiers marching in swift formation, intent on their errand. "What's our plan?"

"Get close enough to where Al is to see if we can locate Cilla, Zoe, and Marc," he said, his eyes darting around the camp. He pulled me in front of him to avoid the unicorn caretakers hauling a cart of food toward the habitat. Must be dinnertime. "See if we can get a better read on the situation. Go from there."

"This feels a whole lot like flying by the seat of our pants." I moved back to his side and took his arm once we were clear.

"Flying by the seat of our pants?" Wells's eyebrows lifted toward his hairline.

I pressed my lips together, choking down a giggle. "Earth saying. It means operating without a plan."

"Then you should be perfectly comfortable." One corner of his mouth tipped upward.

"And yet."

We stopped whispering as it became clear that we were walking back toward our old tent. My stomach churned. I wrapped my hand tighter around Wells's arm. There was no way the king was going to let us out of here. I alternated between wondering what the hell we had been thinking and telling myself that no matter what, we couldn't leave our friends trapped in our stead. Worst-case scenario, we would be locked up in the palace and told to make babies. I still had a few more months of sterility from the blood spell. Maybe we could figure something out before that ended.

Al and the king were definitely in our old tent. It was also heavily guarded and shielded. We carefully circled the entire perimeter without learning anything else.

Anyone not of the blood is muted by whatever wards are in place, Wells 'pathed.

Shouldn't I be able to get in and get a read on them if they're in there? I asked.

Not the way this particular spell works, apparently. The rules are different if you're inside the tent and outside of it. As king, Allestair has use of several blood kromas that the rest of us don't. It would be too draining for anyone else to keep this kind of ward up for long, but...

What do we do? I asked, my stomach swirling. We'd only discussed the worst-case scenario in passing. Neither of us would stand for our friends taking the fall for us. Neither of us wanted to be at the king's mercy. We also knew that Allestair would ensure that it was much more difficult for us to escape this time. If we could keep him from learning about my blood status, then we perhaps had some other loopholes.

Wells hugged me under the shield. *I don't suppose you'd agree if I volunteered to go in on my own?*

Hell no. What good would that even do? I 'pathed viciously, wrapping my arms possessively around his waist. *He'd probably just publicly torture you until I came out. I don't suppose you'd let me go in alone?*

Absolutely not.

Good, so neither of us is going to hide behind the other. I leaned into him and closed my eyes, nerves squeezing my lungs. The bond delivered Wells's resigned dread straight into my own stomach.

We stood together for a moment, savoring our last few moments of freedom. But there were no other options. Perhaps going willingly would make things easier on us. Anger spiked in a hot flash. We'd been in his army, literally fighting his war. I was using the powers he coveted so much on behalf of his kingdom. It wasn't fair.

At least we'll be together, Wells 'pathed, pulling back to look at me. He brushed the backs of his fingers across my cheek. *And someday we will find a way out. I'm sure of it.* We sighed simultaneously.

My anger burnt out quickly, leaving only raw nerves behind. Drawing this out was only making it worse. *Ready?*

He nodded and we stepped away from each other. I let the shield drop. Wells took my hand and we walked side by side to the tent's entrance.

CHAPTER THIRTY-NINE

There is no success without the risk of failure. And success is never guaranteed. Often, it comes down to having the courage to fail again and again.
—King Demian Gallagher

T he guards instantly stepped aside for us, even going so far as to pull back the tent flaps. I checked their auras.

They're nervous and confused, I 'pathed.

Not surprising. I'm sure they've been told nothing other than to let us inside and no one goes out, he replied as we stepped into the tent.

The sudden change from Sephrya's hot blanket of moisture to the kromatically cooled air inside had my skin erupting in goosebumps. Wells tried to stop just inside the tent, but we were firmly pressed into the room by the interior guards. They stepped behind us and snapped the tent flaps shut.

Dread hugged my stomach as my eyes adjusted. Wells squeezed my hand. Through the bond his anise pang of resolve hit the back of my tongue.

The interior of our tent had changed. The bed was folded up and shoved back against the far end. The table had also been dragged to the edges. In their places were settees and lounge chairs.

Perched in one corner, on their own settee, were Cilla and Zoe.

Zoe's black eyes were devastatingly calm. She sat rod-straight, balanced on the edge of her seat, one dark arm resting across her partner's pale legs. Just blocking Cilla. My best friend was tucked into the corner, peeking around Zoe's shoulders, her blue eyes locked on me. As if I were the one thing she'd been looking for. My attention was snagged by a flicker of movement near her midsection. She was holding their new baby.

I'd never seen an infant sidhe before. Little Kris was perfectly tan. Her skin almost exactly between Zoe and Cilla, edging a little on the darker side, with white-blond curls.

My heart twisted. I stumbled forward, lifting my arms toward Cilla—Wells yanked me back. Not to his side, but in front of him. His body curled around mine, intensely protective in a way he'd never been. His face was hard, eyes on the red end of russet.

I followed the line of his gaze.

King Allestair stood behind the desk, which had been moved to the center of the room. His icy eyes gleamed, aura dancing with satisfaction. He leaned forward; fingers splayed near the edges of the wood. His lips curled upward.

Wells's desk was clear, save one sheet of paper and a long iron rod.

Aloysius, Adgemon, Kavlo, and Marc stood behind the king. Their auras tumbled with distress.

Marc's face was ashen.

This alone had my bones going soft.

"You're not touching her with that," Wells snapped, his eyes darting to the rod on the table and then back to the king. "She's done nothing to deserve it."

His long fingers wrapped my biceps as he pressed me against his chest. Two breaths later, I realized that he was trying to wink. And failing.

That was part of the wards on the tent then. Only the king and Al could wink out. I wondered if I could.

I took a closer look at the metal rod. The end curved into a swirling S like a cattle brand from an old Western. My breath caught. I'd read about this in Marc's military books. Slave brands, their metal forged with poison so the mark would never heal. But those were rarely used, and only for prisoners of war, traitors, and deserters. I was none of those things.

"Of course she hasn't," Allestair said, picking up the brand, his voice slick as oil. Out of the corner of my eye, I saw Zoe tuck Cilla into her, her face stricken. "This is for you, Llewellen."

Ice coated my stomach, with the dual sensation that told me Wells was experiencing the same emotion. He moved one hand from its protective barrier in front of me to my shoulder at the base of my neck. If he was branded, an entirely different set of kromatic rules would apply to him. This would go beyond the inability to disobey anything forbidden by his king. Allestair would have complete control. Wells would have no choice but to obey anything he said. There would be no new position in the army, no possibility of ever moving away from the palace. The control would pass to Al once Allestair was gone. I grabbed Wells's arm and tried to wink us out. I'd get Cilla and Zoe later.

But it was like Wells was a weight dragging me back. I couldn't wink with him.

Imogen, go. Find somewhere to hide. If he marks me, I'll have to do whatever he wants—

He can't! "You can't do that to him," I growled at Allestair. "That's for prisoners of war, traitors—"

Allestair's eyes narrowed on me. I wondered if he was shocked at my ability to speak. He'd never lifted that injunction. "And deserters," the king said, tapping the brand against his other palm. "Where have you been hiding the past week, Llewellyn?"

My jaw dropped open. My eyes flew around the room, unwittingly searching for help. The guards were poker-faced. I'd learned while living in the palace that they only experienced mild discomfort at most when the king bullied someone. And then only the newer ones. Cilla and Zoe were hunched together, faces tight with devastation, their auras drenched with guilt. Al's aura spun with anxiety. His face had never been more bloodless. Captain Marc and Admiral Kavlo both looked like they were going to be sick. Fear, disbelief, and helplessness twisted through their auras. Adgemon was the picture of shock, his thick, black hair sticking out in odd places, as if he'd been shoving his hands through it. He was obviously new to Allestair's ways.

The king strolled around the desk, casually tapping the brand against his open palm.

"He was eviscerated by the Sephryans!" I barked, fanning my arms out as if I could physically shield Wells. "You sanctioned him going there! I got him out. He was unconscious for days. *You* assumed him dead and put Adgemon in his place." I pointed toward Adgemon, who nodded, hopefully. As if this were a misunderstanding that could be cleared up. "He wasn't deserting, he was fucking fired. And you orchestrated—"

He cut me off, eyes sharp. "I did promote Adgemon in Llewellyn's place, of course. Llewellyn had surrendered himself in your stead and we needed a general." Allestair smoothly regained his composure, still strolling ever closer with the brand. "However, I merely demoted Llewellyn. I never released him from the army."

Rage tumbled through my veins, a slow burn that grew ever hotter. He was clever. I'd never dealt with someone so devious. Even now, here we were: *his* worst-case scenario. And the king had a plan for that as well. For a moment, I considered blurting out that this had all been Allestair's doing in the first place ... but it was my word against the king's. If Marc came to my defense, we'd risk outing that he'd helped us. Even if everyone in this tent was on my side, Allestair had the Blood. And all the excess magic that went with it. My chest tightened.

I watched Marc, Kavlo, Adgemon, even Al, try to reason with him. Listing Wells's commendations. Citing his loyalty of service. The successful campaign against Sephrya. How his unit survived against impossible odds. Allestair only pretended to listen.

"Father, you know Mother won't stand for it," Al tried. "You'd be humiliating her as well—"

"Your mother will have both of her sons back under her roof again," Allestair interrupted coldly. "I daresay she'll find a way to make do."

Allestair's aura was hungry. Excited. He had us cornered at last. During it all, I rifled through my memory for any information I had absorbed about this brand. For ways around it. I knew there were ways . . .

"I wouldn't worry about Llewellyn," he told the others. "As long as he . . . and his mate," he gave me an oily smile, "cooperate. His servitude will be very light."

"Isn't there some kind of . . . due process?" I asked, my eyes bouncing from person to person. "Surely you can't just trap someone and throw a brand on them?"

He's the king, Imogen, he can do whatever he wants, Well's 'pathed, his hands steady, but cold on my shoulders.

I'm not letting him do this to you, I snarled, continuing to angle myself between Allestair and Wells.

The brand glowed ever more red as Allestair pushed kroma through it. "Any requests as to where we put it? Somewhere easily seen . . . but perhaps able to be covered for your mother's sake . . ." His eyes flicked to Wells's neck.

Finally, something clicked. "I challenge you for him."

Zoe gasped, then the room stilled. All eyes swiveled toward me but I kept mine locked on Allestair's face. Wells's hands tightened on my shoulders and he pulled me back. *Imogen, no. Rescind.* Captain Marc squeezed his eyes shut as if he were in pain. His aura sank into blues and dark violets. Allestair shook his head, smiling condescendingly.

"Only sidhe from another kingdom may challenge a king to spare a soldier from slavery," he said. "You cannot challenge your own king. Although the drive to protect your mate is laudable."

"You are not my king." I stared unblinkingly at him, straightening my spine. Wells's agony twisted through my guts. I ignored it. I was not going to have him become a slave to Allestair. More than he already was. "I wasn't born in your country and you have no power over me."

"Every Earthling turned swears fealty when they sign their consent form." Allestair's voice was coated in ice. His frosty-blue eyes darkened as they bored into mine. I watched the pieces falling into place behind them.

"I never agreed to be turned." I took a step toward him. "So I never signed a goddamn thing. How about you put that fucking brand away so we can set the terms of this challenge." I shouldn't have enjoyed swearing in front of him so much.

Wells yanked me backward. "I'm sure we can come to some kind of agreement?"

"One that doesn't involve you branding someone who doesn't deserve it," I spat.

Wells slammed one arm across my chest, trapping me against him, and wrapped his other hand around my bicep. *Imogen, stop baiting him, you're making it worse. He'll kill you if you go through with this challenge. You just got off potions for hell's sake.*

I'm not letting him brand you, I growled.

I'd rather be a slave and have you alive than free with you dead, he shot back fiercely.

"Father, let's just take them home," Al spoke up, his aura spiky with desperation. "We've found them, they're safe . . ." he glanced around. "No one seems happy about branding Wells, he didn't know he was still part of the army and now that we know he was seriously wounded . . . Maybe we can just get Imogen to swear fealty and move on."

I opened my mouth to argue, but Wells clapped a hand over it. *Imogen, please. We knew when we walked into this tent that we were giving ourselves up. If Al can talk him out of accepting your challenge, let him. We'll deal with the rest as it comes up.*

I watched the king's eyes sweep over the two of us greedily.

His grip tightened on the no longer glowing brand. Ice-blue eyes calculating. I couldn't help wondering what details he was adding up in his head. The longer he looked, the more his aura tossed with the muddy greens of avarice. He wanted control of us badly. I wondered if it were still about my bloodline and the children I would produce or if it had morphed into some kind of vendetta. Conquering us individually.

"What do you desire, should your challenge be successful, Imogen?" Allestair purred, twirling the brand between his fingers, eyes fixed on me.

Wells dropped his hand from my face, now unabashedly wrapping both arms around me. I laid my hands on his forearms, squeezing back. It was only then I noticed that we were both trembling. "Wells and I get to live our lives free from you. We go back to Wells's house until he's fully recovered, he can stay in the army if he wants, or do something else if he chooses. No branding. No signing."

The king nodded, eyes flashing. "And if I win, you *will* sign fealty to me, and I will brand *both* of you." The corners of his mouth curved upward. I'd never seen him smile so much. "These are the terms. If you survive, of course."

"I accept," I said, and only had a moment to congratulate myself on the steadiness of my voice before kroma zinged against my skin, locking me in challenge with Allestair. Everyone watching deflated.

Wells's heart thundered against my back. The other auras in the tent spun more quickly, the bright colors of alarm flashing through.

Allestair's aura remained a muddy green, bronze determination pulsing beneath. "Kroma only," Allestair continued. "As the rules dictate, you may choose one weapon. Know that you may only wield it once. If you are disarmed or your strike fails, you forfeit the weapon."

I nodded. My mouth going dry. Wells's hug tightened.

"Now for location . . ." Allestair glanced around the tent as if he were wondering if it were large enough.

"We're not doing it in here." I flung an arm toward Cilla and Zoe. "There's a goddamn *baby*." I also didn't want to be contained inside a tent shrouded with his blood-kroma spells. I wouldn't stand a chance then.

"Traditionally," Captain Marc broke in, "the monarch being challenged proposes the terms and once accepted, the challenger proposes the location. Terms having been agreed upon, Imogen should choose location."

"The plain across from the Briarwood Forest," I said immediately. It was outside the camp's shield. *If he kills me, you can escape into the forest. The urzen won't hurt you,* I 'pathed.

If he kills you, I'm committing treason and doing my best to rip his throat out, Wells responded. *Imogen, if you lose, but he doesn't kill—*

I'm not entertaining that possibility right now, I told him firmly. *Don't put that energy out there. I just have to be smart.*

Moments later, we were all standing in the field. In addition to everyone who had occupied the tent, a regiment of soldiers had been ordered out by Adgemon as a precaution in case someone from Sephrya decided to interrupt our proceedings or any urzen prowled out.

Like I would be so lucky.

Once free of the tent, I 'pathed Prism with an update as I had promised. He wasn't thrilled about being left out of any violence I was involved in, but there wasn't much he could do about it. By kromatic law, once a challenge had been issued and accepted, it was impossible for anyone to interfere until it was finished. He and Obsidian insisted on being present, however, and winked themselves to the field. No one dared attempt to corral them.

Marc and Kavlo had summoned an open tent for Cilla and Zoe to sit beneath with the baby. Neither of them were willing to stay behind in the camp. I'd been able to wave at them and exchange a quick 'path with Cilla telling her the baby was beautiful and she looked amazing, but nothing else. The palace guards wouldn't let me approach them. Although the presence of several of Wells's soldiers ringing the plain gave me a lift.

Wells and I had been stripped of our weapons in the tent. My dagger, which I chose as my one-strike item, was laid, unsheathed, on a table near

Cilla and Zoe's tent beside the king's choice. Allestair had picked the branding iron as his weapon. As a taunt or a tactical move, I wasn't sure. We were to summon our items when we wanted them. For one strike only.

Wells's long fingers drifted across my clothing as he checked me over. As if an untucked portion of my shirt would tip the scales. *Allestair has powers you've never seen before, Imogen. Remember the things that you do well and don't let him trip you up.*

Care to elaborate? I forced a smile I didn't feel.

He sighed and lifted his hands to cup my face. *He has powers even I haven't seen. And there isn't time.*

Indeed, the palace guards were glancing over at the king, as if wondering when they should rip Wells away from me. I raised my eyes to his, ignoring the fear and worry swirling through his aura.

He brushed his thumbs over my cheekbones. "I'm sure you've realized that this will not end at first blood. It will end with one of you dead, incapacitated, or verbally surrendering." He touched his forehead to mine, lowering his voice to a whisper. "I love you, Imogen." His fingers tightened around my jaw. "There's no shame in surrendering to stay alive. We'll figure the rest out if it comes to that."

"I love you, too. I'm not going to die. And I'm not going to surrender." I gave his arm a squeeze and he stepped back. Tension wafting through his aura. But this was it. I felt it in my bones; this was the only way for Wells and I to free ourselves of this monster. And if someone had to go, it was not going to be Wells, and it was not going to be me.

With my throat desert-dry and my legs like jelly, I turned to face the king.

CHAPTER FORTY

There is no fear like watching a friend fight an impossible battle, knowing you can do nothing but be there to help pick up the pieces when it's done.
—Captain Marcellus Tibercio

As soon as Wells was clear, the atmosphere changed. The air seemed to thicken, like a front coming through. A soldier blew a war horn in one long blast. Time to begin.

My entire body was electric with nerves. My stomach roiled, but my gaze was sharp and my mind clear. As if I was about to step into the ring. I dragged my right foot several inches back, setting myself in fighting stance, in spite of being thirty feet away from him.

Allestair's aura went eye-searingly bright and crackled with gathering power like I had never seen. His lips stretched into a grin so wide it seemed to split his face. As if he'd already won. I'd never seen his genuine smile before today.

I didn't hesitate.

The clouds darkened as I pulled the lightning's energy toward me. Straight for the big guns. If I could end this quickly, I would. I wasn't giving him a chance to play with me.

The king's aura dimmed as he thrust his arms out to the sides. Power surged to his palms. Coalescing into compact, blindingly bright orbs. My world entered slow motion as he hurled two mini-suns at me, overhand, one right after the other. I ducked the first. Clods of hot earth pelted my back as it pounded into the soil behind me. I called the wind as I leapt to the side to avoid the second. I felt its heat sear the air against my legs, just missing its target as the wind lifted me high and fast.

Twin craters marred the turf where I had been standing.

My mouth tightened, nerves fled. Like a switch had been flipped, I was in locked fight mode. I jerked the lightning from the sky as the wind propelled me higher. Electricity wrapped itself around me. Energy zipped along my spine and spanned my torso. I took a breath and narrowed my focus, guiding the energy down my arms.

Then flung a bolt, Zeus-like, at Allestair.

I hurled my second bolt before he could recover, cursing when he winked away. I twisted in the wind's grip. *Where the fuck are you?*

I was thirty feet up when the air stilled.

The wind vanished as if I had accidentally drifted into the eye of a storm. Allestair stood directly beneath me. Arms pressed to the sky. Shaking as if he were holding something aloft.

I tumbled from the breezeless air.

Heart in my throat I called for the wind but it was gone. In desperation, I blasted the field below with lightning. Frantic to slow my descent. My last bolt went sideways and my ribs cracked audibly when I finally smashed into the dirt.

I forced myself to roll to my back immediately. Hurled sticky fire just as Allestair emerged from his wink right at my side. Direct hit. I'd bought myself two seconds.

Ribs screaming, I staggered to my feet.

Allestair gritted his teeth as he fought my fire. Wiping it from his limbs with broad swipes. That he even knew how to combat the spell was impressive. I relentlessly lobbed more. Keeping him cloaked in hungry conflagration. I changed angles. Continually moving. Forcing my lungs to pull in full breaths.

Agony slicing through my ribs like knives with each inhale. Firing flame faster than he could extinguish it. He roared, pain and frustration etched in every line of his face. Then he thrust a hand to the sky. Curled his fingers and yanked down.

I was plunged into darkness.

Fear grabbed me by the throat. I blinked. Jerked my head from side to side. Complete blackness. I couldn't even see Allestair coated in flames. Terror screamed at me to run, to find a way out, but I clenched my jaw and forced my limbs to still. *Don't panic.* Heart pounding, I wrapped myself in a cloaking shield and dropped into a low crouch. Allestair had bought time to deal with the fire. I had time to deal with this. I lowered my head. Took a painful breath. Saw the trampled grass beneath my boots.

I wasn't blind.

I let my gaze travel along the ground. I could see a few inches in all directions. It was as if he had wrapped me in moonless night. Was it everywhere or just this spot? Would it move with me? Had he somehow tied it to me? No matter, I needed to dispel it.

If Allestair had summoned darkness, perhaps I could summon light.

I cupped my hands together as if to scoop water, noticed the red crescent dents my fingernails had carved into my skin and dismissed them. Focused on the energetic wheels at the center of my palms. Thought of light. Searched my essence for it. My blood heated and lightning sparked. I shook it off and tried again.

Light without heat. Just light.

"Come now, Imogen, hiding isn't your style." A lightly barbecued Allestair crept into view, his singed face set in a furious glare. I let his taunting tone roll over me, refusing to allow my focus to waver. He didn't banish the darkness but seemed unaffected by it as he scanned the area. That crackling energy bounced through his aura.

Beneath my shield, a pearl of light winked into existence. It was an effort to tighten my focus as my heart leapt. It was as if I were cradling the brightest grain of sand.

I forced myself to relax into my power as Wells has so often drilled. Breathed a little more energy to my fledgling light. My smile grew as it filled my hands. I caressed its edges. Glanced up. Allestair had inched closer. My grin went feral.

I waited until he turned his face my way. Threw off my cloak.

Flung the light wide.

Blinding him.

And banishing the dark.

He shot a gray stunning-blast sightlessly. I winked away. Sliced the air with blue-black cutting kroma as I emerged. Winking again when Allestair smashed my kromatic blades and chucked a sun my way.

For a breathless eternity, we winked and cast kroma. To emerge without an offensive attack already primed was to be caught unawares. I knew Allestair. Not as well as his family, but he had ensured I was intimately familiar with his cruelty.

I knew he would be going for pain and humiliation. And I met him strike for strike. We flung ourselves in and out of winks. Changing levels. From midair to a tiger crouch. Sprinting or jumping out of the ether.

My entire being was laser-focused. Adrenaline kept the worst of my pain at bay. The rest I shoved aside and tried not to think about the toll this was taking on my not-yet-recovered body. I was expending too much energy to heal quickly. I'd need help mending my ribs.

And I was careful to conserve my power when possible. In the back of my mind, I ran through potential dagger attacks if my kroma were to suddenly sputter out.

At least out here, I had access to the sky. I pulled my lightning into what I thought of as my little battery pack and tossed several cutting blades with a fraction of the energy I might have used normally. I nicked Allestair twice. Slicing face and shoulder. Drawing blood. Hope rose to buoy my heart. I was gaining the upper hand.

Then the ground beneath me split.

I stumbled back from the jagged chasm as it widened. As if the jaws of the earth were yawning wide, hungry for me. A rent now cleaved the field like a carnivorous mouth.

The ground stopped shifting with jarring suddenness. I stumbled to a sloppy fighting stance, looking up just in time to see one of Allestair's suns smack into me.

Pain exploded across my chest when my breastbone cracked.

My body was tossed end over end, no better than a rag doll. The force of the blast crushed the breath from my lungs. I tumbled, stomach-first into a stubbly tree, halting my momentum.

Allestair's second sun had tracked me.

My ribs howled as it rammed me into the packed dirt. My body engulfed in turbulent heat. A burning beyond anything I'd ever experienced shoved itself beneath my skin.

My spine arched off the ground, I opened my mouth to cry out. Snapped it shut as the heat pushed its way down my throat. *Ice! Ice!* I writhed uncontrollably. Spasming in agony. *No, Imogen, think, you have to think.*

I wrenched my concentration inward. Willed my brain to calm. Yes. We're hurt, but we have to keep going. *There is no other option.*

Still thrashing as I was engulfed, I pulled ice to my skin. It wasn't among my most frequently practiced kromas and took all my stored energy. Finally coated in hoarfrost, the heat died. My throat and lungs were seared, burning each time I coughed.

Get up. I ordered my muscles. I rolled to the side, choking up blood. My singed hair fell into my face. Its stinking ends curled and blackened, melting frost dripping from it. Air sawed in and out of my chest in ragged, blade-sharp gasps. I couldn't stop coughing. Slicing torment from my broken ribs accompanied each hacking breath. Blood dripped from my nose. Spotting the ground. I felt the shuddering of the earth as the jagged chasm next to me slammed shut.

Before I could get to my feet, Allestair gripped me by the neck and hauled me up. My toes barely scraped the ground. His nearly transparent aura spun with muddy green. Gold sparks of excitement bursting throughout. His grasp on my throat smothered the coughs. I fought to wrap my legs around his arm. Snap his elbow into an armlock.

He slammed a fist into my hip, spasming the muscle. "Valiant effort," the king panted through bared teeth.

At least I'd winded him. My blackened nails scraped weakly at his fingers.

He shook me as if I were no more than a pesky cat. "Once I've branded you both, I'll allow your mate to heal you. In a day or so." He stretched his other arm behind him. The branding iron flew into his hand. His knuckles whitened around it as he poured heat into the metal. "I should shove this into your insolent face," he growled.

"You know what your tragic flaw is?" I wheezed, one of my hands slipped away from the fist wrapped around my throat, falling against his chest. "Hubris." I summoned my dagger.

Right through his back.

I felt the point stab through my palm before Allestair dropped me. The branding iron tumbled from his grip. He stared down at the dagger, protruding from his front. I guessed I had severed an aorta. Assuming sidhe hearts were set up like human hearts. He staggered back.

Coughing and wheezing, I staggered forward two steps, reached around him, wrapped scorched fingers around the hilt, and jerked it from his body.

Blood fountained from his mouth. He pressed one hand to the hole in his chest. The other clamped onto my shoulder. His aura shuddered with a riot of color.

I stumbled, dropping my dagger and gripping his arms with both hands. My eyes locked onto his just as my peripheral vision darkened. His limbs went slack under my fingers. His aura flew from his sagging body as the light left his eyes. My lungs heaved, each breath searing. I couldn't hold him. My grip slipped and he dropped away as my knees buckled.

"I've got you, Demon." Broad hands caught me under the arms. I fell back against Wells's chest.

Something slammed into us. Hot, fierce, and powerful. The heat and pressure forced their way under my skin, gliding along my bones and wrapping around my organs. My mouth dropped open in a silent, jaw-cracking scream as my spine arched painfully against Wells's grip. My vision darkened. I left my body behind; heard screaming and felt my own throat tearing as if I were listening from a distance. I tried to hang on, tried to stay with Wells, but the world was ripped away.

It was as if my ears existed separate from the rest of my body, which was perhaps lying peacefully in a different room two floors below.

It was nice. No pain, no responsibility, but not alone.

"... suppose we should ask Al. And Mother."

"As everything is in tremendous flux at the moment, I might dare suggest we do things traditionally? If Aloysius agrees, of course..."

My body slowly floated up to join my ears. I had weight and sensation. My lungs smoothly filled and deflated. I braced for pain to seize me again. My ribs didn't hurt. My hand didn't throb.

I risked a deep inhale. Scented no blood, mud, or burnt hair. In their place was sandalwood, spice, soap, and that one indefinable element that made the cocktail my favorite.

Wells.

My heart lifted. I tried to find my muscles. To move.

Gentle fingers pushed hair away from my face.

"I think she's joining us at last." I stretched toward Wells's voice. *We're free. Free. Free.* I felt his warm hand wrap around mine. "Alright, Demon. You're safe now. You can wake up."

My eyelids fluttered. Fluttered. Opened.

Wells smiled down at me. My head rested on a pillow in his lap. "There she is," he whispered, sunset eyes bright.

"Hello," I croaked. No coughing. Air passed easily in and out of my lungs. My throat no longer felt scorched.

"How do you feel, Imogen?" he asked. Smoothing nonexistent stray hairs back from my forehead.

"Not as bad as I should." Pain hadn't grabbed me again. It almost felt like something was missing. Like getting rid of hiccups and waiting for the next one to hit. But I felt fine. In fact, I felt like I was crackling with energy. Which didn't seem right after what I had been through.

I lifted my right hand. Not even a scar where the knife had pierced the skin. I turned my head. We were in a large airship's berth. I was reminded of photos of the "good suites" on cruise ships. The ones regular people could never hope to afford. There was even an oblong window stretched across one wall.

Captain Marc sat at a galley table, attached to the wall at my right, with two long booth-like cushioned benches on either side. Admiral Kavlo was perched on the edge of a sofa on the opposite wall, leaning forward with his elbows on his knees.

I rolled to my side and shoved myself to a seat. Wells steadied me when my head spun, but the world quickly righted itself. We were perched on the edge of a large, circular bed with luxurious, blue satin coverings, too large to belong on a ship.

"Cilla and Zoe?" My voice broke on Zoe's name and I cleared my throat.

A strained smile curved Kavlo's lips upward. "Fine. Resting with their baby. You'll see them soon."

"What happened?" My voice was less hoarse.

A beat of silence.

"Well, for starters," Marc said. "We have a new ruler."

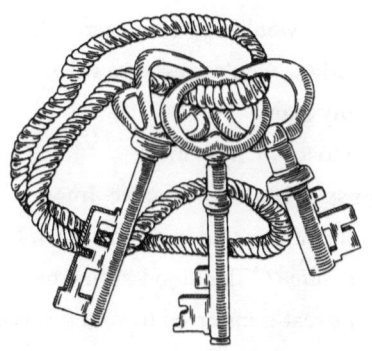

CHAPTER FORTY-ONE

A life worth living is worth fighting for.
—Llewellyn Eigneachan

My stomach swooped. I had been so laser focused on preventing Wells's enslavement and surviving Allestair I hadn't given a passing thought to who would succeed him if I won. I glanced around the room, my hand tensing on Wells's thigh. I couldn't see Al anywhere. My heartbeat thundered in my ears. Surely the throne passed to him. Did he hate me for killing his father?

Wells was rubbing those circles between my shoulder blades. The ones he rubbed when he thought I might freak out.

"So, Al is king right?" I asked, my eyes flicking from person to person when no one said anything. "That's why he's not here. He's doing king... stuff?"

Wells slid an arm around my waist as my shoulders tensed. I couldn't look at him, although I pressed harder into his side. I knew. I knew if I glanced at Wells the truth would be written across his face. But I made myself focus on Captain Marc, who's eyes were still on Wells's. When no one spoke, he finally met my gaze.

My blood turned to ice in my veins.

"Turns out your spell was very effective, Imogen," Captain Marc said, swirling two fingers of amber liquid in a short glass. *Is he drinking whiskey? Are we in a whiskey situation?* "The blood kroma has chosen you, and thus the power of Molnair's seat transferred to you. It was quite the light show. Many people thought it went to Llewellyn as he was physically supporting you at the time."

I went numb, my vision darkening at the edges. My gaze remained locked on Captain Marc, waiting for him to say something else. Perhaps offer a solution. A way to reverse this. I was in no way qualified to rule Molnair.

He merely sipped his cocktail.

I shot to my feet. My lungs expanded in a sudden rush. I hadn't realized that I'd stopped breathing. Feeling charged back into my limbs in an electric surge. My knees buckled, but I caught myself. Wells stood beside me, wrapping a broad hand around my upper arm. "Breathe, Imogen."

My legs steadied as I sucked in a shaky breath. I half-turned to him, one hand curling around a fold in the sleeve of his shirt, holding hard, as if I could use it to pull myself out of this nightmare. Wells merely took hold of my other hand, gazing steadily at me. "We will get through this." Although he projected outward calm, his aura radiated buttery nerves. He dipped his chin in the barest nod.

"Oh, she's awake."

My breath caught as Al strolled into the room, a bottle of whiskey clutched in one fist.

He slid to a seat on the galley bench opposite Captain Marc, letting the bottle thunk to the table. "Congratulations. Your majesty." He drew out the last word in a mocking sneer as he pulled the cork and splashed whiskey into his glass. His hard amber eyes never turned to me once, focused on the middle distance as he sipped his drink.

I forced down a deep inhale and turned forward again, willing my fingers to release Wells's sleeve. My gaze flicked between Marc and Kavlo. "Can we undo it?" I rasped.

They shook their heads in unison.

My knees went watery again and I sank down to the edge of the bed.

Al snorted. "Eventually someone is going to have to admit I was right about that fucking prophecy," he muttered into his glass as he took another large sip.

My chest caved as if I'd been punched in the sternum by one of Allestair's suns. The feeling spread until I felt as if I were breathing through cheesecloth. "The prophecy never said anything about being king."

Al's eyes finally locked onto mine. I had never seen them so hard. "You have to argue about everything, don't you, Imogen. Gods' fucking bones."

Numbness swept through my limbs and all I could do was stare at Al, marking another rare use of my full name. I had killed his father and stolen everything he'd been groomed for. I was certain everyone in the room could hear my heart crashing into my ribs.

Al tossed the rest of his drink back and filled his glass again. "I went to a seer after Solange. She said the human of legend would take up residence in the palace and have great influence on my life." He laughed humorlessly. "She could have been more specific."

"You can keep the palace. I don't want it," I said, eyebrows pulling together. This, at least, was something I could give back to Al. I turned to Marc, not even bothering to hide the desperation in my voice. "I don't have to live there, do I? Can I just let Al and Iphigenia have it? I don't want to live there."

"You have to live there, Imogen," Wells said, his voice painfully gentle. "Although you certainly don't have to kick anyone out."

"Why? I hate it there. You don't like it either."

"The ... current monarch's power is tied to the mountain. It always has been. You have to spend time there to reconnect with it and the moment you stop calling it home, the protections around it cease to exist as they are also tied to you. If you leave it permanently, you leave the mountain vulnerable. Meaning not only its inhabitants, but the seat of Molnair's power."

"But, nice to know how you really feel about my home," Al bit out, already halfway through his second glass of straight whiskey.

Anger simmered, flushing my skin and burning a bit of the horror away. I got to my feet. "I've never made it a secret. And the argument could be made that this mess is all your fault."

"*My* fault?" Al stood and threw his glass into the fireplace—yes, on an airship—where it shattered. "You're the one who absolutely refuses to follow any fucking rules but your own. You have to fight everyone on anything. Do everything the hard way."

Wells stepped up beside me as Al took a step forward.

Al's burning eyes flicked to Wells for an instant before returning to me, a sneer curling his lip. "We could have been happy, Imogen, if you had just trusted me and given things a shot, but no, you had to fight, get other people involved." He slashed a hand in Captain Marc's general direction. "You had to cozy up to my brother, refuse to see me, so *of course* you bonded with him. Even then you couldn't just stay put and stay safe in the palace. No, you had to do things your own way. Lie about everything. Find a fucking ancient potion to change your blood and come to the goddamn war front, nearly getting yourself killed, nearly getting Wells killed, fucking up treaties, bonding to unicorns, stirring up urzen, and now—"

Kavlo stepped up and put a hand on Al's shoulder, his dark eyes sympathetic. Al shook him off with more force than necessary. Marc silently floated the whiskey bottle to his own side of the table.

Al spun back toward me, his eyes flashing back and forth between my face and Wells's before landing on mine. "'Demon' is the perfect nickname for you. Just come in and fuck shit up irreparably." He spun on his heel, summoning the whiskey bottle into his hand as he strode to the door. "I can't believe I thought you were anything like Solange. I wish I'd never seen you."

The cabin door whooshed shut behind him.

We all stared as if he had slammed it.

My entire being deflated as I sank back to the bed. *Wake up. Wake up. Please, God, let this be the worst nightmare ever.* I pulled my knees up in front of me, curling in on myself, shoved the heels of my hands into my eyes, and tried to get air back into my lungs.

The mattress dipped beside me, then Wells's hand landed on my shoulder. "What are you thinking, Demon?" he asked. "What's going on?"

"This is called 'freaking the fuck out,'" I said into my knees. "Do they not have that here?" I forced down a breath and lifted my head. "Great, I'm inventing it."

"Why are you freaking out?" Wells hand drifted to the back of my neck, as if anchoring me. "If it's just Al—"

"*Just Al?* Are you serious?" I stared at him, my hands trembling. "This is ... this is the *perfect* situation for freaking out. In fact, join me, won't you?"

"Imogen, I promise this isn't the end of the world," he said, incorrectly. "Tell us exactly what's upsetting you and we can—"

I shot to my feet. "Is that a real question?" Vibrating with anxiety, I paced the room hoping to dispel the shaking spreading through my limbs.

"You're not alone, Demon, we'll all be here to help you."

"Wells, half the army thinks I'm a fuck-up, the entire country considers me a *child*, and I've deposed their ruling line ..." I choked out the last bit on a hoarse whisper as my throat tightened in terror. Flashes of the parade when I'd first arrived in Molnair stole through my mind. Al dancing among the cheering crowds, dazzling them all. He was Molnair's prince in every sense of the word. And Allestair had kept the narrative carefully controlled so as not to allow a crack in his son's veneered image. "Everyone loves Al. This is a disaster."

"I'm not saying it will be easy, Imogen," Wells said, stopping my frenetic pacing with a hand to my waist before tilting my face up to meet his determined gaze. "But you're not without allies."

I wrapped my hands around his wrist, my eyes widening as I stared into his. "Wells, this planet is completely bonkers. I do not understand half of what goes on here. I've been here less than a year. The army thinks I'm an idiot after what happened with Prism. And now I've killed their monarch." I stepped away from him, dropping my face into my hands before shoving them up into my hair. "I am in no way qualified to be king."

Wells had the audacity to half smile, reaching out to catch my waist. "Technically you're the queen—"

I paused. Considered. "Fuck that. I'm king. You can be queen."

"You're female, Imogen." He narrowed his eyes.

"Am I in charge?" I glanced around the room. Everyone silently stared at me. "I'm in charge now, right? Then I'm king. King Imogen the Unprepared. In fact, let's put that on my stationery so that everyone knows whenever I initiate correspondence—"

"Imogen—"

"I'm freaking out, Wells, the impulse to joke is real, I can't stop!" My face burned, my pacing radius shrunk until I was very nearly spinning in a circle.

He crossed the room and pulled me into a hug. "Okay, shut up." He held me firmly, one hand on the back of my head while I buried my face in his shoulder. "Deep breath," he murmured.

I took one.

"Two more."

I shut my eyes and matched my breaths to his, focused on his heart beating beneath my palm, the worst of the panic ebbing from my nerves. *We're alive, we're together, and we're free*, I reminded myself.

We are, Wells said, a smile in his 'path.

My control must have slipped. *Did I 'path the entire room?*

Just me. He dropped a kiss on my crown and pushed me back, blazing russet eyes locked on mine. "You're not alone, we're all here to help you."

My bones went liquid. I sank back to a seat on the bed. "Can't I abdicate? Surely there must—"

All three of them shook their heads.

"I can't... this isn't good for anyone!"

I twisted toward Wells, my fingers diving into the folds of his shirt again, clinging to them as if I could strangle the answer I wanted from the fabric.

Captain Marc cleared his throat. "I won't sugarcoat it for you: many people are going to be resistant to the idea that the power descended to you. For all of the reasons you stated before." He tossed back the rest of his whiskey. "But let's take one challenge at a time. Things being as they are, we do need to get you back to the palace as quickly as possible."

"And you'll need to address the nation," Kavlo pointed out.

"I don't want to do that," I said, breaking out into a cold sweat at the very thought.

"You will have to address them at some point soon, Imogen," Marc said, lines of tension had etched themselves into his forehead. "Some of them will support you if they were disgruntled with the way Allestair ran things, or if they are in support of Llewellyn—and that number is not small—but you need to make a public address regardless."

My insides curdled. "You don't ever have to worry about me not reading a potion introduction again," I told Wells, then forced down a deep breath before facing Marc. "How soon do we need to go? We're in the middle of a siege, shouldn't I—"

"Adgemon can handle the siege." Marc said, setting his glass aside. "We need to start back to Molnair today. I suggest taking the royal airship, not just for appearances but because your mate is still healing."

I blinked, but before I could say anything Marc went on.

"The most vulnerable time for a king is immediately after coming into possession of the power." He sighed deeply before sharing a glance with Kavlo. "Both for the individual and the country itself. You need to reconnect with the seat of your power before Demian realizes Molnair is under new rule."

Kavlo interlaced his fingers atop the table, "And there are other factions that may decide to attack while Molnair is vulnerable with a very young and untrained monarch inheriting the throne. You need to solidify your relationship with the mountain and seat of power at the very least and we need to gauge national support."

I dug my fingers into my knees, realizing that I might be fighting a war at home as well as one abroad. The new power roiled beneath my skin, almost desperate to be syphoned off. As if I were too small a vessel to contain it.

"There's really no way to just let Al be the king?" I asked. "No way the throne can revert back to him at all?"

"Oh, there is." Marc interlaced his fingers on the tabletop.

I sucked in a gasp, hope flaring beneath my ribs. "Does he know? Let's get him back here, let's—"

Wells stopped me with a look, his russet eyes grave. "Al can take control of the throne. If he kills you first."

ACKNOWLEDGMENTS

There is this mythical image of an author as this solitary, free creature, tapping away at the water's edge, a gentle breeze ruffling their hair as they churn out their next masterpiece with a mug of coffee or glass of wine at their elbow.

I'm not saying I've never written near a body of water, or with the aid of coffee or wine. I've done all of those things. I've also written in the car while my husband drives. In the waiting room at a doctor's office. I've written wearing an eyepatch, sunglasses, and reading glasses after eye surgery when I had severe light sensitivity because a deadline had to be met. In short, I never stop writing, and although I do often write on my own, my best work is never done in a vacuum. This book in particular was raised with the help of a village.

First, I need to thank Alisha Khapleke, Jackie Johnson, Lauren Nossett, and Lauren Thoman for doing at least one beta read. Once *Dagger* was published, I dusted off *A Horn of Onyx*, which I had "finished" years ago when I was a much less experienced writer. Thank you for pulling me out of the forest and pointing out which trees needed to be trimmed.

Thank you, Melissa Grace, for your help on the back end, and your encouragement and advice when it came to throwing spaghetti at the proverbial marketing wall. Thank you to Ashley Hager and Alisha again for advice in that area also.

Thank you, thank you, thank you to Maryann Appel for the incredible cover and interior design. I honestly never want to work with another designer. You've ruined me in the best way!

Thank you, Suzanne Elise Freeman, for your support in bringing Imogen's voice to life and navigating the audio landscape. I knew you were my favorite narrator for a reason.

Thank you to Christine Van Zandt for editing this project. The critique definitely pushed me out of my comfort zone and changed the book.

Thank you to my husband, Dean, for always supporting my creativity, for plunking the occasional chocolate bar or encouraging note on my desk, and for reminding me every so often not to be too hard on myself.

Thanks to my wonderful team of ARC readers, headed by the amazing Teresa Brock, whose passion for story literally lifted this one up.

Thanks to my parents. My mom for always being my first, middle, and last beta reader. And reading as many times in between as I churn out versions. And my dad for saving my books to read on trips and always believing that the next big thing is just around the corner as long as I keep working hard.

Finally, thanks to Lauren Thoman again, for talking me through spirals when I realized I had to make yet another plot change, brainstorming for literal hours at least once to help me make sense of said plot change, for being a voice of reason when I was editing this book in ridiculous amounts of pain after eye surgery, and for believing in me when I could not believe in myself.

Thank you to my cats, Aang and Cloud, for sticking your butts in my face, knocking pens off my desk, clawing my chair, and—very occasionally—curling up in my lap to inspire me.

And thank you, the reader, for traveling with me. For looking at this thing I made for you and going "yay!" I love you so much.

ABOUT THE AUTHOR

Meredith grew up in New Orleans, collecting two degrees from Louisiana State University before running away to Chicago to be an actor. In between plays, she got her black belt and made martial arts and yoga her full-time day job. She fought in the Chicago Golden Gloves, ran the Chicago Marathon, and competed for team U.S.A. in the savate world championships in Paris. In spite of doing each of these things twice, she couldn't stay warm and relocated to Nashville. She owns several swords but lives a non-violent life, saving all swashbuckling for the page. When not writing, she enjoys knitting scarves, gardening, visiting coffee shops, and cuddling with her husband and two panther-sized cats. Her debut novel, *Ghost Tamer*, is a 2023 Amazon Editors' Pick, a 2024 IBPA Gold Winner for Best SciFi Fantasy, and a 2024 IPPY Award Gold Winner for Best First Book. *The Sidhe Chronicles* is her first series.

OTHER BOOKS BY MEREDITH R. LYONS

Book I The Sidhe Chronicles

Keep up with Meredith's other writing at meredithraelyons.com

www.ingramcontent.com/pod-product-compliance
Lightning Source LLC
LaVergne TN
LVHW091618070526
838199LV00044B/838